ALPHA

GAY EROTIC ROMANCE

RJ Scott

Cardeno C.

Bailey Bradford

Amber Kell

Sean Michael

ALPHA GAY EROTIC ROMANCE
Published worldwide by All Romance eBooks, LLC
Safety Harbor, FL 34695
AllRomanceeBooks.com

PUBLISHER'S NOTE
This is a work of fiction and any resemblance to persons, living or dead,
or business establishments, events, or locales is coincidental.

ISBN: 978-1-936387-90-8

First Printing, April 2015

ALPHA
DELTA

ALPHA GAY EROTIC ROMANCE

RJ SCOTT

CHAPTER ONE

"This is the second fucking time we've had to do this and I'm telling you now I'm not staying for the whole thing."

Finn Hallan glanced over at his teammate and wondered if he should check him for any visible weapons. Erik was one of those guys who was never happy about sitting still, let alone in a meeting as seminar dealing with health and safety.

"Cap's not going to like you backing out of this," Finn warned. He was just as restless, too used to action and getting on with things instead of sitting here in a briefing room listening to changes in policy. Thing is, this shit was statutory and Cap had made Finn and Erik attend, in case there was anything important about oil platform safety. Finn was certainly not going up against Cap, and he knew Erik needed to keep his ass in the chair if he wanted to stay on the team.

Delta was a highly sought after group of people to join and if you made it you didn't refuse to sit in meetings that you'd been ordered into.

"We need a serious emergency," Erik groused.

"A hostage negotiation or at the very least a terrorist threat."

The woman in front of him turned and frowned at the words, but she took one look at both Erik and Finn and turned back to face the front. Finn knew they looked out of place. Both in the dark dress colours of the Delta uniform, not long off duty, they probably gave the impression of some kind of hardass security detail. Certainly not the kind of guys you told to shut up. She would know who they were, members of the ERU, codenamed Delta, and the ones who policed for terrorist activities in Norway and out into the Norwegian sea. Which, incidentally, was where most of these NorsDev employees in the briefing worked.

Erik grinned and raised his eyebrows suggestively before cupping his groin and looking pointedly at the back of the blonde's head. Finn shook his head. She was a NorsDev exec and everyone knew the high-ups at the energy company had nothing to say to the ranks. If only she knew how much Finn and Erik could do for her if she was in trouble, if only she was aware of the kind of men they really were—ones who never sat still—then maybe she'd be a little more understanding of the boredom factor.

The presentation on the large screen at the front of the room switched to a new slide with a name in block capitals. Niall Faulkner. Not a name that Finn recognized and he couldn't help the groan when he saw the line under the name. *Platform Decommissioning Engineer.*

"Oh Jesus fuck. Save me from nerds with

clipboards and PowerPoints. I think my last brain cell up and died," Erik muttered.

The speaker indicated the slide, "And now I'd like to hand it over to Niall Faulkner. Some of you will recall Niall was responsible for the X220 additions." A ripple of murmurs around the room indicated that at least some knew what the hell that meant. Evidently this Faulkner guy was someone with a name at NorsDev. A man stood in the front row of the lecture theatre and made his way up the four steps to the stage, tripping on the last step and grabbing at the retreating previous speaker as he left. Luckily the new guy, Niall, Finn assumed, didn't fall flat on his face, but he couldn't help the smile on his face. It was funny shit seeing someone fall over.

Niall made his way to the lectern, looking down at his notes and shuffling them into some kind of order. The main spotlight flickered then focused directly on him, and Finn had an instant gut reaction to the man on the stage.

Short and slim, with dark hair and glasses, he was the hottest safety officer Finn had ever seen.

"Woo boy," Erik said under his breath. "You thinking he's way to pretty to be a man?"

Finn didn't dignify the comment with a response. Erik was the only member of the Delta team who knew Finn was gay and that comment was directly aimed at Finn and the fact Erik kept trying to get Finn hooked up with someone. *Anyone.*

"Not my type," Finn lied very quietly. Actually, this Niall guy was pretty much the epitome of Finn's type. Preppy with a side order of nerdy was just exactly what Finn liked under him, or over him, or hell, anyway which around him. And the glasses? Hell, glasses got him every time.

"You think he's batting on your team?" Erik asked.

"Absolutely," Finn deadpanned.

Erik frowned and peered to the small stage below. "You can tell from here?"

Finn punched Erik in the leg, "No, fucker. I can't."

Erik huffed and pulled out his cell phone, putting it in his lap and shielding the glow with his hands. He was clearly booking out of this presentation. On the other hand, Finn found himself absolutely fixated. He wasn't entirely sure what Niall was saying because he wasn't listening to the words, but Finn could listen to his soft Scottish accent all day. Kind of a cross between Ewan McGregor and Sean Connery.

All too soon this Niall guy, who apparently could remove oil platforms in a responsible and environmentally sound way, had finished the presentation. There was a polite ripple of applause before he threw the meeting open for questions.

Finn had a lot of questions, only none of them were to do with... He peered at the last slide...ethical decommissioning.

Erik leaned over, "Bathroom," he said.

Finn gripped his friend's jacket. "Cap will kill you for flunking again."

Erik shrugged free. "Cover for me," he hissed, then left out the side door. *Fucker.* The woman in front turned to face him, but this time she didn't turn away, in fact she was looking at him expectantly, as was the whole of the row. He scanned them, wondering exactly what to say.

"Sir? Did you have a question?" The soft sexy burr of the Scottish voice asked over the microphone.

Shit. Evidently Erik's leaving had caught Niall's attention and he thought the kerfuffle was a freaking question. The woman in front smirked at him, then raked him with her eyes with a large dose of disdain. She was daring him to say he'd been fucking around with Erik and hadn't listened to a word the presenter said.

"Yes," Finn said smoothly. The woman looked surprised but she didn't turn in her chair. "Is decommissioning of oil platforms what you always wanted to do?"

And no, he had no idea where that came from, but it seemed like a reasonable question. People asked that kind of thing? Right?

Niall stared out at him with a look of consternation. Finn waited for that moment when Niall said that in all of his *however many years* he had never had such a strange question. Then Niall's expression cracked and he shook his head ruefully.

"I wanted to be an astronaut," he admitted. "But mild vertigo and a propensity to being sick whenever I flew meant that wasn't going to happen. Seemed to me the ocean and the unexplored depths was the next best thing."

As soon as he'd answered, another question came from the front row, from the lick-asses who actually paid attention in these seminars. The pressure was off Finn. Damn woman was still looking at him, although the rest of the row had turned back to face front. Her expression had changed and she was looking at him with a speculating gleam. He leaned forward toward her.

"Can I help you?" he half whispered.

She lowered her lashes at him. "I don't know. Can you?"

Finn leaned even closer. "Unless you have a cock under that pretty red dress then I'm not sure I can."

Her eyes widened and she turned her back to him with an audible huff. It was all Finn could do not to laugh out loud, even if he did feel a bit of a dick for saying that. But then, she had been the one staring.

The rest of the seminar passed in all it's boring glory, a combination of industry information, safety notes, and that speech from Niall-with-the-accent. When Finn turned on his cell phone he saw he had three missed calls from Cap, and a picture message from Erik of a cup of coffee and a Danish. Just seeing the food made Finn's stomach grumble and knowing Erik was sat somewhere relaxing pissed him off no end.

He listened to Cap's messages. If the matter had been urgent then he'd have been pulled from the seminar, but these messages were more on the line of is-Erik-there and I-just-saw-Erik-with-coffee.

Like I have any control over Erik.

He sent off a quick text to Cap, assuring him that Erik must have been on a break, then another to Erik saying he'd been spotted. Let Erik and Cap fight that one out. As for Finn, he'd earned points today by staying through the whole thing and he'd seen the edible morsel that was Scottish-Niall, so it was a win/win for him.

In the breakout area with coffee and snacks, Niall was holding court. A gaggle of women surrounded him, all talking, and Niall looked like he was doing okay. Laughing and smiling and talking, and Finn wanted some of that. Using his best seek-and-destroy tactics, he made his way around the edge of the room until he was behind Niall and a single step forward had him up close and personal with the man. He realized a few things in quick succession: Niall smelled of a fresh aftershave, he was a good six inches shorter than Finn, and his voice was even sexier close up.

Please if there is a god, let Niall Faulkner be gay, or at the very least bi or curious.

"So astronaut, then," Finn inserted in a lull in the conversation. Niall looked at Finn sharply, then, obviously realizing he was looking right at Finn's chest because of their height difference, his gaze travelled upward, then down to groin level, then back to Finn's face. Quickly, but with enough focus to have Finn thinking that Niall was checking him out.

Oh yes, he certainly checked me out.

"Until I was eight at least." Niall said with a small smile.

Finn wasn't letting this drop. He wanted to tease Niall, and he sure as well didn't want Niall turning back to the NorsDev women who surrounded him. "I wanted to be a cowboy like Clint Eastwood."

"But you ended up a cop," Niall pointed out with a nod to the uniform that Finn was wearing. "ERU? That's the special team out of Oslo right?"

"Yeah, and same thing," Finn said. "Fighting the bad guys."

"Except you don't have a horse."

"I had to leave the horse outside. He never pays attention in seminars." Finn held out a hand. "Finn Hallan," he introduced himself. "On loan to the Norwegian Emergency Response Unit."

"On loan from where?"

"Metropolitan, London."

"A Londoner working for the Norwegians. I didn't know the *Beredskapstroppen* opened to non-Norwegians."

"My father is Norwegian. And you're Niall Faulkner, the decommissioning expert from Scotland, if I hear right? And you work for NorsDev." There, that turned the whole conversation about what Finn could or couldn't do on its head. He'd much rather hear what Niall had to say about himself. And the interesting twist of a Scot using Norwegian words was just the sexiest thing ever. The women around him, all four of them, melted away and just about on time Finn was in a one-on-one situation with the sexy engineering guy.

"Were you actually listening to what I was saying today?" Niall asked with a tilt of his head to punctuate the question. He had the most intriguing eyes but the light here was too bright to properly make out the color. How did Finn explain he was looking at Niall and listening to the tone of his voice rather than taking in the content of what Niall was saying?

"Of course," Finn lied. "You're an expert in the field of decommissioning."

Niall raised an eyebrow, silently mocking Finn.

"And you're ethical as well," Finn added.

"I can summarise for you now," Niall said. He opened his mouth to begin but a man stepped up next to Niall with a plate of snacks and coffee.

"Eat something," the new arrival insisted. He spared Finn a quick glance and a smile then focused back on Niall. "Seriously, if you don't eat you'll fade away to nothing." The new guy had a similar Scottish accent to Niall's but it wasn't enough to hold Finn's attention. Finn didn't imagine the look of exasperation on Niall's face, nor did he think for one minute Niall would fade away. He may be a little on the small side, but then, most people were next to Finn with his six four in height, to be fair. But there was something solid about Niall, he was all lithe muscles and slim build... In fact he was built for—

"Mr. Hallan, this is my brother Ewan," Niall said. "Ewan, meet Mr. Hallan—"

"Finn."

Niall ignored him and carried on with the introduction. "He's with the ERU."

Ewan whistled and looked impressed. "A real life Delta in our midst. You here for your annual health and safety briefing?"

"Just picking up what we need to know."

"Might help if you listen to me then," Niall deadpanned. "I was examining the fact that when we're deconstructing the oil platforms that security is lower and there is a skeleton staff until handover and that this could well be a security risk."

Finn wasn't entirely sure what to say to that. His role in Delta was the backbone of the war against terrorists in Norway and the locale, which covered the oilrigs in the Norwegian sea. He should really have listened to Niall. So how did he apologize then ask for a recap without looking like a complete dick.

"I heard all that," he lied.

"Yet you asked me about what I wanted to be when I grew up?" He stepped out of the light a little and Finn was blown away by Niall's eyes, a stunning mix of golds and browns. They were damn near twinkling with the teasing.

"I didn't exactly phrase it like that," Finn defended himself. Then he backed down. "Maybe I could get a private consultation," he said slyly. This was the perfect time to test the waters with the decommissioning engineer, or whatever he was called.

"Call your team and I'll do a group talk before I leave on Friday," Niall offered. "It was good to meet you, Mr. Hallan."

"Finn," he repeated in the hope he would hear his name on Niall's lips in that soft bur.

They shook hands again, then Niall was lost to the crowd, his brother at his side guiding him around the different people. Finn resolved to look Niall Faulkner up when he got to a quiet space. There was something intriguing about the man with the hazel eyes and the soft steady voice. Oh and his pants, there was something about what was in his pants, and the way they hugged his groin tightly…and that ass…

CHAPTER TWO

Niall allowed Ewan to guide him away and was thankful for the interruption. "Thank you," he said in a quiet voice.

"Was he making you nervous?" Ewan asked with a backward glance at the man they had left by the back window.

Niall considered the tall, broad, in-your-face, dark-haired, blue-eyed man. Nervous, no. A little turned on, yes. That Delta ticked every single one of Niall's items on the checklist. Taller. Bigger. Stronger. Fuck, even his libido had his cock hardening in his pants and he couldn't allow himself to get turned on like some horny teenager. Not here. In this place he was a respected engineer with years of experience behind him and his opinion was requested. He held a high position leading a team of engineers at NorsDev, one of the biggest energy companies in the world, and he wasn't even thirty yet.

He did not have time to fuck that all up by mooning over Mr. Tall and Sexy in his uniform. And hell, that uniform. It stretched in all the right places, and add in the trim waist and flat stomach and Niall was a goner. God knows what he would have done if he'd actually gotten a look at Finn's ass, but it had to be fine given the way his uniform pants clung to muscled thighs and—

"Earth to Niall," Ewan interrupted is thoughts. "You okay?"

"Yeah, I'm fine… And no, he didn't make me nervous. So who's next on the agenda?"

"Adam's here from finance, something about budgets."

Oh. Hell. No. "You have to get me out of here," Niall said urgently. "That man will kill me with boredom."

Ewan turned to say something but it was too late, Adam was there, folders under his arm, and Niall abruptly saw an hour of his life disappear into a black hole. When he glanced back at where he'd left Finn he saw the man was still there. He was leaning back against the window, arms crossed over his broad chest, and he was staring right at Niall.

Flustered, it was all Niall could do to concentrate on Adam and his wish to cut three million from the budgets for decommissioning the Forseti platform. When next he got a chance to check on Finn, the sex-on-legs guy had gone. Niall couldn't help the bite of disappointment. Yes, Finn Hallan made him feel all kinds of nervous, but it was a good nervous, and he already missed the sight of him.

And what did that say about attraction between two people? Because Niall was ready to jump the man's bones and they'd barely shaken hands.

"I'm going up to get some work done." The time had long since passed eight p.m. and he was off the clock now. Someone else could be the expert, the one who answered questions, all Niall wanted was a tumbler of whiskey, his PJs and his laptop. And sleep.

Ewan passed him another plate of whatever leftovers there were on the main table. Niall took them because he knew it was a waste of time arguing with his little brother. After all, Ewan was just looking after him.

"I know you won't call room service," Ewan said on a sigh. He tucked a plastic bottle of Coke into Niall's laptop bag and handed him the whole thing. "Go. Before Adam corners you again."

Niall did as he was told, edging his way out and making sure not to meet anyone's gaze. He only did these safety audit assessments once a year and it seemed like everyone in NorsDev wanted a piece of him. When he made it out to the main corridor juggling plate and laptop bag it was like the last day of the summer term and he had the long stretch of weeks ahead of him. Okay so it was only one night but that was a long time in a really nice hotel with a shower built for two.

Unbidden, thoughts of Finn in the shower had him groaning at the rush of lust. Jesus, he was losing it big time today. He pressed the button for the elevator and stood back. He was on floor seventeen of the Radisson Blu with a wonderful view of Oslo and he couldn't wait to see it all lit up in the dark again. The elevator was way up there at twenty-four but he wasn't moving. He'd have a long wait but climbing up seventeen flights of stairs would probably mean he'd be found near dead on floor thirteen. He chuckled at the thought but stiffened when a familiar voice spoke behind him.

"Niall," Finn said softly. "You going up?"

Niall turned very slowly to face the object of his fascination and he swallowed. Finn had changed out of his uniform and into jeans that hugged his legs like a second skin, and a scarlet T-shirt that stuck very close to every single muscle. In uniform he looked edible, but dressed like this with damp hair from the shower he looked like every gay man's wet dream. His eyes were so damn blue, his lashes long and dark. He may have showered but he hadn't shaved and stubble darkened his jawline, which gave him an almost dangerous look. Niall needed to say something, Finn had asked him a question. Something about the elevator.

"Seventeen," he said.

Clearly that was enough, Finn nodded. "Are you finished for the day now?"

Niall nodded and heard himself sigh. "All done for another year."

"Except for my one-on-one," Finn pointed out.

"I didn't say a one-on-one. I said I'd talk to your whole team."

The elevator arrived and they both got in. He pressed seventeen and stood back with the expectation that Finn would press for his own floor. When he didn't Niall assumed that they were on the same floor. That was until the doors shut and Finn stepped right up in his space.

"I wasn't talking about the security briefing," he said all sexy-growly. Niall moved back until his back hit the mirrored wall and Finn stepped forward.

Abruptly, Niall was flustered and words failed him. "Wh-what were y-you referring to?"

Carefully, *oh so gently*, Finn used a single finger to tilt Niall's chin up.

"Our one-on-one," he said.

"Ours..." *Oh God, oh fuck, I am going to break the zipper in these pants.*

"Unless I read this wrong and you don't want me to hold you down and suck your brains out through your cock."

Finn hadn't moved any closer, in fact it appeared he was deliberately well out of Niall's space. This was the moment that Niall had to make a decision. He could brush this off, ignore the erection pressing painfully against his zipper, forget the fact that desire and lust fought for every inch of his body. *Hold me down. Fuck...* Or he could take everything those blue eyes promised and have one night of the kind of sex that he imagined he would have with Finn. He heard his brother's voice. *Go for it. No one is ever promised a tomorrow. What do you have to lose?*

Swallowing, Niall shifted the weight of his computer bag from his shoulder, distracted by the flash of numbers as the elevator passed twelve, thirteen... He had to make a decision.

"You didn't read it wrong," he said. His voice came out surprisingly normal despite the fact that his tongue felt too big for his mouth.

The elevator came to a smooth stop and Finn moved his finger and stepped back.

"Is your room okay?" he asked softly.

Niall attempted to remember how he had left his room. The maids would have been in to tidy but Niall wasn't the neatest. He'd been in the hotel three days and was still living out of his suitcase.

It seemed suddenly sensible to set guidelines. "Yes. Tonight, just tonight. Okay? And do you have… Are you…"

The elevator doors made to close but Finn held out a hand and stopped them. "Condoms, lube. Check." He didn't address the whole one-night thing.

"This all seems a bit clinical," Niall said, simply for something to say.

In answer, Finn held out a hand and took the plate of food. He stepped out of the elevator and waited for Niall. When Niall let them into his room he had to concentrate on getting the card in the slot and disengaging the lock. He considered the sad fact that he wasn't exactly coming off as the most competent engineer in the world.

When they were in, Niall placed his laptop bag on the floor under the desk and watched as Finn placed the food on the desk then shrugged off a small runner's backpack. That must be where the condoms were, because there was absolutely no room in the pockets in Finn's jeans. Niall didn't know what to do next. He'd never really had a one-night stand. How did it happen? Did they just get on with it? The first times he'd had with all three of his boyfriends had been after dinner where wine had played a part. "You look really worried," Finn said. He was using a soft tone like you would with a child and that gave Niall a bit of confidence to prove he wasn't actually in need of the tone.

"I don't really do this." He waved between them.

"Have sex?"

"Have one-night stands."

Finn stepped in his space again, and this time,

with the desk at his back Niall had nowhere to move. Then Finn did something that had Niall near melting into a puddle. The damned cop cradled his face gently.

"Who said anything about one night?" He tilted Niall's face and leaned down at the same time. With his hands cradling Niall, he kissed him. The kiss was firm but not pushy. There was none of the shit that happened in clubs whenever Ewan managed to drag Niall to one. Seemed like all that happened there were tongues and teeth and a whole lot of demands. This was...

Different.

Finn touched his lips with tongue, pressing inside. With a whimper that Niall hoped to hell was just in his own head, he opened his mouth and tentatively matched the movements. He didn't know what to do with his hands. Should he leave them at his sides, or could he touch...? He rested them on Finn's biceps but couldn't stop with that touch, instead locking his hands at the base of Finn's spine and pulling him closer. They kissed that way for the longest time, Niall so hard it was painful.

Finn moved one of his hands from Niall's face and trailed his fingers down Niall's back, finally coming to a rest on his ass, pressing and lifting so that Niall was near on tiptoe. If they didn't do something soon, release the pressure, if he couldn't undo his pants, then he might do serious damage to his cock. As if he'd somehow telegraphed the message, Finn's hand moved and this time it was to slip under the top button of Niall's pants. He lowered the zipper, finally pushing his fingers into Niall's jersey boxers and closing around Niall's hard cock. Niall pulled back sharply from the kiss and cursed loudly.

All Finn did was chuckle, *the bastard*, then guide Niall back for more kissing while twisting his fingers and tugging on Niall. Niall could stand like this until he came, held up just with the desk at his thighs and Finn holding him upright, but he wanted his hands on Finn and he wanted it now. Copying Finn's movements, he loosened the tight buttons on Finn's jeans and finally managed to get his hands inside Finn's pants. Just the feel of his hands on Finn was enough to have him deepening the kiss, more frantic in his need to taste Finn. Then Finn released his hold of Niall's cock but before Niall could complain Finn yanked at Niall's hand on him, releasing the hold, then lifted him, hands under his ass, and carried him the short distance to the bed.

They tumbled onto the wide mattress, bouncing and awkward and a mess of uncoordinated limbs. But all too soon they were stripping clothes until finally they lay naked and hard against one another. There were questions in Finn's eyes and Niall instinctively wriggled and spread his legs, letting Finn settle between them. He wanted a lot, he wanted everything: Finn's mouth on his cock, Finn's fingers in his ass, more kissing, fucking. He wanted it now. Finn slid off and grabbed his bag, emptying the contents on the bed. Lube and condoms showered the quilt and in a quick movement he covered his erection and had his hands slick with lube.

Crouching over Niall, with his fingers pressing against Niall, he paused. "Are you sure?" he asked.

Niall didn't say a word. He simply grabbed a

pillow and pushed it under his ass, lifting himself, then held onto to the metal framework at the top of the bed. He didn't want to turn over. If he was going to break all the rules and have some muscled cop fuck him into tomorrow then he wanted the visuals to go with it. Finn groaned and kissed him, a single finger breaching Niall, the burn of it a discomfort that edged away. For the longest time they played. Finn kissing a path from Niall's lips to his throat then from one nipple to another, all the time pressing his fingers inside and adding lube.

"Now," Niall said a little desperately. He didn't know what he was asking for. Finn's lips were so close to his cock, but the fingers in his ass were making him want to screw down on them and he was torn.

"If I suck you, will you come?" Finn asked raggedly and breathing heavy.

Niall whimpered. "Yes, I don't want…need you inside…please…fuck me…"

There was time for blowjobs later. There *had* to be time for blowjobs later.

Finn sat back on his heels and used more lube on his sheathed cock. He shuffled forward, his muscled thighs lifting Niall that little bit higher and guiding himself to Niall's loosened hole. Then he pressed and slowly he moved inside. Niall inhaled sharply. He would never get over this first intrusion, the feeling that this wasn't going to work. Then abruptly that stopped, he relaxed and he tilted his hips and inch-by-inch Finn was inside, until finally he stopped and hunched over to steal a heated kiss.

They kissed until Niall couldn't breathe and he realised Finn was moving, slowly, powerfully, he was pushing Niall to feel. Niall gripped the headboard hard, the slide of pillows under his ass and head meaning he couldn't control his movement. No, the control was all Finn's. With every push, Finn talked. He praised Niall, thanked him, his voice increasingly ragged as he was getting closer.

"Touch yourself," Finn said. Niall didn't argue, circling his cock. He set a counter rhythm that made sense in his head, pushing down onto Finn then up into the circle of his hand. Above him Finn tensed, staring down at Niall, his lips parted. Then he was coming, great pushes into Niall's body and the sight of this big man tensed and hard, his face contorted in pleasure, was enough to have Niall coming hard over his belly. He closed his eyes at the last minute, savoured every ripple of orgasm as it hit him.

Finn collapsed against him, taking care to rest just to one side. Then, as he softened, he eased himself out and dealt with the condom. Niall didn't want to move but someone had to deal with the trail of wet on him. He grabbed the tissues by the bed and wiped himself down.

What happened next? Was Finn going to take his twenty or so remaining condoms, his lube and his tight body and go back to his own room. Or would they cuddle? Or maybe some more kissing?

What actually happened next was not on Niall's list of scenarios. Finn reached for the plate of food and set it on the bed before sitting cross-legged, unashamedly nude, his softened dick still an impressive size against the dark curls there.

"Want food?" he asked.

Niall scooted to sit in a similar position.

Something about the decadence of this, of a one-night fuck, of sharing what they had just shared, had him not caring he was naked with a near stranger. Super-Confident Niall was running this show. Of course, it wouldn't be long before Introverted Niall took control, but he'd work with what he had now.

They picked at grapes and cheese and biscuits and shared the bottle of water. Neither spoke much until Finn opened his mouth and said something that was an unexpected to Niall as sitting naked was.

"We have to do this again."

CHAPTER THREE

"You seeing Finn this weekend?" Ewan asked.

"Hmm?" Niall entered the last row of data and saved the spreadsheet. That was the last of the preliminary workups on the Forseti platform and he had the buzz of achievement. Numbers were not his thing. Pipes and oil and steel and the mechanics of decommissioning, that was what he was good at.

"Tall, dark, cop, gruff English accent, all around bad guy, three months of monkey sex."

"He's the good guy," Niall chose to comment on that one point on a yawn. He pushed himself back and away from the desk and stretched tall, his fingers just scraping the low ceilings. "And no, he's on training manoeuvres this weekend up in Urskar."

"It's been a few months you've been seeing him now. You getting kinda serious?"

Niall huffed a laugh. Finn was the farthest from serious that a man could get. He was all fuck and leave. Yes, they talked, yes, they sometimes shared the same bed, but Finn wasn't all hearts and flowers. He was a Delta and that meant he was on call in the hairiest of situations in Norway. Terrorist threats, hostage negotiation, riot. All the big bads that no one expected in a beautiful, peaceful country like Norway. But it was the oil at the end of the day, the platforms in the Norwegian sea, the proximity to the UK, all of this created a volatile mix that Finn was in the middle of.

They'd only managed five hook-ups in three months. Niall knew this because he counted. Seven days was all they'd enjoyed, but hell, those seven days had been more than enough to keep his orgasm tally at a healthy level. A combination of alpha male who loved to be in charge, with Niall's capacity for apparently being able to push all of Finn's buttons and made their sex explosive. Added to that they talked about a lot of things from engineering to being a cop in London. Niall had fallen in love and he hated the feeling that he wasting his heart on someone who could never care.

"I'm out of here," Ewan said. He picked up his laptop bag and the files from his desk. What very few people knew was that Ewan held the same degrees as Niall, that he was just as much of an expert as Niall. Ewan was just happy being the one in the background. Not that Niall really enjoyed all the talks he had to give, or the conventions he needed to attend, but he was, after all, the big brother and he'd taken his responsibility well enough. "I'll pick up the bags and meet you at the helipad."

"Yeah, okay. But, Ewan, is Mel really okay with you coming to Forseti with me?"

"You already asked that twice today."

Niall shrugged. "I'm just making sure."

"She said, and I quote, 'It's a boy and if he takes after his father he'll be late and I'm having a baby, not dying', so I think we're okay."

Ewan left with a small wave and Niall closed everything down before turning off the lights and locking the door of their shared office. He had about an hour to collect his luggage from his apartment then it was his least favourite thing about working on the oil platforms. Actually getting to them.

The Super Puma was on the helipad, rotors unmoving, the pilot talking to his co-pilot with a clipboard in his hand. There were six passengers. Niall was there before Ewan, who arrived five minutes later, still talking to Mel on his cell phone and gesticulating wildly.

Niall crossed to his brother and caught him just outside the white ring of the landing area. "What's wrong?" He'd never seen his brother as upset as he looked at this moment.

"They've taken her in, I told her she looked all puffy and she just cried and I didn't mention it again, but her blood pressure is climbing and they're saying it could be the start of pre-eclampsia."

Niall laid a hand on Ewan's shoulder. This was a three-week stay on an oil platform in the middle of the Norwegian Sea. This wasn't a quick five-minute drive from home to hospital. Quickly, he assumed big brother mode.

"You stay here with Mel. I can handle this one."

Ewan blinked, his mouth open. He was going to argue but Niall said nothing and waited. He could see all the decisions going on in Ewan's head. The work Niall and he were doing on Forseti and the scheduling for decommissioning was something that with two would take three weeks, but with one would take longer.

"I could come out when Mel's been seen," Ewan said finally.

"There is nothing more important than Niall Jr.," Niall said with a reassuring smile.

"We're not calling him Niall."

The brothers exchanged a hug and grins and Ewan stood on the pad until the Puma wheeled up and away, and both his brother and the station were ever-decreasing dots in the blur of rain.

Sitting as comfortably as he could between the others on the copter, Niall took a moment to look around. The other four passengers were all in the standard black jackets of security and would be relieving the other team looking after the platform. Forseti itself had run pretty much dry two years before and the decision to decommission instead of move led to all the oil workers, except for a skeleton crew of six, being moved off.

Now it was Niall's turn to go in and make decisions. And these would be the men he would be spending the new few weeks with. They were all big men, and he realised they all had the same look about them as Finn did. Determined, sure of themselves.

That just made him miss Finn. Which was stupid. They were fuck buddies, nothing more serious, and the fact Finn disappeared like a thief in the night after most of their hook-ups just underlined that.

He couldn't talk to his companions; the blades were thunderous in the spare metal interior. He was more interested in what was out the window anyway. Rain and more rain. The wind didn't appear to buffet the helicopter but it was enough to cause great blasts of rain against one or other of the windows. He wriggled a little to get comfortable and pulled out his cell phone, selecting a play list and hoping to hell it was loud enough to drown the noise.

They landed in wind and rain, a dramatic moment when the helicopter had to hover away from the platform for a few seconds, but not enough to worry Niall. He'd had worse crossings.

The leaving security team exchanged nods as they climbed into the Puma and suddenly it was just Niall, the new security team and a rather agitated man in a thick slicker waving them over to the sheltered area. The security guys went their separate ways and the guy in the slicker grabbed Niall by the hand and shook it hard.

"Welcome," he shouted over the noise of the driving rain on the steel. "Let's get inside."

Niall followed him in, never happier than to be inside from the cold and rain, slipping off his bulky coat and shaking the other man's hand.

"Jeff Fjelstad, Chief," he said. His words were heavily accented Norwegian but Niall smiled at the tone of it. He'd worked for NorsDev for six years now and loved splitting his time between Edinburgh and Oslo. He spoke more than enough Norwegian to carry on a decent conversation at work if needed but the NorsDev way was English as a common denominator.

"Niall Faulkner."

"Welcome to Forseti, Mr Faulkner."

"Niall. Call me Niall."

"I'll show you to your accommodation then we have the initial planning meeting set up in the media room. Is that okay with you?"

Niall and Jeff made small talk about the state of the oil industry, about NorsDev, about the Forseti platform itself, but nothing that took too much thought because Niall was already in engineering mode. Decommissioning a platform wasn't just a numbers exercise, and it wasn't about dismantling the steel structure. It started a long way before that and could take up to two years to complete. From dismantling staff accommodation to ecological impact on a wider scale, this is what Niall was here for as team leader. This platform would be his home on and off for the next six months at least. A week here, a week there, and how much time did that leave to meet up with Finn? Not much at all.

At least he got a private room. Well, two rooms actually, given Ewan was supposed to be here. The door between the two rooms opened up and that was the first thing Niall did just to get more space. The office was another door off of his room and he opened it to have a look inside. A good, well-lit space with three flatscreens, plenty of wall area, and storage. This would be one of the last places to go before the main structural work, and this was where he would be doing all his planning.

He slipped on his glasses and took a moment to stand at the window, the northern gales smashing into the rig, the rain so hard it sheeted down and Niall couldn't make out individual raindrops. Because of this he could actually see the structure ahead of him, part of the platform and views of the heaving sea beyond. Behind him, out of sight, were the machines and pipes, the steel and concrete, the electrics and the decisions he had to make, but outside of this window was the very thing his job sent him to protect. Mother Nature in all her finest anger.

He stopped in the small bathroom and washed his face; his cold skin was prickly with the heat of the water and he stared at his reflection for a moment. He often wondered what people thought of him. He wore glasses, was an engineer with all kinds of letters after his name, a nerd, but he was respected. Just, sometimes, being so small and skinny he was perhaps not seen as able to handle the sea or the oil or, hell, anything.

Except for Finn. Finn thought Niall could handle anything he gave him. Just the thought made Niall smile. He removed his inner jacket and instead pulled on a thick cable knit sweater. Tomorrow was soon enough to go traipsing around the exterior; today was all about meeting the skeleton crew, talking to security, and learning who his team were.

He sent off a quick email to Ewan asking after Mel, even though he couldn't tell when it would go. Communications would be secure and connected from the drilling deck or the media room when he finally got there. At least he'd made some effort at checking in and he'd send something else as soon as he set foot in the communications area, or as he knew it, comms.

With a last look around the two rooms, he made sure Ewan's door was locked, then his own before he stepped outside. Then, shoulders back, he made his way up in the direction where he recalled the media room was placed. He got lost a couple of times but finally made his way to the same deck as the media room at least.

A loud bang had him startled from his relaxed *I know my way* vibe. Then a rumble and a shake that could only have meant that lightning had hit Forseti. *Thank fuck we landed earlier.* Niall sent a quick wish that the helicopter had landed safely back in Grane and carried on. He rounded the last corner and another explosion rocked the path he was taking. He stopped and steadied himself against the wall. That didn't sound like lightening...

Cautiously he stepped forward to the corner and came face to face with one of the security guards from the ride over. He didn't know who was more startled. The security guard was armed, pointing a gun upward, not at Niall. Then the guard reacted, pointed the gun at Niall, and his demeanour screamed to Niall that he should run.

In the split second it took for all that to take place another explosion rocked the walkway they were on and both men knocked heavily into the wall. The guard flailed and fell back, a bullet embedding itself in the wall next to Niall's head. With years of experience on walkways that weren't stable Niall regained his footing. Without hesitating he turned and ran. Time didn't slow down; it was a frantic terrifying stumble to the next door in the corridor, and a desperate heave through the space, kicking the heavy metal door shut and turning the exterior lock. A bullet hit the door, and the guard, red-faced and determined, was at the handle trying the lock.

Niall stumbled backward, hitting the wall and sliding to the side, falling to his knees and facing the other corridor. Jeff was there. Sprawled on the cold floor, his sightless eyes wide open, a bullet hole in the center of his forehead, and blood pooling around his head.

Terror gripped Niall and shock drove him to stand and back away even more. What was happening? He could see the armed man through the tiny glass porthole in the door and for a split second Niall froze, looking into the dark eyes of the man who had shot at him. Then he turned and ran again. Left, right, along, down—the schematics of the accommodation block changed from one platform to another, but once he was into the bowels of Forseti he'd be able to stop and breathe.

His breathing was tight but his thoughts were suddenly clear as he jumped the last flight of stairs into the drilling deck. He had to grab his glasses as he realised he was losing them and he removed them and shoved them under his sweater. He'd be blind without them.

This is a terrorist threat. This is a hostage situation. He stopped at the base of the stairs and forced himself to focus. Whatever the fuck was going on he had to follow protocol. Information and communication. He bent at the waist and supported his arms on his knees, his breathing easing. He was fit but he wasn't a freaking marathon runner. His long hair flopped in his eyes and, irritated, he swept it back as he stood.

Communication meant one thing. The drilling deck, where the brains of Forseti was, or the media room, where the workers contacted families.

Media room is compromised, he told himself. *What would Finn do?*

Decision made, he jogged through the maze of

the drilling deck and stopped only at the main door out into the open air. The rain hadn't let up; he wasn't going to make it to the other side of the deck without being soaked through. He could go down two levels and come back up in the comms room but that would add time to this.

What if the comms room is compromised as well?

He stepped back away from the window and pulled out his cell phone. It was just a normal iPhone and there was no way there would be anything in the way of a connection. If he couldn't get to the main deck to connect to NorsDev then he had to find a satellite phone and hope to hell the weather let up enough.

What if all four security guys on the Puma were in on this? What if they were working with the crew here? What if they have guns trained on the upper production deck? What do they want? Who wanted to take over an oilrig in the middle of the damn ocean that didn't even form part of the active pipeline for oil? It didn't make any sense.

Time outweighed the worries and Niall pushed open the door onto the deck, the rain finding and drenching him in seconds. He carefully shut the door behind him and edged his way around the large half-football-field sized area, crossing in and among steel and plastic, thanking God he hadn't switched out his boots for his work shoes, and wishing to hell he'd taken a coat to the briefing.

Why would you have even done that, idiot?

A sound over the noise of the rain had him stopping with fright clogging his throat, but it was just a loose plastic cover snapping under the weight of rain. If this was a working platform it would be dealt with but the deterioration of care was the first thing that happened on decommissioning. The sharp edges of it tugged at his sweater and he yanked away before, in a motion of desperation, he yanked at the plastic itself and tore of a thick swathe of it. Stiff and uncompliant, it was the only weapon he could think to find. What he wouldn't give for a steel pipe, or hell, a gun.

He reached the comms area and crouched by the window. In there was a way to contact NorsDev, to contact Finn, anyone. He couldn't see movement but that didn't mean a thing. Then, just as he made to move, he caught sight of a man pacing the comms room with a wicked-looking automatic weapon in his hands. He'd been behind a pillar and out of view but now he was plainly there to see. Niall ducked down. Great. There went comms, which only left the satellite phones. Where would they be? *In the comms room. Idiot.*

But wait. *IT maintenance...*

Working his way back around the main deck, he approached the comms room from another direction, straight to the maintenance room, and after a considered look in through a cracked window, he cautiously moved in. When he shut the door behind him he stopped absolutely still, gauging if anything was there. No signs of movement, no sounds, just an empty room full of storage boxes and a couple smashed PC screens. He opened the nearest box, nothing but ID card holders. Another box held paper, yet another wrappers of energy bars, but no actual bars. His stomach rolled, reminding him he hadn't even got breakfast and it must be way past lunch now.

Finally, maybe six boxes later he found what he was looking for and pulled out three satellite phones and a couple of chargers. Pushing them back in, he lifted the box and glanced at the piles of remaining boxes. There could be more but could he chance it?

In the end, the need to get out of the situation alive trumped everything and he was out of the security room, and scrambling down open stairs. Icy rain stung his eyes and skin as he moved to the lower production deck and into one of the main storage rooms. There he finally stopped long enough to realise he was shaking with cold and he couldn't feel his fingers. When the door was closed against the elements it didn't make him feel any better physically but on the safety level he felt like he could give himself a few minutes to breathe. He pulled off the sweater, which dripped with water. Then, ignoring his wet pants, laid everything inside the box on the table in the darkened corner. Using his cell flashlight, he lit the area, hoping no one was checking the random abandoned rooms on this deck. He'd deliberately chosen a room with three exits and it was enough so he could focus if he knew he had at least two alternative ways out.

Two of the satellite phones were broken, the backs off and the electrics loose, and only one charger had a light glowing to say it worked when he plugged it in.

"Fuck."

He blew on his fingers, trying to get some warmth into them, but his whole body was so cold it was impossible. Wires slid through his hold, the delicate connections a mess that he couldn't at first make sense of.

Frustrated, he stopped. He needed to warm up before he could concentrate. Walking from side to side in the room, over and around crates, he finally felt like he was warming. All he could do was be thankful he didn't appear to be teetering on the edge of hypothermia.

The wiring was easy after that. The box contained satellite phones for maintenance and he was able to cobble together enough to get one phone that might work. Finally, with the handset on charge, he hid everything under crates and crawled into a space he made, dragging his sweater with him and huddling against the interior wall, which was warmer to touch than the cold floor.

All he could do now was wait.

CHAPTER FOUR

The call came in just past fourteen hundred hours, Erik beating him to ops by about two seconds, both men pulling on vests and arranging holsters.

Finn had been reading, spending the quiet down time before dinner trying to get his head around some of the shit that had gone down today. Time at the Urskar training facility was hard work but it wasn't hard physical work that was bugging Finn. He knew exactly what it was.

Niall.

They'd talked this morning; he was working on the Forseti platform in the Heidrun oilfield for the next few weeks. They wouldn't be seeing each other for a while, and that was fine. Finn was good with that. Of course, he didn't like the fact Finn was flying in this weather. The storm passing through near the Forseti platform was a big one. And yes, he had to admit to himself he'd checked. And that was the problem. He'd checked the storm, he'd worried about the flight, and he was already missing the feisty, nerdy, sexy engineer enough to have it consuming his thoughts. All the what-ifs and the whens, and mostly the whys. He didn't usually do serious, but Niall could make him change his mind. One guy with a soft voice and a wicked mouth comes along and suddenly Finn was losing control of his *touch but don't keep* policy.

Then, this morning he'd fucked up. Big time.

He hadn't been paying attention and he'd seriously blown things in training. He'd let his guard down and got a helmet full of pink dye with a spot-on head shot from a crowing Erik. It wasn't so much the kill shot, it was why Finn had been distracted. He'd been thinking about Niall, and not in the *I want to fuck that sideways* kind of way, but in an *I hope he's okay and I'll miss him* kind of way.

Then Erik had to go and manage to kill him. It was the first time Erik had ever gotten the drop on Finn in training. It had taken three hair washes and vigorous scrubbing to get the pink out of his hair and off his left temple.

Fucker.

When they reached the briefing room Erik grinned at him, that shit-eating grin that told Finn he wouldn't be living it down that Erik's team had taken first blood in the mini war game they were taking part in. The grin didn't last long, subsiding as soon as Cap walked in. After all, it didn't matter what had happened this morning; now they were all about whatever had caused them to be alerted.

"About thirty minutes ago four bodies were found at the Grane oil terminal, identified as security assigned to the NorsDev Forseti Platform."

Cap stared straight at Finn and for a brief moment Finn wasn't really understanding the words. Then one thing hit him square in the chest. Forseti. That was where Niall was.

Rising to his feet he didn't know what to say as fear gripped him. "Four?"

"We have reason to believe these four men were replaced so that a team of hijackers could get onto Forseti."

"That's being decom'd." Erik sounded puzzled. "What kind of collateral does an empty oil platform have?"

"Only four?" Finn interjected. "What about the engineers? Niall Faulkner and his brother Ewan?"

Erik looked up at him and Finn could see the moment the information made sense in his head.

"Fuck. Niall is on Forseti?"

"Both of them... Niall and Ewan. Did they go? Does someone know if he...?" The rest of the team all stared at him, Cap included, and Finn realised he was coming off as a mad man. He subsided. No one could get information out if Finn was raving like a fucking lovesick moron.

"The pilots are back, they took one engineer and four security replacements. So, souls on the platform are one engineer, six skeleton crew, and the four security replacements. Eleven souls in all."

The bottom fell out of Finn and dread stole his breath. Was it Niall or Ewan on Forseti? With who? Terrorists?

"Intel is showing no communications, or demands, but chatter has it that this is an isolated cell connected to the Hofstad Network out of Denmark." Cap slid his finger on the laptop and the screen changed behind him to show four faces. Three fair-haired, one dark, all in fatigues with long addendums at the bottom of the photo. Ex-

Marine, one former SAS. The names a blur. Except for one.

Svein Roberg.

"He's dead," Erik said in disbelief, echoing Finn's thoughts exactly. Roberg had a long history of fighting the good fight for whichever side paid him most. Ex-Special Forces, he had finally been taken down by the ERU two years before, just after Finn joined the team. In fact, it had been Finn who faced him down after tracking him to a small holding in Alta. They'd chased him to the Alta Dam, where the murdering fucker had died.

The bastard had tried extortion in the name of environmental concern and had killed three oil workers in an explosion at one of the dry land containment depots. Finn would never forget Svein's face. He didn't even fight when Erik and Finn had him cornered, simply dropped his weapon and raised his hands.

In the best traditions of all grandstanding bad guys he laughed then said, "I live to fight another day," repeating this over and over as he fell to his knees. There had been madness in his words, and cunning in his silver eyes. Only when Finn had stepped forward did the madness manifest in a blur of motion, the two men grappling for the weapon and a bullet leaving Finn's gun and carving into Svein's neck, blood spurting. Time had slowed and Finn had watched in horror and a curious fascination as the terrorist leaped in a grotesque twist of muscles over the dam wall and down into the churning water below.

"They never found his body," Finn said softly.

But Finn hadn't cared then. The fucker had a bullet in his neck and had fallen over six hundred feet. He had to have been dead.

"Until four weeks ago his file was silent, but chatter indicated there was movement and he was implicated right in the center of it all."

"And no one thought to brief us?" Finn demanded hotly. "Why the fuck not?"

Several others in the team, Erik included, added their alarm.

Cap held up a hand and quieted the room. "Wheels up in ten," he said.

And that was it. They knew nothing. They didn't know why Forseti was the platform involved or why Svein Roberg had shown up. But, whatever information they received, they would be ready for action when they knew what the hell to do.

Erik grabbed his arm as Finn made to leave. "Finn?" he asked. The question was loaded. It was, *are you sure you're okay*, *do you know the man you've been seeing is on Forseti*, and *can you handle this*, all in one word.

Finn nodded. Didn't matter how he felt or what he actually said to voice any of it, he was going with the team and he wasn't putting doubt in Erik's head.

"Let's get this done."

* * * *

The helicopter took them to Grane terminal from Urskar, and Finn stayed quiet the whole time. Intel was trickling in, definite that Svein had survived being shot and was on Forseti, with camera footage from

Oslo and at a gas station near Urskar. It hadn't escaped Finn's attention that Svein made no effort to hide his face. He was buying at the counter in the convenience store and looking directly at the camera.

Was he sending a message to Delta? That yes, he was back, and that they should come find him?

Still, why Forseti? Eco terrorists chose live targets, not empty monoliths in the middle of the ocean. What kind of statement could Svein make with no pipeline to threaten? Maybe they wanted some kind of impact of the attack in the press. NorsDev had managed to avoid being caught up in any kind of hijacking so far, the bigger names were the victims, companies like Lundin Petroleum and BP. But somehow Finn knew. People were the only collateral that Svein had on Forseti.

And people meant Niall or Ewan.

As soon as they landed the team jumped down and gathered around Cap, Finn catching sight of someone walking toward them in the gathering rain. For a moment he thought it was Niall, then realised this person was taller. Ewan.

Ewan hurried straight to them. "My brother is on that platform," he said with panic in his voice. Then he saw Finn and stumbled. "Niall is on there with them."

Finn grabbed at Ewan and held him. The man looked white with fear and Finn had to be the responsible one who kept control of everything and didn't let what he was feeling inside be obvious on the outside.

"We'll get him back," he reassured Ewan.

"What do they want?" Ewan asked.

Cap made his way to Ewan and stood between him and Finn. "We don't know anything as of yet."

"But we know it's hijackers," Ewan snapped. "What are their demands?"

Cap raised a hand and Ewan fell silent. "We need to take this inside."

The men went inside, a situation board already in place, Ewan there with a couple others who all looked as worried as Finn felt.

"This was just posted," a man to one side said then turned the screen so Delta could see as well as everyone else. He pressed Play and a familiar voice echoed through the tinny speakers.

"My name is Svein Roberg. I have taken the NorsDev Forseti platform. At midday tomorrow we will be destroying the platform and taking it to the bottom of the sea where it deserves to be. Let the sea swallow it whole." He stopped and smiled. "Come stop me," he added. Then the video stopped.

The threat was there, implied. He hadn't mentioned hostages. Just that he was destroying the platform. There was no oil to leak, no fires to start, the only collateral were people.

"Why would someone be so hell bent on sending over sixty thousand tons of steel and concrete to the bottom of the sea, uncontrolled?" Ewan asked a little desperately. "And how the hell do we get my brother off of there?"

"We need to get on the platform," Finn said immediately. The noise level rose as everyone put in their point of view, varying from "we're fucked" to "let's do this" depending which team was talking, be it the ground crew, or the Delta team.

Delta huddled around maps. Every single one of them knew Forseti; it had been another training post only last summer. One of the remotest platforms, it was a relic to the 70s standing over a tapped well in the Heidrun oil field.

"He's daring us—"

"No point in going in by Puma—"

"Sea it is—"

"Boat—"

"Drop—"

Every member had something to say, every man on the Delta team was a specialist in their own right.

"Can we get in touch with crew? Are there comms to anyone on the platform?" Ewan asked from behind them. Finn bit his lower lip. He didn't want to think this way, but Svein didn't exactly give the impression he was there for money or effect. Finn didn't have to think too hard to know that Svein was only on there to destroy with no hope of a hostage trade off. Which meant everyone could well be dead on there already.

Cap answered for him. "No comms as yet, nothing from the crew, or from the engineer. Apart from the video we've got nothing."

"He wants us," Finn said. He didn't have to say it out loud but everyone in Delta knew it. This was wrong, this wasn't delicate negotiation nor did it have a strong hope of resolution. This had to be nothing more than a trap for Delta.

"He never got over the fact we killed him," Erik deadpanned. Graveside humour, blacker than black, was how the team worked but something in the pit of Finn hated it.

Niall was on there. His Niall.

"So we're walking into a trap," Cap summarised. "We know that. He knows that. We may as well land a freaking Puma on the helipad and just walk out, weapons drawn."

"Which is what he is expecting because he'll know we know." Finn did his own summarising and it made sense in his head. "So we split, half in the Puma, half by sea." He pointed at the main boat deck where they could safely dock a boat. Then he traced the side around and up and under the lower production deck. "Here, we land it here."

"We need a distraction."

"Landing a Puma is a pretty big distraction."

"Erik, Finn, you're by sea, the rest of us will do the frontal assault, land the Puma, draw their fire. We go in, we take them out, try and get the crew out alive."

There was deadly calm in Cap's voice and Finn nodded his agreement like everyone else did. There was one word Finn was refusing to accept. There was no *trying* to get the crew out, and by default Niall. He would rescue everyone or die trying.

That is what Delta did.

CHAPTER FIVE

The battery light flickered red and Niall had never felt such a keen sense of relief in anything before. A red light wasn't enough to use it but at least the phone was charging. He just had to hope that whoever had decided to attack Forseti hadn't somehow affected communications and he could get a clear line out.

What would Finn do, what would Finn do…

A sound had him shrinking back behind the crates but it was nothing more than buffeting wind and rain smashing into the thick walls. Whoever was hijacking the platform would know he was still alive and that he'd gotten away. And was it just one man with a gun, or was this more than one. Niall had only seen a single man with a gun face to face, but there was another armed in the drilling deck control room. At least two.

If they were worried about finding him, if they thought he was of any use, or hell, if they just wanted him dead, then he wasn't safe wherever he was hiding.

Worst comes to worst you could jump in the sea.

And die in seconds, slammed against the

superstructure, or pulled underneath the tumultuous waves, freezing in seconds.

No jumping into the sea unless you have to.

The red light flickered for a second from red to green but then settled back on red. What happened if he used the phone? Would the unknown attackers pick up the comms, find him? Niall was an engineer, give him sixty-three thousand tons of steel and concrete and he could imagine every inch of it and know it like it was his own, but electrics and telecoms were something he couldn't get his head round. Hell, he could twist a few wires together in a rough approximation of fixed but the phone looked like it was going to last about three minutes.

Maybe I should try for the accommodation block. That was self-contained and could be shut off from the rest of the platform in case of fire. It would be safe in there. Unless the hijackers were in there.

Frustrated at the turn of his thoughts he banged his head against the wall and winced when it fucking hurt. He pushed his glasses back up his nose and huddled into an even smaller ball, shivering with cold, and waited.

He imagined Finn next to him, holding his hand, telling him everything was going to be okay. Keeping Finn in his thoughts was a good move; the strength he admired in his lover was enough to keep him calm. At least until the light flickered to green and stayed that way.

Niall immediately picked it up, not knowing who the hell to call. This wasn't a two-way radio, this was a phone and the only number he remembered off the top of his head was Ewan's, and Ewan was in hospital.

Fumbling in his tight pocket he pulled out his cell and peered at the screen. It was soaked through, water behind the screen, but when he pressed the power it worked enough for Niall to get a number for Grane Terminal. He might have one chance to get a message through and everything counted on this one moment.

Shakily he pressed the digits for Grane but there was silence, before a crackle, then the sound of a connection being made. The call was answered and before they said a thing Niall launched into what he wanted to say.

"Niall Faulkner, Senior Engineer aboard NorsDev Forseti platform in the Heidrun oil field. Unknown armed assailants, two by my count. One crew dead. I'm cut off from everyone else." He waited for a response, but could hear nothing. "Over?" he added cautiously. The phone crackled in his hand and he wondered if there was even any point to this. Was it going through to anyone who could help? "Hello, this is Niall Faulkner, Senior Engineer aboard NorsDev Forseti platform in the Heidrun oil field. Can anyone hear me? One of the crew is dead." Nothing. "Please. Is someone there? One crew is dead. Two unknown armed hijackers."

He repeated the message over and over, forgetting the ice of cold, or the wet, or the fact he could be found. If someone was out there listening, if this was actually a connection, then he was damned if he was stopping.

"Niall Faulkner, Senior Engineer aboard NorsDev Forseti platform—"

"Niall!"

Ewan's voice? Was Niall going mad? That sounded like his brother's voice.

"Ewan."

"Thank God, hang on—"

Another voice came on the line. "This is Emmet Adams at Grane Terminal. Is This Niall Faulkner?"

"I'm on Forseti," Niall managed. "Send help."

"Can you talk?"

"I'm safe," Niall said. He didn't feel very safe but no one had found him yet. And he'd managed to connect to the outside world, that had to count for something, meant that the comms weren't totally down?

"I'm patching you in to the ERU," Emmet said.

Niall waited. The ERU meant Finn, but it wasn't Finn's voice, another man who spoke crisply and calmly.

"Talk to me," was all he said.

Niall imagined talking to Finn, what he could say that might make Finn's job easier. "Two armed men that I know of, one with intent to kill." That much was true, the guard he'd met wasn't exactly asking him to put his hands up, he'd gone straight for point and fire. "Guard one outside media room, guard two armed in drilling observation, I didn't see the crew."

"Assume all four from flight this morning are part of hijack cell," the voice warned.

Niall had already come to that conclusion on his own. He didn't need a random ERU member telling his that. His instincts told him he'd be lucky to make it out alive and that no friendly visitors would point a gun at him.

"What do I do?"

"Stay low. We're on our way."

More crackling then a different voice was there. "This is a big ask, but could you give us a distraction?"

"A what?" Niall startled at another bang on the wall outside, his heart racing.

"We have Delta two at your position in thirty minutes, can you make some kind of distraction to pull the assailants to the boat deck for sixteen twenty without putting yourself in harm's way?"

"I can…can do that."

Could he? He could think of a million ways to cause a distraction, from steel to fire, but could he actually move from here?

"Stay safe. If you can't manage this then get yourself somewhere isolated and stay put. Agreed?"

"Agreed."

The phone went dead and at first he thought it was just the end of the call, then he saw the red light and the sparks from the wires. The whole thing was fucked and there wasn't anything else in the box that was halfway salvageable.

Sixteen twenty. Niall checked his phone, wondering if that was even keeping time with the wet. The screen showed just before sixteen hundred and he just had to trust he was going to be doing the right thing. Fear curled in his belly as he carefully pushed all signs he had been there, boxes and wires, into the very farthest-most point in the dark corner. He wasn't the hero hanging from a rope setting explosions as a distraction, hell he doubted there was anything to cause an explosion. All the power around here was in water.

And why the boat deck? Wouldn't the ERU use the boat deck? What about a helicopter? What if they couldn't get here at all?

Closing his eyes, he focused on what he could do. Then it hit him. Water. He could use the valve for the…

Decision made, he still couldn't bring himself to leave his dark space. He was scared. The memory of Jeff dead on the floor with a bullet between his eyes was enough to have him not moving.

"What would Finn do?" he asked himself out loud.

Sucking up every ounce of courage he possessed, he crawled out from the space and cautiously made his way to the main door from the production deck outside. His hiding place was damn near all the way over the other side of the vast platform, and the rain hadn't let up. Carefully, he removed his glasses, blinking as everything blurred a little. He thought about what he needed to do. Section seventy-nine was his first stop, if he could make it there then he could loosen the valve, move around the edge, under the walkway, to the main boat deck. Follow the pipes to section forty-seven, locate the outlet, loosen it, wait for the pressure to build between the two.

He could do this.

He straightened and pushed back his shoulders, then opened the main door. He had to keep close to the sides as much out of the rain as he could for fear of being blown off the platform. Cautiously, he made his way to the edge of the connections for the main rig right to the steel jacket that kept Forseti secure in three hundred and fifty metre depths. The going was treacherous, the howling wind making him wish for the safety rope he may well have thought to use in this situation. He wasn't the kind to take chances like this. He was the solid, safe one, the one who looked out for everyone else. Rain sliced into his face, blurring his vision even more and he stumbled to a stop.

He guessed the only good thing about this was that the bad guys had as limited visibility as he did. And he had one thing they didn't—he knew his way around these rigs with his eyes closed.

He didn't stop to check the time, couldn't stop, couldn't even take his hands off of every handhold he could find. He felt like he was walking against a brick wall one minute, then sagging to the ground in the next when the wind shifted, pressing him down to the metal floor. He just hoped to hell that he was close enough to the first valve now to at least make it to the second. He'd need leverage to turn the valve and he doubted there was anything official to handle like a wrench. Inspired, he grabbed at one of the small water outlet draining pipes and levered the item until it came apart. Armed with a foot of hard metal he continued onward.

Feeling his way along the pipes, picturing the layout in his mind, he couldn't help but think of Finn. Was Finn landing by boat? Was he even part of the ERU Delta team, did he know it was Niall on the platform?

Last week they'd spent a whole night together, Finn on his way north for training, Niall in seclusion working on project deadlines. They'd eaten out, made a whole date of it, hell, most of it even seemed normal. Finn was stealing a small piece of Niall's heart every time they were together and Niall bet Finn didn't even realise what he was doing.

And the sex? Niall slumped to the nearest pipe and gripped hard, knowing he was only maybe six feet from the first valve. He could think about the sex, about the way Finn made him feel, about the way Finn could hold him and make everything outside what they were doing seem unreal. Then he could focus on what he felt like when he stared into Finn's beautiful green eyes, or when he dug his fingers into Finn's dark hair like he never wanted to let go.

The valve was easy to grab and Niall leaned into it. All he needed to do was turn it enough so the seal was broken. With the lack of oil running through the platform the pipes instead were holding back water pressure. This would work. He was sure of it. The valve moved a little, or was that just Niall's wishful thinking? Then, using the metal bar as a pivot, he leaned with his bodyweight, abruptly wishing he were a lot bigger than he actually was, and it finally gave way.

That was the first part done and he gave up trying to walk to the boat deck, instead near crawling on his hands and his knees, the metal pipe, twisted and buckled, pushed under one arm. He'd gone beyond just shivering, he was growing colder by the moment, his fingers numbing, and his head fuzzy.

I'm going to tell Finn I love him, he thought. Over and over he thought the same thing, focused on surviving this, getting off the platform and telling the stubborn cop exactly what he thought of him.

"I can't love someone," Finn had stated when

they woke up in each other's arms last week. "It wouldn't be fair."

"Fair on who?" Niall asked. "You? Me? Who the fuck would even know?" He was furious and he couldn't help asking. He loved this man and all he wanted was commitment to go alongside the sex. Not forever, but an acknowledgment that Niall meant something to Finn other than just being there for only sex.

The rain eased as Niall rounded the last wall before the boat deck and he lay on his stomach in the wet until he could see through the spray to what was below. There was no sign of Delta, no sign of Finn, and there was no one with a gun. He belly-slid forward until he could see over the edge of this part of the platform and despair hit him. There was a hijacker there, still in a guard's uniform, just inside the door to the boat deck, staring out at the water with a rifle in his hand. He was sideways to Niall but that didn't make it any easier. The valve was between Niall and the hijacker and Niall needed to get closer.

Part of him wanted to check his phone, but hell if it would even be working if he did. Would any of these be any easier if he knew he had five minutes or ten? He crawled a little further to the right, the valve in his sight and the rain sheeting at full force as he moved out of the shelter of the overhanging deck. He reached it and hoped to hell no one was above him waiting to shoot him in the back of the head.

What would Finn do?

Utilising the bar he used his full body strength to attempt to move the second valve. As soon as it was open enough he needed to back the fuck off. The build up of pressure would angle down into the boat deck and the force of it would be enough to grab the hijacker and physically throw him to the ground. Or at least, that was what was in Niall's head.

The rain eased a little, an eerie silence that made Niall's chest tighten. He would be seen. All the hijacker had to do was look up and to the right and that would be it, Niall would be dead and he would never have gotten the chance to say anything to Finn.

I love you, I love you, he murmured to himself as he moved as slowly as he could to get his body weight behind this valve as well. Movement out of the corner of his eye and he swore he could see a boat in the stormy sea. The hijacker moved. Had he seen the same thing?

Temper made Niall strong. He wasn't going to let the Delta team down. He was getting them on this platform and he was fucking well going to make it home so he could pin Finn to the bed and force his lover to say how he felt.

I love you, I love you... The valve creaked and groaned as Niall pushed but it was moving, and he saw the rifle point up at him at the very same moment the valve gave way. The force of its movement pulled him to one side and the pain as he slammed to the floor was enough to steal his breath. A spark, a sound, and he was being shot at, the bullet missing him by inches. He couldn't move, the metal he'd used in the valve had pinned his sweater, curled into the thick mess of wool, and as much as he yanked he couldn't get free. He was like one of those butterflies in a display case. Any second now he was dead.

I love you.

The pressure built underneath him; he could almost imagine the water pressing and forcing, gathering enormous strength until it blew. He struggled to get free, the sweater pulling, tearing, and he knew he had to get away as soon as he could. An explosion of air and water rocked the small part of the platform he was pinned to, metal wrenching under the force of it. Niall could hear screaming and knew it was himself.

I love you.

CHAPTER SIX

Finn adjusted his headset until he could get a clear reading on what the hell was going on. Cap laid it down, Niall was alive and he'd somehow managed to get communication out of Forseti. The storm snagged and threw the small boat, and he gripped hard as a sickening lurch had him cursing.

"Fucking bitch," Erik cursed from the front. He was cursing Mother Nature and her ability to literally pick this boat up and slam it down into the sea like it was nothing. Finn didn't want to hear Erik's cursing; he wanted intel. About assailants, firepower, hostages, but most of all he needed to know about Niall.

Pride flooded him at the thought Niall had somehow eluded the hijackers and had contacted the station. He'd shown clear thinking in what must be a terrifying situation. Especially for an engineer more used to the fear of a failing superstructure than facing the end of a loaded weapon. Then that same fear insinuated itself inside Finn's calm acceptance of the situation. This was nothing new. They were trained for this. They could get on the platform, become a formidable team against God knows who. But that was when they knew the parameters. This wasn't the same.

Svein wanted Delta with all the hate-filled focus of a thwarted bully, and he was using innocents to line up Delta in his sights.

The boat surged upward on a swell and Erik guided it through as best he could. They were only a short distance from Forseti but the vast oil platform was even visible in the churning storm that was trying to kill them. To get on the platform would take no small amount of skill and Finn had to just sit there and accept that Erik knew his job.

"Asked the engineer to create a diversion to drive the hijackers to boat deck," Cap confirmed.

Finn's chest tightened. Erik glanced sideways at him; he'd heard the same message. A diversion to the boat dock meant this half of the Delta team had to come around the back, no soft landing. Not that they expected it. They were clearly moving to plan B.

But what scared Finn the most was the casual way Cap had said the engineer was creating a diversion. Niall. They drew closer to Forseti, the superstructure rising like a goliath out of the sea, steel gray against the churning clouds. Erik guided the craft to the left, away from the boat deck, and when Finn looked up he could see the Puma wheeling above them. They would take the main fire, allow the boat to get a foothold somewhere on the metal rising from the sea. Under the platform the sea settled in a couple of places and the two men managed to get themselves off the boat and onto the structure itself. They were on unmoving land when an explosion from the boat deck had Finn scrabbling the rest of the way up to the deck.

Niall was up there.

When they reached the deck it was empty, a great pipe split at a valve, and metal peeled back like it was nothing more than paper. There was no sign of a hijacker and Finn signalled for Erik to cover him. If Niall was anywhere up here then Finn was finding him.

He followed close to the gray walls and, staring through the rain, he attempted to make out anything except crooked pipes and chaos. Then he spotted what he assumed was one of the hijackers. It was difficult to tell because metal had sliced into his face and cut into skin. There was no blood, the sea had washed him clean, but he hung like a grotesque scarecrow and Finn couldn't even think that Niall was here somewhere just as dead.

Above them the Puma was backing off from fire. He could hear at least two weapons firing, and Delta returning fire. That would pull the focus from him and Erik; they had a chance of getting people off this place. Including Niall.

White material caught his eye and he realised it was a sweater. In seconds he was there, yanking at an unconscious Niall, cutting away the wool that had him caught and freeing him. He felt for a pulse. There was one, and just as Finn contemplated where he would be hiding Niall until this was all over, Niall opened his eyes.

"Finn," he choked.

Finn didn't have time to feel relieved. The rest of Delta was taking the heat and he and Erik had a mission. He glanced around at the mess of metal, something that Niall had done here had made things right for him and Erik.

"You did good," he said as he assisted Niall in getting up. "Can you stand?"

Niall groaned and pushed himself to stand, taking a lot of his weight by himself. "I'm okay." The crunch of glass had Niall looking down. On the ground lay Niall's glasses, twisted with one lens shattered. He couldn't look. What if that had been Niall?

"You said one crew dead," Finn repeated.

"Jeff." Niall nodded as he blinked water from his hazel eyes.

Finn spoke into his comm. "I have one hostage alive. Confirmed one dead hijacker, one dead crew."

Niall is alive.

Erik moved out, Niall behind him, Finn bringing up the rear. Niall appeared to get with the plan and didn't for one minute drop behind. They made it as close to the accommodation module as they could then regrouped in silence. Erik gestured to indicate that there was a hijacker in sight and silently pulled out his knife.

Finn held out a hand to stop Niall moving and counted down with Erik. When Erik moved it was stealthy but somehow the hijacker must have sensed something as he turned at the exact moment Erik was on top of him. A short scuffle later and the second hijacker was dead, sprawled with his throat cut.

Erik held up two fingers. Two dead hijackers. Two to go.

Finn faced Niall. "I need you to get inside the

accommodation module, okay?" Niall looked like he was in shock and Finn stepped a little closer. "Can you do that? I need you inside where you can lock yourself in."

"What about the hijackers?"

"The two left are occupied with the rest of Delta, you have to trust me? Can you do that?"

Niall looked at him, shivering, his skin so pale, his eyes bloodshot and his glasses gone. He looked like death.

"I can," he finally said.

"Then I need you to go find the rest of the crew and stay with them." Finn kept his tone level, even when Niall gripped his jacket and opened his mouth to talk.

"Find me, okay?" Niall said firmly. "Come find me."

Then, before Finn could say a word, Niall turned on his heel and hobbled in the opposite direction. He was cradling his arm, limping, but Finn hadn't seen blood.

"We're taking fire," Cap's voice echoed in his head and he pulled himself out of the need to grab Niall and just leaving this place. *Break the firing.* Then memories of what he's seen Svein do, of the bodies in Alta of fellow ERU members, of the laughter as he'd thrown himself off the dam like some kind of action movie cliché, assailed him. The guy was a killer and Delta needed to take him down.

They continued onward and upward, covering each other as they took flight after flight toward the helideck. The ascension felt like it took an eternity. The other members of the Delta team were putting themselves in harm's way in the Puma, drawing fire. Finn and Erik had to get up there and neutralise it so the Puma could land. An explosion sent shockwaves hard enough to have Finn stumbling back downstairs and a crash of twisted metal blocked his way.

"Fuck, we're blocked," Erik shouted.

They turned on their heels and went back the way they came. The only way up was to find the next corridor and approach the deck from another angle. Fire chased them and they ran in the opposite direction to where they'd been heading. They reached the last area before the alternative exit and skidded to a halt. Svein stood at the door facing them. And immobile, gripped by his throat, was Niall, a pistol at his temple. Svein had utter focus and determination on his face and there was an evil light in his eyes.

CHAPTER SEVEN

Finn stopped in horror. In his head Niall was safe and he wasn't held by a madman intent on killing. This was wrong.

Erik had the presence of mind to make connections in his head that Finn couldn't make. He cursed but didn't stop and stare in shock. Instead he scrabbled back and away until only Finn stood in the face-off. They had to get the focus off the Puma and the rest of the team and that was Erik's job now. Because Finn had to deal with Svein.

"Put the guns down," Svein said. If anything that made Finn grip the barrel of his Sig harder, and angle of his rifle just that little bit higher. Sven pressed the barrel of the pistol harder and Niall closed his eyes.

Finn stepped closer, his gun still raised. He could take Svein in one shot but from this angle Niall would be collateral damage. *Niall would be dead.* Deltas didn't let hostages die if they could stop it. But he wasn't dropping his gun. In all the scenarios where he dropped his weapon he was dead in seconds and Niall would be as well.

"You think I won't kill him?" Svein said. His

tone wasn't threatening, more questioning. "Drop your weapons."

"What do you want?" Hijackers had agendas: the release of political prisoners or money being two of them. There had to be some kind of ground that Finn could give way on without Niall dying. Niall still has his eyes closed, his right arm cradled, and now Finn could see blood darkening the sleeve of his shirt and staining the skin at his wrist.

Why didn't he say he was bleeding?

As if Niall had heard his thoughts he opened his hazel eyes and stared directly at Finn. There was fear in them, but also utter trust in the way he wasn't panicking.

Svein huffed a laugh. "I don't want a thing. I want you. Simple. You and your team for killing me, you for missing my heart."

"Let the hostage go." *Don't personalise the hostage, don't show you love that man more than life itself.*

All the time they talked Finn calculated trajectories. He could shoot through Niall, but that would just catch Svein in the shoulder. He had to be calm and focused about this but seeing Niall gripped so tightly was messing with his focus. If he was going to shoot then he needed to be ready. He hoped to God whatever happened that Erik had somehow removed the last shooter from the platform so that the rest of the ERU could land and give backup. That was one less thing to have on his conscience.

"I wasn't aiming for your heart," Finn said clearly. He wanted to engage Svein, try and explain something enough so that this all slowed down.

"Fuck you," Svein said then he smiled and Finn looked into pale silver eyes that held madness. "You think I don't know who Niall Faulkner is? Warming your bed and making you slow, it was just a matter of time until Forseti was going to be your grave."

"I don't know the hostage," Finn lied. Then, like the decision was made for him, Niall slumped in Svein's hold. Finn reacted on instinct and the bullet left his gun even as he moved. It carved through Niall's arm, caught Svein low on his side, enough for Niall to fall, enough for Svein to curse and twist away. Finn was on Svein before he had a chance to regroup, using his bodyweight as a pivot and landing a punch to Svein's face as he fell to a stop. They grappled and neither had the upper hand but Finn knew this was a fight of attrition. Sooner or later Svein would tire as he lost blood and Finn would take his advantage.

He couldn't see Niall, couldn't even take a moment to worry where Niall was as Svein gained the upper hand, his arm around Finn's throat.

It can't end like this. With preternatural strength he twisted and threw until Svein hit the solid wall and for a split second Finn had the upper hand. Then everything went to hell, the whole platform shifting with another explosion. Svein and Finn were thrown to the floor and fuck, Svein laughed, even as he relaxed his hold of Finn and grabbed at a knife of his own. They jumped back and apart. Svein was just as trained as Finn; they were a pretty even match. Up this close Finn could see scarring on Svein's face, and a cloudiness in his left eye. He quickly filed everything for reference even as he caught sight of Niall grabbing at Finn's fallen Sig.

No. Don't use the gun. Don't do it.

He couldn't have Niall killing. Niall wasn't the killer here.

Finn held out his knife and he and Svein circled each other, Finn balancing on the balls of his feet, curving back and away as Svein stabbed at him. He moved the balance and swiped down, his sharp blade passing easily through Svein's thin jacket. Svein didn't falter and when Finn moved in he sensed Niall moving behind him. He realised he'd taken his eye off the ball as Svein's knife sliced across his chest, upward, to his throat.

Finn jumped back but Svein pressed the advantage and forced Finn up against the wall, both men fighting for control with the knives. Svein was winning this battle of strength, madness in his expression and hate in his eyes. Finn relaxed his stance, waiting for Svein to press the advantage and as he did they separated and Svein held his knife in place ready to stab. Finn dropped to the floor and rolled to a crouch in seconds. His temple pounded and dizziness assailed him. Svein saw the crouch, leaned over him, knife high, and in a desperate lunge Finn stabbed up and into Svein's throat.

"Doesn't matter," Svein choked. Finn twisted the knife as Svein weakly batted his hand, blood spilling from the wound then life leaving his eyes in an instant.

Finn shoved him away and pulled out his knife at the same time, the arc of arterial blood splattering his jacket. *This time, fucking stay dead.* He glanced at Niall, who stared at him with horror in his expression. He looked so damn pale with the Sig in his hands, the aim of it right at Svein on the floor.

Finn moved quickly, prising the pistol from Niall's hands. "He's dead," he said.

Briefly Finn embraced Niall but they couldn't stop.

"Tango main is down, Erik."

"Copy that, Delta Seven," Erik replied. "Helideck clear, tango four down."

"Exfil in ten," Cap responded. "Let's get these hostages off Forseti."

"Why did he...?" Niall pointed at the dead Svein on the floor.

Finn didn't have time to talk about this. He had to get to the helideck and get the hostages off the platform, including Niall. Finn checked Svein's pulse one last time, there was nothing. Then he considered direction and with Niall right behind him they headed upward.

"I was going to the others," Niall said as they climbed. "He was just there. I tried to..."

Niall stopped walking, leaning on the metal banister and bowing his head. This was inevitable; he'd been running on adrenalin and abruptly that had left.

"Keep going," Finn encouraged.

"Why did he...?"

"I have a bad feeling about this," Finn said hurriedly. "I need you topside."

Niall nodded, visibly pulling himself together and straightening. "Let's go."

About two flights from open air Niall was pulled short by shouting, Erik's voice loud over the headset. "Abort. Abort. Helipad is wired."

Finn heard cursing from Cap and held his breath. When an explosion didn't happen he assumed they had managed to abort the Puma landing.

"Jesus Christ, Finn, you need to get your ass up here and see this."

Finn considered everything. Svein hadn't given them a way off of Forseti. "Is there a timer?"

"I can't fucking see shit up here past explosives," Erik snapped.

Finn made a decision. "Get down here, Erik. We have to move the crew to the boat to get off this thing." Glancing at Niall he considered whether his lover would be able to get down to the boat deck and passed to where he and Erik had left the boat. He was frighteningly pale and his face was red with the burn of sleet and bruises.

I will keep you alive.

"Erik, get the remaining hostages to the boat deck. I'll get Niall down there."

"I can't," Niall said softly. So soft that Finn almost missed it. "I think…" He slumped against the railing and only Finn grabbing tight stopped him from falling.

"We have to get lower," Finn said. "They rigged the helideck to stop the Puma from landing. Our only way off is with the boat."

Niall looked up at him, focusing in on him, his eyes wide, then he coughed. He opened his mouth to say something but closed it just as quickly. "Let's move," he finally said.

Together, with more of a stumble than a walk they began descending back the way they'd come. Every step was exertion and Niall was becoming heavier with each one. Finn could feel the blood on his hands, the sticky wetness an indication something was seriously fucking wrong.

"I love you," Niall murmured. "I know you don't want to hear it but if we die—"

"We're not dying." Finn hoisted more of Niall's weight and refused to think that there was a world where Niall wasn't in it.

"I love you," Niall repeated. His voice held a hint of question. Finn had spent so much of their time together calling it an easy relationship for sex that he'd held back how he felt, but could he still do that with Niall literally dying in front of him?

They stopped for a second and Finn couldn't even think about how much further they had to go down. Nor how long they had left. Who knew what kind of timing was on the damn explosives. *Fuck.*

"Delta Seven, we're at the boat." Erik confirmed the facts.

Finn cradled Niall's face, looked deep into his eyes even as he spoke to Erik. "Get the boat away."

"Waiting for you," Erik said stubborn and focused.

If the platform was rigged, then they'd all die.

"Five, you see anything, you go…"

"Copy."

Finn pressed a kiss to Niall's cold lips, then pulled back, "I love you," he said. "Now let's move."

And with that declaration of love they began to move again, Finn aware that the whole platform could collapse around them, or that Erik would move the boat, or that hell, he was going to die here with Niall.

They stumble-walked down to the boat deck, the

burning from the knife wound in his chest getting worse then numbing in the icy cold as they moved outside.

"Not far now," he reassured a near-comatose Niall. He could see the boat, the tethering holding, they were six feet, five feet... He could imagine the step to take to get Niall onto the boat. Two feet, Erik was there, grabbing Niall and dragging him into the boat, Finn right behind him, the boat wheeling away, the faces of scared hostages burned onto his retinas. They were away, twenty feet, thirty, fifty, when a huge explosion parted the storm and the heaving seas. Instinctively, Finn covered Niall.

"Down," he shouted, the frightened crew doing as they were told. Finn looked back at the extent of the explosion, at the fire, the hell that rained down on them, and prayed to hell they made it out. Something smacked into the boat, then another, hitting Finn on the back and forcing him lower in the boat.

A hundred feet, two hundred...

Then the terrifying noise of the platform in self-destruct was swallowed by the storm and they were far enough away for Finn to sit upright. They couldn't see Forseti now, and he had to think.

"Cap? We need exfil..." He yanked at an unconscious Niall's clothes, revealing bone cutting through skin in his arm, and so much blood, some congealed and some free flowing. Niall's pulse was thready, thin, barely there.

"Five," Cap answered immediately.

Finn gripped his fear and refused to let it show to anyone. Five may not be enough time to save Niall.

CHAPTER EIGHT

Niall woke slowly, step by step, each a little more painful than the last. He was aware of noise around him, of pain, and the startling white of the lights in his face. People asked him questions, his name, his age, and he was sure he'd heard Ewan's voice on more than one occasion telling him he was an uncle now and uncles didn't do things like die on oil platforms.

Although Ewan's voice was welcome he still craved Finn's lower, huskier tones but there had been no sign of him.

The doctor told him he'd been hypothermic, that his radius had snapped out through his skin, that he'd lost blood and was actually lucky that they'd got him back to land and to a hospital before he died from shock. That had been at least an hour ago and since then no one had even come into his room, let alone talked to him. Right now he'd even give a smile to a nurse if it meant he wasn't stuck here with drips in the back of his hand and his head buzzing with pain.

They'd suspected a concussion from the boat deck explosion he'd rigged with the water at high pressure. They'd worried he'd been hit by pieces of

Forseti self-destructing but at the end of the day seemed like his brain had come out of this fairly much intact. Go figure.

And talking of Forseti? Niall groaned at the thought of what had happened. The platform was a hazard now. The destruction hadn't been systematic and project managed. It had been rent in two from the helideck down to the lower production deck. Apparently, according to Ewan, there had been so much explosive wired up that there was no chance of anyone getting off alive. Fires had raged in the accommodation block, the comms room, and the small room where he had hidden, and there was nothing left recognisable as an oil platform part from twisted metal rising out of the sea.

Forseti had died dramatically and horribly and its death throes had very nearly taken him and others with it.

A nurse came in to check his vitals and he grabbed the chance of talking. He asked the same question that he'd done every single God-damned time he'd spoken to anyone.

"The team that got us off of the platform, are they here?"

The nurse, still smiling, shook her head. "Sorry, this is my first shift this week, I don't know of another team in the hospital."

"ERU," Niall persisted. "The Deltas."

The Nurse frowned briefly, then resumed her smiling, this time with raised eyebrows. "Oh, I think I'd notice a Delta in the place," she joked. "And no, there aren't any. But you do have a friend who is waiting to visit."

Ewan was back again. This time Niall hoped he'd bought his son with him so Niall could at least see the new baby.

The nurse leaned over to add details to his chart then adjust the drip into his non-splinted arm. They'd had to operate on the bones, knitting them and holding them in place with a metal plate and it fucking hurt today.

"Although," she added thoughtfully, "the guy out there is very rugged and sexy, could easily be a Delta." She left and all of a sudden Niall had hope inside him. Ewan was a good-looking guy, as brothers go, but no one had ever described him as sexy or rugged. To be fair though, not that anyone would to Niall. Was it possible that Finn was here?

The moment they'd shared on the stairs, just before Niall lost his last connection to consciousness had been intense. But that had been three days ago now. Three. And Finn had said he loved him, but where was he now? If Finn really loved Niall then shouldn't he be here or something?

The door opened a little, then more fully and Niall's breath hitched in his chest. Finn. His lover looked tired. No, beyond tired—exhausted. He wasn't shaved, his hair a mess of spikes, and he looked uncertain, wary to step in the room.

"Finn," Niall said with more than a little excitement in his voice.

"Hey," was all Finn said.

Niall wriggled a little to sit more upright, sickness washing over him at the pain in his arm. Finn immediately crossed to him, placing a hand on his chest. "Don't move," he said, concerned.

Niall couldn't concentrate on not moving. "Where have you been?"

Finn shrugged then glanced behind him at the closed door. "Tidying up loose ends with Svein," he explained. Niall imagined that was all he was going to get out of Finn, secrets and all that mess associated with hijackings and hostage situations. Then to Niall's amazement Finn continued. "Svein had been tracking you," he admitted. "Had a whole wall of crazy in this place outside of Oslo. Saw a connection between the two of us."

Niall considered the words. He could sense what Finn was doing. All that heroic shit where he kept himself out of Niall's life in order to keep Niall safe.

"Don't do that," Niall snapped the conclusion of his internal thought process.

"What?" Finn looked confused.

"Start all that shit about how we're better apart."

Finn looked down at Niall. "What the hell are you talking about?"

"You're going to give that whole speech about how we're better apart just so I don't get targeted by a mad man intent on killing a Delta."

Niall watched as realisation passed over Finn's face. Then Finn chuckled. "I wasn't going to say that at all. Hell, he wasn't after you, he was using you to get to me, different scenario."

"So what do you want to say?" Niall couldn't help the suspicion in his voice. He was used to the fact that this whole relationship was a temporary thing, had even come to terms with it in his head.

Finn moved to sit on the bed next to Niall, and somehow in that curiously graceful way he had about him for such a big guy, he was in a position to cradle Niall in his arms. Niall sunk into the strong hold and attempted to relax.

"My place has two rooms," he said. "You could move in with me and have the second bedroom as an office. I'd move in with you but I need to be near HQ in Oslo."

Niall said nothing, the words sinking in slowly. "What?" he finally asked.

"Will you move in with me?"

"In with you?"

"Yes, in with me," Finn chuckled as he repeated the words. "I love you, Niall Faulkner, and I'm done with this self-sacrificing bullshit that has me fucking and leaving. I want forever with you. You up for it? I'm not much, my time is up with ERU in ten months or so and I'm back in London, and you'll just be dating a cop again. And I—"

"Shut up and kiss me," Niall ordered.

So he did. And Niall enjoyed it so much that he even forgot he was in pain.

Well...very nearly anyway.

EPILOGUE

Forseti was a mess.

Three weeks on the platform and Niall was a mess as well. Not only was it one of the hardest things he had to do, going back to where he'd nearly died, but he missed Finn. And that was just ridiculous. The very nature of who they were would mean they'd spend time apart, weeks, months even, but this was all so new, and there was no way Finn would be missing him. He'd be busy, focused on the important work he did.

"You okay?" Ewan had asked that a lot over the last three weeks, and was still asking it now as the Puma landed back at base. So far Niall had managed to gloss over how he was feeling, but with his feet on solid ground he felt like maybe now was a good time to clear the air and get his worries out there. His brother was a good listener and maybe all he needed was for Ewan to tell him everything was going to be okay, and that relationships like the kind he and Finn had could work.

"I miss Finn."

"Yeah, I know. I miss my family as well."

Finn wasn't family. Not officially, but the way Ewan casually implied Finn was family to Niall was a nice thing. They entered the station and Niall offloaded his case and laptop onto the first table they came to.

"How do you do it? How do you deal with time apart?" Niall immediately asked.

Ewan crossed to the coffee maker and poured two mugs, exchanging insults with the security team who had shadowed them on Forseti. Real security guys this time, not gun toting terrorists with hidden agendas. Seemed like Niall would have to wait for his answer until caffeine was consumed. Ewan began talking as soon as he was back at the table.

"It's exciting, you know, I get home and I see Mel and it's like we're newlyweds again. Although she's had Adam on her own and probably needs more of the baby care help than the hot monkey sex."

Niall frowned. "I don't want to hear details about what you do with Mel."

Ewan poked him. "Well I'm not a virgin, you know, I'm a married man."

"I just… I'm not sure Finn will be missing me as much as I miss him, okay? He's probably out there saving the world and not giving one ounce of thought to the idiot who nearly died on his watch."

"I thought he said he loved you." Ewan looked puzzled, then his expression brightened. "I think you need to go now."

Niall picked up his coffee and sipped at it tentatively. "After debrief and coffee," he answered.

"No, I'll cover debrief. I promise you really need to go." He nodded to indicate something behind Niall and it made him turn. To see Finn standing just inside the door in his heavy coat. Something inside Niall snapped into place and in seconds he crossed to where Finn stood and pulled him into a hug.

"Glad you made it back okay," Finn said into his ear.

Niall made a split second decision and returned to scoop up his laptop and case. "Tell them I'll debrief tomorrow," he said to Ewan. "We'll do it together. Go home to Mel." Then he turned on his heel and followed Finn outside. He wanted to kiss his lover, to hold him so close and never let him go, but he didn't, because if he started he wouldn't stop.

"Where to?" Finn asked cautiously. He looked uncertain, his eyes wary.

"Anywhere warm." As if to underscore that the wind blustered around them, and with it came the hint of icy rain. Finn tugged Niall towards a car and they drove in silence away from the station. They turned off the main road and pulled up outside the cluster of apartment buildings where Finn had a room. Niall had been here before once and it was a nice room right in the middle of a group of them used by the rest of the Deltas when they were on site. Finn killed the engine before turning to face Niall, seemed like he wanted to talk but didn't quite know what to say.

"Did it go okay? On Forseti?" he finally asked.

Niall nodded. "We managed to get a workable plan to salvage." He didn't want to be talking about work. He wanted to talk about him and Finn and the future. "Look, before we… go inside and do… whatever…"

"Are you okay?" Finn asked with a cautious tone.

"No." Niall didn't mean that to come out quite so forcefully and wished he could take it back when his big-bad-Delta flinched.

"Niall—"

"I have to say something, and what I say may make you run for the hills, but I'll understand, okay? I mean, I get you're this super cop who lives for the danger and keeping us all safe, and I know we connected, but when I tell you this you might not want to do that... in there." Niall failed miserably at explaining one single thing in any form of coherent fashion.

"Niall, what's wrong?"

"I missed you, okay? I thought about you every minute of the freaking day, and I need to know whether you did too."

"Whether I did what? Missed you?"

"Yeah."

"It's important to you?"

"I'm sorry."

"Jeez, don't be. Because I thought about you every minute I could. When I was on downtime, when we were in Oslo, when I wasn't busy fake killing everyone on training." Finn reached out and cupped Niall's chin. "I love you. You're the other half of me and I hope to hell that is what you need to hear, because I don't have the words like you do."

"And we *can* make this work." Niall wasn't questioning, he was making a statement of fact.

"I thought it was working already. Let's finish this inside."

They made it halfway up the stairs before Finn stole a kiss, which led to more kissing, which led to them fumbling for the key when they got to the small apartment, so much so that Finn couldn't get the door open and Niall had to help him. With the door open they finally stumbled into the room, Finn pushing the door shut and pressing Niall up against the wood.

In seconds they were undressing each other— coats, sweaters, pants, socks, boots, everything flying from them—and Niall kissed every inch that Finn uncovered on his muscled body. This was so right, this was fire and passion and Niall craved Finn with an intensity that burned in him.

Somehow they tripped their way to the large bed and tumbled back in a tangle of arms and legs to the mattress. Niall whimpered in his throat as Finn pushed and shoved him up the bed before covering him with his body and sighing into their kisses.

"Here is where we belong."

"In bed?"

"Together." Niall answered. "So we'll be apart sometimes, and we'll miss each other, but we'll always be in love, and we'll make so many memories that you won't have space in your head for there to be any doubts."

Niall arched up into Finn and gripped hard to his lover's forearms. "Can we start now?"

Finn deepened the kisses, shifting and pulling until they were in just the right position, an arm's length from the cabinet next to the bed. Finn reached over and located lube and condoms and Niall relaxed against the mattress, Finn would take care of him. They kissed as Finn stretched and prepared, and the kissing was endless, only interspersed with soft spoken words of love.

"Now," Niall said, "Please."

Finn pressed inside, so slowly, all the time kissing, and groaned as he moved. Finn stopped when he was inside, and for the longest time they rocked gently until Niall couldn't handle it anymore.

"Finn…"

Finn pulled out a little, then pushed back in, staring down at Niall, complete concentration on his face. Niall loved that about him, how he took this all so seriously. Then he didn't have time for thought at all as Finn moved faster, setting a pace that robbed Niall of breath.

"So close, touch yourself," Finn pleaded. Niall gripped his hard cock and tried to set a rhythm but it was too much, Finn pegging his prostate with a punishing accuracy. Niall closed his eyes as his senses went into overload. He gripped his cock with one hand, Finn's bicep with another, and groaned his release as he lost it between them.

"Open your eyes, Niall, please."

Niall opened his eyes and that seemed to be what pushed Finn over the edge as with a cry of completion he was coming hard. He rested on Niall, still inside him and just a little to the side, supporting his weight on his arm.

"God, I missed you," he admitted again. "Don't ever think I don't."

Niall could never tire of hearing the words. He hadn't been expecting love with a Delta, but that was what fate had given him.

"And we'll make this work."

Finn pressed one last heated kiss before pulling out and to one side. Laid on their backs, they both looked up at the white ceiling, hands grasped tight.

"Every single day you'll know I love you," Finn promised.

Niall smiled to himself. That was all he could ask for and it was just what he wanted.

"Every single day."

RJ Scott has been writing since age six, when she was made to stay in at lunchtime for an infraction involving cookies. She was told to write a story and two sides of paper about a trapped princess later, a lover of writing was born.

As an avid reader herself, she can be found reading anything from thrillers to sci-fi to horror. However, her first real true love will always be the world of romance where she takes cowboys, bodyguards, firemen and billionaires (to name a few) and writes dramatic and romantic stories of love and passion between these men.

With over sixty titles to her name and counting, she is the author of the award winning book, *The Christmas Throwaway*. She is also known for the Texas series charting the lives of Riley and Jack, and the Sanctuary series following the work of the Sanctuary Foundation and the people it protects.

Her goal is to write stories with a heart of romance, a troubled road to reach happiness, and most importantly, that hint of a happily ever after.

www.rjscott.co.uk

Also by RJ Scott

Love Lane Books

A Reason to Stay
All the King's Men
Angel in a Book Shop
Bodyguard to a Sex God
Book of Secrets
Broken Memories
Capture The Sun
Chase The Sun
Child of the Storm
Christmas In The Sun
Darach's Cariad
Deefur and the Great Mistletoe Incident
Deefur Dog
El Chico Indigente en Navidad
Face Value
Follow The Sun
Full Circle
Guarding Morgan
Heat
Il miracolo di Natale
Jesse's Christmas
Jete a la rue pour Noel
Kian's Hunter
Last Marine Standing
Love is in the Hallways

Love is in the Message
Love is in the Title
Natale a New York
New York Christmas
Noel aÂ New-York
One Night
Oracle
Shattered Secrets
Spirit Bear
Still Waters
Texas Christmas
Texas Fall
Texas Family
Texas Heat
Texas Winter
The Christmas Throwaway
The Decisions We Make
The Ex Factor
The Gallows Tree
The Heart of Texas
The Journal of Sanctuary One
The Only Easy Day
The Soldier's Tale
Valentine 2525
Worlds Collide

Totally Bound Publishing
Back Home
Crooked Tree Ranch
Moments
The Angel and the Model
The Barman and the SEAL
The Carpenter and the Actor

The Doctor and the Bad Boy
The Fireman and the Cop
The Paramedic and the Writer
The Teacher and the Soldier

Extasy Books
The Demon's Blood
The Guilty Werewolf
The Incubus Agenda
The New Wolf
The Third Kingdom
The Vampire Contract
The Warlock's Secret

For an up to date list of all books please visit
www.rjscott.co.uk

Jumping In

Alpha Gay Erotic Romance

Cardeno C.

CHAPTER ONE

"Hey, handsome. You're back a day early, ain't ya?" Sally Bouvier said. She smacked her gum and twirled a strand of her blue hair around her matching blue manicured finger. "I wasn't expecting ya till tomorrow."

"Tomorrow's Saturday and I have the weekday shift."

"Like ya'd be gone for two weeks and not come see me the second ya got back." She rolled her eyes at the ridiculousness of that possibility. "Clint Rivera, what kind of fool do ya take me for?"

Technically, he was coming in to check if any of his cases needed his immediate attention or if the sheriff was short-staffed and wanted him to work that weekend. Both possibilities were unlikely in sleepy Hawthorne, New Mexico, but it wasn't as if anybody was waiting for him at home, which was the very reason he'd packed his two dogs, thrown his camping gear in the back of his truck, and driven out of town two weeks earlier. Clint wasn't normally one to take a vacation, but he'd had hours accrued and it was use it or lose it. His temper, not the time. And the last thing he needed was another round of anger management classes. Besides, Sally wasn't all wrong about his reason for coming to the station.

"I picked you up a couple of those date shakes you like on my way into town." He set a plastic bag filled with ice and two Styrofoam cups on Sally's desk. "I didn't want them to melt."

"Aww, honey, ain't ya sweet." Sally jumped up from her chair, hurried around her desk, and threw her arms around him. Well, she tried, anyway. Between the size of her breasts and the width of his chest, it was more like a half-hug. "Did ya get one for yourself, sugar? Ain't they just the cat's meow?"

"Uh..." He had in fact gotten one of the infamous date shakes at the truck stop off the interstate, but he didn't like the sickly sweet flavor and after he'd encountered chunks of what he could only hope were dates, he'd tossed the whole thing. Not that he wanted to admit such sacrilege to Sally. The woman might be half his size, but she ran the sheriff's office and she'd become an adopted mother of sorts to him since he'd arrived in Hawthorne.

Thankfully, she saved him from answering her question when she leaned back, looked him up and down and then crinkled her nose and said, "Although I do declare, honey, ya surely could have gotten washed off first instead of bringing the campground in here with ya."

After two years working with Sally, Clint still had no idea what kind of dialect she had or where she'd picked it up. Nobody else in the town, or for that matter, in the state, spoke with her particular twang and as far as he knew, Sally was a Hawthorne native.

"I stopped at home and took a shower." Rubbing his hand over his smooth cheeks, he said, "I even shaved."

"Humph." She walked back to her chair, brushing off her dress as she went. "Darlin', I got more dirt on me from huggin' ya just now than I did when Tommy Elders and I necked out by Eagle Nest Lake."

"Who's Tommy Elders?" Clint asked as he pounded his hands on his flannel shirt, denim jacket, and jeans. Based on the poofs of dust, he could see Sally's point. Washing his truck was next on his agenda, otherwise any shower followed by a drive would be pointless.

"He was my high school beau." Sally sighed happily and smiled at the memory. "Tommy was a real looker." She appraised Clint. "He had black hair and brown eyes like ya, same with that constant tan, but he was more delicate, like them runway models."

At six feet two inches tall and one hundred and eighty pounds, nobody ever called Clint delicate.

"You went to school with a model?" he said, surprised that someone from Hawthorne was anywhere near famous and he'd never heard about it. Of the thirty thousand residents in town, twenty-nine thousand were active participants in the rumor mill and the other thousand were too young to talk. Although, to be fair, Clint didn't interact much with folks outside of work and he'd never been one for gossip.

"Oh, no, honey. Tommy's a mechanic. Ended up marryin' a gal just as pretty as him, movin' down south, and havin' a couple of babies." She leaned forward and lowered her voice conspiratorially. "Now I didn't say nothin', but those kids of theirs were plumb ugly, darlin'. I mean, bless their hearts, but ya couldn't even look at 'em for more than half a minute without gettin' queasy." She straightened up and shook her head. "It just goes to show ya."

He arched his eyebrows in question.

"A positive times a positive makes a negative." She untied the plastic bag, picked up one of the cups, and stuck her gum on the lid. "Just like in math, honey."

"You mean a negative times a negative makes a positive."

"What's that, darlin'?" Sally took a big sip of the shake and moaned. "Mmm, mmm. Even better than I remembered." After another sip, she put it back in the bag and stood. "I'm going to head on home and put these in the refrigerator for later." She patted her hips. "Ya know what they say, honey, a moment on the lips, a lifetime on the hips and with that shindig tonight, I surely don't need the extra calories."

"What's going on tonight?" Clint asked with a chuckle.

"Oh, that's right, ya left before they sent out the invitations." She leaned down and battled with the bottom desk drawer. "It's the biggest ticket in town, honey. All the muckety-mucks are goin' to be there." Eventually managing to wedge her purse free, she started digging through it. "Earl Landers invited me as his plus one. Nice man. Shame about his wife but honestly, after her first two divorces, nobody expected her to make this one last long." She clicked her tongue and shook her head disapprovingly.

Clint decided not to point out that she herself had three divorces and two annulments under her sequined, bright teal belt.

"Bill Chiders sure is pullin' out all the stops for his little girl's wedding."

Though he didn't know Bill personally, Clint had spent half a year listening to his ex say Bill's name in variations of the same theme: "Bill said reputation is the most important part of being a lawyer. Anyone can put in hours, but to earn the big money, clients have to like you. Once I get a few more clients, Bill will have to make me a partner."

Clint didn't suppose there was anything inherently wrong with those ideas, but when a good reputation meant hiding any sort of relationship with him, he couldn't help but take it personally.

"This was the inside envelope." Sally yanked a gold envelope out of her bag. "It came tucked in another one. Two envelopes, honey." She waved it in the air. "And this is just for the engagement party!" She carefully pulled a shimmery package tied in ribbon out of the envelope. "As fancy as they got on the invitations, ya just know the meal's going to be special." She thrust the invitation at Clint. "It's so pretty, I'd have had it framed if that Ewan Gifford wasn't such a jackass. Pardon my French." She patted Clint's shoulder. "I need to go home and do my face, honey. Thanks for comin' by."

And with that unwitting launch of a bombshell, Sally walked out of the station and left Clint holding an invitation to his ex-boyfriend's engagement party. Not that she had any way of knowing that given that their breakup was caused by Ewan's refusal to come out for fear of ruining his precious reputation and Clint's frustration at living in the closet after having moved halfway across the country to build his own life. Well, those reasons and, it now seemed, Ewan's having a fiancée. Fucker.

Clint had been out of town for exactly two weeks. Fourteen days. Nobody went from a first date to a lifetime commitment that quickly, which meant Ewan had been seeing his boss's daughter while they'd been... He couldn't call it dating considering they'd never gone anywhere outside their apartments, but didn't fucking the same man on a regular basis for going on half a year mean something? It did to him.

Six years in the army, almost all of them deployed to Afghanistan, followed by a two-year stint on the Detroit police force, had taken away any romantic notions Clint once might have had. But a man didn't need a child's fairytale dream of happily-ever-after to be loyal.

The sound of crinkling paper snapped him to attention. He looked at his hand and saw the previously smooth layers smashed into a ball. Shit. Sally was going to kill him. He set the invitation on her desk and tried straightening it out, getting as far as seeing the distorted words "Ewan Gifford's" next to "engagement" before muttering, "Fuck it. I'll buy her flowers," and tossing the whole mess into the trashcan.

"Nice shot."

A unique combination of whiskey smooth and gravel rough, sometimes in the same word, Clint didn't need to see the speaker to identify his voice. Only one man sounded like that: Hawk Black, the new deputy mayor. He'd moved into town shortly after the November election and taken over the post from a man who had decided he couldn't wait for his boss to retire so instead he ran against him in a remarkably ugly campaign. Clint didn't know what was more surprising: the fact that elections in Hawthorne could get contentious or the fact that a stranger was appointed such a powerful position. Then again, it was possible he paid more attention to the new arrival than other people. And not because of his job title.

Reminding himself to keep his eyes on the deputy mayor's face and not leer at his imposing body, especially not his groin, which Clint already knew looked damn enticing in a suit, he took a deep breath, plastered a smile on his face, and turned around.

"Thanks. Those four years playing in high school are coming in handy now in trashcan basketball."

"You have the build for playing ball." The deputy mayor dragged his gaze from Clint's shoulders to his feet and back up again, making Clint feel as if he were nude despite his boots, jeans, undershirt, flannel, and jacket. "Guy your size, I bet nobody could penetrate your defense."

The comment didn't fully make sense, same for the look he was getting, but Clint chalked it up to his brain working at less than full tilt. He had that problem whenever the deputy mayor was near—a direct effect of giving up a good bit of focus to that tall, muscular body, strong square jaw, bright blue eyes, and midnight black hair, and losing the rest of his focus on trying to hide his physical response.

Even Clint's ex had noticed his reaction to Black, which was really saying something because Ewan had been terrified to be seen with him. But one afternoon, Ewan had happened to walk into the coffee shop where Clint was sharing a table with Black after unexpectedly running into him. In an uncharacteristic move, Ewan had acknowledged him, just a brief hello and an introduction to the deputy mayor. But for weeks afterward, Ewan had tossed out snide remarks that Clint had rationalized as jealousy. It had made sense at the time, but knowing what he knew now, Clint wondered how a man who had been dating someone else himself had the nerve to be jealous of Clint's reaction to anyone or anything. Asshole.

"There's that growl again." The sides of Black's mouth turned up in an almost-smile. "I'd ask what you were thinking about that has you so roweled up, but—" Black flicked his gaze to the trashcan. "I don't think he's worth another second of your time."

Once again, Clint was lost in the conversation. He really had to listen to Black instead of fixating on the color of his eyes. They couldn't be contact lenses; he'd looked closely enough to have noticed the tell-tale lines. But never in his life had Clint seen a blue that deep yet clear. Like his rough but smooth voice, it was a contradiction, one of many.

Two hundred pounds and six and a half feet meant Hawk Black was too huge to pull off a fancy suit, but pull it off he did. The smooth fabric draped his broad shoulders and tight ass so enticingly that Clint often fantasized about ravaging the guy with his clothes on, something that had never been his kink.

And it wasn't just Black's appearance. Though Clint didn't know what a deputy mayor's duties included, he would have thought it'd be mostly glad-handing, but this man wasn't the type to kiss up to people or blow smoke up their asses. Hawk Black was more stoic than bubbly but, in yet another contradiction, he was also friendly. As a detective, Clint reported to the sheriff so he didn't have cause to interact with Black for work, nobody at the station did, and yet, Black was frequently there, making conversation and inspiring hard-ons.

"Sally prefers chocolate."

"Sally?" Clint had been paying attention that time, just not to the conversation. But, honestly, who could blame him with that bulge on display? He wondered if Black wore underwear.

"Ms. Bouvier," Black said, arching his eyebrows and grinning. "Your friend. You said you were going to buy her flowers. I thought you might want to know that she'd rather get chocolate."

"Oh." Though he wanted to ask how Black knew anything about Sally, Clint couldn't think of how to phrase the question without being insulting. Aside from which, the answer was none of his business. "Thank you."

"How was your camping trip?" Black asked as he leaned his left shoulder against the wall, folded his arms, and crossed one ankle over the other.

If he wore underwear, they were loose, like boxers, because the tube snaking down his right thigh couldn't be anything other than a cock and it looked the furthest thing from restrained.

"Clint?"

After shaking his head to clear the hormonal haze, Clint blinked and cleared his throat. "I, uh …" With the thin fabric of his pants, if he wore boxers, wouldn't lines be visible along the legs? Clint was a jeans guy through and through. He owned a couple of pairs of Dockers for formal occasions but not a suit so maybe he was wrong.

"From the look of your truck, I'd say you must have gone off-road."

"Oh. Yeah." Clint licked his lips. "It was great. I did some hiking, found a lake and fished." He caught his gaze dropping again, internally smacked himself, and looked the deputy mayor in the face. "Cooked over a fire at night."

"No phone, no computer, nature surrounding you." Black nodded. "That sounds like almost the perfect trip."

"Almost?"

"It'd be even better if you had someone with you." He paused. "Someone who'd enjoy the surroundings and appreciate the company."

"I took my dogs." Even if he hadn't left town to get away from Ewan, Clint never would have invited his ex to go camping. The man wouldn't have been willing to walk away from his phone or his computer for that long. And while Clint would have loved to fuck out in the fresh air, having Ewan around for other parts of the day would have been less enjoyable. They didn't share the same interests and Ewan would have complained the entire time about insects, wildlife, and not having access to a shower. "My girls are good company."

"Speedy and Fluffy, right?" Black chuckled. "I

bet they enjoyed having you all to themselves day and night."

He didn't remember telling the deputy mayor his dogs' names but who knew what he said when his brain was on hiatus and his focus was on his dick. And on Black's dick. Seriously, if Clint didn't get this unusual attraction under control, he'd end up embarrassing himself and making Black uncomfortable. Unfortunately, he didn't have anyone to help him out with that project, so he needed to go home and beat off alone. Again.

"Yeah, they did. Good pups." Clint knocked both hands against the desktop and straightened. "All right, I better get going." He cleared his throat. "Sally said I need another shower."

Shoving himself off the wall, Black raked his gaze over Clint again. "You look fine to me." He stepped closer and inhaled deeply. "Smell fine too."

Suddenly, Clint wondered if Hawk Black was coming on to him. The idea seemed preposterous. Even if Black was into men, something Clint had never considered as a possibility, they were standing in the middle of the police station. Sure, nobody else was around, but that didn't mean someone couldn't walk up at any moment or that somebody couldn't hear them from an adjoining room—two things Ewan often pointed out as his rational for why they needed to stay away from one another.

"Thanks." Clint furrowed his brow and looked at Black appraisingly, but all he saw was a large, handsome man with intelligent eyes looking back. He didn't know what he'd expected—for the deputy mayor to drop to his knees and ask to suck his cock?

He snorted at the ridiculousness of his own thoughts.

"I'll, uh, see you later." He paused and wondered whether that comment could be misconstrued. "Next time you're here, I mean." He gulped. "If I'm working, which I probably will be because I have the weekday shift and that's when you come here for…" He had no idea what the deputy mayor did when he was at the station or why he came there. "Sorry." He dragged his hand through his hair. "It's been a rough day." And he needed to stop rambling like an idiot. Disgusted with himself, he raised his hand in a wave, said, "See you," and turned on his heel.

"Clint?"

He twisted his head and looked at Black over his shoulder.

"Yes?"

"Nothing to apologize for. Let me know if you need…" Black quirked one side of his mouth up in a lopsided grin. "Anything."

Grateful his back was to Black so his now barely repressible hard-on wasn't visible, Clint dipped his chin in thanks and then uncomfortably walked out of the building. He'd go home, beat off, take a shower, beat off, find something to eat, beat off, and then, maybe, his mind would be clear enough to figure out if the deputy mayor was flirting with him. Whether or not he'd come up with an answer, at least he'd be distracted from thinking about Ewan Gifford's upcoming nuptials.

CHAPTER TWO

As if being relegated to a dirty little secret from the man he...liked, most of the time, and returning to town only to hear his ex was engaged to be married and starring in the town's most exciting social event hadn't been bad enough, Clint came home to more bad news.

When he'd lived in Detroit, Clint's apartment window had faced a dilapidated church. When he'd looked at the crumbling building, he'd thought about the war-ravaged neighborhoods he'd been in during his time abroad, but as he stood next to the mailbox in front of his current apartment, it was the fading sign painted on the flaking church wall that he remembered. *The Road to Hell is Paved with Good Intentions.*

He had *intended* to come home and stay there. He had *intended* to have a quiet night putting a dent into his bottle of lube. Unfortunately, his *intentions* didn't last because he was being evicted.

Reading the letter a second time didn't change the facts. His landlord was selling the building to a developer who was going to tear it down, which meant Clint was being evicted. The thirty-day notice had arrived on the same day Clint had left so he now had two weeks to find a new place to live. He tried to shake off his frustration at the latest knee to the nuts.

Short on distractions, he flipped through the mail as he walked to his door. Solicitations, bills, and a heavy cream envelope.

No. There was no way he was holding what he thought he was holding.

His fist itching to punch a hole in the wall, he tore open the paper and saw another envelope inside. A gold one. Had Ewan Gifford lost his damn mind? Who invited a person he'd been fucking to a party celebrating his engagement to the other person he'd, it now seemed, been fucking?

The pain hit Clint before the realization that his foot was inside the stucco wall. Kicking a hole in the side of his house was better than kicking Ewan's ass and getting fired, but it wasn't nearly as satisfying. Plus, he was sure to lose his deposit.

"Damn it!" Clint wiggled his foot free and tried to find his way back to calm.

The cause was hopeless anyway, but when he noticed the rip across the top of his boot he fell deeper into the abyss. He loved those boots.

"Fuck!" he shouted. And there went another hole in the wall.

After counting to ten three times, Clint decided he could walk into his house without scaring his dogs. He shook off his only-slightly sore foot—those were damn good boots—and put his key in the lock while making a mental list of everything he had to do. He'd washed his truck on the way home from the station, but he still had to do laundry, go grocery shopping, find a new home, pack, possibly fix the holes in the wall, and repair his boots.

His hard-on was well and truly gone. He could probably resurrect it if he focused on Hawk Black for thirty seconds because the man was that hot, but right then, Clint was pissed as hell and the only logical course of action was to get pissed as hell. He'd skip dinner and go straight for the beer. Getting off would have to wait.

With his evening plans laid out, he pushed his front door open and tossed his keys and mail on the chair slash coat rack slash everything-holder. Waiting for him inside was good news and bad news.

Excited puppies rushing up to greet him were always a welcome sight. Fluffy wasn't the brightest bulb in the box, but nobody had ever been happier when he came home. She whined and wiggled, her entire back end shaking from side to side. Speedy was on her tail, nosing Clint's thighs in a combination greeting and request for scratches.

For a few seconds, Clint's bad mood started to lift, but then he saw the white poof from the corner of his eye. Not understanding what it was at first, he squatted low and petted his dogs. He noticed another white something, and then another.

Squinting across the narrow portion of the living area he could see from his position in the small walled-in entryway, he straightened and said, "What is that?"

The answer became clear when he took one step and got a view of the entire room. The entire *destroyed* room. Clint's jaw dropped. The source of the white fluff, also known as his sofa, was spread around—the frame was close to the original location and what once were cushions were strewn everywhere else. The coffee table top was flat on the ground with the legs splintered and, if he was seeing right, chewed. He took a moment to be grateful that he had chosen to spend the extra money for the wall-mounted plasma television. But then he saw the cord, which he'd had to plug into the outlet near the floor because the rental house didn't come with an outlet at television height.

"You ate the TV cord?" he asked his still wagging dogs. "Why?"

He walked toward the television, at first carefully moving over the debris and then giving up and stepping right on top of it. The occasional crunching sound was both disconcerting and oddly satisfying.

"You did," he said when he reached the TV. "You two never destroy things." He paused. "Almost never."

Squatting down, he picked up the cord.

"Why?" He shook the cord at his dogs.

They ran over and licked his face.

"Stop."

They didn't.

"Cut it out."

After coordinating a dual-jump where three paws landed on his chest, they did. Unfortunately, he had toppled backward by then.

"What is it Sally says about bad things?" he asked himself. "They come in threes, right?" The dogs didn't answer. "So we have Ewan's a fucker, I need a new place to live, and my furniture is destroyed. That's three." He shoved himself up. "But my boots make it four." He brushed his hands down his sleeves, trying to get the various sofa and table particles off, when he encountered something sticky. "What the...?" He moved his palms to his face and sniffed. "What is this?"

The dogs still didn't answer.

"Fuck it, never mind."

He shook his head, stomped into the kitchen, and yanked the refrigerator door open. Not surprisingly given his day so far, the top hinge snapped and the door started tilting toward the floor.

"Damn it!"

He tried to catch it but then his heel slipped on something—not the sticky substance from the living room, because this was slimy—and he went down, taking the door with him. The refrigerator followed but, in what might have been the only good thing to happen that evening, it hit the floor directly beside him instead of landing on top of him.

"Is this a joke?" he shouted as he jerked his gaze around the room. "This is a joke, right?"

The sound of shattering glass followed by the sight of amber liquid seeping out from underneath the destroyed appliance told him there was nothing funny about the situation.

"Not the beer!"

He scrambled to his knees and, with a grunt, flipped the refrigerator onto its side. He hadn't gone shopping since he'd returned home so there wasn't much in there: condiments, baking soda, bottles of water, and beer. Everything except the beer had survived. The only thing he wanted was beer.

"You know what?" he yelled to the still empty

room. "I know where to get a drink."

He stood up and marched toward the front door.

"Biggest party in town, huh? Bet that means an open bar."

He scooped up the mail he'd left in the entryway along with his keys and walked out.

"Ewan thinks it's funny to invite me to this bullshit? The least that asshole owes me is a beer."

* * * *

The engagement party was being held at the golf course country club. Clint had been there once for a wedding and another time for the animal shelter's big fundraiser. Neither event had valet parking but when he turned to pull into the parking lot, he was thwarted by orange cones and a sign reading *Reserved for Valet.* Why people would have trouble parking themselves in a lot not thirty feet from the front door, he didn't know, but the orange cones gave him no other alternative. With a sigh, he changed course and went to the circle drive in front of the entrance where a handful of men wearing bright blue vests stood around a temporary podium.

"They're closed today for a private event, sir," said one of the valets when Clint pushed his truck door open with a squeak.

He added oiling the hinges to his to-do list.

"I'm here for the—" Clint ground his teeth, "—event."

"Oh!" The valet looked at Clint's clothes and shifted uncomfortably from foot to foot. "Are you sure because you're not dressed like—"

"I'm sure." Clint leaned back into the car and retrieved the invitation from the mail pile he'd tossed onto the passenger seat. "See? I have the golden ticket."

The valet leaned forward, looked at the envelope in Clint's hand, and then flicked his gaze up to Clint's face.

"It isn't open."

Looking down at his own hand, Clint remembered that he'd opened the cream outer envelope and, once he'd seen the shimmery gold one, assumed he knew what was inside. But given the if-it-can-go-wrong-it-will day he was having, he suddenly worried that if he looked inside the inner envelope, he'd find something else entirely. Like a letter from the bank foreclosing his truck, even though it was a 1990 he'd bought used for cash.

"But don't worry about it. I recognize the envelope." The valet leaned forward and, in a quieter voice said, "I heard other people say they want to keep the invitation in good shape too, sir." He glanced down at Clint's hand. "It really does sparkle."

After carefully examining the valet's expression, Clint decided the guy wasn't fucking with him.

"Here." Clint thrust the envelope at him. "Keep it."

"Oh, no, I couldn't do that," the valet said but he looked at the envelope longingly.

Clint arched his eyebrows and shook his head "Consider it a tip."

"The valet services are free for guests, sir. The happy couple arranged it."

At that moment, Clint fully expected someone to walk up and admit that he was being recorded for a reality television show aimed at seeing how much insanity you could throw at a man before he lost his damn mind. Sadly, no such miracle occurred, which meant he was, most likely, experiencing real life.

"Well, I like you and I want to tip you extra," he said as he pushed the envelope against the valet's chest. "It'll be our little secret."

"Thank you so much, sir," the valet said in an excited whisper. "I won't tell any of the others." He quickly darted his gaze around, presumably to make sure nobody would run over and snatch his prize. "And I'll make sure to park your—" he glanced at Clint's still-creaking truck, "—uh, vehicle in a great spot."

As long as he got his ride back at the end of the night, Clint didn't care where they parked it but he said, "Thanks," and even managed an almost-smile before he stepped away from the truck and toward the country club entrance.

The restaurant was in the back of the building, with an attached patio overlooking the golf course. For the last two events he'd attended at there, he'd walked down the green carpeted hallway, passed the dated seating area, turned left next to the doors leading to the restrooms and tiny gym, and then reached the restaurant. The route from the entryway to the restaurant hadn't changed and if Clint looked carefully at the edges of the hallway, he thought he could see the green carpet peeking through, but otherwise, the space felt entirely different.

The walls and ceiling were covered with a gold

and silver balloon archway. A gold fabric runway lined the floor, with rope lights along its edges, highlighting the sparkle in the fabric while silently directing guests in the right direction. The hallway started in one spot and ended in another and the doorways were hidden by balloons, so there was in fact only one possible direction people could go, but logic, like the budget for this party, was apparently irrelevant.

Internally patting himself on the back for not slamming his entire body against the balloons just to hear them pop, Clint put one foot in front of the other and hoped that some dirt, drywall material, and unidentified sticky or slimy substance from his house was on his boots and being smeared onto the runway. He dragged his feet a little to help the cause.

Piano music greeted him as he left the balloon hallway and stepped into the restaurant. Though this space was slightly more identifiable, the decorating had still been taken to an extreme.

A silver disco ball hung from the middle of the ceiling and gold fabric streamed from it to the outer walls in every direction, like a giant Liberace flower. The fabric then slid down the walls in flowy rows spaced at exactly the right intervals to avoid the wall sconces lighting the room. The normally nondescript chairs were covered in a similar silky fabric with thick gold ribbon wrapped around the bases in bows. The tablecloths, of course, matched.

As Clint stood at the entry to the room, his jaw hanging open and his eyes unsure what over-the-top item to focus on, a waiter in a tuxedo walked by holding a round tray of champagne flutes.

"I'll take one," Clint said hurriedly.

The man stopped, turned to him with a smile, and then frowned as he dropped his gaze to Clint's clothes.

"Make that two." He snatched two flutes from the tray before the waiter could make a run for it with the alcohol. Speaking of alcohol. "Where's the bar?"

He slammed back one drink and then the other.

"There's a bar in the north corner and another on the patio." The man paused. "Sir."

"Thanks." Clint put the empties on the tray and picked up two more flutes. "I appreciate it."

Before he finished speaking, the waiter rushed off. Good call, really, because if he'd stayed there, Clint would have skipped the bar and downed the whole tray of champagne. Speaking of which, who drank this shit? He was on his third and it wasn't tasting any better. That didn't stop him from downing the fourth, but why couldn't they have beer? It was gold colored, like the rest of the décor and, if the sparkling glitter covered candles on the table told him anything, it was that Ewan had seen that particular decorating decision through to the last detail.

His ex always had been a detail-oriented guy. Clint had actually admired that quality when it came to how hard Ewan worked and how nicely he kept his home. He hadn't liked it as much when Ewan fixated on any possible way their relationship could be discovered and then used those reasons as excuses to keep from being seen together. In fact, he'd disliked it enough to break up with the now about-to-be groom.

Just then, he heard Ewan's familiar voice. Clint stepped to the side so he could see around the crowd that was already filling the room and found Ewan, standing next to a table, his arm around a pretty brunette's shoulders. He was smiling and chatting with the people at the table and he looked...happy.

Fair enough, Clint thought. *Everyone deserves to be happy.*

If he were being honest, he and Ewan had never been happy together. Content sometimes, but not happy. About the only thing they had in common was a mutual desire to get their rocks off. Thinking of their relationship in those terms, Clint wondered if he'd made such a fuss about hiding the nature of their relationship because he wanted to take Ewan out in public or because he didn't like being told he couldn't. The wind of righteous indignation blew out of his sails and he sighed.

Coming to this party was a bad idea, but he was there and Ewan had invited him, so the least he could do was wish him well. Then he'd get his truck from the special parking space, stop by the drive-thru liquor store, and go home. He remembered the state of his house and decided a bar might be a better destination. Speaking of bars, he needed to visit the one there to get a little more liquid fortification before he could bring himself to do the right thing and congratulate Ewan.

With one more sigh, Clint dragged his fingers through his hair and made his way to the north corner, weaving through the crowd. The line was half-a-dozen people long but he eventually reached the front and handed the bartender the empty champagne flutes.

"I'll have a beer, please," he said. "An amber or

a lager if you have them. Otherwise, anything cold's great."

"I'm sorry, we don't have beer."

Clint blinked a few times, thinking over the sentence and, after coming up with no alternative meaning said, "Is this the bar?"

It looked like a bar, there were wine bottles and glasses behind the bartender, but a bar meant beer.

"Yes." The bartender smiled at him.

"Oh." He furrowed his brow in thought. "Did you run out?"

"With the amount they ordered, we're never running out of anything." The bartender laughed. "Besides, the guests have been here less than an hour." She leaned forward and lowered her voice. "The customers wanted to portray a certain *atmosphere* and they felt beer didn't fit."

Huh. That sounded quite a bit like Ewan, actually. Clint had never fit in the atmosphere he wanted to portray either. At least he was in good company. Him and beer.

"Tell me you have something other than that champagne," he said pleadingly.

She tilted her head toward the bottles of wine and raised her eyebrows in question.

Clint sighed in defeat.

"I'll tell you what," the bartender said, chuckling. "You keep this on the down low and I'll make you something special." She bent over, shuffling underneath the bar, and then stood, holding a bottle of Scotch. "I found this Dewar's when I was unpacking." She picked up a tumbler and started pouring. "Guess it was leftover from the last job." She set the bottle down and reached for the small refrigerator behind her. "I can add in soda water and you'll have a decent drink."

"If you can skip the soda, that'd be perfect."

She snorted. "That kind of night, huh?"

He shrugged.

The bartender picked up the Dewar's, poured another finger, and handed it back to Clint.

"I have to say, you don't look like you belong here." She paused. "And I mean that as a compliment."

"I really don't," he agreed and took a sip, wincing as the liquor burned down his throat. "And thanks." He raised the glass to his lips again.

"If I write my number on a napkin, any chance you'll call me?"

Initially surprised and more than a little flattered, Clint kept drinking as he tried to come up with the right words to let the nice woman down gently. But before he thought of an answer, a too-tight squeeze to his arm stole his attention.

"What are you doing here?" hissed Ewan.

Clint raised his glass to the bartender in a silent thank you slash apology and turned around to answer his ex's not-so-nicely-asked question.

"You invited me, remember?" Clint said. "I wanted to—"

"You're supposed to be camping until tomorrow! I didn't think you'd actually show up."

Until that moment, Clint had never heard a whispered shout. It was impressive. He slammed back the drink, set the empty glass on the side of the bar, and wiped the back of his hand across his mouth.

"Why did you invite me if I wasn't supposed to come?"

"To be polite!" Ewan rolled his eyes. "And what are you wearing?"

Initially sneering, Ewan ran his gaze over Clint, but when he looked up again, his expression had turned hungry.

"Come on now, Ewan." Clint threaded his thumbs through his belt loops and let his hands hang down, bracketing his cock. "You know you like me in my jeans and shitkickers."

"The invitation said black tie optional or business formal," Ewan said, his voice shaky. He licked his lips. "And you know we can't be together in public."

Was he supposed to apologize for coming to the party after being invited, for wearing the wrong clothes, or for talking to Ewan after Ewan had initiated the conversation?

"What's black tie optional business formal?" Clint asked, because he wasn't going to apologize to Ewan for shit and flirting with him felt dirty and pathetic.

"You need to leave," Ewan hissed. He quickly darted his gaze around, gulped, and leaned forward as he whispered. "You can call me later and we can …"

"Call you for what?" Clint asked. "You have a fiancée."

"Keep your voice down. She doesn't have to know. We can still …"

No fucking way, no fucking how. He hadn't been willing to keep seeing Ewan in secret before he knew the man was dating someone else. Why on earth would he downgrade from being a dirty little secret to being the other man after Ewan got married?

"Never going to happen, Ewan," he said, shaking his head, which might have been a mistake because the entire room started spinning. Maybe downing four glasses of champagne followed by a tumbler of scotch hadn't been his brightest move. "Best of luck to you on the marriage." He turned around and stumbled toward the door, muttering, "Fuck knows you'll both need it."

CHAPTER THREE

"Are you sure about this, sir?"

Was Clint sure he wanted to get the hell out of Dodge? "Yes."

The valet fidgeted in front of the truck door. "You haven't been in there very long and you seem a little, uh—"

Though Clint tried to stand patiently and wait until the valet moved, he found himself suddenly tipping sideways. But only his top half. He managed to catch himself by grabbing onto the side of the truck, which left him pressed against the valet.

"Sorry about that," Clint slurred.

The valet whimpered.

"Did I hurt you?" Clint pushed himself back to a standing position. He gripped the side of the truck bed to help him stay stabilized.

"No," the valet croaked. "I'm fine."

"Great." Clint looked at him meaningfully. When he didn't move, Clint added, "So, I need to go."

Still nothing from the valet.

"And you're blocking the door."

"You're really muscular."

Clint stared.

"I mean hot," the valet said in a panic, his neck turning red. "Drunk!" he shouted. "I mean you're drunk."

"I'm fine," Clint assured him as he patted his shoulder. He was aiming for the shoulder, anyway. He made actual contact with his chest.

The red moved up the valet's face all the way to the tips of his ears and he started hyperventilating.

"You look like you're going to be sick," Clint pointed out.

"I... I... I..." The guy stopped, took in a deep breath, held it for a few seconds, and then blew it out. "Please, sir. You're not in any condition to drive and I wouldn't want you to get hurt."

Though his natural inclination was to get angry about anyone telling him what to do, Clint took a mental count of how much he'd had to drink in a short period of time and realized the guy was probably right.

"I need to get out of here," he said, more to himself than the valet. "And it's not like there are any taxi companies in Hawthorne."

"Oh." The valet gulped and looked up at Clint from underneath his lashes. "Things have slowed down with all the party arrivals. Maybe I can take you home and, uh, stay for a little bit." He coughed. "Just to make sure you're okay."

Clint must have been drunker than he realized, because the offer wasn't adding up.

"I'll take him home." Whiskey and gravel.

"Mister Deputy Mayor," Clint said as he turned to the side and found himself face to face with Hawk Black. "It's good to see you." He would have offered to shake the man's hand, or suck his dick, but if he let go of the truck, chances were high he'd fall.

"Call me Hawk," the deputy mayor said to Clint and then he turned toward the valet and said, "I'll take his keys."

"Yes, sir." With a disappointed sigh, the guy handed them over, looked at Clint sadly, and then shuffled away.

"I think he might be drunk or something," Clint whispered. At least he hoped it was a whisper. His ears were ringing so it was hard to be certain.

"Somebody sure is." Hawk smiled at Clint fondly as he circled his arm around Clint's waist. "Let's get you in the car."

"I can walk."

Hawk looked him over appraisingly. "Doubtful." He started walking, taking Clint with him. "Besides, this gives me a chance to feel all those muscles that kid was talking about."

"What kid?" Clint asked in confusion.

"The valet." Hawk shook his head. "Damn, you're toasted if you didn't notice him drooling over you."

"Huh?"

"Never mind." Hawk opened the passenger door, moved his palm up Clint's back to his nape, and massaged him gently. "I've waited long enough. He's out of luck."

"Huh?"

Dipping his face forward until his breath blew across Clint's cheek, Hawk rasped, "Get in."

A full-body tremor made its way through Clint

and he lost the power of speech. Not that he'd been speaking so much as grunting.

"Come on, baby." Hawk nudged him into the car. "Time to go."

Had Hawk just called him "baby"?

"Huh?"

"Buckle up," Hawk said with a smirk. He shut the door, jogged around the front of the truck, and got into the driver's seat.

Clint could do nothing but sit and stare.

After staring back for a couple of seconds, Hawk said, "You need to put on your seatbelt." He reached across Clint, snatched the seatbelt, and slowly pulled it across Clint's chest. Every part of that process involved Hawk's shoulders and chest rubbing against Clint's nipples and Hawk's scent permeating his being. "Safety first," he said hoarsely as he clipped the buckle into place.

If he'd been a little less drunk, Clint was pretty sure he would have come in his pants. As it was, he had to tip his head against the seatback and close his eyes so he could calm his libido. There was no avoiding hard-ons in Hawk's presence. With a groan, he reached between his legs and adjusted himself, hoping Hawk didn't notice, or that if he did, he didn't mind.

"You left the party early."

Just the man's voice was enough to make Clint's cock throb. In his entire life, he'd never reacted to another person like he did to Hawk Black. Of course, he'd never met anyone as ruggedly handsome, powerfully confident, and quietly intelligent.

"As opposed to loudly intelligent?"

"Huh?" How could Hawk know what he'd been thinking?

"Because you're thinking out loud." Hawk grinned. "I'm glad you like how I look. That'll make this much easier."

"I didn't…" Clint stopped himself mid-denial because, first off, he had very little chance of convincing Hawk he hadn't meant what he'd said and second, anybody with eyes would come to the same conclusion. "What do you mean *this*? What's the *this* that'll be easier?"

"Making you realize you need to stop playing around with silly boys and start getting serious with a real man." Hawk turned the key and shifted the truck into drive.

Though he wasn't completely certain due to the veil of alcohol clouding his brain, Clint was pretty sure he was being insulted.

"I'm not silly," he said defensively.

"I agree." Hawk flicked his gaze over and dragged it down Clint's body. "There's nothing silly about you."

"But you said—"

"I was talking about Ewan Griffin." Hawk flared his nostrils and clenched his jaw. "Why you wasted all that time with that limp dick, I'll never know. He'd wouldn't come close to being good enough for you on his best day, and from what I can tell, he has only bad days."

Clint's jaw dropped and he stared at Hawk in surprise.

"How'd you know?" he eventually asked.

"That Ewan's a spineless ass who isn't worth your time?"

"No." Clint shook his head. Ewan's abrasive personality was hard to miss so he wasn't surprised that Hawk didn't like him. "That we were—" He stopped mid-sentence. Hawk couldn't know about his relationship with Ewan so he probably meant something else and Clint was misunderstanding.

"That the two of you were fucking?" Hawk said.

Okay, so Hawk did know.

"Damn but you're cute."

"Guys my size aren't cute," Clint protested.

"Those red cheeks and dimples say different."

"It's too dark to see my cheeks." But his face did feel hot.

"I see you just fine, Clint."

There was a world of meaning behind that drawl but try as he might, Clint couldn't figure out what it was. He was usually much sharper than this.

"I drank too much," he muttered.

"You're a cute drunk."

"Again with the cute." Clint snorted and shook his head. "I'm almost your size."

Slowly turning his head to look at Clint, Hawk arched one eyebrow and said, "I've got a couple of inches on you."

That time, the meaning behind the words was clear. Clint was drunk, not dead and he couldn't miss the interest in Hawk's appraisal. Or at least that was what he hoped. Either way, he was going with it.

"Doubtful." Clint pawed at his groin. "I have a great dick."

"I'm sure you do, baby." Hawk licked his lips,

making Clint whimper. "And I've been waiting a long time to get a look at it."

So he was right about Hawk's meaning, but he was completely outmatched by the man in the flirting department. Well, as long as the night ended with the two of them naked, he supposed they'd both be winners.

"Are you gay?" he asked, needing to know what he was walking into. Or driving into. Or, more accurately, being driven into. What the hell were they talking about?

"I just told you I want to play with your cock." Hawk arched his eyebrows, but didn't take his gaze off the road. "Doesn't that answer your question?"

"You said look, not play." Clint adjusted himself in his jeans, his growing erection not comfortable in the constrained space. "And you could be bi." Or he could be so ashamed and scared that he told everyone he was straight, including the guy he was fucking.

"I'm gay," Hawk said, his voice firm, unapologetic, and the furthest thing in the world from scared or ashamed. "And I'm going to look at your cock while I play with you." He groaned and, with one hand still on the wheel, reached into his lap and rubbed the heel of his hand against the prominent bulge in his slacks. "Or maybe I should start with your ass." He gulped. "God damn, but do you have an ass made for jeans."

What he had was the world's most painful erection.

"Who said I'll let you do any of that?" Clint asked, needing to push back a little even though they both knew he was so eager for it, he'd drop trou on the side of the road if Hawk pulled over. Normally he wasn't this big of a slut, but a man didn't get more than one chance to sample something as delicious as the deputy mayor and damned if Clint was going to turn down the opportunity of a lifetime.

"I'm very persuasive."

The only persuading Clint would need to go to bed with Hawk was an invitation. And even that was negotiable.

"We're here." Hawk put the truck in Park and turned it off. The engine continued rattling. "This truck's seen better days."

"Serves its purpose. I don't need fancy." Clint squinted out the windshield. The sun had set completely and there wasn't much moonlight. "Where are we?"

"I think you proved that by wearing jeans and boots to that party." Hawk looked him over and narrowed his gaze. "Or were you trying to get your ex's attention?"

"Nah. I already did that for longer than I should have," Clint confessed. "I came to the party to get a beer 'cause my refrigerator broke."

"They didn't have beer."

"I know." Clint shook his head. "I guess beer's not good enough." He twisted sideways and looked at Hawk. "What the fuck's wrong with beer, huh?"

"Not a thing. Give me a steak hot off the grill, a beer cold from the fridge, and a guy to share 'em with and I'm happy."

He'd just described Clint's perfect evening, which begged the question...

"Why were you at that party tonight, man?"

Maybe hob-knobbing with the big names in town was part of Hawk's job, but if that was true, he would have had to stay longer. "And why'd you leave? From the look of things, it was just getting started." Not that Clint had looked at anything except the bottom of a glass and, for a few minutes, Ewan's angry face.

"Same answer for both questions," Hawk said as he pocketed the keys. "I wanted to spend time with you."

"Huh?" Clint was back to one-word answers.

"You heard me." Hawk grinned. "It's warmer inside. Let's go."

Remembering his earlier question, Clint leaned forward and looked from side to side.

"Where are we?"

"Home."

"No." Clint shook his head. "I live in one of those four-plexes off Main. We're set back a ways to the left of the Nowhere Diner." He dragged his hand through his hair. "Or at least I live there for now. Got to get out in two weeks. Landlord's selling the place."

"Kismet."

"Huh?" Clint said before he could stop himself. If he didn't start forming complete sentences, or at least real words, he was going to kick his own ass.

"It's cold and I need to get some coffee and food into you." Hawk pulled the door handle and stepped out of the truck. "Let's go inside."

Clint opened his door and tried to get out, but couldn't.

"Take off your belt."

Looking from Hawk's face, which was suddenly in his doorway, down to his own belt buckle, and then to Hawk's face again, Clint said, "We're doing it out here?"

"Your seatbelt." Hawk barked out a laugh as he stepped forward and reached around Clint. "Besides, I'm still in the wooing-you stage. I figure that means I ought to do you in a bed a few times before I attack you in the front seat of the truck."

"Nothing wrong with screwing in a truck, man."

In fact, if Hawk didn't stop rubbing his shoulder blade against Clint's erection, he'd be coming in the truck.

"Nope, nothing wrong with that at all." Hawk finally straightened. "When the weather warms up, we can throw some blankets in the back and fuck under the stars."

It was February. The weather wasn't going to warm up that night. Was Hawk talking about getting together again? The alcohol in Clint's veins and the hard-on in his pants were making it nearly impossible for him to think clearly.

"I don't understand."

"You will." Hawk took his hand and waited for him to climb out of the truck.

"I can walk," Clint said, unsure how he felt about the gesture.

On the one hand, he'd always prided himself on his strength and self-sufficiency. He'd enlisted in the army right out of high school and built his own life, never needing anyone's help. But on the other hand, there was something undeniably enticing about having someone to lean on.

"Like I said before, I like touching you." Hawk yanked on his arm. "Quit being stubborn and get your fine ass out of that ugly truck and into my house so I can play with it."

Laughing, Clint tightened his grip on Hawk's hand and hopped out of the truck.

"I thought you wanted to play with my dick," he said as he cupped his crotch.

"I said I want your ass too." Hawk tugged him forward until their noses touched. From this close, his blue eyes twinkled as brightly as the stars. "I want it all," he whispered. "I want every last part of you."

CHAPTER FOUR

Needing to clear his head so he could assimilate Hawk's words with some type of logical meaning, Clint peeled his gaze away from the distractingly handsome face and stepped away from his truck.

"This is your place?" Clint shoved his hands in his pockets and looked at the earth-colored pueblo.

"Yup."

The inconsistently sized windows and flat roofline differentiated it from the modern versions of the traditional Native American houses. "How old is it?"

"Nineteen thirties." Hawk stepped up behind him, wrapped strong beefy arms around his waist, and rested his chin over Clint's shoulder. "The inside's been updated over the years. Nothing fancy, but it's sturdy, warm—" he slid his lips over Clint's neck, "—solid."

"Sounds like a good place." Clint's voice shook along with his body. The soft lips and scratchy whiskers were doing nothing to curb his arousal.

"I like it." Hawk found a spot behind Clint's ear and suckled while he moved one hand beneath Clint's jacket and the other down to his groin. "Going to like it even more with you in it."

He'd suspected the deputy mayor was interested in him earlier that day, but he hadn't anticipated how strongly the man would come on to him. The attention was flattering, enticing, but also a little disconcerting. Was he willing to be another man's secret?

No. Clint had promised himself to live life on his terms and that meant not hiding. Not even for someone as enticing as Hawk Black. But maybe he was getting ahead of himself. Maybe Hawk wanted nothing more than a fuck for the night and the sweet talk was just that … talk. His wanting it to mean something didn't mean it did.

Finding a guy to fuck wasn't difficult. Hawthorne was small, but there were neighboring towns and bigger cities a car drive away where Clint could walk into a bar on almost any night and meet someone who wanted to get off. But finding a guy who wanted to touch and talk was hard. Finding a man who wanted to hold him and was large enough to do it was harder. And finding someone he was drawn to anywhere near the way he was to Hawk Black was impossible.

With a sigh, Clint tipped his head back against Hawk's broad chest and let himself enjoy the rare romantic moment for as long as it'd last. No other buildings were visible, just some faint glimmers on the horizon that could have been lights or could have been stars.

"Are we outside the city limits?" he asked, keeping his voice low to match the intimate mood.

"Not quite."

"Town center's ahead of us and to the left, yeah?"

He felt Hawk's nod against the side of his face, their cheeks rubbing together.

"I didn't think there was any private property out this way," Clint said, finally getting his bearings and realizing where they were. "I thought it was all Hawthorne land."

"It is." Hawk buried his face in the side of Clint's neck and inhaled deeply.

"What're you doing?" Clint asked, trembling at the action.

"Smelling you." Hawk breathed in deeply. "You smell fucking amazing." He squeezed Clint tightly for a flash, then released and slipped his hand around Clint's. "You're shivering. Let's go inside."

Although the shivers weren't temperature related, it was cold outside so Clint followed without argument. He stomped his boots in front of the door by habit and then stepped inside the warm house.

"I'll hang up your jacket." Hawk rubbed his hands over Clint's arms and up his shoulders, massaging for a few seconds before pulling off the denim jacket and draping it over one of the hooks beside the door. "You can take your boots off too, if you want. The wood floors aren't too cold."

As Clint stepped out of his boots, Hawk flipped a few switches, bathing the house in warm light.

"Bedroom's to the right. There's a great beehive fireplace." Hawk flipped back around so he was facing Clint, his blue eyes dark and his pupils dilated. "Your skin's going to look amazing in the firelight." Hawk stepped closer. "Do you know how many times

I've jerked off thinking about you naked in that room?"

"No." Clint shook his head, completely off-balance. "I didn't know you, uh, felt that way."

"God damn." Hawk stepped even closer and combed his thick fingers through Clint's hair. "For such a skilled cop, you have no idea what's staring you in the face."

"Maybe I suck at my job," Clint said, trying to lighten the mood.

"You're great at your job. Here and in Detroit. And your military record's impeccable. You have a Distinguished Service Medal and a commendation." Hawk grinned. "Seems like your people reading skills just short out when it comes to me." Hawk tipped Clint's face up. "Why is that?"

"You know why," Clint said, seeing no point in playing games. He was at Hawk's house for one reason and they both knew what it was.

"You want me." Hawk leaned down and brushed his lips across Clint's jaw. "Not the same way I want you, but it's a start."

At twenty-eight years old, Clint wasn't a stranger to the concept of going home with a man to screw. Hawk Black probably had close to ten years on him, so he had to know the score too. Which meant he had to understand that the things he was saying, the intensity with which he was looking at Clint, and the tenderness in his touch weren't standard fare for a hook-up.

"Did you plan this?" Clint asked, remembering Hawk saying he'd gone to the party that night hoping to see him.

"Oh, yeah," Hawk admitted easily. He slid one palm to Clint's neck and massaged him while he cupped Clint's cheek with the other.

"How'd you know I'd be there?"

"Where?" Hawk dipped forward until their lips were only a breath's distance apart.

"Ewan's party." Clint dragged his palms beneath Hawk's suit jacket, over his muscular chest. "How'd you know I was going?"

"I didn't." Hawk skated his lips over Clint's in a barely there kiss. "But after seeing you at the station, I thought there was a chance you'd show up and I wanted to be there for you."

Be there for you.

After a few seconds gazing into Hawk's eyes, Clint grasped Hawk's jacket collar with both hands, tugged him close, and pressed their mouths together, licking, nibbling, and sucking. The kiss was bruising, passionate, and full of pent-up need Clint didn't realize he carried. Without thought, he rubbed his groin against Hawk's thigh, ramping his arousal higher.

"So hot," he mumbled. Hawk was even better in person than he had been in Clint's fantasies. He couldn't believe how lucky he'd gotten, and then an uncomfortable thought occurred to him. He pulled away, leaving Hawk panting. "How'd you get in?" Clint asked.

Hawk licked his lips and blinked.

"Do you know Ewan? Is that how you got in? Is that how you knew about the two of us?" An even worse possibility slammed into him. "Was he fucking you too?"

The soft, hazy arousal disappeared from Hawk's eyes in a flash. "No," he growled and pulled Clint forward, slamming their bodies back together. "There's only one man I'm interested in." He ground his cock against Clint. "And that's you."

"They weren't going to let me in without an invitation," Clint pointed out. "How'd you get in?"

"The bride's father is smart enough to know who he needs on his side to succeed in this town so I was invited. I hadn't planned to go, though. Not until I realized you were back and you might show up." Hawk curved his palm around Clint's chin and cheek and looked into his eyes. "Listen to me carefully. I didn't say the words while you were with that guy out of respect, but that shit's over and I'm done holding back." He bit Clint's lower lip, hard. "I want you. Do you finally hear me?"

"How long?" Clint rasped, his lungs burning, his heart racing, and his balls tight as stones. He bucked against Hawk, making contact with his thick erection. "You know what? Never mind. We can talk about it later." He licked Hawk's lips and when they parted, he moaned and slid his tongue inside. "Show me that bedroom, man. I need…" He drew in a shaky breath, the desires coursing through him too deep and intense to put into words. "I just need."

"Yeah, me too." Hawk moved his hand over Clint's chest, found his nipple, and twisted it through his shirt. "Going to do you so damn good, baby. You'll see." He kissed Clint again and then stepped away, looking like it was the last thing he wanted to do.

"Why'd you stop?" Clint asked before he could stop himself from sounding so needy.

"Because I need to get some coffee and food into you first." Hawk flipped around. "Kitchen's this way. Come on."

"Not hungry," Clint said, but he followed Hawk, his gaze darting between his broad shoulders and his backside. He wanted Hawk to take off his suit coat so he could get a better look at his ass.

"Yeah you are. You're still drunk too."

Not nearly as much as he had been twenty minutes earlier. That little scene in the entryway had infused him with shots of sobering adrenaline and arousal.

"I'm fine," Clint assured him as they passed by a den furnished with brown leather sofas and colorful native blankets.

"Once I know you get it, I promise to fuck you sober, drunk, and everything in between." They walked into the kitchen and Hawk went straight for the coffee maker. "But right now, you need some coffee, food in your belly, and a little more time to let the alcohol pass."

"You trying to sober me up enough to drive home so I get out of your hair?" Clint joked.

Hawk froze and looked at him over his shoulder. "I'm trying to sober you up enough to decide the opposite."

Clint furrowed his brow.

"You're not ready." Hawk tilted his chin toward the bar stools around a wood-topped island. "Have a seat. A little wrestling in the bedroom's fun, but only when it's a game. I'm not into doing guys who aren't willing."

"Aren't willing?" Clint asked incredulously. "I

know you didn't miss the seven inches of wood in my jeans."

"Too drunk to know you were in no condition to drive home isn't willing." Hawk arched one eyebrow and grinned as he grabbed his dick. "And I've got eight and a half."

Clint snorted. "Congratulations, man." Realizing he wasn't going to change Hawk's mind, he sat on a stool. "Bet I'm thicker, though."

"Thick's good." Hawk's voice was husky. "You won't get any complaints from me about thick."

Tearing his gaze away from Hawk before he started drooling or begging, Clint distracted himself by looking around the kitchen. The space was bigger than the tiny corner in his apartment where he cooked, but it wasn't huge. The cabinets were oak, probably a few decades old but in decent condition, and the countertops were a traditional Saltillo tile.

"I'm good on a grill but in the kitchen, about all I can make are scrambled eggs and spaghetti." Hawk walked over to the fridge. "Pick your poison."

"Eggs are good." Clint's stomach growled at the mention of food. "Toast too, if you've got it."

"Not hungry, huh?" Hawk chuckled. "A heaping plate of eggs and toast coming up."

"Want some help?"

"Nope. I'm wooing you, remember?" He put a frying pan on the stove and turned on the gas.

"I don't need wooing, man."

"No?" Hawk looked at Clint as he untwisted the tie on a bread bag.

"Weren't you the guy I was dry humping five minutes ago? I'm as good as gotten."

With a smile and a shake of his head, Hawk picked up an egg and cracked it against the side of the pan. "I figured out your dick liked me a long time ago." He tossed the eggshell back into the carton and moved on to the next one. "I'm aiming for an organ located higher up." One by one, he added the rest of the eggs and then scrambled them with a fork while they cooked. "They say the way to a man's heart is through his stomach. That means I have to show you my mad cooking skills."

"My stomach's not that picky, man. I'm much more interested in my dick."

"So you're saying I should bypass the stomach because the way to your heart is through your dick?"

"Something like that." Clint laughed.

"Then I'm golden."

Hawk plucked the toast from the toaster, tossed it from palm to palm until he reached the plate, and then began buttering it.

"That sure of yourself, huh?"

"What can I say?" Hawk plated the eggs. "I'm great in bed."

"I'll believe it when I finally see it."

"You're speaking in whole sentences and all your words finally make sense, so I think that'll be pretty soon." He put the plate in front of Clint along with a fork and knife and then stepped over to the coffee maker. "Eat up." He poured the coffee into a mug and set it in front of Clint.

"Aren't you eating?" Clint asked through a mouthful of scrambled eggs.

"I'm good. I grabbed dinner with Gabriel before the party."

"Gabriel?" Clint reached for the mug and drank some coffee.

"Martinez." Hawk walked to refrigerator. "The mayor." He came back with two bottles of water.

"Work dinner or do you hang out with your boss socially?" As soon as the question was out of his mouth, Clint realized it was invasive. "Sorry. Forget I asked. That's none of my business." Clint opened the bottle and began chugging down the water.

"Yes, I spend time with Gabriel socially. We've known each other since long before he became the mayor of Hawthorne." Hawk sat down on the stool next to him. "And of course it's your business. Everything about me is your business. That's the only way this thing is going to work."

"This thing," Clint repeated while finishing up his eggs. "You mean the whole wooing your way into my heart bit?"

"It isn't a bit."

"No?" Clint pushed away the mostly empty plate and folded his arms on the counter. "Then what is it?"

Hawk turned in his seat so he was looking directly at Clint and then, without flinching, said, "It's me telling you I'm in love with you and I'm going to do my damnedest to get you to feel the same way about me."

Facing down a criminal with a gun pointed at his head would have been easier for Clint than making that kind of confession, so he had to give Hawk credit for bravery, even if the man was insane.

"You can't be in love with me."

"Really? Why's that?" Hawk asked, sounding amused. "Enlighten me."

"Because you don't know me."

"I've spent the past two and a half months finding every excuse under the sun to get to know you, Clint." Hawk reached for Clint's hand and curled his fingers around it. "You were born on November 11, 1986 in Flint, Michigan. You have a brother, John, who works in a bank and another brother, Derrick, who teaches school. Your mother's a nurse and your father does books for medical offices. You're not particularly close to any of them. You enlisted in the army out of high school, served for six years, then went back to Michigan and became a cop. Two years after that, you moved here to Hawthorne. Your favorite color is red. Your favorite beer is Full Sail Amber. You like animals more than people. You have a high sex drive and a great sense of humor." One side of Hawk's lips turned up. "Two of my favorite qualities in a man, by the way."

"How do you…?" Clint blinked rapidly, trying to remember everything he'd talked about with Hawk over the past few months. When he thought about it, he realized that he ran into Hawk at the station or around town four or five times a week and every single time, they ended up chatting. "You're a good listener," he admitted. "But some of those are just guesses."

"You adopted a dog who got hit crossing the road and lost a front leg, paid for all of her medical bills, and named her Speedy. You did the same thing with Fluffy, the fire survivor without fur on half her body." Hawk smiled and shook his head. "Only a man who loves animals and has a wicked sense of humor would do that."

"Fine." Clint laughed along. "But the sex drive thing's just a lucky guess."

"The only thing lucky about it is the orgasm count I see in my future. My analysis is based on data, pure and simple."

"All right, Mister Presumptuous." Clint folded his arms over his chest. "What data are you relying on?"

"You spent half a year fooling around with Ewan Griffin. The guy's good looking, but there's no way you were interested in anything else about him, which means you were with him to get laid. I figure a man's got to have a higher-than-average libido to put up with that dickwad for as long as you did."

That analysis had Clint throwing his head back and laughing deeply. "You know what? I have no idea how you figured out I was with him at all, but I'm not going to argue with you about the rest of it because you're right."

"I'm always right." Hawk grinned. "And I figured it out because I watch you." He leaned closer and lowered his voice. "You want to know what else I figured out about you, baby?"

"What?"

"You think your feelings run too shallow to fall in love, but that isn't true."

"No?" Clint rasped, his throat suddenly thick.

"Nope." Hawk shook his head. "You've just been waiting for me to come into your life and show you how good it can be."

CHAPTER FIVE

"You're sure there isn't anything else we need to do before we can finally go to bed?" Clint asked, only half joking.

"Ha ha." Hawk shoved him against the bedroom wall and nibbled on his neck while he unbuttoned Clint's shirt.

"Laundry?   Dusting?"   Clint   said,   the breathlessness in his voice taking away from his attempt to sound serious.

"A man tries to be honorable and this is the thanks he gets." Hawk shoved Clint's shirt off his shoulders.

"What's honorable about working me up and leaving me hanging for over an hour?"

"Wanted you sober enough to know what you were doing." Tugging Clint's undershirt up his chest, Hawk said, "Shirt's coming off. Raise your arms."

"I'm not a kid, even if you keep calling me baby."

"I know you're not a kid." Hawk shoved his knee between Clint's thighs and rubbed up against his balls. "That doesn't change you being my baby." He pulled the shirt over Clint's head. "But if you want to be stubborn, I can keep the shirt on your arms." He tugged the fabric down behind Clint's back. "Some guys like getting tied up in the sack."

"I don't—" A particularly well-placed nudge to his nuts distracted Clint mid-sentence. "No more games, man. Please." He swallowed hard. "I need it."

"I know." Hawk slammed his mouth over Clint's, shoving his tongue inside and plunging in and out while he furiously worked Clint's belt buckle and jeans open. "Going to give it to you," he said as he dropped to his knees and peeled Clint's jeans and briefs down. "Over and over again." He rubbed his cheek against Clint's hard cock and moaned. "Fuck yeah. Look at you."

"You like that?" Clint asked, gazing down at the huge, gorgeous man on his knees. "Told you I was thick."

"You weren't exaggerating." He cupped Clint's balls and followed a prominent vein in his shaft with his tongue. "You have a great cock."

"I'm so hard." Clint tipped his head against the wall and brushed his trembling fingers over Hawk's head. "Suck me."

Without another word, Hawk did exactly that. He licked his lips, parted them, and then dropped his mouth over Clint's erection.

"Yes," Clint hissed. "Like that."

Hawk's lips remained tight around him as he bobbed up and down, his saliva slicking the way.

"Close." Clint wanted to wait, wanted the pleasure to last longer, but he'd been lusting after Hawk for so long that he couldn't contain his excitement.

"Mmm," Hawk moaned and grabbed Clint's hips, his hands so big that his fingers dug into Clint's ass cheeks. He popped his mouth off Clint's cock, licked his slit, and said, "Fuck my mouth, baby. I can take it."

His entire body shaking with barely pent up need, Clint said, "Are you sure?"

"Give me everything you've got," Hawk said and then he jerked Clint forward, causing Clint's cock to sink fully into his mouth.

"Fuck!" Clint shouted, all semblance of control shattering. He twined his fingers through Hawk's hair and moved Hawk's head back and forth as he rocked his hips, pumping in and out of tight, wet, heat.

Rather than fighting him or trying to wrestle back control, Hawk moaned in pleasure and let Clint use his body however he needed.

"Oh god." Clint's balls tightened almost painfully. "Oh god, Hawk!" With a final thrust his orgasm hit, stealing his voice and his breath as he pulsed into Hawk's waiting mouth. "Oh," he rasped once he was drained. "That—" His teeth chattered and he realized all of his muscles were spasming. "Good." He released his hold on Hawk's hair and massaged his scalp. "So good."

"Clint," Hawk groaned as he stood up. The front of his dress pants pushed forward obscenely.

"Yeah." Clint reached for his belt buckle. "Let's take care of you." Within seconds, he had the front of Hawk's pants open and his long, rigid shaft fished out of his underwear. "Damn, this is nice." He curled his fingers around the smooth, hot skin and stroked. "So nice." He swiped his thumb over the damp glans and kept a steady pace. "Want to feel this inside me later."

"You like bottoming?" Hawk asked as he moved his hips forward and back, humping into Clint's fist.

"I love sex." Clint twisted his wrist and tightened his hold on Hawk's dick. "Every which way, man." He leaned up and dragged his tongue from the bottom of Hawk's chin up to his lips. "Fuckin' crave it."

"Aw, hell," Hawk groaned. "You're so sexy."

"After you fuck me, I'm going to do you." Clint moved his mouth to Hawk's ear. "I hope you like having your ass eaten, because I'm going to feast on you, Hawk."

"Now. Now. Now," Hawk said, his voice desperate. "Yes!" He cupped Clint's cheeks, and gazed into his eyes as hot seed shot from his dick and fountained over Clint's fingers. "Clint," he whispered reverently as he brushed his lips over Clint's in a gentle kiss. "I knew it'd be amazing with you." He buried his face in Clint's neck and licked at his sweat-slick skin. "I knew."

"Lucky guess," Clint responded as he turned and caught Hawk's lips with his own.

"Call it what you want." Hawk chuckled and returned Clint's kiss. "We're good together."

"You want to be good together in that big bathtub you were bragging about during the house tour? If my eyeball measurements were right, there's enough space to fit us both."

"So that's what you were thinking about when I was proudly showing you my home?" Hawk asked, his blue eyes twinkling.

"I had the hard-on from hell and you refused to do anything to help me with it until I could pass a roadside sobriety test! What did you expect me to do? Focus on your color scheme?"

"With what you drank at that party, you couldn't pass a field test now. I just wanted you sober enough to avoid morning-after regrets."

"The only regrets I'm going to have are not following through on the ideas I had during the tour." Clint circled his arms around Hawk's waist and smiled up at him, enjoying the lighthearted conversation in the wake of their passionate encounter.

"Well then we'll definitely add shower sex to tonight's agenda," Hawk promised.

"My ideas expanded beyond the shower."

"Oh?" Hawk arched his eyebrows. "Care to fill me in?"

"Eventually." Clint slipped out from under Hawk's arm and walked to the adjoining bathroom, making sure to put an extra sway in his step. He wasn't used to flirting, didn't know if he was any good at it, but he was having a hell of a time playing. "For now, you can be satisfied knowing I have plans for you on every surface and in every room of this house."

Behind him, Hawk groaned.

Maybe he wasn't too bad at flirting. Clint grinned and looked at Hawk over his shoulder.

"You said you could keep up with me, right?"

"Count on it," Hawk growled. He caught up to Clint in two steps and yanked him back against his still-suited body. "I have everything you need." He pinched Clint's nipple with one hand and caressed his balls with the other. "I'll keep you blissed out every day, baby."

His sated cock valiantly trying to fill again, Clint

whispered, "I don't doubt it." He turned around and began undressing Hawk. "You're gorgeous." He thought about everything Hawk had said to him that night. "A little intense, but gorgeous."

"I can be laid back about a lot of things, but if you mean how I feel about you, I'm a lot intense." Hawk waited until Clint met his gaze. "I love you."

Reflexively, Clint looked away. "I don't understand how you can just say things like that."

Most people he knew, hell, all the people he knew, took care to guard their feelings. There were entire books dedicated to the concept of playing hard to get. Hawk Black was the exact opposite. He put everything out there without hesitation, which was both terrifying and comforting.

"I don't play games, Clint." Hawk took Clint's chin between his finger and thumb and tilted it up so their eyes met again. "You deserve someone who isn't going to hold back with you."

* * * *

Dirty talk in bed was fun, waking up with a guy's tongue in your ass was even better.

"Ungh, Christ. What're you doing?" Clint mumbled, his voice husky with sleep and his cock thick with arousal. He was prone on his stomach and Hawk was behind him, settled between his spread legs, a hand on each side of Clint's ass, holding him open, and his face buried between Clint's cheeks.

"Enjoying my morning." Hawk swirled his tongue around Clint's pucker and then curled it and pushed into his hole.

"Oh god." Nobody did this for him, not ever, and it felt amazing. Clint kept his head and shoulders down and tucked his knees up underneath his body, raising his back end and opening himself up farther. "Hawk, please."

"You want to get off like this?"

"Uh-huh." Clint nodded, reached back, and grabbed his ass, spreading himself as wide as he could and exposing everything.

His hands relieved from their duty, Hawk slid his palm between Clint's legs and pulled his cock down.

"Damn you're hot." He swiped his tongue up Clint's channel while he stroked his cock. "I love this."

Clint would have agreed, but he'd lost the power of speech.

"Going to make you come, feed you, and then take you back to bed and start all over again."

Still jacking Clint's dick, Hawk pushed a thumb into Clint's hole and followed it with his tongue.

"That sounds... Ungh!" Clint rocked his hips, pushing into Hawk's face and down into his hand.

"What's that, baby?" Hawk said, taking a break from licking Clint's passage to nibble on the sensitive skin along his butt.

"I..." Clint swallowed and cleared his throat, trying to concentrate. "I said that sounds good but I need to go home." He moaned when Hawk twisted his thumb and grazed his gland. "Dogs," he finished, hoping the word was sufficient explanation to end the conversation because he wanted Hawk's mouth focused on the task at hand.

"Bring 'em here." Hawk lapped at Clint's balls

and then sucked each of them into his mouth in turn. "Neither of us has to work until Monday and I'm not letting you out of my bed until then."

"That leather couch in your living room's a good height." Clint's voice was breathless and he couldn't stop pumping his hips, but he was doing his damnedest to get Hawk as worked up as Hawk had him. "Why limit us to the bedroom when one or both of us can bend over that?"

"I like how you think, baby." Hawk licked a swath down Clint's cock. "You can make a list of all those good ideas and we'll tick 'em off one by one."

"Kind of busy right now," Clint pointed out.

Chuckling, Hawk said, "Good point. List later, eating your ass now."

True to his word, Hawk went to work on Clint's backside, licking his channel, sucking on his pucker, and tonguing his hole, all while stroking his dick.

"Going to come," Clint warned.

"Do it." Hawk shoved a finger into Clint's hole, curled it, and pegged his gland.

"Hawk!" Clint shouted, pleasure overtaking his body and mind. He shoved his ass back, taking Hawk's finger in as deeply as possible, and shot, ejaculate pulsing from his dick onto the bed as he shook and grunted.

Before he was done, Hawk's broad body was draped over his and Hawk's long cock was sliding between his cheeks and over his lower back.

"Love how you taste." Hawk curled his arms under Clint's armpits and gripped his shoulders while he thrust. "Love how you feel." He thrust against Clint. "Especially here." He circled his hips, rubbing his dick against the outside of Clint's hole. "Want to do you bare, baby. Want to come inside."

Clint's breath caught at the thought.

"I haven't been with anyone in almost six months, not since I first saw you in September." Hawk kissed the back of Clint's neck. "Tell me I can fuck you raw later." He took Clint's skin between his teeth and then sucked. "Say you want it, baby. Say you want me."

Undeniably aroused by the idea, Clint turned his head, met Hawk's gaze, and said, "Yes. I want you. Come in me."

Hawk's eyes widened, he gasped, and then he stilled as hot wetness coated Clint's lower back.

His body sated and boneless, Clint rolled onto his side and then tugged Hawk down so they were face-to-face. He flung his leg over Hawk's thigh and kissed his chest, shoulders, and neck as Hawk's gasps evened into regular breaths.

"Are you back to the land of the fully-conscious or are you still brain-addled from that orgasm?" he asked.

"Little of both." Hawk sighed contentedly, curled his arm around Clint's neck, and stroked his hair. "Did you mean what you said?" he asked quietly.

Clint took in a deep breath and met Hawk's gaze.

"Did you?"

"Oh, yeah," Hawk said, his husky voice leaving no doubt which question he was answering.

"Not the fucking bare." Clint licked his lips and, when Hawk furrowed his brow in confusion, added,

"You moved to Hawthorne in late November, after the election."

"Ah," Hawk said in understanding. "And you're wondering why."

"No." Clint shook his head. "I know you moved here to work for Mayor Martinez. I'm asking what you meant about seeing me in September when we didn't know each other yet."

The smile that took over Hawk's face was wicked.

"When I told Gabriel I was moving here, he asked me to take the deputy mayor job as a favor to him and I agreed. The job isn't the reason I came to Hawthorne. You are."

Clint's jaw dropped.

"Taking you off-guard is fun." Hawk grinned manically. "And I'm really good at it."

Rolling his eyes, Clint said, "Stop gloating and explain yourself."

"It's simple, really." Hawk shoved two pillows under his head, lay on his back, and pulled Clint on top of him. "I'm a political and managerial consultant based out of D.C. Or at least I was. Gabriel was a close friend of my father's so when things were going south in his reelection campaign, he asked for my help. I came down here to get the lay of the land and I saw you."

He combed his fingers through Clint's hair. "You were at a softball game. Police versus firefighters. I couldn't take my eyes off you. You were wearing a black Rolling Stones T-shirt that wasn't tight but you'd been sweating so it was clinging to your chest. I watched you run the bases, joke around with your teammates, and then wave everyone off when they were going for beers, so I followed you."

"We have a name for that, you know?"

"Falling in love?"

"The technical term is stalking."

"Tomato, tomato," Hawk said, pronouncing the word differently each time. "Anyway, you went to the veterinarian's office to visit your dog."

"Fluffy," Clint said, remembering his frequent trips to the vet when his dog was near death. "She'd whelped her pups in a storage shed behind the strip mall off Fourth. A few high school kids set off firecrackers out there and one hit the brush outside the shed and caught the whole thing on fire. She kept going into the building to get her pups out, didn't stop until every last one of them was safely away from the danger."

"Brave dog."

"She is."

"The receptionist at the vet's said they didn't think she'd make it but you insisted they try to save her, footed all the bills, and came to visit her twice a day." Hawk kissed Clint's forehead. "I fell in love with you right then. Told Gabriel I was going to wrap up my projects in D.C., put my place on the market, and move here to be with you. He asked me to work for him and that brings us to today."

"You changed your whole life because you saw me playing softball and have a soft spot for dogs?" Clint pushed himself up to a sitting position and dragged his fingers through his hair. "People don't do that."

"Well, I did." Hawk curled his big hand around Clint's thigh. "I've never felt that kind of pull. No way was I going to ignore it and miss out on something great."

"I could have been dumb or mean or annoying or straight or—"

"You're not any of those things." Hawk sat up and brushed his lips over Clint's. "You're wonderful and getting to know you only made me fall harder."

A part of Clint he didn't know existed woke up with those words and a longing blossomed in his chest. His heart raced, his lungs burned, and he wasn't sure whether he wanted to run away or snatch what Hawk was offering and guard it with every part of him.

"Mayor Martinez must have thought you'd lost your mind," he said as he wondered the same thing about himself.

"Nah." Hawk shook his head. "My dad did the same thing when he met my mom, so Gabriel knows the drill."

"Your father met your mom and moved to New York?" Clint remembered Hawk saying he'd grown up there during one of their conversations. He also knew Hawk had a younger brother and two younger sisters, that his family was close, and that he'd had Golden Labs as a child.

"She moved to be with him, actually. My mother's family is from New York. My father died when she was pregnant with me so she moved back there and remarried. Black's my stepfather's name. She gave me my father's last name as my first name."

"Your father's last name was Hawk?"

"Hawk's my nickname. My father was Bruce Hawthorne." Hawk raised his hand and pointed around the room. "This was his house."

"You're a Hawthorne?" Clint asked incredulously. Not only had the Hawthorne family founded the town, but their charitable endowment still funded a lot of the organizations and they owned a good portion of the land. "I thought the family had all passed away."

"All except for me."

"How is it I didn't know this?"

"Well, it didn't strike me as important when we were getting to know each other." Hawk moved his hand up Clint's thigh to his groin and caressed his balls and shaft. "I hadn't spent any time here so it doesn't have anything to do with who I am, just what I own."

"So on top of being gorgeous and smart, you had a powerful career and tons of money and you decided to move to Hawthorne, New Mexico, to take up with me?"

"Yup." Hawk wrapped his hand around Clint's dick. "Best decision I ever made."

"You're insane."

Lying on his stomach, Hawk put his face in Clint's lap and said, "I prefer to think of myself as a romantic."

"Fine. You're an insane romantic." An incredibly sexy insane romantic.

"Insanely romantic." Hawk lapped at Clint's hardening cock. "I like that."

"That's not what I said." Another couple of

minutes with Hawk's mouth on his dick and Clint wasn't sure he'd remember his own name let alone the conversation.

"Potato, potato," Hawk said, once again pronouncing each word differently. He licked Clint's balls. "How I got here isn't important." He blew hot air along Clint's shaft. "The point is, I'm here, I love you, and by the time I'm done with my seduction plans for this weekend, you're going to love me too." And with that promise made, Hawk took Clint's dick into his mouth and gently sucked.

"That feels so good." Almost as good as the warmth unfurling in Clint's heart.

CHAPTER SIX

Hawk insisted on driving over with him to get the dogs on Saturday morning. Clint thought about refusing in light of the state of his apartment, but he wasn't sure he'd have the nerve to go back if he left Hawk's place alone, and no matter how crazy fast things were moving, he knew he'd never wanted anything more than a weekend alone with Hawk. So together they went.

"What happened here?" Hawk asked when he saw the holes in the walls.

"Bad day yesterday," Clint answered as he put the key in the door.

Hawk's large hand landed on his back, caressing him, and Hawk's warm breath and soft lips skated across his nape.

"It started out that way," Clint corrected. "Didn't end up too bad, though."

"No, not too bad." Hawk laughed softly and kissed his neck again. "Those dogs sound like they want their daddy. Better open up before they scratch the door down."

"Not sure it matters at this point." Clint pushed the door open and happy dogs immediately rushed him, jumping on his thighs and whining their hellos. "They tore the place up yesterday afternoon."

"Hey, pretty girls." Clint dropped to his haunches and pet his pups, surprised they weren't barking at the new visitor.

He was about to introduce them to Hawk when the man himself squatted next to him, held out his hand, and after a brief sniff, received licks.

"Aren't you a sweetheart?" Hawk said to Fluffy who, despite her name and her loyalty was the furthest thing from sweet. "And you too," he said to Speedy who had planted her one front paw on Hawk's chest and licked his face.

The only visitor Clint'd had to his apartment was Ewan and both dogs had growled and barked at him so much that Clint had taken to putting them in the tiny, fenced yard during their hook-ups.

"They don't usually warm up to people this fast," Clint observed as he stood up.

"Well they must sense how I feel about their daddy and approve." Hawk grinned at him and rubbed each dog's head affectionately. "Thanks for making me look good, ladies," he mock-whispered to the dogs. "I'll pay you in steak later."

"You know the way into their hearts," Clint said, smiling at the picture Hawk made with his dogs and thinking theirs weren't the only hearts Hawk had captured.

Forcing himself to look away, he walked into the living room and sighed when he found the same mess he had left the previous evening.

"Damn." He dragged his fingers through his

hair. "I was hoping it had magically cleaned itself up while I was gone."

"Holy shit," Hawk said from over his shoulder, apparently having followed him into the room. "Your dogs did this?"

"Yeah." Clint walked into the kitchen to get a garbage bag. "They can be rowdy, but yesterday was bad, even for them. Maybe it was a full moon or something."

"How did they knock over the refrigerator?" Hawk asked incredulously.

"That one's on me." Clint squatted next to the downed appliance. "Help me out here."

"What'd this refrigerator do to piss you off?" Hawk mirrored his stance on the other side of the fridge.

"It sided with the wall after our kickboxing match," Clint joked. "On three. One. Two. Three."

In perfect concert, they lifted the refrigerator.

"Door's shot," Hawk pointed out as he pushed the door into place. "It'll stay closed but it's not operational."

"I know." Clint looked around the room. "The good news is the building is being demolished anyway, so maybe the landlord won't notice." He walked to the sink and got a trash bag. "Either that or my deposit is gone."

"I'm pretty sure the holes in the wall already took care of that." Hawk stepped over. "Looks like this is a two-person clean-up. You want me to do the living room or the kitchen?"

"Bet you regret coming over." Clint placed his palm over Hawk's chest and nuzzled his neck.

"Are you kidding?" Hawk circled his arm around Clint's waist. "I got to meet your dogs, see where you live, and now I'm getting cuddles." He dragged his lips across Clint's face until their mouths met and then he slipped his tongue into Clint's mouth. "Mmm. Perfect morning."

"In that case, you take the living room." Clint handed Hawk the garbage bag. "I think the kitchen's worse."

* * * *

"Ready to go?" Hawk asked as he walked into the laundry room where Clint was bagging up the dog bowls and food.

"What's that?" Clint tilted his chin toward the two duffle bags in Hawk's hands, both straining at the seams.

"I packed your clothes and bathroom stuff."

"You must have my whole closet in there." Clint set the dog supplies down and walked up to Hawk. "I'm coming over for two days and I was planning on spending them naked."

Hawk's blue eyes darkened and his nostrils flared.

With his gaze glued to Hawk's, Clint cupped the growing bulge in his jeans. "Hear something you liked?"

"You're playing with fire, baby," Hawk warned.

"Oh yeah?" Clint tugged on Hawk's fly, popping all the buttons open. "What're you going to do to me?"

Before he knew what hit him, Clint was flipped

around, shoved against the washing machine, and disrobed from the waist down.

"I'm going to fuck you." Hawk pinned Clint's wrists against the washer, suckled on his ear, and thrust his groin against Clint's bare ass.

An involuntary sound escaped Clint, one he refused to characterize as a needy whimper no matter how much it resembled exactly that.

"Sounds like you agree with my plan." Hawk licked a swath up his neck and then bit it. "Don't move."

The heat of Hawk's body slid away, Clint heard his duffle being unzipped, and then Hawk was back, spreading his ass open with one hand and slicking his hole with the other.

"Glad I found your lube," Hawk rasped.

"Me too."

"You good without a rubber?"

"Fine on my end." Clint grunted when a finger was pushed into his hole. "But you know I was fucking Ewan up until a couple of weeks ago."

"You go bare with him?" Hawk asked as he twisted his finger and brushed against Clint's gland.

"Never," Clint answered breathlessly.

"He ever top?"

"Nuh-uh." Clint shook his head.

Hawk's finger came out and a slick, hot cockhead pressed against Clint's hole instead.

"There been anyone else?"

"Not in close to a year."

"Then I'm not worried."

Slowly, Hawk pushed inside, his long, thick cock spreading Clint open inch by inch.

"Oh fuck," Clint moaned, dragging each word out. "I missed this." He widened his stance and tilted his ass up, giving Hawk as much room as he possible. "Feels so good."

"Christ." Hawk bottomed out and laid over him, his chest against Clint's back and his mouth next to Clint's ear. "Nothing's ever felt this good." He trembled and circled his hips. "Not sure how long I can last inside you, baby. You're so damn hot and tight."

"'S okay." Clint clenched his ass, adding sensation to Hawk's dick and making him gasp. "I'm already close."

"Going to be hard and fast," Hawk warned as he straightened. He gripped Clint's hips and moved him back until Clint's cock hung over empty air and only the upper half of his chest lay on the washer. "Brace yourself."

Clint grabbed onto the sides of the washer as Hawk made good on his promise, pulling out of his hole and slamming back in, his pace punishing and relentless.

"Ah, ah, ah!" Clint shouted, the pleasure and passion too big to keep inside.

Behind him, Hawk grunted and panted, somehow managing to plunge in even deeper while grazing Clint's gland on every pass.

"Going to fill you up."

"You already are." And not just his ass.

"Clint," Hawk moaned. "Love you."

"Oh, Jesus, please," Clint begged, knowing all he needed was one touch to his cock and he'd explode, but unable to release his grip on the washer to bring himself off.

"I have you." Hawk snaked one hand under Clint's belly and tugged him up to a standing position, his back pinned to Hawk's chest, and then he took hold of Clint's dick and stroked while he continued pumping in and out of Clint's body.

"Hawk!" Clint shouted as his balls tightened and his cock throbbed. "Yes!"

Thick cream shot from his dick, hitting the underside of his chin, his chest, and his belly. Behind him, Hawk made a strangled sound, shoved all the way inside, and stilled as hot fluid filled Clint's passage. They stood together, hearts racing and breaths coming out in loud gasps.

When he finally regained control of his muscles, Clint twisted his head and looked at Hawk. "Now I'm ready to go."

Hawk snorted and kissed the back of Clint's head. "Remember what I said about a high sex drive and a great sense of humor?" He nipped Clint's ear. "I was right."

* * * *

If Clint thought he was falling too quickly for Hawk, his dogs were even worse. Fluffy and Speedy immediately settled into Hawk's warm pueblo, curling up on the rug in front of the fireplace and showing no inclination to continue their recent furniture destruction tendencies. When Monday morning came around, neither dog wanted to go.

"Leave them here," Hawk said. "You're coming back for dinner anyway."

"When did we make dinner plans?"

"I've got way more planned for us than dinner," Hawk said softly.

Even if Hawk hadn't repeatedly told him as much, Clint would have figured that out when he'd gone to get his toothbrush out of one of the duffle bags Hawk had packed and found his entire closet stuffed inside. The responding glow that had spread through his chest had lasted the entire weekend and showed no indication of waning.

"You saw what they did to my place. Are you sure you want to leave them unattended with all your nice furniture?"

Hawk was dressed for the office in one of his perfectly fitted suits and Clint wanted to tear it off him and go back to bed. Two days of continuous contact had made him crave the man even more. He satisfied himself by straightening Hawk's already straight collar.

"I'm not worried about the dogs." Hawk kissed him, took his hand, and led him outside. "They're smart enough to realize they're home."

Clint might have argued, but they both had to get to work. Besides, he suspected Hawk was right.

"You want to drive in together?" Hawk asked. "I'll probably end up making one of my regular visits to the station around quitting time anyway."

"Why do you have so many meetings there?" Clint asked. "I've always wondered."

"Meetings?" Hawk laughed and shook his head. "Baby, haven't you figured out by now that I go there to talk to you?"

"Oh." Clint blinked in surprise but when he examined his feelings, expecting to be worried, he found only happy warmth. "Sure. And if you need to work late, there's always plenty to keep me busy."

Hawthorne had a low crime rate, but two weeks of vacation meant a full desk waiting for Clint. Thankful for the distraction, he dug in, efficiently making his way through the mountain of work and doing his level best not to daydream about Hawk like a lovesick teenager. He had been mostly successful by the time six o'clock rolled around.

"Hi, Hawk," Sally said.

Clint looked up from his computer and saw Hawk walking into the office. His suit coat was flung over one shoulder, his tie was loose, and his shirtsleeves were rolled up, exposing his thick, corded forearms. Even the man's arms were sexy.

"How are you, Sally?" Hawk looked at him, his eyes sizzling, and then he leaned against Sally's desk and focused on her. "Things going all right with Earl?"

Despite having spent five days a week, nine hours a day for two years with Sally, until that moment, Clint had never seen her blush.

"Ya were spot on about him, honey." Sally put her hand on her chest and sighed. "He's the cat's meow."

"I knew you two would hit it off." Hawk smiled at Sally. "I'm glad it's working out."

Hawk walked over to him and Clint realized he'd stood up in anticipation, but anticipation of what? Did he think Hawk was going to kiss him in the middle of the station, with Sally looking on, the sheriff in his glass-walled office, and other police officers wandering around? Disappointment flooded Clint and he kicked himself for once again putting himself in a position where he had to hide.

"Hey," Hawk said quietly as he approached. "You okay?"

Swallowing hard, Clint dipped his head as a silent yes even though he wasn't sure if that was an honest answer. He gripped the side of his desk to keep himself from reaching out to Hawk, the desire instinctive after their passionate weekend.

"You sure?" Hawk kept walking until he was only a breath's distance from Clint, much closer than a colleague or even a friend would stand.

In a flash of clarity, Clint realized that even though he had used Ewan's refusal to come out as an excuse to stop seeing him, he wasn't certain what he would have done if Ewan had agreed to be public about their relationship. When Clint had put his military career behind him and moved to a new state for a fresh start, he'd told himself he was done living on anyone else's terms except his own. He wouldn't hide, wouldn't pretend; he'd just be himself and let the chips fall where they may.

But then he'd been too busy getting settled into his new job and new town to make friends or date or do anything other than be a cop. And when he'd finally had time to devote to a social life, he'd chosen a guy who was so deep in the closet there wasn't a snowball's chance in hell of getting him out. That hadn't been an accident, Clint realized, it had been a shield. Much like the shield he had thrown up every time Hawk had made himself vulnerable by confessing his feelings and sharing his desires for a future by Clint's side.

"I'm sure," Clint said as he cupped his palm around Hawk's neck in a move that spoke of a lover's familiarity.

The smile Hawk gave him in response lit up the room.

"Good," Hawk said.

Although Clint had accused Hawk of being insane and firmly insisted that nobody uprooted his life to be with a guy he didn't know and declared his love to someone before the first date, those things clearly made Hawk happy. More than that, they made Clint happy. And he'd never been truly happy in his safe, sane life.

"You know, I was thinking today." Clint licked his lips. "I need to find a new place to live."

His eyes sparkling, Hawk held onto Clint's hip. "Yeah?"

"Uh-huh." Clint nodded. "Most of my clothes are already at your place and my dogs like it there, so I should probably go ahead and pack the last of my boxes and move in."

"Definitely." Hawk's expression was a mixture of amusement and fondness. "It's the only practical thing to do."

"Right." Clint swallowed down his nerves, gazed into Hawk's adoring blue eyes, and plunged ahead, knowing he'd have company on the emotional jump he was about to take and the lifetime journey that would follow. "Plus, I'm in love with you."

Hawk beamed. "I love you too, baby." He leaned his forehead against Clint's. "We're going to have a great life together."

If Clint knew one thing about Hawk Black, it

was that when he set his mind to something, he made sure it happened.

"I have no doubt." Clint threaded his fingers with Hawk's. "Let's go home."

Cardeno C. –CC to friends – is a hopeless romantic who wants to add a lot of happiness and a few "awwws" into a reader's day. Writing is a nice break from real life as a corporate type and volunteer work with gay rights organizations. Cardeno's stories range from sweet to intense, contemporary to paranormal, long to short, but they always include strong relationships and walks into the happily-ever-after sunset.

Also by Cardeno C.

Dreamspinner Press

A Shot at Forgiveness
All of Me
He Completes Me
Home Again
In Your Eyes
Just What the Truth Is
Love at First Sight
Marriage - A Home Series Celebration
More Than Everything
Perfect Imperfections
Places in Time
Something in the Way He Needs
Strong Enough
The Half of Us
The One Who Saves Me
Until Forever Comes
Wake Me Up Inside
Walk with Me
Where He Ends and I Begin

The Romance Authors, LLC

Blue Mountain
Eight Days
In Another Life
In Un'altra Vita & Otto Giorni
McFarland's Farm
TJ & Finn

MIDNIGHT RUN

ALPHA GAY EROTIC ROMANCE

BAILEY BRADFORD

CHAPTER ONE

There wasn't even a hint of moonlight as Jack Herman ran along the hiking path at Government Canyon. The thud of his paws on the pavement soon changed to soft slaps when he finally hit dirt. He wanted to throw his head back and howl, but it wouldn't be wise considering he was hunting.

And not just any prey. Jack had no intention of eating what he caught. He wasn't on that kind of hunt.

The wind carried the scent of the intruder, spicy and earthy, like peppers rolled in fertile soil. Jack had detected it every night he'd come to revel in his wolf for the last week.

Tonight was a full moon, not that it could be seen behind the heavy cover of clouds. Besides the intruder, Jack could scent the impending rain. A storm was brewing courtesy of Mother Nature, and it matched the one building in him.

San Antonio didn't have many places for a wolf to run. Government Canyon was Jack's, and he'd be damned if he let some other shifter encroach on it. He was an alpha through and through, even if he no longer had a pack to lead.

An old, familiar pain streaked through his chest. He wouldn't think about his past, not now. Possibly not ever again. The pain was too great.

And he had a task to complete—find the bastard trespassing on his packlands. Jack wouldn't stand for someone to take it from him. He needed this space to run and rejoice in what he was.

Thunder cracked loud enough that Jack felt it shake the ground beneath his paws. A few seconds later, lightning brought the surrounding area into stark relief for one brief moment.

Then it was pitch dark again, and Jack's usually acute wolf vision was a bit muddled from the quick reversion from light to dark. Just as when someone took a picture of him with the flash on, white spots danced before his eyes and he shook his head.

It was a good thing his nose worked just fine. He could run blind if he needed to, and let his sense of smell guide him. That, and his hearing, which was exceptional.

Although, in minutes he'd be hearing nothing but the storm itself, and the rain could very well fuck up his tracking ability.

It would figure he'd find someone trespassing on his lands in February. There were two things that could be counted on to occur in San Antonio in January—rain, and colder temperatures than the natives liked.

Jack was a native, but he was an exception to the cold rule. It invigorated him in a way the heat never would. In fact, for the whole month of August, he didn't want to leave the comfort of his air-conditioned home or work.

Give him temperatures in the thirties or even a little lower, and he was thrilled to his webbed paws. Now he had that winter weather, finally. It wasn't surprising that the rain had rolled in considering the overcast skies that had threatened to unleash on them.

Jack put his nose to the ground and inhaled the tantalizing aroma of the other shifter. Not a wolf, he could tell that much. There wasn't the strong, piney scent that came with all of his kind. He ran over the other kinds of shifters he was aware of, but couldn't decide what he was after. The paw prints were non-existent. Either the creature wiped them out or was of such light weight as to not leave prints behind.

That one sniff caused a sensation Jack was becoming used to when he got a good, strong whiff of his prey. His groin tingled, his cock tried to stiffen, and the heat of arousal rushed through him.

Jack tried his best to stomp that shit down. He wasn't in the market for a lover or a fuck buddy. He was a lone wolf now, and always would be.

And that means no fucking? he asked himself.

It was best to ignore his scathing little inner voice. Especially since Jack had no good answer for it.

The loose dirt gave way to rocks, and despite his attempt to be silent, every now and then one gave way under his paw and went clattering against another. With the sky lighting up regularly every few seconds due to the lightning, Jack's vision was a tad screwy. While it wasn't rare to have a lot of rain during February, such a fierce thunderstorm was unusual.

Regardless, it was beautiful in its own way. The

thunder clapped louder, making his ears ring on occasion. The storm excited his wolf, though there was some anxiety as well.

His beast knew the power of a storm, of lightning and the fire it could bring. The human side knew it as well, and reveled in being out in it. There was so much freedom to running full-tilt while the elements raged around him.

Rain began to come down, the drops fat and cold when they hit his nose. His thick black coat kept most of the moisture off of him for a while as he continued running, chasing after that scent.

If he didn't find his prey soon, he might get away. Jack was certain the prey was male simply because the aroma of it aroused him. Jack was, and always had been, a gay wolf shifter. That wouldn't have suddenly changed. Hence, he reasoned his was after another man, in whatever form that man might currently be taking.

The rain came down harder, pelting him like frigid wet pebbles. He tucked his head lower and ran faster, trying to hang onto the thread of the other shifter's scent.

It was no use. Within minutes, he'd lost it. Frustrated, Jack threw his head back and howled.

The pleasure that brought him was undeniable, and he shook his coat before vocalizing again. He could have sat and sang to the moon all night if he didn't have to fear being caught. Granted, there shouldn't be anyone else out there, but it *was* Texas and people did have guns.

Jack trounced through the rocks and mud, no longer worrying about being silent. As heavy as the rainfall was, he doubted he'd be heard by anyone or anything in the nearby vicinity.

Mud squelched between his toes. He'd have a mess to clean off of his paws later. For now, he just let go of his disappointment at losing his prey and instead enjoyed the weather and the run. He was reminded of his childhood, and it was almost like he'd reverted back to the boy he used to be, when he'd run free and fast with his littermates through rain and mud, and occasionally even snow.

Veering off Black Hill Loop, Jack cut through on a path that was barely noticeable. Something else had been out there, some animal big enough to break some branches here and there but not too tall considering where the breakage occurred.

And he caught a whiff of that scent again. Thrilled to be back on the hunt, Jack could only assume whatever creature he was chasing, it'd only just passed through. Otherwise, the scent would have been washed away.

With the overhang of the tree limbs, the rain wasn't doing quite as much erasure as it had been. The thunder and lightning raged on, the wind whipping at him in sporadic, chilly bursts.

Jack didn't care. Excitement was pumping alongside adrenalin in his veins. He was *so close* he was almost salivating with anticipation.

Anticipation for what, he didn't want to really think about, because his dick was harder than it'd ever been, and that wasn't his normal reaction to hunting.

CHAPTER TWO

He'd really screwed up. Malakai had heard a very strident howl and he knew he was being hunted.

It was his own fault for not leaving the area, but he didn't have anywhere else to go. For weeks he'd avoided being spotted. His white coat stood out starkly against just about everything in the area, so he'd really had to get creative. Dirt helped. Shifting into his human form wasn't much of an option. His skin was nearly as pale as his fur.

At least the mud would help. He'd be a matted, muddy mess in no time.

If he survived the storm, and the confrontation with the wolf coming after him. For a while, Malakai had thought he'd lost the predator. Unfortunately, the sensation of being tracked prickled along his spine and his nerve endings like an electrical current.

Hungry and tired, the cold rain chilled him thoroughly—unusual considering what he was. An arctic fox shouldn't be bothered at all by the South Texas winter temperatures, ever. Yet he was shaking with more than just fear.

Not fear. Terror. Another clap of thunder caused his heart to nearly pound out of his chest. Malakai dug his claws into the wet ground and tried to run faster. He was tired, and weak from lack of proper nutrition. He sucked at hunting, which was part of why he'd ended up in the Godforsaken state he was now in.

He hated storms. Absolutely hated them. The fierce power of nature was unlike anything else in the world. Nothing could predict it completely or control it. At any second, Malakai could be struck dead, or have a tree fall on him. He could trip and hit his head, then drown in a mud puddle.

God, he hated storms!

Malakai's nerves were shot. His thoughts became chaotic as panic and dread swelled inside him. His steps became sloppy, his vision dimming with each breath he had to struggle for.

Lightning hit something close to him. A tree, perhaps, judging by the horrendous sound it made.

Malakai didn't look. He whimpered and tried to get as far away from the most immediate danger when he smelled fire. It was probably just from a tree being singed; he didn't think a fire could really get up and going in such heavy rain. Even so, his fox demanded that he run harder, so he did.

Bones aching, he lost track of everything but his fear. He needed to find shelter, needed to get out of the storm.

It'd make him easy prey if he sought a place to escape the weather. Malakai knew he was easy prey regardless. He was tiring too much to keep running. If he was being pursued by a wolf, then he might be able to escape it by hiding in the restrooms by the campgrounds.

With a burst of inspiration, he remembered the lock on the door to the bathroom's entrance. The larger ones, up by the headquarters, didn't lock like that.

But the others did. If he could get in there and twist that deadbolt, he might be safe.

And if the hunter *was* more than a wolf, then Malakai would have a whole different problem on his hands.

Every hair on his back was doing its best to stand up by the time he spotted the building. The rain hadn't let up and it pelted him viciously as he ran for the shelter over a dozen yards away. Every slap of his paws on the ground sent water splashing up his legs, chilling him over and over again.

He reached the slight covering of the building, similar to a porch. With the wind blowing the rain right under it, it provided no protection. Malakai gasped as he began to shift. He hadn't taken a proper breath in too long, his lungs constricted by fear. His head spun and his appendages went numb while his muscles, tendons, and bones reshaped themselves.

If he'd been cold as a fox, it was much worse as a man with no fur or clothing to protect him. Malakai was on his hands and knees, shaking so hard his teeth chattered. He shoved himself onto his feet and hit the door with his shoulder. The second he was able, Malakai slipped into the restroom.

And froze as the large black wolf bared its teeth at him.

CHAPTER THREE

Jack had been coming to Government Canyon for a long time, since it'd opened up years ago. He knew the property like he knew his own face. It wasn't difficult for him to figure out where his prey had been headed. Jack had cut around and taken a much shorter route to the restrooms. He was glad his gamble had paid off.

Especially since before him stood one of the most attractive men he'd ever seen in his life. With long hair so blond it was almost white, and skin that gleamed pale and milky, slick with rain, and features so delicate they reminded Jack of paintings he'd once seen of fairies.

Ethereal, that was the word he wanted. There was definitely an exquisite beauty to the man unlike anything Jack had encountered before.

"P-please don't h-hurt me," the stranger said in a trembling voice. It was deeper than what Jack would have expected, given the man's pretty features. The large blue eyes framed in black lashes were especially enchanting.

A hard shiver racked the pale man's body. His eyes rolled back, and Jack shifted in an instant, lunging to catch him before he hit the cement floor.

He just barely succeeded. Jack landed on his ass hard enough to jar his spine. He locked his arms around his slight burden, grimacing at how cold the man's skin was. "What are you?" he muttered as he stared at the man's slightly upturned nose and lush pink lips. He took in the high cheekbones, the slight dip in the chin, the uptilt to the outer edges of the man's eyes, and the finely arched eyebrows that were several shades darker than his blond hair. Had Jack not seen the pale pubic hair, he'd have suspected a dye job, considering the dark brows and black lashes.

Jack gathered the man into his arms after another hard shiver rocked the thin frame. He needed to share body heat, of which he suddenly had plenty. The fact that he was aroused, too, was disturbing, considering the state of his prey. Jack couldn't seem to help it. His body wasn't listening to his brain.

Part of being a shifter, he supposed. He was, after all, more of an animal than a regular human. Add in him being an alpha, and Jack knew himself to be very different from most of the people he met.

Okay, from anyone he'd met. He was too intense for all but the most casual of lovers, if they could even be called that. A hookup and a scene at Binders, the best BDSM club in San Antonio, was his usual method of interacting with other men, barring his job.

Holding another man, especially one so fragile in appearance, wasn't something Jack did, either. Yet there he sat, cradling his prey, stroking over soft, wet skin.

Goosebumps covered it despite Jack's attempt to bring warmth to the man. He ended up shifting and covering most of that shaking form with his furry body. Shifting had taken care of the wet pelt.

Within minutes, the man beneath him stopped shaking so hard and, with a groan, he opened his eyes.

And shrieked. "*Eek!*"

Jack had never in his life heard anyone actually make that mouse-like noise. He growled a little as he got up.

"Please don't bite me, please — "

Jack didn't back away too far — he couldn't in the small confines of the restroom. He moved as close to the door as he could get, then he shifted again.

"Oh…wow," the man whispered, staring at him with those big eyes.

Jack canted his head to the left, still feeling rather wolfish. He raked his gaze down lean limbs and a flat but unchiseled belly, then further still to the thickening cock framed with near-white hair. Pink balls lay cradled between thin thighs.

"I'm Jack Herman. What's your name?" Jack demanded, his voice gritty, his vocal cords still feeling more wolfish than man.

"M-Malakai."

That was only a partial answer. Jack wanted all of it. "Last name?"

Malakai sat up but hunched over, drawing his knees to his chest and hugging them tightly. "No last name." His cheeks pinked with a blush. "Just Malakai. That's all." He didn't look at Jack when he spoke.

Jack frowned at him. "You have an accent. Where are you from?" It wasn't a Texas accent, that much he could tell on his own.

Malakai turned his head then peeked at him through strands of hair nearly hiding his entire face. "Alaska, but that was years ago. A lifetime ago."

The sadness in Malakai's voice was unmistakable. It tugged at Jack's heart, which surprised him considering he'd thought that particular organ to be impenetrable. "You're on my lands," he said gruffly, "And I know you're a shifter. What kind?"

Malakai blinked. "You didn't see me?"

Jack arched one brow at him. "What kind?" he repeated in a firmer tone.

"Artic fox," Malakai answered. He hugged his legs tighter and ducked his head. "Are you going to kill me?"

Jack blanched. "What? No. I wasn't going to kill you even when we were both shifted. What the hell kind of monster do you think I am?" It pissed him off, but he tried to rein in his temper. Malakai, for all his beauty, looked scared and starved, and he hadn't come by either of those things naturally. Someone, or more than one person, had hurt him. Jack was sure of it, recognizing a certain wariness in Malakai. "This is my territory, though, and I had to know who was trespassing."

"I'm sorry. I...I didn't know." Malakai tucked his head down lower. "I'm sorry."

Jack felt like he'd kicked a pup, which he'd never do. He was an alpha, a Dom, not an abusive asshole. Sighing to himself, he squatted so he wasn't lumbering over Malakai. "How'd you wind up out here? I've been coming for years and only just started scenting you."

Malakai began to shake again. Jack's protective instincts surged to the surface. "Shh, hey, it's all right," he murmured, awkwardly moving to Malakai's side. "I'm not going to hurt you." He noted that his words seemed to have a calming effect on Malakai, so he continued speaking, though he always felt his words were inadequate. They seemed to be helpful this time around. "You can tell me what's happened, why you've ended up here."

He was so drawn to Malakai, to his scent and appearance, even to the way he huddled, submissive, though Jack didn't care for the scared part at all. Well, some fear during a scene was fine, it could add to the excitement for the Dom and sub both, but that was different, an agreed upon set of events that could be halted with one word—the safeword—from the sub.

Maybe Malakai needed a safeword. If he knew he had the power to shut down anything bad or frightening that he didn't like, perhaps Malakai would feel secure. But there'd have to be trust between them for that to work, and Jack's brain was leaping past things like them being strangers and such. Malakai called to him on an instinctive level that shook Jack to the core, even as he longed to explore it.

"Oh." Jack blinked and plopped back on his butt. Wow, he couldn't believe it but—

Malakai watched him nervously as Jack, pulse racing, stood up then walked right to Malakai's side. "What?" Malakai squeaked.

Jack inhaled deeply, his eyelids almost closing as he filled his lungs with Malakai's scent. As it had when he'd been pursuing Malakai, Jack's dick began to grow erect.

Warmth spread throughout his body, from the top of his head, down his spine, around to his shoulders and sternum, then all the way to his toes. He felt lit up from the inside out, and as Jack tilted his head down to look at Malakai, he heard Malakai gasp.

"You feel it," Jack rumbled. He crouched beside Malakai and cautiously pushed back a lank of hair, tucking it behind Malakai's ear—his pointy ear. That was surprising; Jack had never seen a shifter retain anything so obviously from its animal form. When they morphed into humans, they looked completely human, and the same when they went all beastly—there was nothing other than that creature in their appearance.

But Malakai had very pointy ears. Surely it wasn't just the one. Jack touched the tip.

Malakai shivered, a soft moan escaping him before he dipped his head even lower.

Jack moved to squat in front of Malakai. "Look at me." He made it an order, trusting his alpha nature to lead as it should.

Malakai gasped and raised his head. His eyes were wide and the expression on his face was one of stunned arousal.

Slowly, Jack tucked more hair behind Malakai's ears, wanting to see his face without obstruction. "Gorgeous," he said without thinking. "So fucking gorgeous."

Malakai shook his head frantically. "N-no, I'm not. I'm a freak with pointy ears and bug-eyes and—"

"Stop." Jack couldn't let Malakai run himself

down. "I like your ears, and you have eyes that can gut a man in a heartbeat."

That adorable blush stole over Malakai's cheeks again. He licked his bottom lip then bit it, averting is gaze at the same time. "I don't know what to believe anymore."

Those pretty eyes welled with tears. John grunted and before he could overthink the impulse, he tugged Malakai into his arms.

God, the man felt perfect there, so sweet and soft against him. Oh, Malakai was hard in all the right places, but his skin was as smooth as satin. And because Jack was honest, he didn't keep a pressing admission to himself. "I want you," he said bluntly.

Malakai stiffened in his arms.

Jack spoke against the sensitive skin of Malakai's neck. "I want you, but I won't push. Much. You have to feel the connection between us. It isn't just me." He hoped it wasn't just him, anyway. If so, he was fucked. *Or not.* He supposed he could be wrong. Maybe Malakai wasn't his mate. Maybe he was just a really hot man that Jack wanted.

His wolf howled at him, the sound bouncing around Jack's skull but never escaping that boney cage. Apparently, his wolf thought he was a fucking idiot. The beast wanted its mate—Malakai.

CHAPTER FOUR

Confusion almost muted out the desire pooling in Malakai's groin. He was embarrassed that his cock was thickening, had been ever since he'd looked at a very naked Jack Herman. Being aroused by a real man was a new experience. Malakai had fantasized plenty of times when he'd been kenneled and alone, even sometimes when he'd watched Jared and his wife having sex.

It'd never been the wife that had interested him, but rather the fat cock Jared had sported, and the other bits that dangled down there. If he'd been attracted to females, Malakai would have pined after Jared's wife, Rita. She had been beautiful and kind, always making sure to feed and water him when Jared was often forgetful of such things. She'd have hated what had happened to Malakai.

"Where are you?"

At Jack's question, Malakai jolted. Held secure in the man's embrace, his fear ebbed somewhat. "I was...in my head."

"Did I scare you when I said I wanted you?" Jack asked.

The deep timbre of Jack's voice did funny, very pleasant, things to Malakai's cock and balls. "No, I don't think scared is the right word. Confused," he admitted somewhat reluctantly. "Why would you want me?"

Jack snorted. "Why wouldn't I?" he retorted, cupping Malakai's chin. "Look at me."

Malakai found it difficult to do so. It seemed wrong, probably because Jack was an alpha. Malakai wanted to keep his gaze down. He *needed* to show respect and the urge to flop onto his back and show his belly was almost irresistible.

But he also had to obey. Looking in Jack's dark brown eyes, Malakai's heart raced. "Yes, sir." The words rolled off his tongue, feeling so perfect he nearly whimpered.

Jack's eyes darkened, the brown almost black as his pupils expanded. "That's right. You know what I am. In here." Jack moved one hand around and placed it over Malakai's heart. "Look at that. I can almost cover the width of your chest."

Since Jack sounded intrigued and possibly turned on, Malakai didn't believe that was an insult. Still, he wanted to look away—but not bad enough to tug his chin from Jack's grip.

"I can see every one of your ribs," Jack continued. "What happened?"

Malakai was tired, hungry—starving, really—and so confused by the riotous emotions and needs he was experiencing. He closed his eyes. "Everything. I—they died and no one was there to let me out of the kennel, and even when I shifted I was still locked in. The door to the outside run was locked and I—" A sob escaped him and Malakai tried to curl in on himself. "I was so sure I'd die."

Jack murmured that he had Malakai now, and he released Malakai's chin, instead pulling him into that warm, safe embrace again. "It's okay, Malakai. I've got you. Feel how right it is, you in my arms."

Malakai did feel it. How could he not? He hadn't been home since he'd been trapped almost a decade ago. Jared and Rita had been good keepers—well, Rita had—but they'd wanted to own him, not cherish him for who and what he was.

"I spent nine years with them, locked up all the time at first, then gradually allowed out some once they knew I wouldn't attack," Malakai said, the words just tumbling out. "Jared, he trapped me when I was a pup, barely eleven in human years." Malakai still recalled the fear he'd experienced when that cage had slammed shut on him. "I just wanted food, and I was the worst hunter in our pack. It seemed too easy, and it was. The trap closed and he had me. He had me for so long."

As Malakai had spoken, Jack had grown tense, his big body stiffening everywhere that Malakai could feel it. "You were caught as a kid? A pup? And kept as a pet?"

Malakai nodded. "Eventually, a pet. At first I was just a trophy to show off to his friends. I was so scared, and alone. I missed my family. I still miss them."

Jack caressed his back and much to Malakai's surprise, kissed his nape gently.

"Oh," Malakai breathed, hoping for another kiss. He'd not had any affection once he'd been caught, not much in his fox form, and never like this. "Please?"

"Please what?" Jack asked. "Please stop? Please don't stop? Please give you more?"

Malakai squirmed, trying to get closer to Jack. "The last two." When Jack didn't immediately kiss him again, Malakai added, "I do feel it. I'm not afraid of you. I'm…I'm…" He groaned in frustration.

Jack slid a hand down and around until it hovered above Malakai's dick. "You're what? Horny?"

Answering wasn't possible when Jack began to suck on the base of Malakai's nape. At the same time, he let the side of his hand brush over the tip of Malakai's shaft.

Malakai cried out in shock. He'd never felt half as much pleasure when he'd touched himself.

"Did you get to masturbate where you were kept?"

"Not often," Malakai squeaked out. Was Jack going to do that for him?

Jack licked from right between his shoulder blades to the top of his nape. Then he nipped, soft at first, with more pressure the second time, and Malakai barely had a second to grasp what was happening. "Oh!"

He came so hard his gut cramped each time his cock spurted.

"Nice, honey," he heard Jack say. The approval in his voice was such that Malakai couldn't be humiliated for coming so fast. He'd pleased Jack, that was important. More so than his own climax.

"Mmm, you smell so good." Jack dragged his

fingers through a cooling patch of cum. "Lick it clean."

Malakai was going to have an erection again in minutes at the rate his blood was pumping. He parted his lips then stuck out his tongue so he could lap his seed from Jack's fingers. The salty, bitter taste was familiar enough, and he hummed happily while he licked his juices up.

"Done that before?" Jack asked.

Malakai just kept from smacking his lips. "I was curious, and I tried it once. I liked it." Would Jack think he was a pervert?

Jack grinned. "Good, because I sure as shit thought it was hot to watch." Then his smile faded. "You escaped from the kennel. Is anyone going to come looking for you?"

Malakai shook his head. "Who would bother? Rita and Jared are dead. I don't even know if the authorities are aware of it. They died in their home. I didn't know at first. I couldn't understand why Rita had forgotten about me. That was the worst feeling, thinking I'd been forgotten." Worse than the starvation and thirst.

Jack pulled him close again. He tucked Malakai's head against his broad chest. "I'm sorry. That must have been horrible."

Malakai sniffed before he could start crying. He'd already lost it once. He wouldn't do it again. "I dug and dug at the concrete. My paws were bleeding. For days I kicked at that stupid gate leading to the outside. Finally, it gave, and I was able to escape to the outside. By then I could smell them, and I knew they were dead. It took two more days to get out of that enclosure. Usually it carried an electric current, but for whatever reason, it didn't then. Maybe they forgot to turn it on. Even so, I had to dig under the concrete foundation they'd laid under the fence line. If it hadn't rained one day, I think I'd have been dead already." He shrugged. "I'm not. They are. When I got closer to the house, the odor was worse. There were flies and I couldn't look. I ran."

Shame washed over him. "I should have notified authorities, but I knew they'd had a party planned for that night. I wanted to be free." He laughed bitterly. "And look at me. Terrified of everything, and so hungry my spine's about to become my next meal."

"That part I can take care of easily. Your self-esteem is something that will need more time to recover." Jack stood, lifting Malakai into his arms. "The rain is still hammering down, but my place is just across the road from the state park. That's why I can come and go so easily."

Malakai had seen some of those homes. The ones across the road tended to be older, maybe even ranches. Those on the same side of the road, at least that he'd seen, had all been newer houses built entirely too closely together. At least Jared and Rita had owned several acres. Jared had said it was necessary for privacy reasons, and Malakai could only assume it had something to do with the narcotics Jared had both used and sold.

"I could put you down now instead of once we're outside, if you insist," Jack said. "I like holding you. Being protective is in my nature."

"Do you have a pack?" It seemed the logical conclusion, given Jack's statement.

But Jack grimaced. "Not anymore. Seems they didn't care for rules and thought they should all be able to do whatever they wanted. Which went against a wolf's instincts, even those who weren't alphas. I had expected them to all come back, and I'd have taken them in without any chastisement. When they found out that sucked, they turned to other alphas as leaders."

"You lost the whole pack?" Malakai asked, shocked at such blatant disregard for Jack's feelings, for the need he must feel to protect and lead. "Were they stupid?"

Jack shook his head. "No, but I was. I should have been more forceful with them. As it was, I wasn't the only alpha it happened to. It was a mini-shifter uprising, I guess. The funny thing is, all the alphas that were abandoned are still lone wolfs. Our packs never came back to us. Their pride and stubbornness wouldn't let them. Before you think I'm cocky, that's only the truth. They had to tell their new alphas what had happened and why they hadn't returned."

"But why didn't those alphas send them back?" Malakai would have thought honor demanded they do it.

"Because we—the packless alphas—all said no. If our members had wanted to come back to us, we'd have accepted them. That they turned to someone else..." Jack growled.

Yes, Malakai could imagine that was quite an insult. "Pride is a stupid thing when it interferes with what's best for you."

"It's a human emotion. Wolves, animals, they do

what's best for their survival." Jack scowled. "Nothing good comes from ignoring shifter instincts for human logic. Open the door. I wouldn't want to drop you."

Malakai did as he'd been directed. Following orders soothed his nerves. There'd been no true alpha when he'd been a human pet. Jared was the head of the household, but he wasn't an alpha. Malakai had been lost since the moment he'd stepped in that trap years ago.

Now he was finally feeling like his life could make sense again. He'd thought he'd grow old and die in that kennel, then he'd thought he'd die a horrible death there.

Instead he was free, and he was only now able to hope for some semblance of a decent life.

CHAPTER FIVE

The trek to his house took less than fifteen minutes. They were both soaked through and through when they leapt onto Jack's porch. The rain hadn't let up at all. Jack shifted then took his key down from the top of the doorframe. "Not the best place to hide it if I weren't an alpha." No one would mess with him or his property. Humans tended to be uncomfortable around him after too long, and they'd subconsciously pick up on his markings around the place.

Jack unlocked the door then ushered Malakai inside. The poor man was shaking hard enough to rattle his bones. "Come on. I've got a hot shower and some clothes you can borrow."

He took Malakai by the wrist—*such a thin one. The man really needed a month's worth of healthy meals, at least*—and guided him to the bathroom. "Here's a washcloth and a clean towel." Jack set both on the counter. "I don't have a spare tooth brush, sorry." He turned to face Malakai. Did the man feel the primeval bonds pulling them together? The more Jack experienced it, the more he thought he was right. Surely an attraction of this magnitude could only mean that Malakai was his mate.

Yet he hesitated to say as much. It wasn't that he was insecure. That simply wasn't the case. Jack automatically wanted what was best for Malakai. It was part of Jack's being. He had to take care of those who needed him, and it'd been a long, long time for him to have no one to lead or look after.

Having his mate suddenly pop up threw Jack out of sorts. He wanted to claim Malakai fully, to fuck and bite and mark him. To do so would mean Malakai would have to stay with him. Mates couldn't be separated once the bond was cemented between them. A day here and there would be okay, but anything more would bring them both physical pain.

"The water gets hot fast." Jack turned the knobs and got the shower going. "Holler if you need anything."

"Um." Malakai's entire face blushed bright pink.

Jack had an inkling of why. "What is it, boy?"

Malakai sucked in a quick breath. His cock twitched. His pulse throbbed at the base of his neck.

Jack saw it all.

"Boy?" Malakai said it less as a question and more as a hopeful request. "What does that make me want?"

"Want?" Jack could have pressed for an explanation, but he knew what Malakai meant. "It makes you burn with a need for me because you're a sub, and you want to please me. You want me to take control, and tell you what I expect. You want me to reward you, and to punish you, because I am an alpha, and a Dom."

Malakai was already shaking his head, his expression conveying his confusion. His dick was fully erect, that part obviously in line with what Jack said.

"Ask," Jack bit out, testing Malakai.

As he'd suspected, Malakai was aroused even more by the sharper tone. "Why would I want you to punish me? I don't like being punished. I hated it when Jared hit me with things or scolded me. I really hated it when he yelled at me," he added. "I hated that the most."

Jack closed the distance between them. How had he lucked into finding such a sweet, innocent, passionate man? He framed Malakai's face with his hands. "I can promise that I will never yell at you in anger. In jest, or if you're in danger, possibly, but not when I'm angry. A good alpha always controls his temper. Punishment isn't about me hurting you for the hell of it. It doesn't even have to involve physical pain. I'd also never punish you without first discussing it and setting boundaries. Don't think I'd just grab you and hurt you. I wouldn't." Then he did what he simply had to do. He slanted his mouth over Malakai's and kissed him.

At first it was a gentle kiss, as he knew Malakai had no experience with a lover. But Malakai moaned and parted his lips. He pushed his tongue into Jack's mouth, and that was all of the gentle part, gone.

Jack ran his hands down until he had two firm ass cheeks in his hands. He gave them a squeeze as he pushed his tongue over Malakai's, claiming control of the kiss.

Malakai mewled and went pliant against him. He was perfect, and so natural in his submission, it did Jack's heart good.

He kneaded the sweet mounds of flesh in his

hands while he nipped at Malakai's lips and tongue.

Malakai trembled beautifully, his need apparent in every aspect of his being.

Jack could smell it, feel it, hear it, taste it, see it—Malakai laid himself open to Jack, to the pleasure they could share.

The stiff prod of Malakai's slender dick against his thigh reminded Jack that he hadn't come when Malakai had earlier. Jack's shaft was achingly hard, leaking pre-cum, and he wanted to rut away until he sprayed his seed all over Malakai, covering him in his scent.

The idea made Jack growl. He spun them until he had Malakai pressed against the wall beside the towel bar. Jack slid a leg between Malakai's thighs. "Ride it," he ordered, breaking the kiss to speak.

"S-sir," Malakai stuttered, clinging to Jack's shoulders and fucking away at Jack's thigh. Malakai's eyes were huge, the dark blue irises ringed in gray.

When Malakai started to close his eyes, Jack stopped him. "No. You will look at me when you come. Just like I'm going to be watching you." He took one of Malakai's hands and guided it to his cock. "Stroke me. Just like this." Jack wrapped his hand around Malakai's.

"Oh, oh God," Malakai wailed, his Adam's apple bobbing repeatedly. "I'm gonna...I can't—touching you—ungh!" His head would have thumped the wall had Jack not moved quickly and shoved his other hand back there. Malakai jerked against his leg, one, then again. He came with a long, drawn out moan, pumping his cum onto Jack's hip and thigh.

And Jack couldn't wait any longer. He tightened

his grip and kissed Malakai again. There was no sweet beginning to the kiss this time. Jack ached, he needed, and he took what he was given, never pushing too far or too fast. Had he been able to just turn Malakai around and shove right into his tight little ass, Jack would have done so.

But Malakai was a virgin, and Jack would never hurt someone like that.

He could get off, however. "Faster," he demanded in between nipping kisses.

The rough friction over his cock was unbelievably good. Jack had never minded a little pain himself, he just had to be in control when it happened—as he did practically all the rest of the time.

So he held on harder and fucked their joined hands. Pleasure began to spread out from his cock to his balls, then it raced over every inch of his body.

"Fuck," he gritted out, vision hazing. Jack slammed his mouth over Malakai's and thrust his tongue in, matching the tempo of his lower thrusts. He *needed* unlike he ever had before. His canines were dangerously close to dropping down. His wolf wanted them to, wanted him to do all the things he could to make Malakai theirs.

Jack refused. He jerked his head aside and bit his bottom lip until he tasted blood. A second later, he flicked his thumbnail over his slit. As if he'd flipped off a lid, cum jetted from his cock.

He heard Malakai whimper, felt him sliding down the wall. Then the hot, wet vise of Malakai's mouth was around Jack's shaft, sucking, pulling out another shot of spunk, then a third.

Jack's orgasm was drawn out until his knees threatened to give out. "Enough," he rasped, pulling Malakai off his cock. "Good, that was so good, boy."

Malakai's eyes were so expressive. His elation at the praise made them seem more vibrant. That, and the smile Malakai wore was brilliant, his pink lips swollen and wet.

Jack took another kiss, tasting himself on Malakai's tongue. It almost made him hard again. If Malakai's stomach hadn't rumbled, Jack likely would have been ready for round two—three for Malakai— in a few minutes.

As it was, he wouldn't ignore Malakai's needs. The man was direly in need of sustenance. "Get in the shower. I'll fix us something to eat."

Malakai ducked his head. "Yes, sir."

Jack didn't miss the smug curve to Malakai's smile, or the little wiggle to his butt. The man was happy, at least for now. Jack was taking care of his mate, even if Malakai didn't appear to know that's what they were.

Even though Jack wanted to tell him, he wouldn't. Malakai had been a prisoner for over half his life. Jack wouldn't imprison him further, even if it meant giving up his mate. He wanted what was best for Malakai. *If you love something, let it go...* He wasn't in love with Malakai, not even close to it.

That didn't mean he wouldn't be, and soon, if they stayed together. Mates had a bond that pulled them tighter and tighter until they loved each other so fully and well that they often couldn't live with the other. It was common for them to pass away within hours or even minutes of one another.

If the bond was completed. Jack could put aside his own longing and do what needed to be done.

As long as he didn't fully mate with Malakai, he'd be able to let the man go when the time came.

CHAPTER SIX

Malakai woke up with a start, his body aching pleasantly in ways it hadn't before. He stretched, groaning as his back popped. His cock was a little chafed from all the attention it'd gotten throughout the night. Jack was a voracious and dominant lover.

And why wasn't he in bed with Malakai?

Opening one eye, Malakai searched the room for Jack but he wasn't in there.

"Guess I'll have to go after him." Malakai's lips twitched at the idea. Jack was definitely a hunter, and he'd pounce on Malakai in an instant. Maybe he'd even do the one thing Malakai was scared to ask him to. He longed to know what it felt like to have Jack's cock breaching him, filling him up in an elementally necessary way. Malakai needed that from him, though he didn't know why.

His quick attachment to Jack should have freaked him out. It didn't. Malakai was safe with the alpha, and he needed a man like Jack as a partner.

He was thinking ahead of himself. Malakai's cheeks burned. For all he knew, Jack was done with him. His chest ached and he had to press his palm over his heart to stem the pain.

A quick check with his fox, and Malakai knew it wasn't a physical pain. God, he was already planning a future with Jack. How was that even possible?

Little flashes of his past flitted through his thoughts. Malakai saw his mother and father bounding through deep drifts of snow. They'd been happy, in love, if his memory served him. Truthfully, Malakai didn't trust it. He couldn't recall nearly as much about his childhood before being trapped. A part of him had shut those memories down because they'd hurt so bad, made him cry and weep for his lost pack. He'd buried them too well in the recesses of his mind.

"You're awake. Good."

Malakai shook his head and opened his other eye.

Jack stood in the bedroom doorway, dressed in dark blue work pants and a gray button-up with a nametag sewn on. *Jack Herman, Owner.*

Malakai read the line under that and giggled. "Alpha Mechanic and Repair?"

Jack grinned crookedly and shrugged one shoulder. "Why not? I am an alpha and a mechanic. Seemed like a good business name at the time." He stood up straight and pointed to his dresser, where a short stack of clothes was neatly folded. "We never got to the clothing part. Something in that pile should fit well enough for you to be seen out in public."

"An ex's clothes?" Malakai asked, hoping he didn't sound jealous. He was jealous, which was unreasonable, given their lack of relationship.

"No exes, not boyfriends, anyway. Those belonged to some of my former pack members," Jack explained. "Every one of them was too scared to come back and get their belongings. If they didn't take it with them when they snuck off then it was abandoned. Didn't matter that I told 'em they could come pick their shit up at any time."

"Guilt," Malakai said again, thinking about his statement the night before. "Were your pack members inbred or something?" he asked, not entirely jokingly. It happened sometimes when the animal part of a shifter's nature proved too strong to be tempered by human morals.

Jack jutted his chin at the dresser. "Get something on so you can eat breakfast. I have to work today. Got an eight o'clock that's one of my best clients. The oil business is making me a financially comfortable man."

Malakai was confused. It sure seemed like Jack had dismissed him. He told himself not to be stupid of clingy. Jack had a job, after all.

The clothes were old but suitable. Malakai liked the way the sweats felt. He hadn't worn clothes before. It was a novel experience to do so now. He smoothed a hand down over his groin. Underwear might have helped to disguise that bulge. Since there were none in the stack of clothes, he'd have to do without.

Didn't seem a bad thing. Underwear looked restrictive. He rolled his eyes at his musings and quickly pulled on a soft blue T-shirt. The socks he ignored. Having his feet bound in a tube of material would drive him bonkers.

Malakai made use of the bathroom, then he padded down the hall and into the kitchen. The scents coming from there were making his mouth water.

"Pancakes, bacon, and more bacon." Jack chuckled. He set a platter piled high with crisp, greasy bacon.

Malakai's nose twitched. He didn't reach for any of the food.

Jack set a plate in front of him, piled high with pancakes. "Go on, eat. I already had mine earlier. Here's the syrup." He set a fluted glass container by Malakai's plate. "Silverware's probably best for the pancakes. Syrup's sticky."

"Thanks." Malakai hated that he had to be told such things. Having lived almost all of his life as a fox had left him with little human manners in many areas. Last night he'd been relieved to have sandwiches and steaks to eat. He'd only been a little mortified when Jack had corrected him. It'd seemed perfectly logical to Malakai to eat the piece of meat off the plate…without the use of his hands. Now he knew better.

Awkwardly wielding the fork and knife, Malakai cut into the pancakes. Once he had them in manageable pieces, he poured syrup on them.

Between the bacon and the pancakes, Malakai could have eaten himself sick. "So much better than kibble," he said between bites.

"I'd imagine." Jack sipped his coffee and watched Malakai steadily.

Malakai liked the attention, liked being the center of Jack's attention. He'd never been that for anyone before. There was no missing the appreciation in Jack's gaze. Malakai could smell the hint of arousal coming from Jack, too. It made Malakai's lust bubble up like a pot of water brought to boil.

Jack set his coffee cup down and strode over to him. He ran a hand over Malakai's hair then fisted it at his nape. "You are tempting me, boy," Jack muttered, pulling Malakai's head back. "Such need in you, and it calls to me."

Malakai trembled just before Jack kissed him, bringing to life nerve endings and wants Malakai hadn't known he had. With his head held still and Jack dominating him through that grip and the kiss, Malakai could have come where he sat.

He didn't. The last time Jack had pleasured him in the not so early morning hours, he'd told Malakai no coming until he was given permission. It excited Malakai unbearably, and he loved being forbidden to climax, though he might not if he hadn't been allowed to come eventually.

This morning, he was in no such luck. Jack ended the kiss then let go of Malakai's hair. He looked Malakai over, a smug grin in place. "Yeah, that's how you should look all the time. Needing to come, your lips wet and swollen from either kisses or sucking my cock." He ran a thumb over Malakai's bottom lip, then pressed down on it. "Fuckin' perfect."

Even so, Jack stepped away from him. "We've got to go. I'll be pushing it to get to work on time as it is."

That temporized Malakai's budding hurt feelings. He wasn't being rejected. Jack just had a job to do. Later, tonight, he and Jack could have sex.

"Am I coming with you then?" Malakai thought to ask.

"Yeah, you are, so go put those socks and shoes on that I left out. You can't be in a mechanic shop without them on," Jack said. "OSHA will be all over my ass if anyone sees you barefoot in there."

Malakai got up. "What's OSHA?"

"A federal organization that makes sure people aren't working in dangerous situations," Jack answered. "Or not more dangerous than they have to be. Some jobs have obvious risks, others, not so much. They just try to keep people from being hurt or killed on the job, and they aren't anyone to mess with, so finish getting dressed while I wash these dishes."

As Jack's tone brooked no argument, Malakai trotted back to the bedroom. He wasn't inclined to argue with an alpha, and certainly not *his* alpha. The thought froze him on the spot. *My alpha? I don't even know him!*

Even as he struggled with that, Malakai couldn't help but feel that he did know Jack. Loyal, dominant, honest, strong. Even though he was an alpha abandoned by a pack of fools, Jack didn't hate the shifters who'd left. When he spoke of them, there was no anger, only a hint of sorrow and regret.

If he ever got a hand on any of them, Malakai was going to be hard-pressed not to resort to physical violence. He'd like to smack everyone who'd hurt Jack and abused his trust.

And who thought they didn't need an alpha, or a pack? Malakai had missed being part of a pack so badly, it'd left him hollow inside.

"Are you about ready?" Jack called out.

Malakai bit his tongue to keep from squeaking. He tasted blood and cringed. "Almost." It wasn't a lie. He had the socks on in seconds, but the shoes were problematic. Once he figured the laces out, it went a lot quicker. Tying them was a challenge he wasn't quite up to, however, so Malakai traipsed out of the bedroom, the ends of the laces slapping the hardwood floor. He kind of liked the click-clack sound they made.

"Ah, I didn't think about the laces." Jack bent one leg a little and patted right above his knee. "Put your foot right here. Watch what I do, because the other shoelace is your responsibility."

The shoes felt clunky, like he was walking with cement on his feet, but Malakai would deal with it. If he wanted to be a part of Jack's life, he'd have to learn and conform so that he wasn't a problem.

One thing he knew for certain, he needed to be with Jack. Malakai tied his other shoe without any issues and reveled in the praise when Jack murmured, "Good job."

CHAPTER SEVEN

Malakai kept out of the way, and was surprisingly helpful, Jack soon learned. Smart, attentive, eager to serve and learn, he made a good helper around the shop.

Jack didn't let him help anyone else. The other mechanics that worked for him were paid damn good wages to do their jobs. Malakai wasn't going to do it for them.

With his long blond braid tucked under a baseball cap, Malakai's fine features were even better displayed. His sharp cheekbones cast shadows on the hollows beneath them. Malakai's lips were still swollen from all the kissing and sucking he'd done, and they were almost a dark red, too.

"There's something you can put on your lips in the top left desk drawer," Jack called out to Malakai, his mind solely on the fox shifter while waiting for customers to pick up their vehicles.

Chortling from across the back reminded Jack of where he was, and that he and Malakai weren't alone there. "Shut up, Drew."

"Nope, not gonna," the mechanic joked before pointing at the person helping him with an engine.

"Besides, Beth here started snickering first. You just didn't hear her."

Beth smacked Drew with a wrench.

"Won't that get OSHA in here?" Malakai asked worriedly.

Beth and Drew both hissed at each other, the siblings poking and bickering in a playful manner.

"It better not," Jack said. "They're just goofing around." He glared at them. "Instead of working, like I'm paying them to."

"Grump." Beth ducked her head back under the hood. Drew stuck his tongue out at her, and looked like he was about to poke her in the ribs.

Jack only had to stop smiling to put an end to their tussling. Drew got back to work. Now that Jack had a few minutes, he wanted to speak to Malakai alone. Something in the man's hopeful expression warned him that the subject the needed to bring up would be better discussed in private.

And he was putting off the inevitable because he didn't want to do it. Jack knew that, too. He wanted Malakai, and the bond between them was already growing, tethering him to the sexy fox shifter. A few more days, and Jack wouldn't be able to let him go.

"Come into the office. Did you eat lunch yet?" Jack asked.

Malakai shook his head. He wiped at his cheek, smudging oil over his fair skin. "No, sir. I wanted to wait for you."

Jack took the clean rag from his back pocket and gently cleaned off the gray mark, noting how Malakai went so very still, his eyes large and expressing something very close to adoration as he looked up at

Jack through his lashes. "You could have eaten. You need the food."

Malakai glanced down. "I wasn't very hungry. Breakfast kept me full."

Jack arched a brow at him when Malakai's stomach growled.

Malakai pressed a fist to his stomach. "Honest, it hasn't growled until now."

Jack believed him. Malakai had such a telling face, he'd never be able to play poker worth a damn. Jack cupped Malakai's elbow and ushered him to the office. "Take care of anyone that comes in," he directed Drew and Beth. He shut the office door and, unable to wait any longer, pulled Malakai into his arms for a kiss.

Malakai opened for him, moaning and ceding any semblance of control to Jack. Not that there was any battle for it. Malakai just melted against him so exquisitely, it bore noting.

Jack caressed his way down Malakai's back, pressing hard enough that Malakai could feel it, while not hurting him. When he finally cupped Malakai's ass and gave those perfect globes a squeeze, Jack almost gave in to the urge to bend Malakai over the desk and fuck him.

Two things stopped him. First was the knowledge that they'd make enough noise to let everyone in the vicinity know what they were doing. And second, his canines began to descend even though he tried to prevent them from coming down.

He pulled back, still cupping Malakai's butt. Jack flicked the pointed tip of one tooth with his tongue while nuzzling a path from Malakai's jaw to his ear. His grasp on his control was tenuous, something he'd never experienced before. Jack had always had a firm grip on his emotions and behavior. It was what had made him a good alpha. So good his pack didn't fear him, because they knew he'd be fair and let them go.

Now he had to fight to keep from taking Malakai despite the certainty of being overheard. He kneaded Malakai's cheeks, then pinched them.

Malakai wiggled closer, his prick hard under his sweats.

Jack grinned and pinched again, letting Malakai really feel it.

"Oh crap," Malakai whimpered, rutting jerkily.

"You like the pain," Jack stated. There was no room for misunderstandings when it came to such things.

Malakai bobbed his head. "D-doesn't hurt, exactly."

"You'll tell me if it's too much." Jack waited until he got another nod of agreement. He whispered in Malakai's ear, "I'd love to strip your pants down around your knees, bend you over that desk, and spank your ass until it was pink. Then I'd finger you open and prep you, wait until you begged me before I'd fuck you. You'd come so hard you'd collapse on the desk while I finished. I'd shoot my seed into you, and mark you inside." And bite Malakai at the same time, marking him outside as well.

"P-please," Malakai asked, moving his thin hips faster.

"Have to be quiet in here, so for now, this is what you get." Jack got a hand around the back of

Malakai's head. Then Jack guided him until Malakai's mouth was pressed to his chest. "You bite if you need to, but don't break the skin. Can't have blood on my uniform."

"But I'll hurt you," Malakai said, slowing his thrusts.

Jack knew his own smile was all wolf. He could feel the beast rising up so close under his skin, wanting out to mate. "You won't hurt me, little fox. You'll just be doing what I told you to."

Malakai's eyelids closed and he lowered his head back to Jack's chest. "Yes, sir."

"So good," Jack praised him, feeling a pang of regret. They had to talk, as soon as the shot was closed and they were alone.

For now, neither of them needed to think. Jack held onto Malakai, letting the smaller man feel his strength, his power. Malakai whimpered and Jack growled. "Bite."

Malakai's chest hitched. His rhythm stuttered.

Jack shoved his hand down the back of Malakai's sweats and buried his fingers in his warm crease. The moment his thumb touched Malakai's hole, Malakai bit.

Jack damn near shot in his pants. His cock ached with the need for release while Malakai clung to him with teeth hand hands. "Come," he demanded.

The heat of Malakai's release seeped through Jack's uniform pants. He didn't care. They were dark and dirty already, so it simply didn't matter. Only he and Malakai would smell the semen anyway.

Jack kept rubbing that tight little hole until Malakai's climax ebbed. He dragged his hand back up, giving Malakai a light scrape of nails over his left ass cheek.

Malakai whined, his mouth still pressed to Jack's chest. Jack wanted to keep him. Instead he sat Malakai on the worn sofa in the office that sometimes doubled as a bed if jack worked too late. "Let me clean you up."

Malakai flopped onto his back. He was entirely too temping.

Jack eased his sweats down, then bent over and licked Malakai's cock.

"Oh—" Malakai slapped a hand over his mouth, his nostrils flaring as he inhaled.

Jack grinned and proceeded to lick the cum from that silky skin. By the time he was done, Malakai's cock was erect again. Jack gave it a pat, then tugged the sweats up over it. "Time for lunch."

With the flush of pleasure still pinking his skin, Malakai was the image of a debauched lover. Jack was glad his canines had ascended or he might have given in then and claimed his mate.

Instead he went to his desk and opened the containers on it. "Food's cold, but it won't affect the taste much. Anything from Mi Hacienda is going to give you a mouthgasm. Like an orgasm for your tongue, because it tastes so good," he explained before Malakai could ask. "Come on. These cheese enchiladas are so delicious you'll weep with sorry when you're done eating them." He was only laying it on a little thick. The food really was exceptional.

Malakai sniffed and got to his feet. "It smelled amazing when the delivery person brought it in."

Jack got them set up with their drinks and plastic

utensils. It was the most pleasant lunch he could recall having, and the time passed too quickly.

"I've got to get back to work." Jack kissed Malakai—he was coming to need those kisses, and damn, the bond was growing every time they touched. He hadn't thought that was the way it worked. Apparently it did for them.

He wondered if Malakai would realize what was happening. For all Jack knew, arctic foxes didn't have mates, not permanent, together-until-the-end mates. It would explain why Malakai hadn't said anything about it yet. Besides, Malakai's expressions gave him away. He wasn't hiding anything.

Jack had his own reason for being quiet on the subject. Tonight, he'd reveal it to Malakai.

CHAPTER EIGHT

"Who are those people?" Malakai was a little panicked to see the group of men and women standing and sitting on Jack's porch. He'd done all right at the shop with Drew and Beth after a little while, but people in general made him nervous. He didn't know how to behave around them.

Jack stopped the truck right before he should have turned in his driveway. "I'll be damned," he murmured a second later. "They're shifters. I recognize one. That redhead, his name is Rick. Used to be part of my pack."

Ignoring his own nerves, Malakai leaned forward in his seat too quickly. The seatbelt caught and he was jolted. He hated the seatbelt and grumbled under his breath as he studied the people. Most of them were dark headed, with one orange-haired man among them. Almost as one, each of them lowered themselves to either a sitting or kneeling position. "Why are they doing that? Is there anyone else from your pack?"

"It's what they'd do to show submission to their alpha." Jack studied them for another moment before continuing. "Rick's not the only one returning.

Zia, the woman sitting on the bottom step, she was one of the first to take off." Jack started driving again. Only a few yards, then he turned into the long driveway.

"When the pack used to show up, that's what they did. Convene on the porch if I was at work or gone. This is all…familiar, and surprising. But good." Jack's smile might have been barely there, but he was happy.

Malakai could sense it, almost like it was his own emotion.

"If they want to really be a pack again, we'll have to take a celebratory run tonight." Jack looked at him. "Would you like to come with me?"

Malakai wanted that very much. "Yes. I can vaguely remember running with my old pack." He frowned so hard his temples throbbed. "I honestly don't remember much about them. I tried so hard not to think about my home once I'd been trapped. It hurt too bad, and I was so lonely." His eyes burned and Malakai ducked his head. God, he was such a wuss sometimes. He'd cried himself to sleep so often over the years, he should have been dried up inside.

"You don't remember your family?" Jack asked, unbuckling his seatbelt, then Malakai's.

Malakai chewed on his bottom lip, a habit he needed to break considering how tender that flesh now was. "Bits and pieces. I get flashes, like an impression of playing with my littermates, or my parents running or them bringing back food for us. Nothing that lasts very long. It's like I've banished their memories or the past for so long, and now I can't get them back."

Jack took his hand and gave it an affectionate squeeze. "Do you know where you came from? Your parents' names?"

"Yes, to both," Malakai said.

"Alaska, and…?" Jack brought Malakai's hand up to his lips, and kissed Malakai's knuckles.

"Arak, my father." Malakai's throat nearly closed as emotion welled up in him, threatening to escape as a sob. "Irinnia is my mother." More names came to him, brothers and sisters, friends he'd known and played with. He was overwhelmed by the rapidly occurring memories.

"They are all going to be so glad you're alive," Jack said. "I'm sure they've missed you, like you did them."

Something about that last statement set off an alarm in his head that Malakai chose to ignore. He glanced up. They were being watched by everyone on the porch. "You should greet your company," he got out before trying to slink down in the seat.

"Don't hide. They're not going to hurt you, and they can damn well wait a few more minutes." Jack tugged him over until Malakai was right beside him. "I wouldn't let anyone harm you, not that they would."

"It's just, there's so many of them. Beth and Drew were hard enough to be around the first couple of hours. Talking to the delivery guy made me break out into a sweat." He slunk down again, or tried to. Jack held him firmly in place. "When Jared and Rita had guests, I'd shake and try to hide. I was always glad when they put me in the kennel then. Sometimes they'd want to show me off and people kept touching me or teasing and…and…I'm sorry. I wish I was stronger or—"

"None of that. No one will fuck with you or tease you. I won't let them, not here, or anywhere." Jack put a finger under Malakai's chin and urged him to raise his head.

Malakai did so, unable and unwilling to resist Jack's command, even unspoken as it was.

"So obedient and sweet," Jack whispered, moving his finger along the underside of Malakai's jaw.

The pride in his voice and expression was like a caress on his bare skin, or his fur when he was shifted. It felt *very* good. "Thank you, sir." Malakai liked calling Jack "sir". It fit, and Jack clearly approved.

"Social anxiety happens. I don't know if that's what you have or how it'd be treated in a shifter, but don't blame yourself for it. You are who you are," Jack finished. He kissed the tip of Malakai's nose.

"I'll try." Malakai needed to please Jack. It was quickly becoming vital to him. He wondered if he was attaching himself to the nearest alpha after so many years of being without one, but that didn't feel right.

Jack felt right, like he was rapidly becoming a part of Malakai, and vice versa.

"That's all I ask of you, that you try." Jack kissed him gently. "Now, let's go see what these wolves have to say for themselves. I won't be a dick. I do, however, want to make sure they understand that my pack isn't a democracy. It's the rule of the wolf when we're shifted, and even when we're not."

"Do you control their lives when they're humans?" Malakai asked.

Jack scowled. "No, I don't, but there are still pack rules and protocols to follow, respect that must be shown. They still lead their own lives. Now, when we're furry, it's nature's rules, pack rules, in full effect."

"That sounds reasonable. Actually, it sounds perfect." Malakai couldn't help but ask, "Do you think they'll be okay with a fox in their midst? I don't want to get eaten."

Jack growled. "I meant it when I said no one would hurt you."

"Yes, sir. I'm just nervous and—" Oh, he did like Jack's kisses. Some of the tension drained out of Malakai as Jack plundered his mouth. When Jack pulled back, a smug grin in place, Malakai was certain he could walk on air if it pleased the alpha.

"Now, let's greet our guests." Jack opened the door.

Our guests. Ours. Malakai hoped that meant he was Jack's permanently. It was a swift tumble for him, but his animal nature was certain it was right. Malakai was going to trust that part of him.

CHAPTER NINE

Jack stood in front of the dozen shifters on his porch. He growled, more for them than him. As lesser-ranked wolves, they'd be reassured by a show of strength, even if some of them had left because of it before. Their innate nature needed the rules and hierarchy of a pack. It was the human side of them that fucked things up.

A dozen heads dipped lower, and several shifters sprawled on their backs, belly up, neck bared.

Beside Jack, Malakai trembled. Jack had his arm over Malakai's shoulders, and used his hold to curl Malakai into him.

Malakai tucked his face against Jack's chest. Jack rubbed Malakai's shoulder and back, seeking to ease his nerves.

"This is Malakai, and no one will give him any shit, *at all*," Jack stated firmly. "That's the first rule of this pack. If you're here for some other reason, you want something other than to be a part of my pack, then say so now."

Some small part of him would have liked to make them beg. He'd been incredibly hurt when he'd been abandoned. For a while, he'd doubted everything he had ever done for them, and second-guessed his decisions after they left as well. It'd taken a lot of reflection to accept that it hadn't been anything specific he'd done that had caused the departures. Wolves were pack animals, and sometimes they could be lead by a wrong idea instead of an alpha.

Fortunately, it seemed their primitive natures also brought at least two of the original pack members back to him.

"Zia," Jack said, settling his gaze on her.

She kept her eyes on the porch floor. "Alpha, I'm sorry."

While Jack didn't intend to make anyone beg, he'd needed to hear that apology. "It's okay. Welcome back."

Tears leaked down her cheeks. "Thank you, alpha."

"Jack," he told her. There was no need for distance between them, and the honorific needed only to be used in special circumstances, like when he had each member swear fidelity to him. That would come later, under the moon's light.

Jack addressed the shifters he didn't know. "If any of you are here from another pack, you will contact your alpha and apprise him or her of your whereabouts and intentions. Then, if you want to become a part of this pack, you can run with us tonight." Jack kept his voice steady, strong, but inside he was a jumble of excitement and relief. He'd been a good alpha before. He'd be a better one this time.

"Come to me," he ordered.

Malakai wiggled and Jack tightened his hold. "I

need to make sure I'll know every member's scent, and they need to do this, to offer their trust to me. You are fine where you are." He'd hold Malakai while he sniffed necks.

"To the left," Jack directed the approaching shifters. He didn't want any of them even accidentally brushing up against Malakai. "State your name. If you have questions, you can ask once this is done." If there was anyone intent on causing trouble, Jack would know it by their behavior when he checked their submission to him as alpha.

One by one, Jack greeted the potential new members. He repeated their name when they introduced themselves, and he rumbled when he took in their scent. When Rick reached him, Jack received another apology. Jack accepted it and growled louder, knowing Rick needed the stronger vocalization.

Malakai had remained still, with only an occasional shiver, while Jack familiarized himself with everyone. Once done, he nodded at them. "All right. Anyone have questions?"

Zia stepped forward. "Not a question, just something I have to say besides the apology."

"Go ahead." Jack cupped the back of Malakai's head, under the long braid, offering comfort to him in every way possible given the current situation.

"You were a good alpha to us, to me," Zia began earnestly, gesturing with her hands as she spoke. She'd always had to move her hands while speaking, Jack recalled.

"If you'll take me back, I won't be such an idiot again. I know what I did was wrong and won't offer excuses. I just need to be in a pack led by someone I trust again." She stepped back.

Jack nodded. "Thank you for that. I won't turn away anyone who is sincere about this. If you've come from a pack, you still need to contact your alpha there and sever the ties appropriately, with respect."

There were murmured thanks, and soon the shifters spoke with more confidence to one another. The ones who didn't know Jack would be cautious around him, a wise move considering some alphas could be total brutes. They'd all come around in time.

Malakai glanced up at him. "There're no cars."

"That is odd," Jack whispered back. "Maybe they all teleported." He winked at Malakai and was rewarded with a sweet smile. "You are something else."

"Where are the vehicles?" Jack asked the others.

Zia shrugged. "We all met at the last national gathering, and got to talking about how much we didn't like the packs we were in. I knew you were a good alpha, and that I'd screwed up by leaving. Rick felt the same way, and he put together the plan for us to come back. We rode a bus."

Jack did his best to hide his surprise. "That had to have sucked."

"It did," James, an older man, said. "Is there some requirement that says people can't shower for a few days before boarding a crowded bus?"

"Is that why you reek?" joked Elizabeth, James's daughter.

"All buses smell bad," Rick declared. "They carry a scent of desperation and body odor that never can be cleaned out. Too many people in too small of a place, entirely too often."

Already the pack members-to-be were relaxing. It made Jack proud of them. "Everyone's welcome to come inside."

Malakai moved back to his side.

Jack studied him, looking for any signs this was too much for him. All he saw was nervousness and the same pride he felt for Malakai reflected back at him.

Once everyone who wanted to come in had done so, Jack told them to help themselves to any food or drink they wanted. "Malakai and I are going to get cleaned up. Make those phone calls if you need to. We'll be a while."

There weren't any catcalls, but Jack could tell a few people thought about if judging by their smirks.

Jack put Malakai in front of him and patted Malakai's backside. "Come on."

In the bathroom, he stripped Malakai quickly. Malakai was half-hard by then, and Jack took his thickening cock in hand. "You did well, Malakai."

"Thank you, sir." Malakai braced his hands on Jack's shoulders. "That feels so good." He bit his lip.

"What is it?" Jack prodded.

Malakai shook his head, then huffed. "I don't mean to be such a wuss. People scare me, but I like the ones out there so far. They all seem sincere."

"Then what's bothering you?" Jack asked. "Spit it out."

Malakai gulped, and slowly raised his gaze to Jack's. There was a definite pained look in his eyes. "You haven't said I can be a part of your pack. Do you not want me?"

"Of course I want you." Jack nearly gulped

himself. It was the moment he'd wanted to put off. He wouldn't. Malakai deserved the chance to spread his wings.

"You need to go home and see your family," he said, watching Malakai's expression darken. "They have to have thought the worst. I want you to go home to them, and experience the freedom you've been denied. Then, if you want to come back, I'll be here." *Waiting for you, my mate.* He released his grip on Malakai's shaft.

"I don't want to go back to Alaska," Malakai said quietly, his chin quivering. "Please don't make me."

They were mates, Jack knew it without a doubt. Malakai would come back to him—but Malakai needed to return to his pack, and maybe even find some peace there. His parents deserved to see their son, and coddle him for a while.

Jack wasn't going to argue the matter. "You're mine, Malakai, and even though it's only been two days, you know it is the truth. We're mates."

Malakai gasped. "I didn't remember—how can you make me leave, then?"

"Because you owe it to your parents and pack to go," Jack explained. "Just like I was owed an explanation, and more than I was given when my pack split. Go back, then return to me. Run with us tonight, and play under the moonlight. Tomorrow we will worry about everything else."

He had to give Malakai and his parents the chance to recover from what had happened. "Malakai," Jack murmured when the man didn't speak.

"We're mates," Malakai whispered. "I should have known. I've forgotten too much."

"You'll remember," Jack assured him. "You understand why I'm sending you back."

"I do. Not that I want to leave you, but to see my parents and siblings again, that would be…" Malakai trailed off, seemingly at a loss for words.

"I won't claim you fully until you return. The separation would be too hard on us otherwise, and I can't close up the shop to come with you." Jack wished he could. "But tonight, after we've ran and played and hunted, I will take you under the stars." He wouldn't bite. "I'll make you mine, and you'll think of me every day we're apart."

"Yes, sir, please." Malakai tipped his head back and Jack kissed his neck.

"Here's where I'll bite you," he said before sucking on the skin.

Malakai cried out, his hips jutting as he thrust against Jack.

Jack swatted his butt. "No coming." He kneaded the spot he'd smacked. "Not until tonight, after our run."

"Jack," Malakai whimpered. "Please, can you do that again?"

Jack grinned and palmed Malakai's ass cheek. "Is it going to make you come? Because if it does, then I'd really have to spank you for coming when I've told you not to. Do you think our guests would hear my hand landing on your skin? What about the sounds you would make?"

Malakai whimpered again. "I think I'd like the spanking, but not the audience."

Jack nodded. "Which is why I won't push you right now. We have a lot to discuss before we engage in anything even so mild as a spanking. There are safewords to be decided, and limits to be declared."

"I have safewords picked out. After you asked me about BDSM, I knew what I'd use."

"What are they?" Jack enquired.

"The standard ones. Red for stop, yellow to pause, and green for go or all good," Malakai explained. "I want to try everything once, even the things that scare me, like blood play. I trust you with my body."

And once Malakai came back to him, he'd trust Jack with his heart as well.

CHAPTER TEN

Flying wasn't something Malakai ever wanted to do again. The private jet was luxurious and all, but Malakai was terrified the whole time he was on it. Not that he wasn't grateful to Jack for arranging the quick transportation to Alaska. Apparently there were some alphas who were quite well off, and one of them at least was a good friend of Jack's.

The flight attendant, a shifter named Cruz, had kept out of sight after checking on Malakai twice. Once the plane landed on the private airstrip, Cruz appeared out of nowhere—Malakai hadn't been watching for him—to inform him that he'd be greeted by his father outside.

Malakai stared at the white-haired man looking at the jet. Had he ever seen his father in human form? Not that he could remember, but they did live in a frigid land not conducive to being a naked person. Malakai had been raised in a den, not a house, up until he'd been trapped.

The man outside had to be Arak, and the woman who joined him, that was Irinnia, Malakai's mom. His eyes filled with tears. He looked so much like his mother, he would have known her anywhere. He even had her slight build.

While his heart ached to be with Jack, it also filled with a warmth he hadn't experienced since he'd been a pup, safe with his family and pack. He unfastened his lap belt, his heart pounding as tears slipped down his cheeks.

"Are you okay, sir?" Cruz asked.

Malakai bobbed his head and sniffled, then surprised himself by talking. "My family. I haven't seen them in a very long time."

"A reunion! How wonderful! I'm so glad the weather cooperated with us today and we didn't have a delay." Cruz beamed as he stepped aside. "Welcome home."

Malakai didn't correct Cruz. As happy as he was to see his parents, and hopefully his siblings, this wasn't Malakai's home.

Home was with Jack, his alpha.

"Thank you," Malakai said rather than explain that to Cruz. He took his backpack from Cruz after he got up.

Cruz kept smiling as he escorted Malakai to the exit. "Your coat." Cruz handed him the puffy, ugly thing. "It's a lot colder than it was in Texas, sir."

Malakai put it on, shuffling his back from one hand to the other. He could have shifted and done without the stupid thing, but didn't know if he was allowed to. There were probably people around who didn't know about shifters.

Cruz opened the exit door, and the frigid air was shocking even though Malakai had been warned. He gasped and felt like his lungs were freezing. Then he looked at his parents and the joy on their faces.

A pressure he hadn't even known he'd been carrying eased off his chest. His parents were glad to see him; they'd missed him. It was perhaps selfish to have feared they'd moved on and didn't need or want to bother with him now. Uncharitable of him, because Malakai had no memories of them being bad parents.

He traipsed down the steps, gaze never leaving their faces as they approached. When he made it to the asphalt, he was immediately pulled into their arms.

"Son," his dad muttered, while his mother sobbed his name.

"We never thought we'd see you again," his father said. "Malakai." He tucked a strand of hair behind his ear. "You look like your mother. And, you look a little stunned. Don't remember us like this, do you?"

"Old and wrinkled, or human, I bet," Irinnia added, winking despite her tears.

Malakai found his voice once he swallowed past the tightness in his throat. "I think you both look gorgeous, and no, I can't remember seeing anyone from the pack in human form."

"Too cold where we used to live," Arak informed him. "After we lost you, we moved the pack onto private lands owned by another alpha. Became more civilized, if you will. Turns out two alphas can and often do live on the same property without killing each other."

"Come, let's get off this runway. Planes make me have palpitations, even just looking at them," his mom proclaimed. "You are very brave to travel on that tin can with wings."

Malakai couldn't keep from laughing. "I hated it, but Jack arranged it for me so I could come back to see you."

"Jack? He's the wolf shifter we heard had found you, isn't he?" Irinnia asked.

Malakai waited until they were all seated in the SUV before answering. "He's more than just a wolf shifter. He's an alpha, and he's my mate."

Irinnia and Arak turned from their front seats to stare at him.

"Is that a problem?" Malakai asked. Surely they didn't take issue with his mate being a male. He had remembered enough to know there'd been other such pairs in the pack.

Arak turned back and started the car, but Irinnia kept looking at him. "And he let you come here? How, if you've been mated, can either of you stand the separation?"

Malakai blushed so hotly he was surprised he didn't melt all the snow in the state. "We haven't, er, we haven't done that. Jack said he wouldn't, not until I'd had time with my family. He's a good alpha, and I couldn't ask for a better mate."

"He sounds like a special man. I'm glad he chose to give you this time with us. Once we heard you were alive and safe, we would have come to you," Irinnia said, "But this way is better. You can see your brothers and sisters, your nieces and nephews and cousins."

Nieces and nephews? That boggled Malakai's mind. "How many—nieces and nephews?" he asked.

Irinnia grinned, her blue eyes sparkling. "A lot. A whole lot."

* * * *

Malakai didn't know how Jack had done it, and on such short notice, too, but he'd given Malakai the greatest gift possible. The two weeks Malakai spent with his family passed quickly, though each day, he missed Jack more.

Phone calls and video chats didn't cut it. Malakai needed to go back to his mate so badly he ached physically for Jack.

"I want to come home now," he told Jack during their latest video chat. "My family and I've had time together. We've caught up, and we know we all love each other." Just as he knew, after a little more than two weeks, that he loved Jack. His soul yearned for the man, and his heart knew who it belonged to. "Let me come home."

Jack had looked tired but happy. Now he seemed energized as he nodded. "Yes, it's time. We can visit your family once I've got another mechanic hired, and they can always come here." Jack stood and stretched, giving Malakai a lovely display of his well-defined stomach. A dark trail of hair bisected Jack's abs. It swirled around his belly button, then continued below.

Malakai wanted to lick every inch of that treasure trail.

"When you get home," Jack said, and it was only then Malakai realized he'd spoken the thought out loud. "Until then, have fun with your family. Have you memorized everyone's names yet?"

Malakai groaned. "No. How can my brothers and sisters be so prolific? Thirty-two, Jack! Thirty-two nieces and nephews, and more on the way! Christmas is going to be a nightmare. I need a job."

Jack laughed, the sound of it warm and sexy, confident. He sat back down. "You have a job when you get back. The more confident you become dealing with people, the more you'll have to do at the shop. I'm more than happy to have you as my helper there."

It was what Malakai wanted. "Thank you." The prospect of spending every day working with Jack was beyond enticing. "But what if I can't change?" Malakai asked, voicing a concern he couldn't ignore. "If it's not just a matter of me getting used to dealing with people? What if I'm too screwed up and there's something wrong with me because I'm broken and—"

"There's nothing wrong with you," Jack interrupted. "When you get home, we're going to have a serious talk about that and how you talk about yourself. I think that's where we'll begin with our rules and punishments."

The arousal Malakai felt was instantaneous. They'd discussed the D/s relationship before, what each of them wanted and expected. It'd been hard to speak of some things, especially the ones he really wanted to try, like being flogged and plugged, or gagged with a pair of underwear Jack had worn all day. Malakai had done it, though, because his mate demanded and deserved complete honesty, and so did Malakai. Jack was always forthright with him; Malakai had more trouble being that way with himself.

He was learning. "Yes, sir." And he could even

tease some now. "Maybe a spanking would help me to remember." And flirt.

Jack arched a brow at him. "You can damn sure bet that's what we'll start with when you get home."

If Malakai had been able to board a plane in that instant, he'd have been on his way.

EPILOGUE

Jack had ignored the candy and flowers that everyone else seemed to give as Valentine's Day gifts. He had something much better to give Malakai once he got his mate alone.

The jet landed and Jack stood up. He left the waiting area at the private landing strip. "Thanks, Tim."

"Any time," Tim replied. "Always happy to help another alpha out."

Jack would find a way to repay him for his help. Later. Right now, he had a mate to welcome home.

The exit door opened, and Malakai came rushing down the steps a second later. "Jack!"

Jack opened his arms and caught Malakai when he leapt. God, it felt so right to have Malakai back. Jack spun around in a couple of circles, drinking in the sound of Malakai's laughter, the scent and feel of him.

Then he stopped and kissed Malakai, holding nothing back. He tasted blood from the fierceness of it, and moaned as he clutched at Malakai.

"Welcome home," Jack said against Malakai's lips.

Malakai sighed happily. "I am home, and I'm yours."

"You are." Jack scooped Malakai up into his arms, carrying him like he had that first night. "I'm going to make you mine tonight, after your welcome-back dinner with the pack. I won't let anyone bother you, but we have to do this."

Malakai nodded. "I know. I'm the alpha's mate, and I'll never embarrass you. I have to be there for the you and the pack, too."

"You'll never embarrass me anyway. Don't worry about that part." He was proud of Malakai for knowing and claiming his position. As the alpha's mate, Malakai would be sought out by pack members simply because of his status. Eventually, once they knew him, they'd seek Malakai out because of his gentle heart and good nature.

Jack settled Malakai in the truck then jogged around to the driver's side and got in. "It's going to be a quarter moon tonight, and it might rain, but we'll all run anyway." He started the truck and put it in gear. "Then I'm going to lay you out under the moonlight, and make you mine."

Malakai shivered. "I want that, so bad."

"What else do you want?" Jack asked, knowing the answer. He liked to hear Malakai vocalize his wants and needs. It was good for them both.

Malakai peeked at him for a split second. "A s-spanking, please."

Jack could have made him repeat it—was tempted, because it made him hotter than hell to hear those words. Malakai had been brave in asking this time, so Jack wouldn't push. "Good boy. You'll get what you need, and something extra since it's Valentine's Day."

"It is?" Malakai gasped. "Oh crap! It *is*! Rita and Jordan always made a big deal of it and I can't believe I forgot. I don't have anything to give you."

"You have you, and that's the best gift there is." Jack got them on the road. The sooner they got home, the sooner they could eat and get that over with. He wanted to run and mate, and feel Malakai move under him.

They chatted on the drive, but when they reached the house, Malakai noticeably tensed up. "It'll be fine," Jack reassured him. "Stay with me, and if you need space from anyone, tell me. I'll make it happen. I appreciate you letting the pack do this for you. They want to know the beautiful man who is my mate."

Malakai blushed, and relaxed a little. "Thank you."

Jack kissed him but kept it brief. He needed too bad to risk anything more.

Inside the house, a dozen people called out greetings when Jack and Malakai entered. Malakai moved closer to him. Jack kept an arm around Malakai's shoulders, knowing it made Malakai feel more secure than one around his waist.

"Calm down and let Malakai relax," Jack ordered. He considered his and Malakai's chairs for only a moment before sitting and pulling Malakai onto his lap. "You can eat here, with me."

Malakai's shy smile was beautiful to see.

"Can we call you Mal?" asked Sophie.

"No," Jack answered. "Use his full name."

Maybe later on, if Malakai got more comfortable around the pack, that would change. "And he's not used to groups of people, so bear that in mind. He's my mate, and I won't see him stressed."

"I want a mate that gets all protective over me," Sophie said. "Instead I just get asked out by obnoxious assholes that think big boobs equals low IQs. Ugh."

"Hey, that sounds like Jonas here." Alma poked the man beside her.

From there, the conversation took off. Jack contributed when he needed or wanted to, and he fed Malakai, enjoying the intimacy of the act even with the group of people around them.

When the meal was over, and the mess cleaned up, night had fallen. Jack looked at Malakai. He'd ran many times with the pack in the weeks since Malakai had been gone, and once with them and Malakai before the trip to Alaska. This time he'd claim his mate, and though it hadn't been stated, Malakai would claim him in return by biting him as they climaxed.

"Everyone, outside." Jack led the way with Malakai at his side.

The darkness was almost complete. With the waning moon and cloudy sky, it'd be unlikely for anyone to spot wolves running as a pack.

Even so, they were careful. Jack had everyone strip in the garage, and once he deemed it safe, they shifted and took off, loping toward the state park. The weather had been warmer than prior years, something Jack noticed. Each winter was less cold than the one before. With the temperature in the high sixties, it was almost hot as they ran.

The urge to howl was strong. Jack's throat ached with the need to do it. When he had the pack as deep into the safety of the land as he could, he began his song.

Malakai's sweet, yippy howls added a new tone to the ancient rhythm, expanding on it and encompassing the pack as a whole. It was a beautiful melody, and every note it fired Jack's blood.

Then it was time to run. Normally they'd have hunted, but with full bellies, there was no need. They leapt and frolicked, some pack members raced and tussled. Jack and Malakai stayed close together and loped around them all.

Malakai's white fur practically glowed in the dark night. It was beautiful, and soft, silkier than Jack's coat. He licked Malakai's muzzle, and nipped his ear and flank.

Every touch aroused him more, until Jack decided he'd tormented them both enough.

He herded Malakai away from the pack, with a warning growl for them not to be followed. There were other members who would be fucking, the sexuality among their kind not nearly as restrictive as humans. Sometimes a whole pack would be involved in an orgy, save for the mated pairs.

Jack wanted his mate. No one else.

He stopped by the old windmill and let out a new song just for his mate.

Malakai sat perfectly still, his ears perked attentively throughout it. Then he lowered himself to his belly and arched his back, sticking his tail up in the air.

Jack snorted and shifted. "Now, Malakai."

Malakai morphed and stayed much as he'd been, except he lowered himself to his elbows and knees, an easier position for a man.

Jack knelt beside him and fisted a hand in Malakai's wild white strands. He tugged and brought Malakai up for a kiss that left him breathless, staring up at Jack with such need it was damn near palpable.

"Now," Jack said again before nipping a path down Malakai's neck. When he got to the place he'd mark, Jack licked and sucked until the skin there was dark with blood under the surface of it. Then he put Malakai back on his elbows. "Don't move."

"Yes, sir," Malakai whispered.

Jack got up and retrieved the large bag he'd stashed at the base of the windmill behind a bush before he'd left to get his mate. Inside were a few things. A wedge he would use to drape Malakai over, lube, and a thin strip of leather he'd fasten around Malakai's neck after they mated.

"Sweet boy," Jack told him when he knelt behind Malakai. "This ass was made to be marked."

Malakai mewled and arched so that his pert butt was pointing up lasciviously.

Jack took the padded wedge out then set the bag down with the support on top, making sure the lube was open and at hand first. He spread Malakai's cheeks, exposing his tight pucker. "Get your knees further apart. I want you open for me, want to see your balls and cock."

Malakai's groan carried a hint of embarrassment, but was mostly arousal. He followed the order and Jack rewarded him with a caress over his nuts. He palmed the pink orbs and rolled them.

"Jack, sir," Malakai rasped. "It's been so long, I can't—"

"You can and you will." Jack wasn't heartless, however. He gave Malakai's balls a slight tug before letting them go. "You can come while I spank you. You'll get hard again soon enough."

"I will." Malakai bobbed his head. "I promise. I can't not get hard when you touch me."

Jack grinned. "Good. Now, if it's too much, what do you say?"

"Red, sir. Oh, God, I'm so excited!"

Jack popped Malakai on the butt. "You forgot something."

"Sir! I'm so excited, sir!" Malakai wiggled his backside.

"Give me your other words," Jack ordered.

Malakai only whined a little when he answered. "Yellow to pause and green for go on. I can't think when I'm so hard. Sir."

Jack picked the wedge up and put it beneath Malakai's hips. "Lie on that. It'll put your ass up for me and you won't have to worry about falling."

Malakai lay down without more than a, "Yes, sir."

Jack got him positioned perfectly, then he massaged Malakai's legs from ankles to just below his ass. That pretty part got rubbed, too. Jack brought up a blush to it that he could discern, partially because of his enhanced senses, and partially because the clouds had cleared off and allowed the moon to provide some light.

"Ready, boy?" he asked.

"Yes, please," Malakai answered.

Jack started off easy, tapping each cheek repeatedly. Once he got the skin warmed up, he added more weight to his swats.

Malakai began to pant, then moan as Jack heated his ass up.

"Where are you?" Jack demanded to know. "Color?"

"G-green," Malakai stuttered, rocking his hips. "So close, sir, please don't stop."

Considering how fast Malakai was humping against the wedge, Jack was surprised he hadn't already come. He landed two more hard blows to the bottom of Malakai's butt cheeks, and Malakai cried out, the scent of his spunk pungent in the air.

Jack tapped his buttocks throughout the release, keeping the swats light but there. When Malakai's climax ebbed, Jack rubbed his bottom, lowered himself down farther, then parted Malakai's cheeks.

He licked down Malakai's crease from top to pucker.

"Ungh!" Malakai wiggled, trying to push back on Jack's tongue.

Jack added another swat before using his thumbs to press against Malakai's hole. He slipped his tongue inside that tight little opening.

Malakai grunted and squirmed, and soon began humping the wedge again. Jack sat up, grabbed the lube, and squirted out a decent amount. He rubbed some over his cock, but used the majority of it to slick his fingers and Malakai's pucker.

"Ready for more?" Jack traced the wrinkled skin of his opening. "Want me in you, fucking you, making you mine?"

"Yes, yes, yes!" Malakai cried out desperately.

Jack easily slid one finger right into that tight, gripping heat.

Malakai clawed at the ground until he had his hands under him. He came up onto his hands and knees.

Jack let him, moving with him, fingering Malakai's hole, slipping in a second digit.

He twisted his wrist, giving Malakai's ring a little stretch, then curved his fingers and rubbed Malakai's gland.

The sound Malakai made wasn't man but that of a beast. It carried the weight off his need with a strident tone.

Jack bit Malakai's butt cheek and pumped his fingers in and out, faster and faster, all the while imagining how the velvety clench of Malakai's inner walls around his cock would feel.

Until he'd had enough imagining. Jack left off fingering Malakai and growled as he lined his shaft up to that glistening pucker. He gripped Malakai by one hip and one shoulder. "Mine," he declared as he slowly sank his length into Malakai's hole.

The heat and constriction was incredible. He had to exercise patience, stopping until Malakai's body loosened up for him, then he sank his cock in another inch, and another.

By the time his hips were pressed against Malakai's ass, Jack was sweating from his self-imposed restraint.

He lowered himself down, covering as much of Malakai's body as he could. He pushed Malakai's hair out of the way.

With his chest pressed to Malakai's back, Jack began to thrust, small movements at first as he was unwilling to leave the sweet grip of Malakai's body. "So good, Mal," Jack got out before he had to thrust harder. He wound one arm under Malakai, holding onto him, and used his other to fist Malakai's cock. "So fucking hot and perfect."

That was the last thing he said before giving in to the rampant need. He had to mate, to mark and claim Malakai.

Jack unerringly found the dark spot he'd sucked up. His canines had dropped the moment he'd begun to fuck Malakai. Jack tried to say *mine,* tried to say *now,* but lust had stripped him of the ability to do so.

He bit, deep and hard, just like he fucked his mate. At the same time, he moved his wrist up to Malakai's mouth. Bright-hot pain lanced him in the instant Malakai bit him.

Jack's orgasm barreled through him like a tornado, sending his nerve endings into ecstasy-fueled chaos. He thrust roughly, unsteadily, so many pleasurable sensations flooding him that he couldn't comprehend them, could only feel and revel in them.

Beneath him, Malakai keened around the flesh in his mouth, and his cock pulsed in Jack's hand. Together they rode their releases, grinding against each other, sharing blood and sex and a magic only their kind could know.

Later, when Jack could think and move, he gently disengaged his teeth and freed his wrist from Malakai's mouth. "Down," he managed to say before he flopped onto his side, taking Malakai with him. "You okay?"

"Ungh." Malakai coughed and tried again. "Jack, I didn't know it'd be like that. When can we do it again?"

Jack barked out a laugh. "Soon, if you play your cards right. Or play with me right, I should say." He looked at Malakai and brushed his knuckles over one sharp cheekbone. "You are incredible, Mal. I am one lucky alpha."

Malakai snuggled up against him. "I'm the lucky one, and...and I l-love you, sir. Jack."

Jack experienced a rush of pleasure that rivaled that of what he'd felt when he'd came. This was deeper, however, less physical and more emotional. "Mal, I love you too, mate. Sit up with me."

Once he could reach it, Jack took the collar from the back. It wasn't fancy, but it was sturdy, enduring, just like Jack himself. "This is my collar. Will you wear it?"

Malakai's eyes glistened with tears. "Yes, please. I would be proud to wear your collar."

Jack had gotten the perfect gift for his mate, but it paled in comparison to what Malakai had given—his heart, love, and loyalty.

Jack had given the same, probably the first time he'd carried Malakai in his arms.

As he fastened the collar around Malakai's neck, Jack gave him a gentle kiss. "Mine," he murmured, and his spirits soared with more love than he'd ever thought possible when Malakai whispered, "Yours."

Bailey Bradford is a married mom of four who spends most of the day writing, either on stories or at the blog. She loves to write as much as she loves to read. Baily is generally quiet and laid back, choosing to let things slide off rather than stick and irritate her. Although like many authors, she finds it a challenge to talk about herself, but she does answer emails and invites readers to leave comments on her blog if there's something specific they'd like to know.

For more information on other books by Bailey, visit her official website: BaileyBradford.com

Also by Bailey Bradford

Totally Bound Publishing

Unexpected Moments
Off Course
Texas and Tarantulas
Home
Hunt
Levi
Broncs and Bullies
Cliff
Dark Nights and Headlights
Reluctance
Riding and Regrets
Unexpected Places
Gilbert
Hide
Justice
Oscar
Timothy
Isaiah
Nischal
Reckless
Relentless
Rendered
Revolution
Sabin
Whirlwind

SEDUCING RAIN

ALPHA GAY EROTIC ROMANCE

AMBER KELL

CHAPTER ONE

Greg Carter walked through his club. Music vibrated the floorboards masking the groans and gasps from club members as they gave into passion. People seeking privacy slinked in and out of the rooms lining the back walls.

Bored. Greg could admit it if only to himself that his club had lost some of its appeal. His general manager took care of the day-to-day stuff and after years of hiring and firing until he had the right combination of employees, he now had a great staff he trusted to do their jobs. He'd recently expanded and added a nightclub for the non-BDSM crowd. Even the rush of money from that venture didn't dent his boredom. The challenge had faded from his life as soon as the club had opened and proven to be a success.

Shoving his hands into his pockets he scanned the crowd for potential problems. Everything appeared peaceful. Damn it. A hollow ache twisted his heart but Greg refused to acknowledge the pain as anything other than restlessness. It had nothing to do with a stubborn, beautiful sub that refused to stick around or return Greg's phone calls. He'd moved on to sending random texts, but received the same results.

Snarky, gorgeous Rain with his defensive gray eyes and high pain threshold had given Greg one of the best weekends of his life, then disappeared. Over the past few weeks Greg had called Rain several times but when his messages weren't returned he'd stopped. If Rain wanted Greg he knew where to find him. Unfortunately when Rain left Greg's townhouse without a backward glance he took Greg's libido with him. Even standing in a sea of gorgeous and willing twinks Greg's cock didn't even twitch. Now, nothing. Fuck.

He pulled his phone out of his pocket and sent another text to Rain with little hope. What had he done wrong? Rain had left smiling and relaxed even if no promises had crossed either of their lips.

He spotted his brother and headed toward his table. The boy Greg had watched over his entire life had transformed into a grown man with a thriving art career and a devoted lover of his own. Every struggle in Greg's life had been worth seeing his brother happy.

"How's it going, bro?" Stephen grinned up at Greg from Victor Jones's lap. An ever-present sketchbook lay across his knees and he clutched a pencil in his right hand.

Victor nodded in greeting but Greg could tell every millimeter of his attention was focused on Stephen, as it should be. Greg had struggled with their relationship at first, not wanting his brother to get involved with the older and much more experienced Dom. Now, Greg couldn't imagine his brother without Victor; they were two halves of a matched set.

"Everything's great. How about you?" Stephen appeared happy but his brother tended to have an easygoing outlook on life. Luckily Victor protected Stephen with the zeal of a hungry guard dog watching over a plate of steak. Examining his brother's face, Greg spotted nothing but joy. Good, one less person he wanted to kill.

"I'm taking care of him," Victor said. The Dom met his gaze with an amused one of his own as if he could read Greg's mind and knew even now he was still on trial.

Greg nodded. "Good."

From conversations with Stephen the only complaint his brother had involved Victor's reluctance to introduce Stephen to deeper forms of submission. Stephen longed to enjoy Victor's expertise with a whip. Victor still refused. Greg tried to keep out of their business but he had encouraged Stephen to talk to his lover.

Relationships were too much fucking work. He subdued the little voice in his head whispering that Rain would be worth the effort. Scowling, he gagged the nagging voice and tied it up in a St. Andrew's cross in the corner of his mind.

"Have you heard from Rain?" Stephen's compassionate gaze prodded Greg, urging him to spill his secrets. Greg resisted the temptation. He'd been the one to perfect the look, after all.

"No. I think we're over. He's ignoring me right now." He played it off as unimportant. For anyone else it would've worked but Stephen knew Greg better than anyone on the planet.

"He'll come around. If he doesn't I'll talk to him." Stephen stated, confidence filling his tone.

Greg laughed. He'd love to be a fly on the wall for that conversation. Skittish, cautious Rain chatting with Stephen who never met an obstacle he couldn't overcome with sheer perseverance. Hell, he'd sell tickets. "I'll keep that in mind, but I'm not going to chase someone who doesn't want me."

If Rain refused to be caught Greg would have to admit defeat.

"Just because he's not calling you back doesn't mean he's not interested. Maybe he's a complex guy. Don't give up on him yet. He could still come around," Stephen urged.

"Maybe." Greg patted Stephen on the shoulder, refusing to grab that bit of false hope. "See you later. You two should come have dinner with me next week."

He hadn't missed the tightening of Victor's grip. The Dom still worried Greg would try to separate them. Greg didn't know what to do to allay Victor's fears. He might have tried to keep them apart at the beginning but he could see how his brother thrived in Victor's care. All he'd ever wanted was his brother to be happy.

Stephen grinned. "I'll call you and we'll find a time."

Greg met Victor's gaze. Victor nodded his agreement. He had no doubt Stephen had the Dom wrapped around his little submissive finger but he didn't want to cause a fight between the pair. "Great, see you soon."

Leaving the happy couple, Greg continued

searching the crowd. It struck him that his gaze always stopped at slim brunets. He might have convinced his head that pursuing Rain was a big mistake but his heart still liked the idea.

* * * *

Rainier Lemmon traipsed through puddles and mud searching for crows. Usually they were all over the place but the one day he was trying to finish his photography series they completely disappeared. Evil little bastards. The black birds had it in for him. Crows did well in photo sales on his web store but he needed more of them to expand the line. His last series on crows had sold like hotcakes on a freezing winter day. People liked the mythology behind them and the way he captured their spirit. If only he could get the feathered beasts to cooperate today.

Sighing, he continued his walk, ignoring the bright flowers and blue skies. Ever since he left Greg's bed everything had seemed darker. Depression weighed him down almost as heavy as when he'd first left the army without any prospective jobs or ideas of what he wanted to do with his life. The rainstorm the previous night had perfectly reflected his mood. He needed to get his shit together and either get over Greg or call him and beg Greg to take him back. He didn't even care if their relationship devolved into a series of booty calls. He craved the Dom with a fierce need he'd never experienced before. Doms in his past had come and gone with little regret. Greg consumed Rain's dreams both day and night and left him jittery during his waking time as he fought to resist the siren call of the hard-eyed Dom.

Greg had stopped leaving him messages a few days ago. The lack of contact had Rain checking his phone with the ferocity of a junkie waiting for his drug dealer to call. Groaning, Rain pulled out his phone again. Nothing. He shoved it back into his pocket.

Idiot.

Why had this one man gotten under his skin? Rain didn't do relationships. He'd not once had a boyfriend who wanted to stick around and he'd rather have one bright shining memory than months of slow decline. Sure, he might have a few abandonment issues but nothing a good run from his problems couldn't fix.

A crow hopped through a puddle of water in front of him but before Rain could do more than pull off the lens cap and bring his camera up for the shot, the bird flapped away. Rain tracked its flight and smiled when it land in the mouth of an alley a few yards away.

Finally! The blister on his right foot ached and his arms hurt from holding his camera for hours trying to get the best photo. He was ready to call it a day even if it had barely passed noon.

Eager to finish his shoot, Rain walked as fast as he could without spooking the bird. He slowed when he came closer. He crouched down and took a rapid series of photos, the camera clicking madly away as he held down the button. The crow tilted its head and regarded Rain with its beady black eyes.

"Thanks for the photo op," Rain muttered as it

flew off, indifferent to a photographer's need to put food on the table.

Surely one of those pictures would work out. Quiet satisfaction eased through him. The last crow shots he'd taken had sold well as both photos and postcards. His friend Ruth had talked about transferring some of them onto the aprons she hand sewed for her small craft store downtown.

He'd worry about more plans after he saw what he'd shot. Sometimes pictures came out completely different than he'd envisioned when he took them. Rain loved how images could be transformed with a few strokes of his keyboard. He'd often thought he'd been born at the perfect time. He adored technology.

After sliding his camera into his backpack equipment bag, he headed home. He eyed the espresso shop on the corner with a wistful glance but he barely had enough money to pay his rent. Buying the triple mocha he yearned for wasn't in his tattered deck of cards.

He forced his feet away from the shiny brass door across the street and resisted temptation. If he imagined drinking down a hot peppermint mocha on the way home, no one else was the wiser. Ten minutes later he was climbing up the four flights of stairs to his apartment. The elevator hadn't worked since he moved in three years ago despite the sign plastered to the front claiming repairs were coming.

Stepping up his usual pattern Rain skipped the third step, walked on the second half of the fifth step and jumped over the next three. Rain didn't trust the rotting wood with his weight. Some of the other tenants had fallen and broken bones. Management counted on them not having enough money to sue. Assholes.

Rain shrugged it off as one of those things. Overall the building was clean, they might not do repairs but the janitorial staff did good work. Rain made them cookies every Christmas as thanks. He doubted the two ladies were properly compensated. He knew for a fact most of their pay came in the form of a free apartment on the ground floor.

He shoved his key into the lock and jiggled it around before it popped open. The wood had warped a bit and didn't budge without a good shove. Rain didn't relax until he got inside and the homey atmosphere of his apartment surrounded him. Turning, he closed then locked the door behind him.

His meager belongings left quite a bit of empty space. Not a fan of knickknacks, Rain left gaps in his bookshelves without bothering clutter them up with stuff. Bright colors burst over the carpet and brilliant pillows tumbled across his secondhand couch in a riotous display only another visually oriented person would appreciate. Would Greg understand his design style? Considering the Dom kept his brother's artistic touches splashed across his walls, Rain suspected Greg would tolerate his taste if not condone it.

Rain set his camera on the kitchen table that doubled as his work desk. Because of the small size of the one-bedroom apartment, he kept his place clean and made sure no food was left out to encourage the growing rat population. He'd thought about getting a cat once but he could barely take care of himself, and cat food got expensive. "I need to get myself a Sugar Dom to take care of it all."

Rain laughed hysterically at the thought. He'd never be obedient enough to be anyone's kept boy. He only played at the lifestyle; it didn't consume him. A twenty-four/seven sub lifestyle would result in him killing the asshole trying to boss him around. It was also the main reason he didn't call gorgeous Greg back. Greg had possessive Dom stamped all over him with permanent ink and Rain refused to belong to anyone. He'd seen subs who hung on every word dripping from their idiot Dom's lips like it was ordained from the skies. Rain preferred to think for himself. Granted, he'd love to have a regular partner who understood his needs but the tiny pool of good potential Doms was buried in a tumultuous ocean of bad ones.

Rain brushed away the negative thoughts regarding his love life and opened his laptop lid. He had once considered getting a dark room and going old school, but he didn't have the funds for a proper setup. Scraping by got old sometimes but Rain didn't like to fixate on the bad things in life. He preferred to concentrate on the good. Right now his pile of positive things had shriveled to collection of anemic ashes but as long as he could make out a few happy nuggets Rain would get by.

Plopping down on his computer chair, Rain plugged the USB cable attached to his laptop into his camera then clicked on the button to start transferring his pictures. He'd put every dime he had into a top-of-the-line computer and camera. He watched the numbers add up as he uploaded all one hundred and twenty-three pictures he'd taken that morning. It had rained the night before and the city streets had shone with reflective pools of water. Rain couldn't resist the imagery despite his ultimate goal of taking crow shots.

The pictures began to pop up across his computer screen. He smiled at the beauty of some of the captured images. Photography was a combination of luck and skill, getting the perfect frame at the right time. Luckily computers helped fix things, but if the initial photo was poor he didn't bother wasting time enhancing it.

When it finally finished loading he scrolled through until found his latest crow pictures. The camera hadn't been centered but the perspective had an interesting angle. Some blurry shapes in the background had him scowling. "I hope to fuck those aren't people I need to Photoshop out."

Rain knew all kinds of tricks to change the background of pictures but he could almost always tell when a photographer used a Photoshop cheat to rearrange a shot and he didn't like how they looked. He clicked onto the next picture to see if the blurs had vanished. Why were people in the alley anyway? Maybe they were restaurant workers?

Rain clicked his mouse trailing the pair from picture to picture. They slid into focus in the second shot and he wished to hell they'd remained fuzzy.

"Oh fuck." It was like watching a sick flipbook. One scene flowed to the other and the sequence of events became clear. The first picture showed a man pulling out a gun, the next two showed him shooting his companion. Even in the dim alley lighting the shine of the shooter's badge glowed. With his high definition camera Rain had picked up the gun firing and the subsequent murder in brilliant detail. In the clear shots he could make out the familiar structure of the killer's face.

"Where do I know you from? Fuck, that wedding!"

Despite his aversion to bridezillas, Rain had agreed to take the photos for a friend of a friend. He would bet his camera that the guy in the photo had been at that wedding.

Rain's stomach churned when he got to the last shot. The second man lay on the ground, his eyes open and unmoving. The bullet hole in his head came across as a vivid red splash of color against the man's pale skin. Racing from his computer Rain made it to the bathroom just in time to purge the small amount of food he'd consumed. He continued to hurl until there was nothing left but stomach acid burning his esophagus. He slumped to the floor enjoying the feel of the cold linoleum against his cheek. Germs were no doubt fighting to swarm across him, but he didn't care. Weak and close to tears, Rain pondered his options and came up blank.

CHAPTER TWO

Rain didn't know how long he stayed lying on the cold tile but eventually he pulled his ass up off the floor. His head spun from the sudden shift of position and the many possible scenarios that all ended in him being a murdered witness.

"This isn't my fucking day," he groused.

What the fuck was he doing to do? If he took this to the police he couldn't be certain it would go to the right person. After all, a cop was the killer in his photos. Besides, what if the man hadn't been working alone? Just because the camera had only picked up two people didn't mean there weren't more around somewhere. For all he knew a carload of accomplices could've been sitting in a vehicle around the corner. One wild scenario after another ran through Rain's head. Ideas spun and spun until he sat on his kitchen chair paralyzed by fear.

Fuck! What should he do? Who could he call?

After he got back from Iraq Rain had been too much of a mess to let anyone close. His job as an independent photographer didn't exactly give him workplace friends, and the people he did know kept at a distance. He only kept in touch with a few old friends and even they weren't the type he could bring into this kind of danger.

He'd joined the army after his family kicked him out for being gay. It hadn't been the grandest of reasons to join up but he'd given them four solid years before a suicide bomber decimated his unit. Even after that incident he'd finished out his tour then returned home with a tidy amount in the bank. Unfortunately, life had chipped away at his money and he'd flirted with bankruptcy on more than one occasion.

Rain's life flashed before him, a lonely existence that kept him isolated from others. Before his weekend with Greg he'd thought his coping skills were good. This forced him to peel back the shiny lacquer of "everything is okay" he'd slapped over his life.

Being a loner sucked at times like these. Not that he'd experienced a psychotic gunman shooting down one of his own before, but still, his number of friends could be counted on one hand with a couple of fingers left over.

He couldn't go to his dear friend Ruth; she was in her seventies and had health issues. If someone came looking for him he wanted her to be able to say she hadn't seen him. She didn't lie well.

"What am I going to do?" He dragged himself to his feet.

Standing only led to pacing. He walked back and forth in a twisty path across his apartment floor, circling his footstool, sliding past his couch and wandering through the kitchen before turning and starting the entire trek again. He bit at his nails as he walked, nerves overcoming sense. Rain's mind skittered back and forth like a mouse trying to escape a maze and finding a dead end at every turn.

Rain returned to his computer to check for other clues. It wasn't until he reached the last photo that he considered returning to the bathroom to throw up his guts and possibly his liver. In the last picture the killer had turned and faced Rain. He'd been so intent on his crow picture, Rain hadn't seen the murderer staring at him. Triple fuck!

His phone buzzed. Startled, Rain jumped. Plunging his hand into his pocket he pulled out his phone. A message flashed onto the screen.

Are you all right? Just checking in.

Greg had texted him again. Despite the horror of his current situation Rain clung to his phone and reread the words, seeking solace between the lines. Just when he thought the Dom had given up Greg reached out to contact Rain again. Rain slid his thumb over the screen. Maybe he could stay with Greg for a few days? They'd had an amazing weekend together, no reason he couldn't crash at the Dom's house for a week or so.

He didn't have to tell Greg anything about the cop. Rain couldn't let the Dom get involved. He liked Greg—hell, he more than liked him, which only added to his determination not to drag Greg into his problems. Rain just needed to get away from everything while he figured out what the fuck to do. Unfortunately, Greg might consider this more of a commitment than Rain was ready for. Rain shrugged; runaways couldn't be picky.

Before he could chicken out Rain pressed the button to connect him to Greg. Why did he feel as if he were calling his lifeline?

"Hey, babe." Greg's deep voice rolled across him, welcoming as a hug.

Rain cleared his throat and brutally pushed away the rush of giddy delight racing through him. *Focus!*

"Greg." His words trembled and his voice broke. He took another breath and grabbed back control. "I was just thinking of you."

Thinking, praying, and wishing he had the confidence to talk to the Dom again.

"You could've called. I've been texting and calling you for weeks." Greg's sharp tone had Rain snapping to attention even though the Dom couldn't see him. Something about Greg always had Rain searching to put his best foot forward. He failed miserably, but he tried.

"Um, yeah sorry about that. I'm not good with emotions." Truth. Or commitment. Or dealing with long-term, demanding Doms. He bit his lip before he over-shared.

"And you think I am?"

Rain almost blurted out "yes". Greg took amazing care of his brother in his own way. Rain had seen the pair together and had been warmed by the affection in Stephen's eyes. The artist had forgiven Rain for kneeling beside his Dom with surprising swiftness. Maybe Greg's hand around Rain's waist had defused Stephen's suspicions. Rain had never actually slept with Victor before, they'd been good friends who attended the same club for a few years before Rain had moved. Only now were they in the same city together and Rain kept a careful distance, mindful of Stephen's feelings.

"I didn't mean to insult you," Rain settled. He refused to debase himself. Greg would get used to his issues or dump him, Rain would discover his choice soon enough.

"Did you decide to come back and be my sub? I would take good care of you," Greg coaxed.

Crap. Rain froze, trying to put his words in a discernable order before he blurted out his problems. He didn't usually have difficulty speaking, but Greg overwhelmed him. The big Dom wouldn't take a toe-in-the-water approach. Greg lived life on his terms and expected everyone else to bow to his will.

"Rain?"

Rain winced. He'd been silent for too long. "I'm not making any promises but I'd like to come stay with you for a few weeks to see how we get along. If things work out maybe I'll stay longer."

He winced. Yeah, there was a deal no Dom would turn down. His stomach churned and swirled eager to return his attention back to the toilet.

"A few weeks?" Greg's voice took on a more welcoming tone as if he liked Rain's idea.

Surely it wouldn't take more than a few weeks to get a psycho killer off the streets? Was he fooling himself? Did justice take longer? More importantly, could he leave Greg after that much time living in his home? It had taken all Rain's resolve to walk out the door the first time.

"Yeah, is that too long? I can come for a day or so if you'd rather." Rain bit his thumbnail. *Please don't say no.* If Greg turned him down Rain would have to take the first bus out of town. He couldn't afford a plane ticket anywhere. He needed to get out of his apartment and into hiding as soon as possible. Since Rain and Greg hadn't been seen together in public maybe no one would think of the connection between them? The cop had to find Rain to kill him.

"Meet me at my townhouse by two p.m. sharp. You should be able to find it, you left it easily enough." Greg hung up before Rain could reply.

Rain bit back his annoyance. "Bastard."

He could tell the Dom was going to hold a grudge over Rain's previous defection. He couldn't help it if he'd panicked at Greg's long-term plans for him. Wasn't it subs who were supposed to want to move in after the first date? Rain had been thrown when Greg began planning their lives. He didn't know if he'd be able to trust someone else to run his life. Not that he'd done a bang-up job of it so far but to just hand over control to someone else took more submission than Rain could comfortably muster.

However, if he'd had a proper Dom he probably wouldn't have spent his morning taking pictures in the park. He doubted Greg would let Rain out of bed before noon. A peek at the clock on his microwave jolted him into action.

"Fuck, I need to get going."

He ran to the hall closet. Pushing aside coats and shoes, he pulled his battered suitcase from the inner pits of the hell of the forgotten. He took it to his bedroom then tossed it on the bed, unzipped the bag and flipped it open. The small pack didn't hold tons of things but it would hold his clothes for a week's stay. If he figured out how to report the cop he'd be done in a few days but if it took a few weeks he needed to be prepared. Besides, Greg would make him come back to get more if he didn't have the appropriate amount of clothes. Rain couldn't chance returning.

Shivering from fear and shock, Rain packed clothes, his camera, his laptop and some basic essentials, including the large jar of lube he'd purchased a few days ago. He didn't know when he'd be back here but he sure as fuck wasn't going to leave behind his equipment. Some things could be replaced but his camera and computer weren't among them. He'd used some of his meager funds to purchase his gear and he didn't have money to buy new ones.

He shoved his phone back into his pocket then headed out the door wheeling his suitcase behind him. He picked it up by the handle to carry it down the stairs. Good thing it wasn't too heavy. Despite what he implied to Greg he had no intention of moving in with the man for any permanent basis. He ignored the twinges in his heart. Stupid organ had never done him any favors.

The busy sidewalk had Rain jumping at shadows. The cop could be hiding anywhere. He wished he remembered the guy's name but he'd just been another face in a sea of wedding guests. What if he'd followed Rain home? It wasn't like Rain had been paying attention. His mind had been focused on possible photo shots not on cops shooting him.

Rain brushed away the tears streaking his cheeks. He couldn't show up at Greg's place with red eyes and a Rudolph nose. Greg would question him mercilessly if Rain appeared upset.

"Paper?"

"Crap!" Rain clutched his chest as the homeless vendor waved his newspaper at Rain. He usually gave them a few bucks for their paper because at least they were working to get off the streets. He never forgot he could easily be one of them. He treated people with the same courtesy he wanted to receive no matter where they were in life.

"Sorry, didn't mean to scare you." The paper seller grinned, unrepentant.

"That's all right." Rain knew his smile lacked its usual joy but he couldn't dig up much happiness right now. He pulled a few dollars out of his jacket pocket and handed them over in exchange for a paper. He never pulled out his wallet on the street but he almost always kept a few bucks within easy reach, for charity. Rain understood there were a few beggars who made more money than him and some spent their money on drugs and alcohol. Still, he had a few regular folks around the neighborhood he liked to help out.

"Thanks, man. You have a good day."

"You too." The odds of his day turning out well were so astronomical they were practically in a different galaxy. His legs ached by the time he reached Greg's townhouse. Last time he'd visited he'd taken a cab home. This time he didn't want to waste the funds or leave a trail behind. Taxi drivers kept records. Better to walk here and leave less of a trace.

Damn, he already had a fugitive mindset.

The familiar painted door came into sight. Rain's feet hurt and his nerves were so stretched they might never bounce back to normal. Searching the street around him one last time, Rain walked up the three steps to Greg's front door. He pulled out his phone and checked the time. He had two minutes to spare.

Fuck it. Unwilling to stand outside as a possible target he knocked on the door.

A noise had him spinning around, heart pounding, only to spot Greg's neighbor putting the lid back on his trashcan. He gave the man a weak smile and a nod. If he didn't get inside soon he'd faint in the doorway and Greg could pick Rain up off the steps.

A lock clicked in front of him and Rain turned back around to meet Greg's hard gaze. "You made it. Good timing."

"Thank you, Sir."

Greg must be one of those Doms who believed if you weren't early you were late. He'd met a few of those before. He usually skipped past them when he went into clubs. He needed a Dom with more flexibility.

"Come in," Greg moved back to allow Rain space to step inside.

He barely took two steps before Greg slammed the door shut. Rain's suitcase clattered to the floor as Greg pressed him against the wall. Rain gasped at the delicious full-body contact. He went to his tiptoes to align their erections. A small whimper left him.

"So sexy," Greg purred. His hot breath bathed Rain's neck.

Rain inhaled deeply. All things good and right entwined through Greg's scent.

Home.

Fuck he was screwed.

"Th-thank you." Rain barely squeezed those two words out. He'd be incapable of forming entire sentences if Greg stayed this close.

"Hands over your head."

Rain slid into position before his brain had completely processed Greg's request. A blush burned his cheek. The last time he'd been this embarrassed he'd been seventeen and getting blowjob tips from the football captain.

"Good boy," Greg ran his fingers from Rain's wrist to his armpits. Rain flinched.

"Ticklish?" Greg raised his left eyebrow in inquiry.

Rain bit his lip.

"I asked you a question," Greg's hard tone twisted Rain into a submissive knot.

"Yes sir. I'm ticklish."

Greg kissed Rain. A gentle brush only lips no tongue. "Why wouldn't you want to share that information with your Dom?"

"Because you might use it against me," Rain confessed.

Greg kissed Rain's cheek. His deep chuckle vibrated between them. "There's no might, pretty boy, there's only will. I will use every twitch, every jerk, every sensitive part of your body against you until your body knows it belongs to me."

The whimper was completely warranted. Lust clouded his thinking. Damn, he needed this. Rain relaxed as he gave himself over to Greg's command. He didn't need to worry about anything anymore— Greg was in charge. The burden lifted and relief cut through him, so sharp it took away his breath for a moment.

"Easy, babe, damn you're strung up tight." Greg pressed their foreheads together as if he could combine their souls through flesh-to-flesh contact.

"Sorry," Rain leaned into Greg's touch. "It's been a tough week. I missed you."

Both true things, but not the entire truth. Rain hated himself for not spilling his guts to the controlling man but he didn't want to put Greg in danger. The less Greg knew the less he'd get involved. Rain gripped that determination in a tight fist.

"I missed you too. That's why I kept calling and texting. I'm glad you decided to give us a chance." Greg kissed Rain. Not the soft, almost-tender kisses of before but a hard, hungry claiming kiss that burned Rain to the ground like a bush fire clearing a mountain and leaving nothing but ashes in its wake.

Rain melted against the wall, certain his bones had dissolved beneath Greg's passionate assault. It had been like this before, but Rain didn't know if he could gather the energy to leave Greg a second time.

Finally, when he lost feeling in his legs and his cock had reached the same hardness as granite, Greg stepped back. "Go put your bag in my bedroom, then join me in the living room."

Rain nodded. He could understand Greg's psychology. The Dom had put himself out there once, now Rain had to prove he truly wanted to be there by coming to him. Rain took a deep breath before retrieving his abandoned suitcase from the floor. "I'll be right there."

He ignored his aching erection. It urged him to hump against Greg until they both reached orgasm. Discipline. Rain had to gain some if he hoped to make Greg proud of him. Greg wouldn't be impressed by Rain's disobedience. Right now presenting the proper submission wasn't just a condition of trying to find the right sex partner but a line between life and possible death. If he wanted to stay off the cop's radar he had to stay with Greg. Few people knew of their time together and he doubted the ones who did would say anything.

Hurrying down the hall, Rain only made one misstep while trying to locate Greg's room, but it didn't take a genius to determine Greg wouldn't be sleeping in the tub. The second door he opened had a familiar look. He'd been tied to those bedposts a few weeks before. Rain bit his lip and set his suitcase down. Until Greg told him where to put his things he wouldn't do one step more than asked. Greg didn't strike Rain as the type of Dom who appreciated a pushy sub. For the next few weeks Rain would work hard to be the type of sub Greg wanted. After that he'd have to determine if they were well matched or not. He adjusted himself as memories of the kiss in the hall threatened to make him come.

Rain sucked in a deep breath, then left to seek out his new Dom. He found Greg in the living room as promised. A bottle of wine with two half-filled wine glasses, a tray of cheese, preserves and crackers sat on the table.

"Looks good," Rain commented, his appreciative gaze sweeping the scene. "You didn't have to go to so much effort."

Greg shrugged. "I want you to know I don't take your offer of submission lightly. I don't know if we'll work out but I'm serious about trying."

Rain pressed his lips together before he

confessed everything. He'd never hold out in a real interrogation. Not when one heated glance turned him to putty in Greg's hands. Hell, putty probably had more stiffness than Rain's spine.

"Thanks," he said when he trusted his ability to speak again.

Greg patted the couch. "Have a seat beside me. I want us to be comfortable during this conversation. There will be plenty of time for kneeling later."

"Okay," Rain settled beside the Dom waiting for his next instruction.

Greg spread a knife's worth of soft cheese on a cracker along with some fruity spread then held it up for Rain to eat.

He opened his mouth and allowed Greg to place the snack in his mouth. Flavor exploded across Rain's taste buds. He chewed and swallowed before he spoke. "That's really good."

"I'm glad you think so. I like to take care of my subs. Part of that is feeding them."

"I thought Doms wanted the sub to do all the cooking." That had always been Rain's experience and he sucked at cooking.

Greg scowled. "I remember you burning toast when you were here. I think I'll save myself the food poisoning."

Rain opened his mouth to argue. Greg shoved another cracker into it.

"Don't even bother. Besides, cooking relaxes me. You can clean up afterward."

He thought about arguing but it was a great deal. Rain hated to cook and if Greg wanted to be the one who fed them he wouldn't say no to that. He finished his cracker. "Deal. What's next?" No doubt Greg had an entire list of things to go through.

"Did you want a regular job or to stick with freelance photography? I'm happy with either."

Rain couldn't let that slide even if the thought of taking the wrong picture again scared the crap out of him. "I want to stay with my freelance work."

"No problem."

Greg was the most laid back Dom Rain had ever met. Nothing seemed to put him off for long except Rain leaving, that had done a number on the Dom. Rain pushed back his sense of guilt over using Greg for safety. He would help out where he could so he wasn't a complete leech on Greg's resources. "I do have an idea about a job, though." He'd been thinking about this since he'd last gone to Greg's club.

"What's that?" Greg prepared another cracker, this time eating it himself.

Rain tried not to pout from the loss. He enjoyed it when the Dom fed him. He'd never reached that level of intimacy with any of his lovers before. All of his submissive time had been spent in clubs like Greg owned, never in a domestic setting like this. He realized that was why he'd freaked out so much. "I was thinking if I could set up a small studio in one of your rooms I could take boudoir shots of men in their leather. You know, ones where they could be themselves."

Greg opened his mouth then shut it again without speaking.

Rain twisted his hands together, waiting for Greg's verdict. The more he thought of the idea the more he liked it. Sure, anyone could take a photo, but Rain was thinking of something more intimate, romantic. Besides it would keep him busy and out of sight while he avoided a certain killer cop.

"I like the idea. How about we put out some feelers to test the level of interest. If it's high enough I'll give you one of the new rooms I haven't outfitted yet for a trial run."

Rain grinned. "That sounds fair."

He loved the idea of helping capture an intimate moment between two men who might not otherwise get the chance.

"Now let's focus on other aspects of our relationship. I want you to list your hard limits and safeword."

Rain didn't hold back his puzzled look. "Didn't we do all that when we got together before?" He could've sworn they'd had this same conversation.

"We didn't go into specifics. I need to know more so I don't accidentally bump into something you don't enjoy. The point of this is to make it pleasurable for both of us. It isn't just me or just you in this relationship and the more we make sure our interests align the better things will go."

"True." Rain couldn't argue with that kind of logic even if he wanted to. "I don't do anything involving bodily fluids other than semen, no scat or golden showers. I insist on a condom every time and no blood play or anything that will cause permanent harm."

Greg stroked Rain's cheek as if he couldn't help building a connection between them. "Fair enough. Those are reasonable limits. Also if I do anything you aren't comfortable with I expect you to tell me. I'm not the type of Dom who will ignore your safeword no matter when you use it. Understand?"

Rain nodded. "Yes sir, my safeword is cheddar." He had complete confidence Greg would follow the rules of consensual play. His body would be protected during their time together; his heart was still up consideration.

"You never told me. Why cheddar?" Greg took a sip of wine as he waited for Rain's answer.

No one had ever listened to him like the Dom before him. Rain sat up straighter as he spoke. "Because my first addiction was to cheese when I was a little boy. I used to eat the stuff so much that I began to get sick whenever I saw it. It's a reminder to me that everything is good in moderation."

Greg smiled. "I like that." He perused his cheese board. "Good thing I didn't pick up any cheddar. I love the Irish stuff."

"I'm over that now, it just serves as a reminder." Rain smiled.

"Do you have any food allergies?" Greg asked. "I'd hate to make you sick."

"No."

"Great. Now tell me what it is you want from this relationship?"

A safe haven. To stay alive. He pushed those thoughts away to come up with answers Greg would accept.

"I just want to see if it's possible for us to build a relationship. We already know we're sexually compatible but sometimes it's other stuff that causes problems," Rain answered. Once again he'd told the truth and even if his answer didn't contain the entire truth it didn't make it less real.

"Great. Me too." Greg's white smile turned Rain inside out. No Dom should have that much sex appeal it wasn't fair to innocent subs who lacked the ability to protect against his charm. "I'm sorry if this sounds more like a job interview than a relationship talk."

Greg fed him another cracker. It took Rain a few minutes before he could answer. The sparkle in Greg's eyes revealed to Rain the Dom had done it on purpose.

"I agree, Sir, it's important to get this straightened out in the beginning." Calling Greg sir became more natural each time he said the words.

"I'm glad you think so."

Greg's approving smile sent a warm shaft of delight through him. Greg held another cracker to Rain's lips. Greg started to hold a glass of wine out to Rain but paused midway. "I forgot to ask if you drink."

"Fuck yeah." And right now he wished to do it excessively. Between trying to set relationship rules and the stress of running from a killer Rain longed for a drink with an unreasoning passion.

"Don't curse. Next time I'll have to punish you," Greg warned.

Rain shivered as he accepted the glass. His last punishment consisted of his cock being bound and Greg sexually torturing him for an hour. "Sorry, Sir. It won't happen again."

Greg took a sip of wine. "That's almost too bad. I have thought of many inventive new punishments."

Rain gulped down half his glass. His mind

might be confused about accepting punishment but his cock was all on board. Despite Greg's words Rain didn't want to disappoint him. He'd forgotten how much bad language bothered Greg, probably a lingering habit from living with his younger brother. Rain hated having to watch his words. If he wanted to say "fuck" he would, unfortunately he needed Greg and he'd rather hold back a few curses than offend the only man offering him a shelter in this fucked-up storm.

Rain finished his glass in a series of long swallows.

"I see our second lesson will be about enjoying quality wine."

Rain blushed. "Sorry. It's been a hard day."

"Yeah, why is that?" Greg's compassionate expression almost had Rain spilling his guts. Damn it, maybe the wine had been stronger than he thought.

He tried to shrug it off and allay suspicion. "Nothing, just one of those days. I'm happy to be here, though," Rain bounced back. He didn't want Greg to feel unappreciated. The Dom was the only bright spot in Rain's fucked up day.

"Maybe I can do something about making it better." Greg's over the top lecherous grin had Rain laughing.

Rain set his glass on the table. "I think we should seal the deal."

"Do you?" Greg asked, amusement shining in his eyes. "You might lose a few sub points for your aggression."

"Understood." Rain nodded. He slid to his knees on the floor then crawled over until he kneeled between Greg's legs. He trailed one finger down Greg's zipper. "May I, sir?"

"Hmm, you definitely earned them back. Help yourself," Greg said. "I'd hate to ruin your fun or turn down your excellent idea."

"Good." Rain unsnapped Greg's jeans then slid down the zipper in a slow, careful motion, not wishing to pinch anything important. Ah, just as he suspected, Greg had gone commando. During their weekend together Greg had never worn underwear. Rain groaned at the sight.

He pulled Greg's pants down his legs then off completely, not wanting to scrape his Dom's cock on the metal zipper. Rain took a moment to fold them before setting the jeans on the table.

"Nice," Greg approved.

A bead of pre-come dripped from the slit of Greg's erection. "Neatness do it for you?"

"It's not only straight women who find a tidy man an object of porn."

Rain laughed. He'd forgotten how much Greg made him laugh. The Dom had a commanding air to him but in the privacy of his home he let out his sense of humor. Rain wished Greg relaxed more outside his living space.

Rain kissed each of Greg's hairy thighs then ran his hands across the texture. Although he waxed himself perfectly smooth he liked his partners to be more manly. All those wiry hairs sliding across Rain's waxed skin increased the sensuality a hundred times in Rain's estimation.

"Get to the good part," Greg ordered.

"You're demanding," Rain teased.

Greg plunged his fingers into Rain's hair and yanked him closer to the tip of his cock. "Yes, I am. And you like it."

Rain shuddered. He couldn't deny his kink. Lighthearted Greg had vanished beneath his Dom persona and Rain couldn't be more turned on. He lapped at the spongy head and moaned when Greg's grip tightened. Yes. He pushed close enough to wrap his mouth along the cock's tip and pressed his tongue inside the slit.

"Do that again," Greg demanded.

Rain did as ordered before applying suction and using all his years of practice to try to suck out Greg's brains through his cock.

"Oh fuck." Greg's grip tightened but the Dom still didn't hurt him. It was as if he knew the exact point Rain liked pain but didn't go past that barrier.

Rain almost reached down to unzip his own pants but he stopped in time. They hadn't gone over all the rules but most Doms didn't let their subs take control of their own orgasms.

"Clothes. Off now."

Rain lifted his mouth. He frowned up at Greg, deprived of his tasty reward. "What's wrong?"

"I want to come in your ass." Greg pulled a condom and lube from under the couch cushion and handed over the tube keeping the metallic square for himself. "Strip, then prep yourself."

Rain grabbed the lube, grateful one of them was prepared. He'd been ready to toss aside all his rules in order to swallow Greg down but the Dom was sticking to Rain's guidelines. Rain removed all his clothing in slow, smooth motions, giving Greg a bit of a show before folding each item and placing them beside Greg's pants.

The Dom stripped off his shirt and tossed it onto the other side of the couch. He spread his arms, opening his muscled body for Rain's perusal. Rain let out a soft groan.

"Damn, you're beautiful," Rain said.

"I think that's my line." Greg's mouth quirked up on one side. "Now get yourself ready."

Rain nodded. He popped open the cap and wet his fingers thoroughly.

"Turn around and give me a show."

Damn, Rain was going to die of lust overload. The god who looked over clueless subs running for their lives had ripped Greg from Rain's deepest desires and wrapped him up with a sparkly bow.

Rain spun around. He scooted the cheese to one side, glad Greg had an enormous coffee table. Splaying himself across the surface he presented Greg with his ass. One by one he slid a finger into his hole back and forth a few times before adding another. He ended his preparation by plunging three fingers into his ass before Greg spoke and pulled Rain back from the brink.

"Oh yeah, come here babe," Greg growled, the words barely understandable through his rumbling growl.

Smiling, Rain slid his fingers out. He turned to find the condom already covered Greg's erection.

"How do you want me, Sir?"

"Add some lube to the condom then sit on my cock," Greg ordered.

"Yes, Sir." If Rain's hands shook neither of them

mentioned it. He smoothed a thick layer of lube on Greg's cock.

"I think you have enough." Greg said after the third pass of lubricant.

Rain shook his head. "You can't be too careful with a piece of meat this size."

Greg chuckled. "If I remember well you had no problem taking this log a few weeks ago."

"I think you grew," Rain said. He grinned when Greg made a scoffing noise in the back of his throat. Too funny.

When Greg's expression changed to impatience, Rain climbed up on the couch and lowered himself onto Greg's erection. "Oh fuckety, fuck fuck."

Greg slapped Rain's ass. Rain gasped and titled forward until his hands rested behind Greg's shoulders on the back of the couch. It placed his ass a little higher for further spanking if needed.

"Hmm, I think I'm going to have to revise my punishment ideas."

"No, Sir, I'm certain I'm learning my lesson." Rain slid down a little farther and his eyes damn near crossed. "So fucking full."

Another spank had him crying out and pressing down even more until he had fully seated Greg.

"Yeah, definitely a new punishment," Greg mused rubbing Rain's ass.

Rain whimpered. Damn, he would've liked a few more spanks.

Greg kissed him, a ferocious claiming clash of tongues and lips ending with a bite to Rain's bottom lip. "I didn't say I wouldn't spank you other times. Now ride me."

Rain nodded. Stringing vowels and consonants together would take too much effort right now. He obediently moved up and down on Greg's lap until neither of them could do more than groan and pant.

Greg's callused hands wrapped around Rain's cock. "Come!" he commanded.

Unable to resist the order Rain poured his release across Greg's fist and parts of his chest. The sight of his come strung across Greg's hairy abs had him grinning like a fool.

"Like marking me, do you?" Greg asked.

"Yes, Sir." No sense lying. Greg could tell Rain had enjoyed the sight.

Greg gripped Rain's hips and after a few more pumps let out a groan and filled the condom. Once Greg regained his composure he encouraged Rain to get up. Rain removed the condom, tied it off then went to throw it away in the kitchen trash.

He returned to find Greg watching him intently. "I could've taken care of that."

"No. I insisted on the condom I'll take care of it," Rain said.

Greg pinched Rain's chin and forced him to look his way. "Whoever made you feel guilty about using a condom is an idiot. Your health is the number one priority. Don't let anyone, even me, make you feel bad about that."

"Don't you want to take me bare?" He'd never met a Dom who didn't want to fuck Rain without a condom. He never let them, but they all tried.

"Maybe one day when we're both comfortable with the idea and have recent tests we can show each other. Until then we'll use protection. Deal?"

Rain grinned and took the hand Greg held out. "Deal, Sir."

Relaxed, Rain melted against Greg. "What else are we doing tonight?"

"I have to go work at the club. You can either come with me or stay behind and put away your clothes."

"I'll stay here." No way did he want to expose his presence to an entire club of people. Cops had snitches, didn't they?

"Are you sure? It'll be kind of boring here alone."

Rain rubbed Greg's arm in a soothing motion. "I'll be fine. I'll unpack, review some photos and watch a bit of television. Do you have anything to eat?"

"Yeah, a bit of leftover pasta and a salad, and I think there are sandwich fixings. I hate to leave you here alone. If you came with me I could get you a proper meal," Greg said.

"I'll be fine. I'm not super hungry anyway." Rain resisted the temptation for a meal at the club. Greg's chef had awesome taste buds and everything always had amazing flavor.

"Okay, if you're sure." Greg kissed Rain on the forehead. "I'll call to check on you later."

CHAPTER THREE

Greg headed to his club but his thoughts remained with Rain. Complex didn't even begin to describe Rain's personality. Between running away then returning to Greg, he suspected the sub didn't know what he wanted.

Nodding to his bouncer, Ralph, Greg entered the club. Music pounded and flashing lights flickered across the crowd. From the screaming and dancing, people were having a great time. This part of the club had been converted for the average club hopper. In the past year he'd bought the space next to him and begun expanding his business. If he could keep Rain he would buy them a nicer place. Maybe he could set up a nice studio for his sub to work from.

He'd miss all the artistic touches his brother Stephen had added to their home while growing up, but Greg knew he could get Stephen to help decorate his new house too. His brother had a generous heart and loved to share his talent. Greg shook his head as he realized how much he was getting ahead of himself. First he had to get the guy to stay for more than a night. He half expected Rain to be gone when he returned home despite what the sub said. Rain had the skittishness of a feral cat in a room with a thousand rocking chairs.

Greg examined the people around him. Each weekend the crowd grew larger until a line now wrapped around the building with people eager to get inside. Greg had servers offering free sodas and peanuts for customers while they stood in line; this kept people from becoming cranky while waiting to get in. The happier the customer the more likely they'd return with their friends.

Greg passed the noisy dance floor and headed to the quieter members only side. The first section had been established as a quiet zone for Doms and subs to bond without all the noise and clatter of the more active portions of the club.

Sometimes a sub sat at attention with a ball gag in his mouth, other times the sub and master sat side-by-side soaking in each others' company. Greg couldn't wait to bring Rain here and have him sit at attention and meditate. Rain had a busy mind and it would be good for him to have a bit of solitude. Maybe he should instill that into Rain's routine.

No one sat in the quiet area tonight. Saturdays were when most of the partiers and some of the hardcore Doms came out and showed the newbies how things were done. Greg reached his office and sat behind his desk with relief. The club had made him wealthy in his own right but more and more Greg wondered if maybe it was time to hang up his leathers and let someone else run the place. He was getting too old for this shit. Sitting at home with Rain sounded much better than coming here every night hoping to score.

He tried to focus on the invoices he'd left to do tonight. The orders tallied up properly and he emailed the mess to his accountant to sort out. A knock on his door pulled him from his thoughts.

"Come in."

Billy, one of his new employees, entered; his skin had an unnatural pallor. "You've got a visitor boss. A cop wants to talk to you. He says his name is Dalrey."

From Billy's expression Greg doubted he'd enjoy the visit. "Send him in."

Billy nodded. He returned in a minute escorting a uniformed policeman. The cop's flat brown gaze swept the office as if searching for illegal substances in the pristine room.

Greg stood, not willing to be seated while the cop towered over him. "How can I help you?"

"I'm Lieutenant Dalrey from Narcotics, I'm looking for Rainier Lemmon. Have you seen him?"

"Not recently," Greg had no problem lying to the man. The detective gave off a bad vibe. If Rain had done something wrong Greg would find out. He let none of that show in his expression. "Can I ask what this is about?"

"No. If you see him call me." Dalrey handed over his card. "If I find out you knew where he is and didn't tell me I will come down on your ass so hard you'll wish you were hiding drugs in your filthy club."

"I see. Would you like me to call your Chief of Police and tell him that? He's a golfing buddy of mine."

Dalrey sneered. "I just bet he is."

Greg had seen the flash of fear in the cop's eyes. Whatever Rain had done it wasn't anything this guy would accuse him of. Greg recognized a bully when he saw one and Dalrey was the worst sort, the kind with a badge. "I'll be sure to let you know if I see Rainier."

Dalrey nodded. "You do that."

The chill in Greg's bones didn't leave until Dalrey had exited and he watched him leave the club across his camera feeds. A cop looking for a criminal didn't come by himself. Something didn't add up here. He had a feeling Rain had come to him not so much because of his winning charm but for safety. Rain was hiding and he didn't trust Greg enough to tell him.

Crap.

Greg ran a hand through his hair, rumpling his already messy locks. Anger surged through him. He didn't like being used. Rain could have his secrets but Greg would make sure he paid. When he was finished with the sub Rain wouldn't even think about leaving Greg's side without written permission and his ass would be so red it glowed in the dark when Greg finished with it.

He didn't make any phone calls in case the cop had tapped Greg's phone. Dalrey didn't seem like the type to go through proper channels before running a wiretap. Instead, Greg turned off his phone so Rain couldn't make any incoming calls that Dalrey could trace.

Despite knowing the Chief of Police Greg didn't want to call in any favors until he knew what he was facing. He brushed away his first instinct to run to Rain's side and find out the truth. If he left early it would only trigger the cop's suspicion that Greg knew Rain's location.

Shoving his worries to the back of his mind, Greg focused on his paperwork, walked through the club for his usual meet and greet and when it was time to go home he stopped by the grocery store to get food.

Exiting the car, a tingle went up Greg's spine and lifted the tiny hairs on the back of his neck. Someone had followed him. He didn't need to be a genius to know when he was being watched.

Greg cast a quick look around trying to find the source of his unease. He didn't spot anyone. Weird. Either Dalrey had mad ninja skills or Greg had imagined eyes watching him.

He grabbed a basket then headed down the vegetable aisle to check out what was in season. He'd taken up cooking lately as a way to de-stress and eat better. He'd started putting on a bit of weight at the club with his diet consisting of fried foods and few fresh veggies.

After several trips up and down the aisles he settled on a basket full of bright vegetables and lean meats. He threw a bag of brown rice among the lot at the last minute then went to checkout. Still not convinced he'd escaped unnoticed, Greg took the long way home on the off chance his stalker hadn't given up. Someone had told Dalrey that Greg knew Rain and the cop wouldn't just leave at Greg's say so.

He pulled up in front of his townhouse and stared at it a moment. Nothing looked different. He exited the car then grabbed the two bags of groceries in one hand so he could unlock the front door with the other.

Greg needn't have bothered. The entrance swung open as he approached.

"Oh, I've got it." Rain grabbed the bags out of Greg's hold and carried them to the kitchen. Greg locked the door behind him before following.

Rain put everything away, careful to fold the grocery bags and tuck them under the sink before facing Greg again. He leaned against the counter and watched Rain. It only took a few minutes before the sub began to twitch.

"Is there something you want to tell me?" Greg raised an eyebrow and waited.

Rain's nervous smile had Greg's heart sinking. "Um. It's nice to see you home, Sir?"

"Good try, boy. Come with me." Greg headed down the hall, not turning to see if Rain followed. After his brother moved out he'd turned the spare room into a playroom. Stephen wasn't coming back home; Victor would never allow it. To date, Rain was the only sub ever to see his new setup.

If he hadn't heard the soft footsteps behind him Greg never would've known Rain followed him. The elegant man walked with a dancer's grace. He resisted taking Rain on the nearest flat surface. They had things to discuss first. Rain should've told Greg he was in trouble right away and not let Greg hear it from a stranger. What if he'd told the officer where to find Rain? Most people would want to help out the police. Luckily for Rain this particular cop put off bad vibes by the bucketful.

Still fuming, he opened his playroom door and motioned for Rain to go inside.

"Strip!" He ordered. There wouldn't be a discussion about this. Rain could safeword if he objected.

"Is there something I've done wrong?" Rain followed Greg's orders but his hands weren't completely steady while he undressed.

Not unless ripping out my heart is a problem. Greg refused to appear weak in front of Rain. The sub would never know how much his betrayal hurt Greg. He wanted to protect Rain from all the outside forces of the world but Rain didn't trust Greg in return.

Once naked Rain took a proper stance, shoulders back, feet apart and hands clasped behind his back.

"Go to the cross." He didn't offer any of his usual small touches or reassuring smiles. Right now he didn't have it in him.

Rain flashed Greg a nervous look, but didn't safeword. "Do you want me facing you or away?"

"Facing me." He needed to see Rain's eyes when he answered Greg's questions.

Rain walked over to the St. Andrew's cross and positioned his body for strapping in. Greg attached cuffs to Rain's wrists and ankles. Rain sucked in a breath.

Greg ignored him and went to the cabinet. He would get his answers one way or another. Rain needed a keeper and Greg refused to let anyone else have the job.

* * * *

Rain almost safeworded. He didn't know what happened at work but Greg's eyes held a disappointed expression Rain had hoped to never see in his lover's gaze. Greg might not be a man of many words but he used his voice to calm Rain whenever they were doing a scene.

This version of Greg didn't have the same warm smile. "What are we doing, Sir?" He threw in the honorific hoping it would gain him some attention. If he were going to be tied to a St. Andrew's cross he wanted to be noticed. He'd rather be whipped than ignored.

Greg pulled out a tassel whip with velvety soft leather strands. Rain recognized that evil device. It had almost broken him before.

"Oh, no, no, not that." Rain struggled against the cuffs as Greg approached. He could take a hard whip, a caning, once he'd even been hung from the ceiling by hooks, but this was his downfall and from the Greg's wicked expression the Dom knew it.

"Are you going to safeword?" Greg asked in a curious tone as if he was indifferent either way.

"No, Sir." He wasn't a pussy; he could do this. He took a deep breath, his entire body tense as he waited for the first touch.

Greg slid the soft strands across Rain's right inner thigh. Rain gritted his teeth.

"I was visited by a policeman this evening. He's looking for you. Now what could my beautiful sub be doing that would call the attention of the cops, hmm?"

"Nothing, Sir." He gasped the words out. A fine shiver ran through his body and pimpled his skin. Could he hold out? How had the cop found him so fast?

"Really? How strange that a cop would waste his

time searching for a random person. Are you sure you can't think of a single reason he might be looking for you?" Greg flicked the soft lashes across Rain's cock. "Oh wait, I forgot something."

Rain clenched his fists, his gaze pinned on the Dom rifling through his cabinet. Greg forgot something? Not likely.

Before the suspense could build up too much, Greg returned. Without a word he fastened a cock ring around Rain's erection. "There! Much better. Isn't it?"

Rain swallowed.

"Now, where was I?" Greg slid the soft straps across Rain's chest then flicked them randomly against his left nipple then his right. "Anything you want to say?"

"It must be a coincidence, sir." Fuck, he was so screwed.

"I don't believe in coincidences." Greg flicked the tassel across Rain's left thigh, disturbingly close to his testicles.

Rain whimpered.

"I'd like to think you were here because you wanted a relationship between us. I'd hate to think you were here just to hide out."

There. The hurt in Greg's voice sank through Rain's denial. Somehow Greg knew and Rain couldn't let him think he was being used. He swallowed his pride. "Cheddar," he whispered.

Greg immediately dropped the whip and unfastened the cuffs, freeing Rain from the cross. "Talk to me, Rain. Tell me what's going on."

"Can I get dressed first?" This would be hard

enough to discuss without his erection bouncing in front of him.

Greg took off the cock ring. "Go. Get dressed."

Rain nodded. He didn't look up when Greg walked away. He should get used to that, the Dom would be throwing him out once Rain confessed what was going on. Only an idiot would keep a loser like him. He'd photographed a fucking murder and didn't even notice. Who did crap like that? Rain wished it took longer to dress but too soon he finished and headed for the living room. Even after dragging his steps he reached Greg's side quicker than he would've liked.

"Sit!" Greg pointed to the couch.

Rain sat.

"Now tell me about this cop."

"H-how did you find out?" Various scenarios raced through Rain's head. Maybe he could make a run for it? If Greg knew someone must've told him. The cop must've made the connection.

"I had a visitor at the club this evening." Greg's expression didn't imply in any way it was a good visit. "If I'm going to be threatened by the police I want to know why. What have you gotten yourself mixed up with, Rain?"

Rain's hands shook as he slid them through his hair. "It wasn't my fault."

"Really?" Greg folded his arms across his chest. His measuring look pinned Rain in spot more effectively than the cuffs on the cross. Damn. A spurt of sympathy went through him over Stephen. The poor kid must've been on the other end of that level stare more than once over the years. He made a mental note to be kinder to Stephen in the future if he made it out this situation alive.

Rain wiggled on the couch, guilt pressed down on him like a two-ton weight.

"You should've told me you were in trouble right away," Greg said.

Rain nodded. He couldn't deny Greg's words. If he weren't such a fucking coward he would've confessed as soon as he came over. "You're right."

"Tell me."

Rain would only get one shot at this. If he screwed up Greg would throw him out and he'd lose the possible start of a relationship he hadn't realized he wanted until that very moment.

Rain tucked his hair behind his ear. "It's better if I show you. Can I go get my computer?"

"Yes, but come right back here. No stalling."

Rain blinked back tears. Greg knew his habits. He shouldn't find that so completely endearing. Rain stood then rushed from the room. He didn't know how long Greg's patience would last. At least he was willing to hear what Rain had to say before dismissing him from Greg's life. Rain stumbled over his feet as he ran. He grabbed the wall before he took a header onto the hardwood floors. Crap, he needed to get it together.

He slowed down his steps when he reached Greg's bedroom. He pulled his suitcase out of the closet where he'd shoved it out of the way and retrieved his computer. Hands shaking he returned to Greg's side and set the machine on the coffee table.

"I brought you some water." Greg pointed at the class sitting on a coaster beside him.

"Thanks." Rain took a grateful sip of the cold beverage. "You have to understand that when I'm taking pictures I'm completely focused. I don't pay attention to what's going on around me."

He dared to glance over at Greg but only got an impatient look.

"Continue." Greg waved for him to go on.

Rain took another sip of water before blurting out the rest. His stomach gurgled its discontent as he remembered the look in the killer's eyes. Before he lost his nerve he forced himself to continue. "It isn't anything I did on purpose, but I accidentally took photos of a cop killing another cop. I'm guessing it was your Officer Dalrey. I don't know any other reason the police would be looking for me."

There. Now he'd told Greg everything. His heart rate sped up in his chest and he wiped his sweaty hands on his pants as he waited for Greg's response. The Dom's expression didn't give him any clues, probably one of the reasons he was such a great dominant.

"Show me." Greg's hard tone didn't reassure Rain but he wasn't in any position to complain. He'd come to Greg for help and either Greg would help or he'd show Rain the door. Hopefully without calling the cops.

After a few minutes of the laptop booting up, Rain retrieved the file and turned the screen so Greg could see his evidence. There hadn't been any sign of a struggle before the shots. No one could look at those photos and think there had been a mistake. One man had definitely shot the other.

Greg clicked the laptop touchpad a few times going back and forth between pictures.

"Fuck!" Greg glared at the screen before turning his attention to Rain. "That's Dalrey in the picture all right. Does anyone else know you have these?"

Rain shook his head. "I didn't know who to trust."

Greg tilted his head. "How did he know where to find you? It's a big city and no offense but there are a lot of photographers. How did he pick you out from all the others?"

"I recently took pictures at a cop's wedding. I recognized Dalrey's face but I didn't know his name. It's pretty common knowledge that I like BDSM. If he asked around he might've just been casing possible clubs." Rain remembered Dalrey drinking to the new bride and groom and hamming it up for pictures. Just went to show people had many facets. Fun man one day, killer the next.

Greg frowned. "Wait, I thought you hated commercial photography."

"Really? That's what you got out of my statement?" Rain scowled at Greg. "I like to pay my bills so sometimes I'll take on commercial gigs. Weddings pay pretty well when I have a steady stream of them. I told you about my plan for your club. I like pictures of people I just don't want to be one of those photographers who takes shots at sports events or other crap like that." Rain had some nice referrals by the wedding crowd and although he hated getting the bridezilla types, a nice couple starting their life together got to him every time. He could usually judge in the first few meetings if he wanted to photograph the wedding. If the bride seemed too high maintenance or the groom came off as an ass, Rain politely declined.

"You can take pictures for an ad for my club then," Greg said, a victorious smile crossed his face as if he had won the argument.

Rain groaned. "Can we stay on track? You're forgetting a cop-killing cop is on my tail." His voice, rising higher and louder with each word had reached a piercing shrill tone by the end of his sentence.

"I haven't forgotten. I'm thinking over what we need to do. I have to make some phone calls. Although I know the chief your evidence might not be enough to hold the guy unless someone can produce a body," Greg admitted. "We need someone to watch you until Dalrey is arrested."

Rain didn't bring up the fact that Dalrey might not ever see the inside of a jail cell. A good lawyer could probably get Dalrey off unless there was more evidence.

"And by watch you mean get a bodyguard," Rain said. He didn't need things sugarcoated he knew how much trouble he'd stumbled into. It just proved his mother had been right when she said he'd get into trouble he couldn't escape some day. She'd meant his being gay not taking a killer's picture but that didn't make her words any less true.

"Yes, I mean a bodyguard." Greg pulled Rain into his arms, hugging him tight.

Rain could sit there and breathe in Greg's scent all night. Greg created a calm oasis within his arms as if nothing could hurt Rain as long as Greg stood there. The stress of the day caught up with him and

Rain burst into tears. He hid his face against Greg's shoulder.

Greg cuddled him close. "Did you just come here to escape? Do you have any interest in being my sub at all?"

Rain sniffled but sat up straight. Greg deserved to see him, ugly crying face and all, while they had this conversation. "I'm fucked up, Greg. I want you but I don't know if you'll want to keep me. I have huge commitment issues, but for you I want to try." He wasn't quite ready to swear undying love but he definitely cared more for Greg than anyone else he'd subbed for.

Greg cupped Rain's cheek. "Remind me to punish you later for cursing."

Rain gave a watery chuckle. "Okay, Sir."

"I'm going to call my friends. I don't know if they can arrest this guy on the evidence of some photos. Especially since digital pictures can be doctored. At least if there is some evidence against Dalrey he might be less likely to come after you. It's hard to clear up a mistake if there are dead bodies."

"That's why I didn't want you involved. I knew you'd want to fix this." Rain couldn't see a way out and now Greg could be getting himself killed trying to save him. Greg was naïve if he thought Dalrey would let this go. If he would shoot another cop in an alley, offing a photographer with no family couldn't be that much more of a problem. If Rain disappeared it could be months before anyone came to investigate unless Greg kept track of him.

"Enough! I'm going to make some phone calls and rally the troops. We'll get you out of this."

"I appreciate the sentiment but you can't promise that."

"You'd be surprised at what I can do. Get yourself a snack while I call around."

Rain nodded. He already made it sound like he didn't trust his Dom but he didn't want Greg to put himself in danger just because Rain was an idiot and took pictures of a murder.

CHAPTER FOUR

In the end Greg called Lindi Samms for help. He might be a gallery owner but he had connections, or at least his sub Will did. "Hey, Lindi, I need to talk to your boy."

"No." Lindi didn't even try to sweeten his response. No one talked to Will unless Lindi cleared them. Will was a serious lifestyle sub and didn't even eat without Lindi's nod. Greg found that sort of dedication laudable but too time consuming for him. He wondered what sort of sub Rain would be in a long-term relationship. He had a feeling if he told Rain not to eat the feisty brunet would punch him. Greg smiled.

"I'm not screwing around, Lindi. This is a matter of life or death. A crooked cop is hunting Rain. I need to see if I can have Will contact his family and either find me a good bodyguard or at least see if there's any dirt on this guy."

"I see. Normally I'd tell you to fuck off but Will likes you. Let me get him on the phone."

Greg heard the soft murmur of voices talking in the background then Will came on the phone. "What can I do for you, Greg?"

Greg quickly recounted what was going on.

"Why don't you call the chief and I'll call my brothers. It will work best if we approach this from both sides I think." Will's take-charge tone took Greg by surprise. The sub generally let Lindi run everything. Maybe he'd misjudged the man all these years.

"Thanks, Will. I'll do what I can here. I appreciate any help you can give."

Will bid Greg goodbye. Lindi got back on the phone. "I'm not going to let him get involved in anything dangerous."

"I'm only asking for his contacts. I don't expect Will to come here and get in the line of fire."

"You think there'll be gunfire?" Lindi asked.

"I'm trying to avoid it. Rain took a photo of a cop shooting another cop. I'm trying to get the officer arrested before he hunts Rain down."

"Fuck!" Lindi cursed.

"My thoughts exactly."

"I'll let you know as soon as Will hears something from his family."

"Thanks." Greg cut the connection. He went through his contacts until he found the chief's number. He pressed Manuel Garcia's name to connect. He'd known the Dom for years but hadn't ever used him for his police contacts before. Greg didn't like to pull in favors unless necessary. He'd introduced Manuel to his sub, Terry. The pair had been together for six years now.

"Hello."

"Hello Manuel, this is Greg Carter."

"Greg, how are you doing?" Manuel's deep voice boomed across the line.

"Well, that's what I'm calling you about. My sub is having a problem I was hoping you could help us with."

"You have a sub? When did this happen? Last I heard you were a lone wolf. You'll have to bring him by to meet Terry. He could always use some sub friends."

"I'll do that," Greg promised. "First I need to get him out of his current problem."

"Well, I'm not fixing his parking ticket. I don't care how pretty his eyes are or if he can suck like a dream."

"I only wish it was something that simple," Greg muttered. "He's a photographer and he took pictures of one of your cops killing another one. As you can imagine he's afraid to go to the police."

"What cop? How come I didn't hear of anyone getting killed?" The chief's hard tone told Greg heads were going to roll.

"Officer Dalrey is the cop and I don't know why no one told you of the cop's death. Maybe they don't know yet."

"Send the picture to me. I can try and identify the dead man. If Dalrey killed one of our own he's going down for it I don't care that he's the governor's nephew." Manuel rattled off an email address for Greg to send the file to. "I'll call you after I look it over."

Fuck.

"Sounds good. Bye." Greg hung up and went to join Rain on the couch. "I need you to send the photos to the chief's email address. He's going to try and identify the victim."

"And you're sure he's not corrupt?" Rain frowned. Worry creased his forehead.

Greg considered everything he'd observed about the chief over the years. "As sure as I can be."

"Okay." Rain opened his email account and minutes later sent the attached files to the chief. "Now what?"

Greg wrapped an arm around Rain and pulled him closer. "Now we wait." There wasn't anything they could do before hearing back from the others. Exhaustion pulled at Greg. Closing his eyes and shutting out the world sounded like a great idea right now.

"I really do like you," Rain said.

"I like you too." Rain was an enigma, both a hardened soldier and a young man who needed a hug when things got tough.

Someone banged on the front door.

"Grab your laptop," Greg urged.

"I need my camera!" Rain jumped up and ran down the hall.

"Fuck!" Greg whispered. They were panicking and they didn't even know who was at the door. If it were some Girl Scout selling cookies he'd never tell anyone of his terror at the possibility of a cop standing on the other side of his door.

Trying to walk as quiet as possible, he approached the front window and peeked beneath the curtain. Dalrey stood on his doorstep. Greg jumped back before the cop could see him.

"I know you're in there!" Dalrey shouted.

Greg shoved his feet into his shoes then scooped up his wallet and keys before racing after Rain. The sub had his camera around his neck and his laptop tucked beneath his right arm.

"Come, love. Let's get out of here." Greg wished he could pull out a gun and go out blazing but he didn't believe in them. His gut told him Dalrey had come alone. Now wouldn't be the time for his instincts to be wrong.

Walking to the big picture window he blessed the fact he'd bought new windows last year. The glass slid open with a quiet shush of sound. Greg stuck his head out but didn't see anyone. He climbed out first. "Give me the laptop."

Rain handed it over then let Greg help him out the window. After Rain cleared the ledge, Greg closed it as well as he could. Hopefully no one would break in and steal everything he owned.

He kept hold of the laptop and grabbed Rain's wrist. "Stay quiet so he won't hear us."

The townhouse wasn't so large Dalrey wouldn't hear them if they were too loud. If they ran the cop might see them. Greg patted his pockets, then did it again. "Fuck!"

"What's wrong?" Rain asked.

"I left my phone on the coffee table."

"Damn." Rain reached into his pocket and cursed. "Mine must've fallen out in the play room."

"Fuck." Greg continued walking at a fast pace, but not so fast they'd attract attention. "We need to get somewhere we can make a phone call."

"Freeze!" a deep voice shouted. Greg exchanged looks with Rain. In unison, the pair ran. Greg kept a tight grip on the laptop.

"Run!" Greg wasn't fast but Rain had a sleek

build and Greg knew he jogged.

"Give me the computer!" Dalrey shouted. "I'm going to shoot."

Greg stopped in his tracks. Silently he urged Rain to continue. If Rain didn't run off he'd tan his ass later. "Don't you want the camera instead?"

"You think I'm stupid?" The cop scowled at him while Greg held back the obvious response. "I bet he downloaded them already or you wouldn't be taking the computer with you."

"It's too late. We already sent them to the Chief of Police." After he said those words Greg knew he'd made a miscalculation.

A crazed look filled Dalrey's eyes. "Then I don't have anything to lose anymore by killing you."

Dalrey lifted his gun to shoot him. Greg ran forward and slammed the laptop into the cop's hand. The gun went flying into the tall grass. Greg fled. If he stayed there Dalrey would shoot him.

He turned the corner. A hand reached out and grabbed his arm. Greg lifted his fist to punch when he recognized Rain's face. "Fuck, babe. I almost hit you."

"You're an idiot! You should've run," Rain said in an angry whisper. "How dare you put yourself in danger. He could've shot you!"

"He still might." Greg looked around to get his bearings. "Come on. My friend lives a few blocks from here. He'll let us use his phone."

"Okay." Rain cast a scared glance down the alley. "Let's go."

They peered around the corner but Dalrey was nowhere to be seen. "Where did he go?" Greg asked.

He didn't like this at all. Dalrey was a loose cannon and appeared more than willing to kill them to hide the evidence.

"I can't believe he thought all the evidence was on the computer. Hasn't he heard of cloud storage?" Rain snorted.

"Don't mock the psychopath," Greg said absently. His entire attention focused on getting them out of there alive. "I wonder how he found us so fast."

"He probably ran your license," Rain said.

"Fuck. You're right." It would've been a simple thing for him to run Greg's license and get his address. He didn't even have to tail him for that.

There was no sign of Dalrey as they approached Lindi's apartment.

They were steps from the front door when a car screeched to a stop on the street. Dalrey slid out from behind the wheel, a pistol clutched in his hand. Damn. He must've found it. How did they not see him trailing them? He was a sneaky fucker.

"Run," Greg grabbed Rain's wrist and ran toward the building dragging Rain behind him. Gunfire echoed in the courtyard. Greg didn't look back. He couldn't waste valuable time. He needed a phone.

The apartment security met them at the door. When Greg slid inside the security guards looked seconds from finding weapons of their own to stop them from coming closer.

"I need a phone. That cop out there is trying to kill us."

One of the security guards smirked. "Likely story."

"No, I recognize him. He's one of Mr. Samms's friends." a different guard said.

The other guards took a step back.

"Yes, I am. Can I borrow a phone?" Greg asked.

"I can call the police," one of the guards offered.

"He is the police," Rain said.

"My brother's a cop. I'll call him," said a security guard with the name Frank written on his badge.

"I don't feel so good," Rain whispered.

Greg tightened his grip but that didn't stop Rain from falling to the ground and smacking his head on the granite. Blood splattered across the white marble from where he fell like bloody angel wings.

"Call an ambulance," Greg shouted. Another shot rang out. Greg instinctively ducked. Screams reached him from people on the street.

"Bring him over here," Frank called out.

"I don't know if it's safe to move him."

Rain's eyes slid closed. "Run, don't get killed for me."

"Don't you leave me!" Greg shouted. Rain couldn't die. That wasn't how things were supposed to go. He still planned to see Rain's beautiful eyes light up when Greg offered him a collar.

Sirens pierced through the air, a welcoming sound. Greg hoped an ambulance wasn't far behind. The doors slammed open and cops filled the foyer. A uniformed blond with kind green eyes dropped down beside them. "What happened?"

"Dirty cop," Greg said.

The blond didn't say anything more. "They have him surrounded out there and an ambulance is on the way."

"Good."

"Where was he shot?" the cop asked.

"I don't know." With all the blood he'd been afraid to disturb Rain to search for the wound. "He said he didn't feel good."

"Did he hit his head when he fell?"

Greg nodded. "Yeah. I broke his fall a bit but he still hit pretty hard."

The doors opened again and two paramedics rushed in. After they braced Rain's neck they lifted him onto the gurney. Greg got to his feet. "I want to go with him."

"Are you family?"

"His husband," Greg said without hesitation.

"Then come with us," one of the paramedics said.

Greg snatched up Rain's camera and laptop and ran after them. No way would he let Rain go anywhere without him. The drive to the hospital starred as one of the most horrific moments of Greg's life. Rain began gasping and they had to give him oxygen.

"Shh. I've got you." Greg tried to be reassuring and stay out of the paramedics' way at the same time.

Rain's eyes met his and the relief in his sub's eyes reassured him he'd made the right decision to come along. At the hospital they sent him to the waiting room where he sat clutching Rain's laptop. Rain's camera had a broken lens and would take some repair. If it couldn't be fixed Greg would get him a new one. Rain had to be okay. There weren't any other choices.

A cop approached and Greg immediately tensed.

"Are you Greg Carter?"

"Yes."

"The chief told me to come by and tell you they captured Dalrey. He'll be going to jail for attempted murder."

"What about an actual murder?" Greg asked.

"I don't know anything about that," the cop said. "I just know what I'm told."

"Thank you," Greg said. He resisted the urge to tear the cop a new asshole. Killing the messenger wouldn't be fair.

"I want to tell you I'm sorry it was one of our own. Dalrey used to be a good cop. I don't know what happened to him."

"Yeah, me neither." So many factors could go into someone turning into a killer. Money usually played a part. As long as Dalrey stayed in jail Greg didn't care what he went there for.

"Chief said to call him if you need anything."

"I need my boyfriend to not die. Can he do anything about that since it was his one of his men who did it?" Greg snapped. So much for his resolve.

The officer shook his head. "I'm going to head back to work. I'm sorry about your guy."

Greg nodded. The cop did sound sincere and it wasn't his fault Rain had been shot. Greg let him go without further comment.

"Greg!" Will ran down the hall and slid to a stop before him. Lindi followed at a more sedate pace. "Is Rain okay?"

"I don't know. I haven't had an update yet." His chest ached and his stomach churned while he waited to hear anything at all about Rain's condition.

"I called Stephen. He's on his way," Will said.

"Thanks." Greg could use the company. Waiting to hear Rain's status had shattered his nerves and he was one toxic cup of coffee away from destroying his stomach lining.

Will sat beside him and patted Greg's leg. "That's what friends are for. I did some research on your cop and he was into some bad shit. Internal Affairs has been watching him. Apparently he had his own drug gig on the side."

Greg raised an eyebrow over Will's information. "And how do you know this?"

"Yes, how do you know this, my sweet boy?" Lindi asked.

Will blushed. "My dad might know some people."

"Uh huh. I don't think I want to know any more," Greg said.

Will let out a deep breath. "Good."

Lindi laughed. "Greg might have given you a reprieve but we will be talking more about it when we get home."

"Yes, Sir," Will said.

A doctor came out. "I'm looking for relatives of Rainier Lemmon."

Greg raised his hand and stood. "He's mine." The rightness of those words sank down to his soul.

"I'm Dr. Henner and I performed the surgery on Mr. Lemmon. I'm happy to report that although the bullet went into Mr. Lemmon's chest it missed all major arteries and organs. I was able to successfully extract it. With a bit of care, Mr. Lemmon should make a full recovery."

"Can I see him?"

"They are pulling him out of ICU now. When he is in his new room there is no reason why you wouldn't be able to visit."

"Thank you, Doctor."

Greg shook hands with the man then went back down to wait.

EPILOGUE

"Jake, could you turn just a little to the left? I want to get a better view of Paul's harness," Rain said.

The couple moved into position. Rain took a series of shots before repositioning them again. When he had a dozen shots he liked he stopped. "I think that's enough. I'll email you your pictures and you can pick which ones you want me to clean up and print out."

"Thanks, man." Jake towered over Rain but his smile lit up the room. He tucked Paul beneath his shoulder while Paul beamed up at his partner.

"No problem. Thanks for coming by."

"No, thank you," Paul said. "We saw the photos you took of Derek and Sam. They were amazing."

Rain blushed. "I'm glad you thought so." The pair had posed in some extremely intimate positions, but Rain wasn't surprised they'd shared their photos. The couple had asked Rain if he wanted to join them some time. After stammering out he doubted Greg would want to share they'd left quickly with much apologizing. Still, their photos had turned out great if Rain did say so himself.

"I think opening a studio here was a brilliant idea," Paul gushed.

"It has gone over well," Rain agreed. Greg had opened the studio to keep an eye on Rain. He'd told Rain as much. Apparently if Greg had to be at his club to oversee things he wanted Rain near and since Rain didn't exactly like to sit around and twiddle his thumbs they'd worked out a compromise.

The couple waved goodbye and went on their way.

"Done for the evening?" Greg asked, stepping into the studio.

"Pretty much. I'm going to weed out the photos tomorrow." It had been a long day with four sessions. Rain tried to get the best photos to suit each couple or in one case, trio. He didn't judge, he only tried to match everyone photographically.

"Good. I have some news for you."

"Yeah?" Rain continued walking around his studio and tidying up. He hated to leave his equipment haphazardly tossed around.

"Dalrey was killed in prison today."

Rain froze. "Really?" He'd had constant nightmares about the guy getting out and coming after him again.

"Some guard accidentally released him into the general population. One of the people he had put away shanked him."

"Huh, well accidents do happen." Rain watched Greg carefully but his lover didn't meet his eyes, not once. "Let's go home. I could use a celebratory bubble bath."

They'd bought a new house two miles from the

club that came with a spa tub. Rain couldn't get enough of it.

"Excellent idea." Greg kissed Rain's forehead. "A night of relaxation sounds like just the thing. Did I mention I received a velvet tassel whip in the mail today?"

Rain groaned. His cock hardened in his pants as he followed his lover out of the club. Stupid cock didn't know what was best for it.

"Don't worry, love. You'll get to come eventually," Greg tossed over his shoulder as he sauntered out the door.

Rain didn't comment. His world had narrowed to the sight of his Dom's leather-clad ass. Yep, tonight would be a stellar night.

Amber Kell has made a career out of daydreaming. It has been a lifelong habit she practices diligently as shown by her complete lack of focus on anything not related to her fantasy world building.

When she told her husband what she wanted to do with her life he told her to go have fun.

During those seconds she isn't writing she remembers she has children who humor her with games of 'what if' and let her drag them to foreign lands to gather inspiration. Her youngest confided in her that he wants to write because he longs for a website and an author name—two things apparently necessary to be a proper writer.

Despite her husband's insistence she doesn't drink enough to be a true literary genius she continues to spin stories of people falling happily in love and staying that way.

She is thwarted during the day by a traffic jam of cats on the stairway and a puppy who insists on walks, but she bravely perseveres.

For more information on other books by Amber, visit her official website: AmberKell.com

Also by Amber Kell

Extasy Books
Destiny of Dragons
Protector of Dragons
To Catch a Croc
To Kiss a Killer
To Enchant an Eagle
To Have a Human
The Alpha's Only
To Bite the Bear
Oliver's Online

Totally Bound Publishing
Ganging Up on Love
Zheng's Heart
Elijah's Ghost
Farren's Wizard
Overcoming His Pride
Jaynell's Wolf
Kevin's Alpha
In Broussard's Care
Accounting for Luke
From Pack to Pride
Robert's Rancher
Gamma's Choice
Catching Mr. Right
Kissing Orion

Magically His
Protecting His Pride
Saint Returns
Taking Care of Charlie
The Case of the Cupid Curse
The Case of the Sinful Santa
The Case of the Wicked Wolf
Tyler's Cowboy
The Prideless Man
Chalice
More Than Pride
Nothing to Do with Pride
Talan's Treasure
The Case of the Dragon's Dilemma
Zall's Captain
A Prideful Mate
Back to Hell
Bonded Broken
Duke Betrayed
Hellbourne
Modelling Death
Politician Won
Prince Claimed
Protecting Francis
Protecting His Soul
Soldier Mine
Teasing Jonathon
Testing Arthur
William's House
Blown Away
Convention Confusion
Keeping Dallas
Matchmaker, Matchmaker

Mate Test
My Shining Star
My Subby Valentine
Samhain's Kiss
Saving Valor
The Vampire King's Husband
The Wizard and the Werewolf
Trials of Tam
Twisted Rose
Vampire Wanted

OmniLit/All Romance eBooks, LLC

Mastering Will
Considering Carlyle
Wooing Master Jones

Resplendence Publishing

The Helpful Swan
The Swimming Swan

TWO HOWLS

ALPHA GAY EROTIC ROMANCE

SEAN MICHAEL

CHAPTER ONE

Max Starling headed down the road, pushing his bike as fast as it would go. He'd burned every bridge ever built from Miami to Nashville to Detroit and now he was headed across the border.

Fucking assholes. Fucking liars. Fucking moon.

He made it past customs and into Canada around midnight, his body exhausted, his mind racing like his Harley. He'd whine about never finding a place to settle, but no place was big enough to handle the trouble that followed him like a mist.

He hadn't bothered to stop in Toronto, roaring through the big city like the plague was following him. He didn't even stop for a fucking coffee, just got the hell through the city and continued north. He'd gone damn far north, it seemed, leaving behind civilization and decent roads long ago. Which sucked, because, coffee.

His eyes were exhausted, burning and fuzzy around the edges. On top of that, it was going to be dark soon enough and he was going to have to find somewhere to stop and put his sleeping bag down. No way he could drive through another night. Not without falling asleep right there on his hog.

Not long after carefully crossing a less than stable wooden bridge onto a small, unpaved road, he found a trail—not even something as big as a road—and headed up it. There would be a place to shift, to cuddle in and sleep for a day or two. Surely there'd be something. Somewhere off-road where he wouldn't be disturbed.

He thought he heard the howl of a wolf over the roar of his engine. Was that even possible? He guessed so. It was the Great White North, right?

He kept going, the trail he was on getting harder and harder to follow. So far he hadn't found anything very sheltered, but he was far enough from the so-called road he'd left that he was possibly safe to stop. He'd give it a few more minutes.

Finally he gave up, turned his motor off and walked his bike off the trail into the woods. He stowed the bike, hiding it beneath some underbrush among the trees.

The wind blew hard, bringing leaves and scents with it. He'd never been anywhere that felt so deserted of humans.

Whatever. He just needed a safe place to sleep.

He grabbed his pack and started walking, heading up along the trail, eyes peeled for a place to hole up. Something dark that might be a building, or a larger rock, was off to the west, so he headed for it, delighted when it slowly coalesced into a log cabin.

Please be deserted. Please be deserted.

The door opened easily, the place empty. It smelled strongly of occupancy, though. Hell, it almost smelled like wolf. Dammit.

Still. One afternoon. Just let him get one after-noon of sleep and he'd be gone. Poof. He swore.

He stripped out of his leathers and got into his sleeping bag, curled up and went fuzzy. Oh, better. Sleeping. Just for a little while.

Sleeping.

CHAPTER TWO

Ulf was restless, running along the edges of his territory. There had been noises and the faint hint of scents that didn't belong. It had been a long time since his territory had been invaded.

The tiny path from the road proved to be the source of the foreign smells. Metal and gas, oil. And something not quite human. It didn't take him long to find the hidden motorcycle and the trail after that went almost straight toward his cabin. Tilting his head back, Ulf howled then took off at a run.

He followed the trail to his cabin, lip curling at the scent of male. Some fucking wolf had shown up. If this invader thought for a second that Ulf was going to roll over and present his belly or turn tail and run, he had another think coming. This was Ulf's land. All of it.

He nosed the door open, the sound of snoring filling the air. The smell of man was more hidden now, the scent and sounds more wolfish. Growling, he pounced where the noise was coming from.

A slim grey wolf popped up, fur ruffled and eyes bright as the sun.

Ulf snapped and snarled, but he was caught by

those eyes. He saw those eyes every time he dreamed.

The little wolf growled, refusing to back down, standing his ground on shaky legs. Ulf snarled again. He was Alpha here and this was his land. It would be his only warning.

The little wolf sighed, trying to pull together its bedding while not breaking eye contact. He stalked over and vocalized. He expected his due—he would demand it if he had to.

He could read the second the little one gave up on trying to protect his things and simply ran, moving faster than he'd ever seen one of his kind. The wolf leapt over him and scrambled, zipping out the door. Ulf gave chase, having the advantage of knowing the area and where the wolf was headed. This little grey would not make it to his motorcycle with enough time to shift and leave.

The little grey was smart, though, doubling back, leading him on a merry chase. It was almost fun.

Ulf moved a little faster—he hadn't had a good all out run like this in a long time. The exhaustion was beginning to show on the grey now, though, in the graceful lines of his body. Ulf put an end to the chase, pouncing the grey and taking it down, holding the grey in place with his big paws.

The little shit was a fighter, crying out and barking, biting the air. Ulf was bigger, though, and stronger. He snapped back at the other wolf and finally wrapped his teeth around the grey's muzzle. Those gold eyes closed, soft whimpers on the air.

He let go of the grey's muzzle, then opened his mouth over the grey's throat. He could feel the way the pup's heart beat, so fast, so frightened. He was making his point. Growling softly, he let go and stepped back, watching the pup closely.

The little grey hurried to his feet, chest heaving like a bellows.

Ulf knew he should send the little grey on his way, but he couldn't. There was something in those eyes, something that said this one was a loner like him. More than that, this one was his; he smelled it on the air. He growled softly, demanding some sign that the little grey knew it, too.

The grey bowed and then backed off, looking for a way out. No, Ulf didn't think so. Now that he'd decided the grey was his, the beast was staying. Ulf began herding the grey back toward the cabin.

He kept getting tired, confused looks and by the time they got back to the cabin, he was literally pushing the grey toward his home. A soft whine sounded, the pup beginning to dig in.

He moved in and snapped at the grey's muzzle. The little grey danced away, barked at him. He growled. Inside.

He snapped at the lean haunches, and once they were inside, the pup went for the sleeping bag again, curled into it.

Using his hindquarters, Ulf closed the door and moved to his nest in front of the fireplace. Lying down, he kept an eye on the pup, making sure the grey went to sleep and didn't try to run.

* * * *

The big male never slept. Never. Every time Max opened his eyes, the big male was watching. He couldn't believe it. A low growl would sound, like a warning, or an order. He was being told to sleep—he was sure of it.

He would doze off, forcing himself to wake again and again. Finally, the big male came over and put his muzzle over Max's, forcing his head to stay down. The pressure and warmth was intoxicating, undeniable. Odd.

Soon, though, he heard the soft snores of the big wolf.

Move. Move. Come on. Now was his chance! He was so heavy, though. So tired.

The big wolf stretched to lick at Max's muzzle, then settled back in again. Max's nose wrinkled and he settled. Maybe a little nap. Maybe, just maybe, he was safe here. At least for a minute.

He could feel himself, body synching with the Alpha's. It was ridiculous, to trust. He needed to go. Like the big male had heard Max's thoughts, he growled softly.

His body melted into the sleeping bag and he sighed. He was warm and so tired. Maybe he could just stay a minute longer.

The male licked Max's muzzle again. Licked him like he was being marked. The scent was oddly familiar. Weirdly comforting. And the low growling was soothing to his nerves.

His eyes rolled and he moaned, vocalizing. The male sounded back at him.

He'd never had anyone who wanted him to stay, who insisted on it. Never. When it came to him, the opposite was usually true. He moaned, deep in his chest.

One dark blue eye opened up, looked at him. He squeezed his own eyes shut tight.

The wolf holding him down chuffed, laughing at him. That didn't work for him. He pulled away, scrambling back. The big male growled and pounced when his back legs went over an edge. He didn't fall very far, and it was into softness, pillows and comforters in a half-foot deep area in front of the fireplace.

"Ooph." All his breath huffed out of him.

The male began to lick him, marking him. *Marking him.* He shifted and rolled, unsure of what to do. Then the big wolf all but sat on him, keeping him in place.

Max sighed and went boneless again. Fuck. It was clear he was supposed to stay put. Was he in for some bizarre form of punishment for having invaded this guy's territory? If he wasn't so fucking tired, he'd shift and demand the guy let him go. On the other hand, if he shifted, that put him at a huge disadvantage against the big wolf. He was better off staying as he was.

He just needed to sleep. If he was lucky, he'd wake up before the big guy, get his shit and run. He had to be able to get his keys.

He was tired enough that sleep still pulled at him and if he felt safe rather than worried by the big male, well, he was going to put that down to exhaustion.

* * * *

The longer the little grey slept in his bed, the surer Ulf was that he belonged there. Some instinct had brought the wolf all the way to him and it was a good thing.

Ulf dozed, waiting patiently for the grey to wake again. The pup was obviously exhausted, and clearly not from anywhere close by. Northern wolves grew larger up here.

He licked at the sweet muzzle again, not to try to wake the grey, but just because he could. Because he wanted to. He needed to fill himself with that amazing scent. He found one ear and gnawed gently on it.

The pup's eyes popped open, the rush of worry immediate. Ulf growled softly, soothingly. Now he felt utter confusion.

He thought he might have to shift so he could tell the grey to stay put, the little wolf was still fighting him. He held the grey down, grooming the pup with firm, steady strokes. Surely his pup knew about grooming. Understood what it meant.

Their scents mingled, and he sang with pleasure. Good pup. This felt good, right. Ulf had to admit that he was surprised. He'd been a loner for so long and didn't believe there was anyone for him.

Why the moon would send him a wee grey, he wasn't sure, but there was no denying the wolf was here now. Or that he felt this one was entirely his.

Only foolish wolves argued with the moon. And he wasn't foolish.

He settled close, nose on his paws. The grey stole one curious glance after another. Ulf wondered, couldn't the little one feel it? Maybe the pup wasn't used to being a wolf. Maybe he'd been a man for too long and didn't understand his instincts.

Ulf saw that all too often, people lost in their humanity, refusing their wolf.

He couldn't imagine living like that. He was very well used to being in this form, to living this way. Running free. It was so much easier to be wolf than to be human.

Now he could run with his little wolf. Play. Hunt together. He put his head back and howled, then waited for the pup to respond.

The grey finally howled, softly at first, then louder. Ulf howled back, entirely pleased by the response.

Good. Good. The pup had a strong voice, a sure one. He rubbed their muzzles together.

Slowly, carefully, the little grey lost his fur, becoming a lean little blond with the most amazing eyes. Oh damn. Ulf was going to start drooling. It took him a little longer to change—he didn't do it very often.

"Hey." The man found his jeans, pulled them on.

"You didn't have to do that," he noted. He tended to go naked as a man. There was no one to hide himself from.

"Do what?" Oh, rough voice, gravelly. Ulf liked it.

"Put on clothes. You have a fine body."

"I…" Lean cheeks turned bright pink.

Ulf put his hands on his hips. "I'm Ulf. This is my land, my territory."

"I'm sorry. I was tired and I didn't know this was someone's digs. I just needed a nap."

"No, you were guided here." Ulf leaned close and sniffed the grey as a man. He smelled good.

"I am Ulf," he said again. He would know his pup's human name.

"M....Max. I'm Max."

"Mmm. My Max." It suited the little grey. Blond. Whatever.

"I'll get out of your hair. Thanks for letting me stay."

"You don't feel it?" Ulf asked. Could Max really not feel the same things he did?

The scent of arousal filled the air, sudden and heady.

"You *do* feel it." Good. That pleased him. "You were brought here."

"I was…" *Running.*

Ulf heard that thought so clearly it stunned him. "You were running to me." Maybe he'd only imagined he'd heard Max's thought.

Max stared at him, but that pointed chin dipped.

Ulf smiled. "We'll bring your bike in and leave it under branches by the cabin."

"Is there going to be snow soon? I'm from Florida."

"Fuck yes, there's going to be snow soon. And a lot of it. You are going to freeze that pretty little ass off. Good thing I'm here to keep you warm."

"I… I don't."

Max's confusion was luscious.

"You don't what? Don't worry, I have supplies and this place is warm enough with one. It'll be more so with two." It might be nice to winter with someone. He'd never even contemplated it before, but Max made such things seem not only possible but… wanted.

"I…" Max looked like he had shorted out.

His pup was overwhelmed. Ulf went over and started undoing Max's jeans so they could share his nest. It was his duty to help his pup understand their places here. Still, it was a testament to Max's tiredness and confusion that he let it happen.

In seconds Ulf had Max naked again, and he tugged Max back down to his bed. He covered the man completely, mouth on Max's throat. His. Every inch. His teeth grazed Max's skin.

Max groaned, trying to shift away and Ulf pressed down harder against the lean little body. Max reached down, cupped the filling cock, hiding it, shame evident on the skinny face.

Ulf pushed Max's hand away. "You see? You are mine and your body knows it."

Max's eyes went wide. Huge. "I can't."

Ulf frowned. "You can't what?"

"I. You're. We're dudes. Wolves. I know better."

Ulf's eyes narrowed. "You're one of them?" Why would Max have been brought to him if he was one of the ones who believed males loving each other was wrong?

"I… Look. I've had my ass kicked a lot, okay. I swear, I wasn't coming on to you. I promise."

Oh. Ulf thought he understood now. Max wasn't one of them, he'd been tortured by them. His poor wolf.

"No, you weren't. But I'm coming on to you."

Max stared at him, eyes wide, worried. Sweet pup.

He stroked Max's cheek. "You are mine, Max. I know you can feel it."

Max covered his cock again. Growling, Ulf grabbed Max's hand and held it up above his head. It was a very good look. Lowering his head slowly, Ulf pressed their lips together before rocking against the lean body beneath him.

Max's lips opened in a gasp and Ulf knew, without a shadow of a doubt that this was Max's first kiss. Groaning, so pleased that his mate had come to him untried, he slowly moved his lips against Max's before sliding his tongue between the warm lips.

The rush of arousal between them was fierce, huge, making him growl. His prick had hardened to its full length and pressed against Max's smooth belly.

"I shouldn't…" Max began.

"You shouldn't what, Max?" Rolling his hips, he let his hardness rock against Max's skin.

"This. They'll smell it on us."

"Who?" He snapped at the air. He'd take on anyone who tried to come between him and Max.

"Others. Pack. Anyone." Max rolled back, showed a series of scars on his shoulder, his side.

Ulf growled, his fingers not shying away from Max's skin. "They did this because you didn't want to mate with a female?"

Max nodded, crawling off, going for his clothes.

Ulf stopped Max, grabbing his hand and pulling him back in close. "This is my territory, there are no others, no pack. Just us."

"You…" He could see Max drawing himself up, trying to wrest control from Ulf.

"Yes. My territory." He put both of Max's wrists in one hand and slammed their bodies together.

"No..." Max's lips parted and those bright eyes rolled.

"Yes. Mine." He ran his hand along Max's spine, showing he meant all of Max. Ulf knew his place here, and he would teach Max his. "I make my own rules here. No one hurts for being different." And whether there was only himself, or him and Max or thirty, no one would.

Not that he would ever be leader of a pack of thirty. He was quite happy here on his own. Maybe happier now that Max had been brought to him, but he had no intension of overseeing a large pack. None whatsoever.

Max's cock was needy, filling and growing heavier by the minute. Ulf circled it with his hand, fingers squeezing. Hot and velvety against his palm, Max was a good size, not too long, but thick. A very happy handful.

"Mine. My rules. My pup."

"Not a pup."

Ulf chuckled, the sound rough, unused. "You are mine."

Max shook his head, but the needy cock in Ulf's fingers didn't lie. He rubbed his thumb back and forth across the top, spreading the single drop of pre-come that had beaded at the slit.

"Such a needy pup." Ulf would have never thought he wanted someone so needy, but Max felt so right. His hand continued to move along Max's cock. The things he wanted to do to this pup...

"N...not a pup."

"Are too. My pup. Mine. Every inch. Gonna show you."

Max buzzed against him, the energy electric. Growling loudly, Ulf took a kiss, his hand working that pretty prick. Max whimpered, the sound a mixture of need and denial.

The pup could deny it all he wanted, this was real. This was instinct. This was true.

Ulf kept stroking, determined to make Max come. To rub the scent of his pup's seed into his skin.

"I can't do this," Max cried.

Ulf thought Max could. "You're doing it, pup. You're doing it right now." He rubbed his thumb across the tip again, then pressed against it.

The sting made Max gasp, groan. So Ulf did it again.

"Uhn." Max jerked, expression shocked.

"Sweet pup." Grinning, he rubbed that little cockhead, threatening with his thumb. Max shook his head, and licked his lips, over and over.

With his other hand, Ulf rolled Max's balls. Seed poured over his fingers, hot and wet, the scent heady as hell. Groaning, he spread the come between them, smoothing some into his own belly, and then Max's.

Max swayed, knees almost buckling. His arm went around the lovely body and he pulled Max up to him. "I have you."

"I don't know what's happening. I don't just… I don't do this."

"You just did, Max. You spilled all over our bodies."

Those lean cheeks went a deep, dark red.

"It was good. And now it's my turn."

He got a wide-eyed look, a mixture of desire and fear.

"You got to come," Ulf pointed out.

"You made me!"

"I did." He laughed. "Now you make me."

"You won't tell on me?"

"I'm not telling anyone, pup. It's no one else's business."

"Just once and then I have to go." Max reached for him, fingers trembling.

"We'll see about that. But yes, you should return the favor. It's my due...."

"Your due?" Max's touch made his eyes cross, calluses dragging on his skin.

"As Alpha." His words were hardly more than growls.

"I don't have an Alpha."

"You didn't have an Alpha." Who had hurt his pup so badly that he felt so alone?

"That's what I said."

Max clearly wasn't getting his meaning. "You do have an Alpha now."

"Shh." Max stroked him, base to tip, just once.

"Did you just shush me?" He didn't know if he was amused or angry. Possibly just shocked.

"Uh-huh." Max gave his cock another stroke.

"No shushing." The stroking, however, could continue.

"Mmm." Two more touches, slow, easy, rolled over his hot flesh.

"Drawing it out. I like that." Ulf thought Max was doing a fine job for someone so clearly untutored.

"Uh-huh. Shh."

"You keep shushing me and I'm going to have to start spanking you." He would too.

"No way." Max kept touching, over and over, the strokes getting stronger.

"You don't believe me? Shush me again. Go ahead. See what happens."

Max stared at him, fingers working his prick. He smiled, hips pushing, encouraging the touches. He knew that Max was intending to leave, to run, but he also felt the connection between them, the heat. And just because the pup ran, didn't mean Ulf couldn't give chase.

"More," he told Max, arching into the touches.

Max grabbed hold with his other hand, stroking Ulf's prick steadily. Yeah, that was better. Ulf leaned in, pressing their lips together. Opening Max's lips with his tongue, he breathed into his pup.

The hands around him squeezed, gripped him tight. Flicking his tongue into Max's mouth, he began fucking it, taking it like it was his. Because it was. Max began stroking him in time, jacking him with a fury. He tongue-fucked Max's mouth faster, moaning as those hands kept pace.

It wouldn't be long now. His first orgasm with his pup. Marking his mate with his seed. Oh, that thought burned him to the ground.

He cried out, come spraying from him. Max moaned, and didn't jerk away like he was creeped out. Perfect.

Ulf rubbed his come into Max's belly, making Max smell like him. There. Joined. Marked.

"Mine." The world growled out of him and he met Max's gaze.

Max's pupils dilated, huge and black and

eating up the irises. Ulf didn't back down for a second, continuing to stare, repeating the word in his head again and again.

He'd never expected to have a mate of his own. He was holding on to this one.

CHAPTER THREE

The world was deeply fucked up. Deeply. Max was naked and smelling of sex, his whole universe on sideways. It was beginning to snow too. He needed to get on the road, get moving. Get out of here. The sky was steely grey, the clouds heavy and ominous, and he knew he was going to have to make a move soon or he'd lose his window.

The big body spooned up around him, one arm wrapped around his waist, said that that might be easier said than done. A low snore sounded, Ulf's breath hot on his skin.

Max shivered, and he rolled carefully, body sliding on the blankets. A groan followed his movements, then Ulf began snoring again. He grinned at the sound of Ulf's snores, low like a chainsaw. It was comforting.

It also made him a little jealous. Ulf sounded like he slept as if nothing could ever get him.

Max knew better. There were all sorts of hunters out there. All forms. Human, lupine, they were lurking everywhere. He shuddered, suddenly goosepimply with cold. Okay, time to go.

Ulf tugged him back into the warm body again, fingers petting his skin.

"I have to go, man. I'm on the run." He couldn't stay.

"No, you're staying. Mine."

"I have to. What if someone finds me?" They wanted to keep him beat down, not let him run away and find a life.

"Who's going to find you up here?"

Max shrugged. There were hunters in a hundred forms.

"Who's going to protect you here?" Ulf asked next, hand hard on his hip.

"What?"

"I asked who would protect you here? The answer is me. I was trying to make a point."

"The snow is coming." And it was warm in here.

"It is. It's a sign. You're supposed to stay." There was a very stubborn note in Ulf's voice.

"I don't know where I am." This whole thing felt very ordained and he wasn't sure how he felt about that.

"What do you mean you don't know where you are—you drove yourself here, didn't you?"

He nodded, more than a little embarrassed. He'd been running, exhausted, more than a little out of his mind.

The hold on his hip tightened. "What did you mean?"

"Nothing. Nothing at all."

"We're north. A lot north. Trouble tends not to come this way and when it does, I take care of it. This is my territory."

Max nodded. He got it. This wasn't his place.

"And you're mine. So anyone who comes here

will be driven off. And if they're here for you, that goes double." Ulf growled menacingly.

"Yours? We've known each other an hour."

"You don't feel it?"

Max shook his head, but he couldn't meet Ulf's eyes because he heard something—a deep song that seemed to ring through him.

"Liar." Ulf didn't seem upset about it.

Max's cheeks went red-hot, fiery.

Ulf tugged him close again, nose sliding along his neck, over his shoulder. "You smell so good."

"I haven't... I don't know how to..."

"You going to finish one of those sentences for me?"

"No." No, he was going to run away. He was very good at that.

Ulf snorted. "Well, at least that was honest."

Max sighed softly, not sure what the fuck he was supposed to do. Ulf it seemed, knew, sliding his nose along Max's neck, mouth on his skin.

Oh. Oh, fuck.

Max's balls tightened, the sensation so much more erotic than his own hand on his prick.

Ulf's breath tickled his skin, then it was Ulf's hot, wet tongue. Someone was making a wild keening noise, someone was crying out. Max was pretty sure it wasn't Ulf.

Teeth followed Ulf's tongue, scraping along his neck. His hips snapped, his body suddenly burning, aching. Needing. Ulf's body met his, hot cock rubbing against his ass.

Oh, no. No. He couldn't. That was too much. Too far.

Then Ulf rocked against him again. More bites and licks covered his throat, threatening to drive him crazy. The hand on his hip slid forward to stroke his belly. His toes curled, the pressure in his center growing, tensing his abs.

"Mmm. I can smell your need, Max."

"I'm sorry." See? This was what happened.

That had Ulf chuckling. "Don't apologize, pup. I like it. I want it. You don't have to worry about those fucking assholes who think it's a mistake here."

Max touched one of his scars. They thought it was more than a mistake.

Growling, Ulf followed his fingers. "Who did this to you?"

"The pack." There'd been a cleansing, violent and sudden.

"They'll never hurt you again," Ulf promised, hand stretching to touch all of his belly.

"I can hand…" Oh, fuck, that felt good. "…handle myself."

"But you don't have to."

Ulf's hand slid lower, wrapping around his cock.

That's not what Max had meant. Not at all.

Ulf tugged at his cock, palm sliding along it.

His eyes crossed and he shook his head. "Can't possibly go again."

"Oh, you've had time to rest. I'm sure you can."

Max shook his head and Ulf chuckled. "If you do, you'll stay another day."

Well, he couldn't, so that was a safe deal.

Ulf chuckled knowingly.

That put Max's back up. "Fine. It's a bet."

"That I'm going to win." Ulf stroked him slowly.

"No. I'm done. Tired. Worn out."

"With your mate."

Max snorted. Males couldn't mate. Everyone knew that.

Nobody seemed to have told Ulf, however. He was still working Max's cock, fingers wrapped tightly around him. The man just didn't seem to understand the dangers of doing this.

Kisses pressed across Max's neck—warm, soft, good. That wasn't fair. The skin there was super sensitive and Max couldn't decide whether to offer more or growl and pull away.

Then Ulf's teeth threatened. Max's growl was immediate. Ulf bit down in response, teeth sharp, but not breaking the skin. Max stilled, his brain racing, trapped between defense and intense arousal.

Groaning, Ulf moved his mouth a little bit and took another bite. Max shook his head, his hips moving into Ulf's touch.

"Yes." Ulf rocked against him, cock hot as a brand.

"Please. I don't understand. I've tried to be a good wolf."

Ulf stilled. "We're together. You're my mate."

"Two males can't. That isn't allowed."

"We can and it's allowed here."

His eyes rolled and Max panicked, the mixture of touch and need and the change too much, and he ran. He threw the door open, the ground frigid beneath his feet. He needed to shift or he'd freeze.

He stumbled and rolled, then came up fuzzy, still running in a pure panic, not even sure what he was racing from.

There was a howl behind him and the sound of huge paws on the ground. He ran faster, then faster still. Please. Please. Please.

For a while he thought he'd lost Ulf. Then he realized he was being slowly herded back toward the cabin. The big male didn't growl, in fact the song was more insistent. Solid. Peaceful. Like his capture was inevitable. Like the best thing, the easiest thing to do was give in.

Suddenly the wolf was beside Max, nudging him more firmly. He whined softly, sharing his confusion, his worry. Ulf rubbed against him, muzzle against his. The scent of Ulf's breath was a comfort, warm and right and they kept moving, Ulf rubbing and licking.

His legs were trembling when they entered the cabin and the bedding was so soft, calling to his aching body.

Ulf pushed him into the nest of covers and pillows and began licking him, starting with his nose.

Max moaned softly, rumbling his thanks. The licking continued, Ulf seeming determined to get all of him. Finally Max turned over, exposed his belly. Ulf licked it as well and Max didn't feel vulnerable when it happened, he felt... protected.

Max smelled like Ulf now. Ulf nuzzled in, groaning over Max's belly. He grew warm from the nuzzling and licking, the soft, pleased sounds. His body melted, and he let go, let Ulf hear his peace.

Ulf moved on to his paws, cleaning and warming them.

Such care. He'd never had anyone love on him like that before.

Slowly, he began to nuzzle and lick, play back.

Ulf chuffed, biting at his muzzle. Max groomed Ulf's whiskers, carefully smoothing them. Ulf let him, eyes dropping closed as he enjoyed Max's ministrations.

Together they began to breathe, to sing together. He'd seen others do this, heard them, but he knew it wasn't for him. His kind didn't get this.

Ulf growled softly, nipping his ear. It was as clear as if Ulf has spoken. *Pay attention.*

Max blinked, head tilting.

Ulf's pleasure was clear, and Max's ears were cleaned next. That was ticklish, squirmy. He wriggled around, flailing some. Chuffing, Ulf put a solid paw on his head and kept going. He chewed one of his paws, to distract himself from the maddening tickle.

He could taste Ulf there, on his paw, smell the big wolf on him. It soothed him to the bone, and he felt wrapped in it.

When Ulf was done, he lay close, vocalizing softly, trills and little growls that spoke of pleasure. Max's bones felt heavy, and he grunted a bit as he settled. With Ulf's scent on him and the wolf's muzzle resting against his, it felt like he belonged. It felt a lot like home.

He didn't want to think like that, though. That was dangerous. Still, Ulf made it tempting. Ulf made it hard to ignore.

* * * *

Pleasure clearly made Max nervous, so when he woke again, Ulf bounded up. It was time to go hunt. They were both hungry and there would be plenty of rabbits waiting to be found. And it would be something they could do together, that Max should feel safe doing.

Max rolled up, shook himself hard.

Come on! Come on! The snows were coming! They had to go hunt!

Ulf barked happily when Max followed him out and they headed north together, noses to the ground, searching for prey. He couldn't wait to see how Max hunted, how they would work together.

His mate had an amazing nose, following one trail after another. He let Max take the lead, find them their prey. It would help Max feel like this was home.

Max slowed, nose working hard. Then he stilled for a heartbeat before leaping into a bush. Ulf was ready, cutting around the bush to pick up the rabbit's trail as it shot out of the bush with Max hot on its tail. Oh! Oh, there were two of them, fat and juicy and ready for winter.

Ulf and Max turned right, running together as they chased down the rabbits. Ulf made sure that Max pounced and caught one before he bounded and took down the second. He shook it, killed it and then ripped it open, blood hot and wet on his muzzle.

It was so good. He licked his muzzle, looking to make sure Max had successfully taken down his own meal.

Max brought the heart to him, nosed it over. So polite. Such a good pup. Ulf touched his nose to Max's, then ate the heart up, barked once in thanks before tearing into his rabbit.

Max ate quickly, snapping up the food before burying the carcass and heading off to explore.

The pup had good manners, Ulf would give him that. It made him angry, that Max had been ostracized, hurt because he wanted to mate with a male instead of a female. It wasn't like most packs could support too many fertile couples anyway, not these days.

Putting it behind him, he went after Max, proud to show off his territory. Max proved to be curious, and quick, if a little distractible. Every now and then Ulf would pounce the pretty tail and nip at Max's muzzle, play. So good-natured in his true form, Max never growled or grumbled. He was eager to play, to dance and run in circles to tempt Ulf with his joy.

Ulf had never felt so free, so young.

He could see when Max began to droop, his mate's stamina not what it should be. He herded Max toward the cabin. In this cold, with Max not at full strength, it didn't make sense to stay out here while they rested. Besides, he needed to go out, get Max's bike in somewhere protected, bring in any supplies. He could do that while his mate slept.

It had been a good night, bonding. There would be more like it. Like it and more. So much more.

CHAPTER FOUR

Max slept the sleep of the dead, snoring hard, tail over his nose, warm and settled and so very comfortable. He couldn't stop dreaming. Dreams of running with Ulf. Dreams of… other stuff with the Alpha. He ran from those dreams, they made him nervous. But it was good here. Tempting. And he hadn't had such good dreams in a long time.

He felt a frisson of desire as wicked, naughty fantasies danced through his mind. He could smell Ulf so strongly in his dream, as if the Alpha was right there.

He found the tip of his tail wagging, bouncing off his nose. Ulf's happy chuffing sounded very real. He stretched, his pads spreading wide. The careful licking of his paws was not a dream. He was pretty sure about that.

He vocalized happily, rolling on the blankets. Rubbing up against Ulf. Ulf who called back to him. He head-butted Ulf playfully, rolling over to show his belly. That tongue on his stomach was definitely not a dream.

He let himself wake up, let himself stretch and open his eyes. Dark eyes watched him, Ulf's tongue lolling out.

He wagged carefully, panted. Ulf licked him.
There was no censure, no threat of pain. He relaxed,
resting his chin on his paws.

He muzzle was licked again, lazily, like Ulf just
wanted to taste him. Or make him smell like the big
wolf. Max chuffed softly, hid his nose under his paw.
Ulf knocked his paw out of the way and licked
again.

Oh! Play! He hid his muzzle again.

Ulf knocked his paw away again. Licked, Twice.
So Max blew his lips and rolled over, tail thumping
once.

Making a satisfied sound, Ulf bit at his belly.
Max kicked and wiggled, feeling like a pup.

Chuffing and holding him down with the big
paws, Ulf licked and bit at him, all of it light, all of it
play without a hint of nastiness. He gnawed on Ulf's
paw, just lightly. Ulf batted at him gently, still playing.
Oh, if only the world could stay like this...

Even as he was wishing it, Ulf slowly changed,
the human version of him large and muscled. Not as
beautiful as the wolf, but still. Max leaned in, inhaling
the scent of the human Ulf, filling his lungs.

Ulf rubbed his head, fingers digging into his fur.
Oh. Oh, that was... No human had ever touched him
in this form before.

Ulf hummed, the sound not quite a growl.
"Good, pup?"

He rolled over Ulf's lap, nose nudging the man's
heavy balls, the musk there heady.

Ulf laughed. "Tickles."

Max dared to lick, taste the salt on Ulf's skin. Ulf
tasted so strongly of male.

"If you were your other self, we could do more of that."

He licked again. It was simpler, to be like this, to not have to think.

Ulf spread his legs, and the scent intensified. That was all it took for his eyes to roll up, his body shuddering.

"Come on, Max. Bring me your man."

His ear was tugged, and like Ulf had pulled his human free, he lost his fur, shifting in a rush.

He shivered, but Ulf wrapped around him, body hot, warming him. The slide of skin on skin was an addiction, his cock coming to life all of a sudden.

"You see?" Ulf's mouth covered his, tongue pushing in.

Yes. No. He didn't know. He wasn't sure he had enough sense to care. Ulf's tongue woke up all sorts of things inside him.

One hand wrapped around his hip and tugged him closer, even as he tried to hide evidence of his erection from Ulf. But he couldn't, it knocked up against Ulf, who was also hard.

Ulf's growl sounded happy, satisfied to the bone. The hand on his hip slipped down to grab his ass and he was pulled in even tighter. Then Ulf rolled atop him, hips rocking as they slid together.

One of his hands was grabbed, tugged up over his head and held there as Ulf devoured him. He cried out—not from fear, but from wild need.

"Yes." Ulf growled, the sound settling right in his balls. "Give me your need."

Max shook his head from side to side, his balls tight.

A sharp bite split his lower lip, Ulf then soothing the hurt, sucking on it as the rocking of their hips intensified. Max couldn't stop the sounds that escaped him any more than he could stop the leaking of his cock.

Ulf's mouth moved, sliding on his jaw, down to his neck. The sharp teeth threatened, then sank into his skin, the mark of claiming clear. Max arched, seed spraying from him, spreading between them.

Ulf sucked for a moment longer before moving down Max's body to lap up his come. The act, so unbelievably erotic, had him twisting, sobbing out his need.

When Ulf was done, he took Max's cock into the heat of his mouth, lips tight around it. It was more than anyone could ask, to not buck up, hips driving his still-erect prick into that perfect suction. Ulf's fingers slid over his balls, tugged them gently and the suction grew fiercer, the head of his cock squeezed by Ulf's throat as the man swallowed.

"Please." Max reached down, his feet kicking restlessly.

Ulf came off and kissed his way back up to Max's mouth. "I want you, pup."

He nodded, utterly overwhelmed, caught in his pleasure and his orgasm.

Ulf's knees opened Max's legs, spreading them as Ulf's kisses consumed him. He swallowed, groaned as Ulf stole his breath. Ulf's fingers were busy, sliding on his body. He was touched everywhere, and his nipples pinched. That little sting seemed huge, burning through him.

Ulf's fingers continued on, stroking Max's belly

and cock before tugging on his balls. They ached for more, but Ulf moved on. Max yipped softly, the sound pure wolf. Ulf swallowed his noises, fingers pressing back to his ass and touching his hole.

Oh. Oh, he… Max froze, caught in indecision.

Ulf's teeth caught his lower lip again, sinking in as the big fingers pressed against him. The pain focused him, found him rolling his hips and taking Ulf inside. One finger breached him, slid into him like it belonged there.

He stared into Ulf's eyes, and he could see himself reflected there.

"Mine," Ulf whispered, finger going deep before sliding out again. Then in all the way.

His entire body felt that simple touch, to the bone. The rhythm was undeniable, in and out again, then in and out again, time after time.

It was still a huge shock when Ulf touched something deep inside him that made his entire body go crazy. Max bucked, almost losing Ulf's touch. Growling softly, Ulf grabbed his hip, holding him place as that touch came again. His sob shattered the air, wild and feral.

"Yes. My pup. Mine."

Ulf's finger disappeared, but a moment later it was back, slick now, but wider, two instead of one pushing into him. The pressure burned, scraped along his nerves.

He thought Ulf would tear him, but he stretched, opened up to those fingers and it moments, they were sliding in and out of him with ease. The burn became heat, became pure desire.

When he was rocking up into every thrust of those

fingers inside him, Ulf pulled them out completely.

Max shook his head, cried out. "Please!"

"Needed to make room, pup. I'm not leaving you hanging."

Make room? He was so empty.

Dipping his fingers in oil, Ulf gave his cock a quick swipe, then settled with it against Max's hole. "You are mine."

"You're too big. You can't fit."

"I will. You'll let me in." Ulf nipped at his lower lip again, one hand gripping his hip tight enough Ulf had to be leaving bruises.

Max shook his head, but his body betrayed him, pressing closer to the invading cock. It stretched and stretched him, spreading his hole impossibly. Then suddenly it was inside him, sinking deep and filling him up.

"Help me," he cried, although he could feel his body stretch.

"Breathe, pup. You were made for me." There was no doubt in Ulf's voice, just a calm assurance.

The huge cock continued to move into him, all the way in until Ulf's hips were pressed up tight against his ass. His body fought the intruder, squeezing and fluttering around Ulf.

Bending to his neck, Ulf bit at his throat, marking him once again. Max bore down, squeezing tight and Ulf barked once, teeth sinking in. Shaking his head, Ulf broke the skin, made the mark so deep. Max fought for a moment, lost in panic, but it faded, leaving him at ease. Melted.

Ulf wriggled his hips, the cock inside Max rubbing as it shifted.

"Good pup. So good." Ulf moaned, offering the soft praise. "So tight. So hot."

That was when Ulf began to move, pulling out until just the head was still inside him, then slowly pushing back in again. A soft touch to that spot inside him, multiplied everything by a hundred.

"Please." Max's heart raced, going a million miles an hour.

Ulf did it again, not quite all the way out before filling him all the way up again. Teeth letting go of his skin, Ulf licked at the place where he'd grabbed hold of Max and that burned, so badly.

Then Ulf breathed on it, hips punching the thick cock into him so it banged up against the sweet spot inside. His entire body convulsed, his orgasm slamming through him in a rush.

Ulf put his head back and howled, the sound clear despite the human throat. Max didn't have the air to answer, but he still called out with his heart and soul.

A few moments later, Ulf began moving again, pushing into him over and over. This time the pressure was more reasonable, something less overwhelming. The thrusts were hard and sure, necessary somehow.

"My pup. Waited for you."

Max wasn't sure what Ulf meant, but he nodded.

The speed of Ulf's thrusts increased, the pleasure building with it. His head lifted from the mattress, breath huffing from him. Ulf's lips pressed against his, stealing his air. Their gazes locked, the song inside him swelling impossibly. Max swore he could feel

Ulf's song joining his, even though he knew it was impossible. That was for mates.

Mates.

The word began to grow inside him, pushing at his ribs. Their bodies slammed together, the pleasure coiling tighter and tighter, getting ready to explode. Mates. Mates. Mates.

Max howled, the sound tearing from him. Ulf's voice answered him and they came together, Ulf's come pushing deep inside his body and marking him. His seed marked Ulf in return, spreading over the fuzzy belly. Ulf rubbed it in, then brought his hand up and licked it clean.

Max blinked, dazed and confused, feeling almost drunk. Lying down on him, Ulf pressed him into the covers and pillows. The weight was perfect and Max snuggled in, too stunned to complain.

Ulf rumbled, the sound happy, pleased, as one hand stroked him, keeping him at ease.

CHAPTER FIVE

Ulf felt lazy and happy, at ease in his skin. Such a pretty wolf he had as his own. He'd never expected to find a mate, and now one had been brought to him. Gift-wrapped in denim and leather.

Grinning, he stroked Max's belly. He had so much to teach his mate. So much about pain and pleasure and the things mates could do together. Max chuffed softly and Ulf stroked the nape of Max's neck, fingertips finding a tiny lump. Frowning, he shifted, turning to look as he pushed the hair aside. There was a scar there, a square bump right under the skin.

"What's this, pup?"

"What?" Max stretched, shifted.

"What's this scar from?" It didn't look like the other scars Max's body carried.

Max reached back, touched it. "I haven't the foggiest idea."

Ulf went and opened the drapes wider. Then he returned to his mate, turning Max's head into the light. "It looks surgical."

"I've never had surgery before."

"Well this scar begs to differ." It was a mystery.

And it felt wrong. He rubbed his fingers over the spot again. It was hard and square. That wasn't natural. The wolf in him tried to rise up, wanting to tear it out. He scraped it with his fingernails instead.

"Ow!" Max glared at him. "That hurts."

"Sorry. It's… it doesn't belong. My wolf wants to bite it out."

"That would really hurt."

"I didn't say I was going to do it. I just… I don't like it." At all. He had to fight the urge to remove it very hard.

"Sorry." Max stood up on shaky legs, hand on the back of his neck.

"It's nothing of your doing, pup." There was no way Max could have done it, not behind his neck like that. The thing was too neat, stitches too precise.

"No. No, is it a bug?"

"Like a tick?" Ulf shook his head. "It isn't natural."

"Take it out! I don't want something inside me."

"You sure?" He was already up, though, finding a knife and a match to sterilize it.

"I don't want something inside me," repeated Max.

"Yeah, I don't either." He came back and nodded at the kitchen chair. "Sit."

"Okay. Okay." Max jittered, arms and legs bouncing.

"It's going to hurt." He was going to have to cut it out.

"Just be quick."

"Okay, lean your head forward." He pushed Max's hair out of the way.

"I can't believe I'm letting you do this."

"I can. This is something unnatural, of course you want it out." He sterilized the knife. "Take a breath." That was all the warning he gave before slicing open the skin over the lump.

Max sucked in a quick breath, but he stayed still, trusting. Using the tip of the knife, Ulf worked it under the edge of the thing and flipped it up and out of Max's neck. The little thing landed on the floor.

"What is it? Is it a bug?"

"I told you it wasn't anything natural." He bent and picked it up with the tip of his knife. "It's something electronic."

"Electronic?" Max stood up, hand slapped against the back of his neck.

"Yeah." Ulf held it close to his face to look at it, but all he knew was it was something manmade that looked like it should be in a computer. "It's a fucking piece of electronics."

"I. Kill it. Kill it." Max sounded almost hysterical.

Laying it on the table, he rammed the knife through it. "What the hell?"

Max shook his head, eyes huge, fear pouring from him.

"Who did this to you?" Ulf went over and got a hammer, bringing it back and smashing the thing. "Who are you?"

Max blinked, then he paled. "I'll go. I'm sorry. I knew I wasn't meant to find a place."

Ulf grabbed Max's arm, shaking his head. "I didn't mean it that way. I meant who are you that they would tag you? That's for like royalty, rich folks."

"I'm no one. I ran in Miami."

Ulf had heard rumors about Miami, about control-freak Alphas and crazy-ass elders. They were like a religious cult more than a pack. "I've heard stories. You think they'll chase you down and try to bring you back even though they clearly don't want or respect you?"

"Maybe this time they'll just kill me." Max finished pulling his clothes on, one hand sticky with blood.

Ulf growled, getting a towel and beginning to clean both the hand and Max's neck. "They'll have to go through me this time. This is my land—you're my mate. Nobody messes with either of those."

"I can't stay. What if they hurt you?"

"You're not leaving. And I'm not letting them take you." If he got hurt defending his own, he got hurt. He wasn't letting Max twist in the wind here.

Max shivered, trembled against him. Sweet pup. Silly, but dear.

"We're mated now. You know that means I'll always be able to find you, that I'm not complete without you here with me." He knew Max didn't believe that males could be mates, but Ulf knew better.

"I have to save you, protect you," Max countered.

That made him smile. Max might not believe it, but the pup had all the right instincts.

"Then you'll stand with me and we'll fight together." He stroked the line of his pup's spine, lips on Max's throat. His pup had dealt with so much, so many things in such a tiny amount of time. But they would deal with whatever came for them together, standing as one, and he would give Max a good life.

He sucked on his mark on Max's neck, darkening it.

Max whimpered softly. "Have to go..." The hands that held him were tight, clinging, belying Max's words.

"Don't you dare. I will hunt you down and drag you back where you belong." This was the one for him. And they had the weather on their side too. "The roads will be impassible soon." After a few more weeks they would be untouchable for months.

The expression that crossed his pup's face was one of unbelievable hunger. Someone wanted to find a place to light, to find where he belonged, as much as Ulf needed Max to. He took Max's mouth, tongue invading as he made silent vows to protect his pup.

He pushed the heavy leather coat off Max's shoulders, hands sliding over his pup's arms. Max pushed into the kiss, gratifyingly desperate for him. Sucking on Max's tongue, he pushed his fingers beneath Max's shirt, stroking the beautiful abs.

That's right, pup. Feel me. Together, they would defend their land from anyone.

He could feel Max's prick firming, pushing up against him, trying to get to him through Max's jeans. There. There. He smiled, groaned softly as he let himself wallow in Max's desire.

He tugged Max's shirt up over his head and let his fingernails drag down along Max's chest. He flicked the little nipples as his fingers went by them. Max wriggled a bit, reached for his hands. He let Max have them, curious as to where Max wanted them.

Max brought them up, kissed them, one at a time.

His heart melted. His pup was a dear, sweet wolf.

He drew Max into the blankets, the furs that made their nest. They were safe here. Easily defended. They could lose themselves in each other here.

Taking Max's mouth again, he worked off his mate's jeans, getting the sweet body as naked as his own once more. Then he rolled Max beneath him, still devouring Max's mouth.

"I'd just managed to get dressed," Max murmured, between kisses.

"Clothes are overrated." They didn't need them indoors and he rarely left the cabin without wearing his wolf.

And was that a laugh? Was his pup relaxing enough to laugh?

Grinning, he bit at Max's lower lip. The little jerk he got was gratifying.

He pulled the covers around them, creating a sweet cocoon, in their nest where the air was scented with them.

Max's legs spread for him and Ulf settled between them, rocking them together. Their cocks bumped and slid, squished between their bellies. Max wasn't fully erect yet, proof of his pup's worry, but they were getting there.

He found his mark on Max's throat and licked at it a few more times. His. Max was his. Every inch. The moon had provided.

Groaning, he moved to nip at the small little bits of flesh that hardened in between his lips. Max chuckled, the sound husky and rough. Smiling, he used his teeth, not biting down hard, but letting Max feel them. Giving his pup a thrill.

When his pup reached down and pinched his nips in response, Ulf's eyes widened. Half groaning, half growling, he bit at Max's other nipple. Max stiffened, but responded to the bite with a harder pinch. Chuffing, a delighted shiver going through him, Ulf kissed his way back to the first nipple, worrying it between his lips.

He could feel Max's heart pounding, slamming against the man's ribcage. His pup's prick was growing harder by the second and Ulf wrapped his hand around it, encouraging more.

"I ache inside." The whisper was partially shocked, perhaps a bit ashamed, but mostly curious.

"I'll make the ache become almost unbearable, and then I'll ease it. I swear."

"I let you take me, fuck me. I came."

"And we're going to do it again," Ulf promised. "That and more." So much more. They would have all winter with nothing to do but play and love on each other.

He reached down and touched the tiny, swollen ring of muscles, knowing that it would be so sensitive. Max moaned for him and he stroked it again.

"We shouldn't…" Max whispered.

"One day you'll believe that my cock is your right."

"My right?"

"Yes. It's yours—made for you, to bring you pleasure." He stroked that swollen hole again. "You'll beg for it, crave the sensation of being filled."

Grabbing lube, he got his fingers good and

slippery, then played with Max's hole again.

"I... I ache." Max offered the words to him.

Ulf knew. Nodding, he pressed his middle finger into Max, the lube making everything slick and easy. The cool touch would feel good, too. He added more lube and pressed in a little deeper, fucking Max with just the one finger. Max moaned softly, legs restless against the blankets.

"Spread your legs for me, pup. Let me in." With his free hand, he pushed on Max's knee, guiding the movement.

Max moaned, the sound so deep, and Ulf had to fight the urge to howl. He took a kiss instead, pushing that compulsion and the emotion behind it into Max's mouth. Max whined, head shaking from side to side, hips rolling up to meet his touch. Such a sweet pup, conflicted, but getting better at following his instincts.

Ulf pressed another finger in with the first, going slowly, carefully, remembering that this was only Max's second time. Max cried out, but the sound wasn't pained, raw. No, that was need.

Sending his fingers deep, Ulf managed to push up against the little pleasure gland. Max's eyes went wide, began to glow. Ulf hit it again and again, focusing on doing that instead of stretching Max open. He could see the arousal, smell it on the air, and he growled happily.

Grabbing Max's hand, he put the lube in it. "Get me ready to take you."

When his pup hesitated, he pushed in hard, hitting Max's gland roughly. That earned him a jerk, a low cry, and lube spurting out onto trembling fingers.

"All you need to do now is touch me, pup." He

wrapped his own free hand around Max's heat and stroked. "Make me feel as good as I'm making you feel."

"Touch you." Max could do that. Ulf saw the eagerness in the way that Max reached for him.

"That's it." He groaned as Max's hand wrapped around him, his pup's touch so welcome.

Max stroked him from base to tip, once, twice, then again. The way was smooth, slick from the lube still coating Max's fingers and he pumped his hips, encouraging more. All the while he banged against Max's gland with his fingers, wanting his wolf mad with need. He would make his pup howl for him.

Moving in again, he rubbed their noses together, breathing in deeply to pull the smell of Max into his lungs. There was nothing as good as this—as the scent of sex and mate and home.

When Max started whimpering with need, Ulf pushed harder, wanting more. Max's thumb dragged over the slit in his cock, a low cry sounding.

"Yes!" Ulf could come like this, spill over Max's hand, his need was so great. He made himself hold back, though. He wanted to be buried inside his mate. He wanted to stretch that tiny hole, spill himself inside. "Tell me you want me."

"I want you." Max's words were worried, but immediate.

Yes! Ulf put his head back and howled as he slid his fingers away.

"Don't go…" Max's fingers tightened around his cock.

"I can't have my fingers and my cock in you at the same time."

Grinning wildly, he set his cock at Max's hole and pressed in. The sheath of Max's body accepted him, wrapped around him and held him tight. He stayed buried for a long moment, looking into Max's eyes and the whole world went away.

Mate.

The thought was total, encompassing, and it came from Max. Ulf howled again, letting the air carry his pure joy at that.

Then he began to move, thrusting into Max's perfect heat over and over. His thoughts shattered, the wolf there, rejoicing at his mate. They rutted together, Max beginning to meet Ulf's thrusts, to participate.

Yes. Yes, pup. Just so.

Howling again, Ulf sped up his thrusts, his hips moving double time. Neither of them spoke, there was nothing to say. He got his hand around Max's erection, tugging in time with every thrust he made.

Come with me, mate. There was joy, pouring through him, through Max. He could feel it.

Ulf squeezed the head of Max's cock, rubbing his finger across the tip. That perfect ass milked his cock, the squeezing starting a second before Max began to shoot. Ulf howled again, the sound sustained as he came, filling Max with his seed. Marking his pup from the inside.

He would need to find a dildo, a plug, something smooth as glass to hold his seed inside Max's body. The thought made a bit more come spurt from him.

Groaning, he collapsed onto Max, panting against his pup's throat. He nuzzled, licking and nibbling so that the fine skin stayed sensitive.

"That's what it means to be mine, Max."

"Only yours."

"Only mine," Ulf agreed, growling. He would not let anyone else lay claim, let alone take his mate.

"And you?" Max asked.

He met Max's gaze. "I am your mate. Yours alone."

Max's face shifted, the wolf so close. His own wolf was eager to respond, so he slipped out of Max's body, letting the wolf have him.

Max panted, head down between his shoulders. He licked at Max's muzzle, rubbed them together. Max nuzzled back, obviously hungry for connection, reassurance. He bit and teased, giving Max his full attention.

This was his pup, his mate. The center of his world. He was glad Max was finally here.

CHAPTER SIX

The snow was falling and Max knew his bike needed to be protected, so he headed down when Ulf was napping to bring it closer. There was no way to ride it now, so he'd just push it up the makeshift road. There were things they could use in his pack too. When he got to where he'd hidden the bike, though, it was gone.

Damn it. Damn it. Had someone stolen it? Had the pack found him?

The snow was only just beginning to cover the ground, so he checked the area closely, finding tracks from the bike, headed back the way he'd come. He growled softly, beginning to follow the trail. He had to protect his mate.

The trail he followed lead him right toward the cabin, like whoever had taken it knew exactly where they were going. Max ran faster, not wanting to take the time to undress, shift.

Ulf met him along the trail, wolfed out and snapping and snarling, Ulf's worry for him clear.

"Someone took my bike and came here toward you."

The big wolf shook his head from side to side,

grabbed Max's wrist in his mouth and headed the way back toward the cabin — the same direction he'd been headed in while following the faint trail of his bike.

Max went with Ulf, heart pounding. "I thought they might be here. I worry."

Ulf stopped to lick at his fingers, then loped to a tiny shack about fifty yards from the cabin that Max hadn't noticed before. It was well hidden and he'd only left the cabin a couple of times, flat out running away the one time, and hunting for prey the other.

The cabin was locked with a big chain, but Ulf brought him over to a tree with a little hole in the trunk that held a key.

"Oh. Oh, did you bring my bike here?" That was at once the best possible answer and one he hadn't considered.

Ulf breathed out noisily and moved to stand at the door, waiting for him to open the lock on the chain.

Max unlocked the lock with cold fingers, working the chain open. Inside was his bike, along with an SUV that looked a little like a tank. There was also a shovel, an axe and other tools. In the back were stacks of bottles of water and cans of food.

"Oh. Well, I have a little I can add," he offered, feeling little more than relief.

Ulf shifted, one moment the big wolf next to him, the next a handsome, naked man.

"Emergency supplies," Ulf told him. "I usually make do hunting, drinking from the river, but it's good to know these are here in case they're needed."

"Sorry. Sorry, I was worried about you." It was

still nagging him, that he could have brought trouble to Ulf. That he still might.

"I moved your bike when you were sleeping the other night. I forgot to let you know."

He nodded and grabbed Ulf, hugged him. Thank the moon.

Ulf wrapped around him, shivered. "Your clothes are cold." Then Ulf grinned. "You have an unnatural love of them."

"I have a fondness for not freezing my nuts off." He was beginning to learn how to play.

Laughing, Ulf kissed him. "I'll keep your nuts warm."

His testicles were cupped, the touch firm, rough, enough to make him go up on tiptoe.

"Come on. We have a perfectly good spot in front of the fire and this snow is not going to end any time soon," Ulf told him.

"Will there be more?" It was just the beginning of winter, right?

"More snow? Are you serious? The road will become impassible. We'll be snowed in for months."

"I'm from Miami." This was his first winter.

"Right. No snow. Well, if we have a typical winter it'll be up to the top of the windows around the cabin.

That wasn't possible. No way. That wasn't even comprehendible. Ulf had to be pulling his tail.

Ulf chuckled. "You'll see. It's normal here. There'll even be game throughout. Deer, rabbits, foxes. And we'll be warm together in front of the fire."

Ulf turned him and led them back toward the

cabin. Max nodded and followed along, his heart pounding as he focused on Ulf's ass. It was an amazing ass, and what a treat, to be able to watch it as the muscles moved, no one around to have to hide his admiration from.

He reached out, stroked with one finger. Ulf turned toward him, a wolflike sound of pleasure coming from his throat.

"It's okay?" Max had meant no offense and he didn't think he'd caused any.

"It's better than okay, pup. It's wanted." Ulf gave him another wide grin and slid into the cabin.

Max stomped his boots clean, then removed them, hanging his leather jacket up to dry. Ulf's hands were on him immediately, plucking at the rest of his clothing.

Max chuckled. "Clothes are good." Especially with all the snow that was supposed to be coming.

"Totally unnecessary."

For someone who disliked clothes so much, Ulf sure knew how to get them off a man very efficiently and Max found himself naked in moments, vibrating as he stood there, bare to Ulf's sight. Bare and hard.

"Have you ever been sucked, my mate?" Ulf asked.

Max arched, fingers wrapping around his prick, the words unbearably erotic.

"No." Ulf grabbed his hand and pulled it away. "Sucking is my mouth and your cock."

He bucked, his body out of his control.

Grinning wickedly, Ulf sank to his knees, mouth right there by Max's erection.

"I'll... Like a teenager." Right into Ulf's mouth.

"Like a man with his mate," Ulf corrected, mouth wrapping around him, Ulf pulling him in.

Max wasn't going to last. No way. It was impossible. Ulf's lips were tight around his cock, head bobbing down as Ulf took him in deep.

"Mate!" Max arched, his balls emptying like he had no control, just as he'd predicted.

Ulf drank him down, still sucking until he'd finished jerking and shuddering. Then Ulf pulled off, licking his lips. "See? Clothes get in the way of things like that."

Max's legs were trembling. "Uh. Uh-huh."

"Come to bed." Ulf stood and took his hands, tugging him to the nest in front of the fireplace.

"Yes..." Something made a noise outside. *Something.* "Ulf?"

Ulf growled softly, one hand up. Max could smell Ulf's wolf, right there, ready to take over.

"Someone's here." Max knew it. He shifted immediately, body going fuzzy as he became his wolf.

A moment later Ulf was with him, nudging him toward the back of the cabin. When he hesitated, Ulf growled and pushed him harder.

He snapped. No. No, if they were here, they wanted to hurt him, not Ulf.

Ulf bit at his paws, insistent. *Safety.*

He growled, but followed Ulf's urging, his head moving side to side as he fought to hear what was going on.

There was a tunnel hidden at the back of the cabin and they slipped through it, loping along until suddenly they were out in the trees well beyond the cabin.

Oh, better. Max moved, running with Ulf. They circled the cabin, doing reconnaissance. There were three of them—wolves like him, nowhere near the size of Ulf.

Ulf quickly circled the cabin, then looked at him, nodding toward the right, then swinging his head left.

Yes. Yes, mate. Max understood. He went to the right, moving silently.

At Ulf's howl, he leapt for the closest wolf, trusting that he wasn't fighting alone this time. Ulf had his back, his fur and his tail.

In the time it took him to dispatch of the wolf he'd attacked, Ulf had taken care of the other two. He stood there, panting, breathing hard, his muzzle aching.

Ulf yipped at him and came over, licking at his muzzle, cleaning him.

Mate. Mate. Mate. He finally began to believe it.

Yes.

Mates.

Ulf continued to clean him for a few moments before shifting into his human self. "We need to bury them."

Max shifted too, suddenly freezing, shaken, but refusing to show weakness.

"What will they do when these three don't return?" Ulf spat on the body of the closest wolf.

"I don't think they're anyone I know." He certainly didn't recognize any of them, not by sight or by scent.

"You mean they aren't from Miami?"

"I mean they aren't my pack. Hired hands maybe?"

"Ah. I see. I guess that makes sense." Ulf went to his haunches and began to examine the wolf bodies. "Why won't they just let you go? They don't want you in the pack anyway. I would have thought you took away the problem when you came up here."

"It's more than just not wanting me in the pack. They don't think I should exist and just knowing that I do..." Max shrugged. "I know it doesn't make sense."

"Hatred never does."

"They need the bloodline to be pure." Max had heard that enough times to be able to spout it back.

"It's not like you'll be reproducing."

"I don't think they want to take that chance. Besides, my living is an affront to them. Actually, no, they didn't mind me living so much, as long as I was miserable and in reach to taunt, to use as an example of what happens if you don't follow pack law."

Ulf touched his arm. "That's crazy."

"That's the Miami pack. Nobody's ever accused them of being normal, sane, or fair."

"I still say it's overkill to send people for you."

"There were rumblings among the youngest about how maybe times needed to change," Max admitted. "After the last beating I took nearly left me for dead. I bet dragging me back and giving me a very public execution would keep the rumblers in line."

Ulf snorted and spat on the bodies again. "And people wonder why I left the pack behind."

"I'll go get my boots and a shovel," Max suggested. They couldn't just stand there and look at the bodies for the rest of the day.

"Maybe you should get some pants on, too. So those nuts of yours don't freeze off."

He looked at Ulf, blinked. Was that a joke? Ulf gave him a slow wink.

"I... Okay. Yeah." He didn't know what to do.

"It's going to be okay, Max. The big snow will be here soon. Then no one will be able to touch us."

"I hope so. I'll be right back. You... you still want me to stay?" He'd brought trouble with him, just like he'd thought.

Ulf grabbed his jaw, fingers digging in. "You're mine. I expect you to stay."

"I want to stay. I want to, but I'd understand if I had to go."

"You're my mate. You're staying." Ulf sounded very sure.

Something deep inside Max eased. "I'll get my boots."

"Mine too. We have some graves to dig."

* * * *

After burying the bodies, Ulf had Max help him set traps around the place so they'd be warned sooner if more wolves were sent after his pup. It made him growl, that anyone else thought they had the right to dictate to *his* pup. The snows were coming and the roads couldn't be impassable soon enough for his liking.

Satisfied that they would be warned before they were invaded again, Ulf brought Max into the cabin and lit the fire for them. His pup needed to be warmed up. Max was silent, shaking and shaken, all at once. Once Ulf had the fire built, he tugged Max into the middle of their nest and wrapped around him.

"I'm sorry." Even Max's words shivered.

"What for?"

"Bringing them here."

"You're worth it." Totally. Ulf would do a lot to keep his mate alive and happy.

Max didn't respond, his eyes down.

Ulf put his fingers under Max's chin, tilting his face up. "I will fight a hundred wolves for you. A thousand."

"A thousand...Goddess, don't say that."

"I'm not tempting fate, I'm showing you how important you are to me." Ulf highly doubted even a cult-like pack would be able to send a thousand wolves after one.

"I'm just me. You know that."

"Don't you know how wonderful just you is?" Ulf thought that his pup didn't.

Max didn't answer, only stared at him.

Ulf had no more words. They weren't his best forum anyway. He spent months not talking to anyone. So he leaned in and kissed Max. Hard.

Max's eyes flew open, so wide. Ulf stared into them, giving himself to his mate. He kept kissing until the shame and fear were gone from Max's eyes, until all Max knew was him. Then he began touching. He started with Max's jaw, fingers finding every part of it.

The snow was falling outside, the sky steely and dark, but the cabin was warm, perfect for this, the snow isolating them further.

Ulf kissed his way along Max's arms, then drew them up over his head. Max gave him a curious look, but allowed it without argument. Ulf took both wrists in his hand and kept the muscled little body stretched out for him.

"Ulf?" It was heady, the way Max responded to everything he did.

"Yes, pup?" Ulf flicked his finger across Max's right nipple.

Not answering with words, Max moaned for him, tugged at his grip.

"You're mine and I'm going to make you scream with pleasure." It was a promise.

Max blinked at him, obviously caught in pleasure. So he flicked Max's nipple again, then did it a little harder. That made his pup jerk, pull hard at his hands. Ulf didn't let go, though. This was *his* pup.

"I have things to teach you, Max. So many things." And they had all their lives for him to do it.

Leaning in, he bit at Max's other nipple.

"No biting." Max rolled, fighting to escape him.

"The biting is the best part." He nipped Max's shoulder, his jaw. At Max's lower lip, sucking when he drew blood.

Max's cock was diamond hard against him, heated where it pushed against his hand. He pressed his fingers into Max's slit, watching Max's face and wanting to howl at the expression he found there.

One of Max's legs drew up, the motion immediate and no doubt instinctive.

Dragging the liquid from Max's slit, he laid a trail along the thick cock, right to Max's balls. Max watched him closely, eyes glowing, heated. He rolled each ball in his hand, then stroked back to that little hole. His pup clenched, but the heat in those eyes didn't fade.

Stroking until Max eased, he then pushed his fingertip right in. Max opened for him, body responding beautifully. That was it. This was his pup.

Bending, he pulled his finger away and licked at the little hole instead.

"Ulf!" There was pure need in the sound and Max rolled and went up on hands and knees, offering him that fine ass.

Oh yes!

He spread Max's ass with his fingers and began to lick at Max's hole vigorously. Max cried out, begging him, so eager, so hungry. Rubbing Max's perineum with his thumbs, he tongue-fucked his pup. The scent was perfect, and Max's eager acceptance was more so.

Ulf's fingers dug into Max's flesh. He would leave marks, his marks on his mate's ass. He growled deep, imagining the sight of his handprint on Max's flesh. Fingernails pressing against skin, into skin, he searched to drive Max wild.

His pup howled, pulling away and then pushing back onto his tongue. That eagerness, that's what he wanted, for Max to take his need, to accept it and share it with him. Growling, Ulf flicked his tongue faster, more.

"Please. Please, touch me," Max begged.

"No, you'll come like this first. Without a touch to your cock." He pushed a finger in with his tongue, pressing against Max's gland.

"Ulf!" Max arched, muscles clenching tight.

He grinned for a moment before concentrating on making Max come with his tongue and his finger, from only this.

Max tried to balance, tried to reach for his cock. Growling, Ulf smacked Max's hand, his finger and tongue leaving Max's ass. "No touching yourself."

"Ulf! Mate!"

No. This was his pack. His rules. "I said no touching. I get to choose when you're touched, when you come."

Max didn't respond and Ulf growled, laying down a swat on Max's butt, drawing a low cry.

"Did you hear me, pup?" He was ready to swat Max's amazing ass again if he didn't get a response.

"Yes! Yes, I heard, you ass!"

He smacked Max's other butt cheek for that. "It's Master ass to you."

Max cried out again, but didn't pull away. Ulf carefully licked at Max's ass, moving slowly toward tongue-fucking his pup again. He added a few, gentler slaps, warming the skin. The backs of Max's thighs also received a couple of swats, the skin just very lightly pink. Then he pushed his tongue back into Max, ramping things back up now that the rule of no touching had been laid down.

Max pushed back into him, eager for the thrusts, for the swats.

Good pup.

Ulf worked his finger back into Max, finding his gland again.

"Please." Max shook his head, back and forth.

He knew what Max wanted, what his pup needed. "You're going to come like this," Ulf reminded Max, hitting that spot again. He used his free hand, swatting steadily, gently. "Answer me, pup."

"Yes. Yes, mate."

That was more like it.

Ulf pushed his tongue in with his finger, working that little hole and soft sounds filled the air, Max wild for him. He drove his mate higher and higher, finger touching Max's gland every second, tongue keeping everything slippery and wet, intense.

Max gripped down, squeezing him like a fist. Ulf knew Max was close, so he swatted that amazing ass again, pushing his tongue in hard.

The sting seemed to push Max over the edge, the scent of male need, of Max's come, heady. Groaning, Ulf kept licking, working the sweet hole. Max began to tremble, muscles jerking and rocking.

Finally, when he felt Max on the verge of collapse, he pulled his finger and tongue out and, in a quick, smooth motion, he rose up and pushed his cock into Max's ass. Grabbing Max's hips, he yanked the tight sheath of Max's body over his prick.

Putting back his head, he howled at the pleasure he found there.

Slapping his hips hard against Max's ass, he let them both sting and feel every inch.

More than just good, this felt right. Powerful.

Ulf worked hard, hips sawing back and forth. Finally, Max began to drive back, meet his thrusts, his need. That's when he wrapped his hand around Max's cock, giving his pup the stimulation he was craving.

"Mate!" Oh, yes. This pleasure should be marked by his name.

He pulled harder on Max's cock, timing it with his thrusts. His pup would come again, and perhaps again today until the only thing Max was worried about was what Ulf was going to do to him next. Ulf would see to it.

His thrusts sped, all his focus on his mate. Max's song—needy and joyous—swirled about him. He joined in with his own, making their home ring. Max shuddered around him, hot and tight.

"We come together this time, when I say."

"Together. Together, please." Max begged so very prettily.

"When I say." Which was going to be any second now—he was as close as Max was.

"Yes. At your will."

The words made him growl, and latch onto Max's nape with his teeth. He bit hard and made sure the mark was deep. He let go only to give the order. "Come now." He slammed in hard, jostling Max's heavy balls.

His own come poured from him as the scent of Max's filled the air once more.

Sweet pup.

Ulf lapped at the bite on Max's nape. That was his, his mark, his way of showing others that Max belonged to him. He nipped again, humming low. He pressed Max down into the ground, staying right there with his mate, his cock rested inside the perfect heat, holding his seed within.

"Mate." Just the one word with a soft growl. He had faith that Max would understand that meant everything.

Max reached up, twined their fingers together and squeezed. Oh yes. His mate understood.

Now all they needed was for the snow to come before anyone else could invade their territory.

CHAPTER SEVEN

Max ran the perimeter twice a day—once at night and once in the morning. The ground was covered in snow, but not enough, not deep and he knew they would come again. Knew it. Ulf didn't tell him not to patrol, and even came with him now and then. That told him he wasn't the only one who believed more wolves would be sent to take him.

He ran hard, driving through the cold, searching the road, the trees. Ulf was chopping more wood and Max was eager to get back to the cabin, to watch that stunning body move.

Something moved in the trees, catching his attention, and he stopped, vibrating from nose to tail. Then came another movement, this time from the other side of him and there was a noise from straight ahead.

He was surrounded.

He had enough time to howl, to sound the alarm before a needle sank deep into his shoulder and the world went black.

Mate! Mate, run!

* * * *

The moment he heard Max's howl, Ulf dropped the ax and shifted, not even waiting to remove his clothing first. It was easy enough to shuck as he ran. Moving quickly, he headed in the direction of Max's call.

His mate's voice went silent, missing from his mind so quickly that he stumbled. He knew he had to be careful, so the moment he became aware of a foreign scent, he stopped, nose in the air. There were four this time and in human form as well as wolf. And something chemical, wrong.

Fear stabbed through him. No. No, he would not lose his pup, his beloved mate. His own. Max had only just come to him and he would prove his worthiness by saving Max from this attack and keep him safe for eternity.

Moving slowly, carefully, Ulf found the place where the interlopers had attacked his mate. One wolf and three men, though he could tell the men were shifters as well. He wasn't letting them have his mate, no matter what tricks they used.

Moving silently, he followed the trail back to the road where he found the tracks of a four-wheel-drive vehicle. Damn it!

Ulf had to make a choice, run after the vehicle, or go back for his own SUV? He didn't like either choice very much. He would much rather just meet them head on, right now. Of course, they would have to move slowly until they reached the bridge.

The bridge. The bridge! He ran as hard as he could, ignoring the road. If he could get to the river gorge bridge and pull the boards from the end, they'd have to stop. They might even turn around thinking the road actually led somewhere.

When he got to the bridge, he found the tracks coming across, but the snow was falling and there were no new tracks to indicate they'd returned this way yet. Cheering, he shifted to get the job of dismantling a portion of the bridge done.

It was fucking freezing, but he didn't care, using all his strength to pull up enough boards that a vehicle couldn't make it over the bridge. He was pretty sure three would be enough to make a hole big enough for the invader's vehicle's wheels, but just to be sure, he removed four. Then he hid the boards behind the thick bushes that bordered the bridge.

There. There. This was his home. His world. His mate. He would never allow interlopers to take what was his.

Shifting once again into his wolf form, he slunk behind the cover of some trees, waiting for the assholes who'd taken his mate to get there. When they got out to investigate, he would make his move.

A Jeep came trundling down the road, squealing to a halt as the driver saw the broken bridge, the wheels stopping just before the hole. That had been close.

From here, though, Ulf could see through the Jeep's windows and he could see Max's body bound in the back, rolling back and forth. Unconscious? Dead? Bound so tightly he could not control himself from the Jeep's movements?

Ulf wanted to snarl and growl, but he forced himself to stay quiet, to observe and wait for his chance. His mate was not dead. He would not accept that answer.

Why would they come for Max if not to return him to Miami? Ulf decided that Max was just waiting for a chance to escape.

Two of the humans stepped out of the Jeep, standing around, looking for him he presumed, and for the boards.

Ulf had to wait, had to be patient and choose his moment well. There were four of them and at the moment, two were still in the vehicle with his mate.

"Guys. Guys, come help." One of them waved the others over to where the bridge met the road, its missing boards leaving a large gap.

"What about Max?" asked one of the others.

"What about him?" the first one asked. "He's secure, yes?"

"Yeah. He's out for the count."

Ulf's lip curled and he had to hold back another angry snarl. Patience would serve him well here. Patience would free his mate.

The four assholes all went over to the hole in the bridge, gesturing and arguing with each other, voice raised slightly.

If he ran for them, Ulf could maybe knock two over the edge before they even knew he was there. It was a bold plan, but would cut his enemies in half.

Mate.

Ulf heard the soft whisper.

Mate.

Max! I'm here!

Mate. I can't move.

Ulf wasn't sure he could take all four by himself, not and escape with Max if Max couldn't move. It was then he noticed the Jeep was still idling. And there it was. The solution he needed.

He'd take the Jeep and strand the men. Then, once he'd freed Max, they could fight the four together. He could see that Max was already fighting hard to free himself, fighting to get loose and make a stand.

Keeping his wolf form in case he was seen and needed to make an escape, Ulf crept silently toward the Jeep. He made it to the side of the vehicle without being noticed, the men at the bridge still arguing, voices louder, more angry now.

Shifting into his man form, he opened the Jeep's door and slipped in. He managed to get it in gear and moving before anyone noticed. Max was flopping and biting now, working the ropes.

Ulf backed up in reverse for a dozen or so yards, then turned the Jeep and floored it, one of the men managing to jump and grab onto the back of the Jeep as they sped away.

Refusing to slow down despite the narrowness of the road, he bumped along, the asshole clinging to the back being thrown around. Perfect. Ulf could take one on easily. That would bring their numbers to three.

Ulf made it nearly back to where he'd first discovered the Jeep's tracks before he slammed on the brakes and leapt out, shifting mid-air. Snarling, he went for the man still clinging to the back of the vehicle.

Out of the corner of his eyes, he saw Max pop free enough to shift, diving for the back seat.

Ulf took his target down, going for the jugular and opening the intruder's throat. Snarling, he stepped up, his front paws on the man he'd taken down.

Max came around the Jeep with a dart gun in hand, growling deep in his chest, glaring at the dead guy at Ulf's feet.

Shifting, Ulf again ignored the cold. "Three more, back at the bridge, headed this way." He nodded at the dart gun. "We take one of them out with that and send him back with a warning." The other two were not going to make it. He would see to that.

"Yes." Max nodded immediately. "I have had enough. No more."

Good. It was about time his mate stood up for himself against the people who'd hurt him, and who wanted to keep on hurting him. "Let's go get them."

Before they could decide whether they were driving or shifting and running, the three remaining wolves from Miami burst out of the woods around them. Max shot immediately, hitting one of the wolves in the chest, felling him. One down, two to go. The odds had just come firmly into their favor.

Snarling, Ulf leapt at the closest of the two wolves left, once again going straight for the jugular. Meanwhile, Max shot again, but nothing happened, so when the other wolf leapt, Max swung the gun like a bat.

Tearing out the neck of the wolf he'd brought down and making sure his mark was dead, Ulf then turned to make sure his mate didn't need assistance.

The other body—either dead or badly injured— lay there, Max panting, caught between wolf and man.

Ulf shifted and called to Max, needing his mate

human so they could deal with the one intruder they'd let live. He went and stroked the furry head, knowing that kind of mid-transformation was painful, and hard to finish.

Max managed, bruised and drugged, but his mate did it, shedding the last vestiges of his wolf and finding his fully human form.

"Good pup." Ulf drew Max in and kissed him hard.

Max leaned, shivering violently. "What do we do?"

"We tie the one we spared up and put him in the Jeep, go back and fix the bridge. Then we send him across it with a message. If they can't leave us alone, we'll go back and take care of the Alpha there."

"Then we pull the boards from the bridge again," Max told him.

His pup was smart.

"You got it. If we hide the boards, we can still use the bridge when we need it, but nobody else can." There would be occasions where they'd want to go to civilization and stock up on things.

Max nodded. "Please. I'm done running."

"That's what I like to hear."

Max helped him drag the bodies to the back of the Jeep and load them in, but his mate was moving slow.

"Stay with me, Max." Ulf shook Max's arm.

"Trying, mate."

"I know. We need to get this done before you can rest, though." Sleep would work the drugs out of Max's system, but they had to do this first, make their home safe.

"Yes. Yes, we need it done."

Nodding, Ulf climbed into the jeep. "Why don't you shift until we get back to the bridge?" The wolf healed better, would get rid of the poison in Max's body more quickly.

Max crawled up into the seat next to him, shifting almost immediately.

Ulf rubbed his hands in Max's fur, fingers digging in. "Such a beautiful pup."

Max whined softly, leaned in. He rubbed his cheek along Max's muzzle. He could feel Max's urgency, though, his pup's worry.

"We're going to get through this, pup. We're going to protect ourselves for good."

Max nodded, and they headed down the road, Max shifting again to help him once they got back to the bridge. Ulf hated this, hated how every change was slower, more painful for Max.

He worked extra hard and as quickly as he could to restore the boards on the bridge. It wasn't perfect, but it should hold and he would be on his own when he came back, only the weight of his wolf to strain the loose boards.

When it came time to drive the Jeep to the other side, he told Max to stay. "Rest here, mate. While I get these assholes and the Jeep on the other side of the bridge. A Jeep full of dead wolves and a wounded man licking his wounds should send a fine message to the Miami pack Alpha.

Max shook his head. "I'm coming with."

"I'd worry less if you stayed here."

"I know, but we'll work faster together," Max insisted.

Ulf growled, but it was true. "Fine. We go across the bridge together."

"Together. Let's go."

Ulf drove the Jeep slowly across the bridge, the loose boards holding them. He continued to be careful as the wood had been made slippery by snow. On the other side, he parked the Jeep several yards down and they sat there for a moment, staring at each other.

"I want to send it over the edge, but if we don't send a message, I'm worried they'll just keep trying." Ulf would defend against anyone who did come, but it would be nice to know their message had been received and he wouldn't have to do it every few days.

In the end, they left the dead wolves in the back of the Jeep and dragged the unconscious man into the front seat, putting him behind the wheel and leaving the keys in the ignition.

"Is there anything to write with?" Ulf asked. Both he and Max were naked. He'd hate to have to leave the Jeep here and risk the man waking up before they got back with paper and a pen.

"Look in the glove compartment," Max suggested.

Ulf did and sure enough, there was a pen and a couple of maps, one of which could be used to write on.

"These were your people. What kind of language do we need to use?" He knew what he wanted to say, but that wasn't necessarily what he should say. Max would know.

"I'll do it." Max grabbed the pen and simply wrote, "NEVER AGAIN. LEAVE ME ALONE. I AM NOT PACK. MAX."

"Nice." There was no mistaking that message.

"Clear enough?" Max asked him.

"Very clear."

He pinned the note to the man's chest with the dart that had pierced the guy's neck, then closed the door of the Jeep. That was it. Ulf didn't think they could have done anything more.

"Okay." He nodded firmly. They were good. "Home."

"Home. Home, please." Max nodded slowly, his body clearly growing weaker, giving into the drug that demanded he sleep. "As soon as the bridge is removed."

"Yeah. We need to make sure our home is safe."

Ulf shifted, his wolf padding out across the bridge. Max followed, and when they got to the end, they removed one plank after another. They took out more than the four he'd originally done. Ulf taking three away, tossing them back to Max, then leaping across to the road. From there, he took the last four away, making the gap seven wide. Surely that would keep anyone from crossing successfully.

Together, he and Max hid the wooden planks, spreading them out in groups of two beneath the brush. The snow would hide them and only he and Max knew where they were.

Finally convinced they were safe until spring, Ulf shifted, encouraging Max to do the same, then got them moving back toward the cabin. It was a long way to go on foot and Max wasn't at top speed, but Ulf continued to snap at Max's heals and keep him moving.

The snow was falling harder, and night had fallen

when Max finally stopped, refusing to go on. Ulf pushed his mate beneath the shelter of a fir and wrapped around him. It wasn't so cold they couldn't make do here tonight.

Go, mate. Go home.

Like he was leaving Max here on his own. Together, they could stay warm enough.

When Ulf refused to leave without Max, his mate forced himself to stand again. *Home. Home. Home.*

Ulf barked in approval, so proud of his mate. If Max would go with him, they would go home rather than stay in the relative shelter of the trees. He nipped at Max's heels, making him move faster.

They did make it, barely, Max collapsing on the doorstep. It was far enough, though.

Shifting, Ulf grabbed his mate and dragged Max to their bed. Once there, he lit the fire, making sure it was blazing, then he shifted again and laid himself around his pup, protecting Max from anything that decided to come their way.

CHAPTER EIGHT

Max slept and slept, the drugs working their way through his system. He dreamed the wildest things, but the constant in the dreams was that he was searching for his mate. For Ulf. Sometimes Ulf was close enough Max could smell him, other times, Ulf was well beyond his reach.

He sighed, barking, running and calling. *Mate. Mate. Matematemate!*

There was a sharp bark and something wet dragged across his face.

Mate! Ulf, is that you?

Another bark sounded, this one close. Loud.

Mate. Need. He reached out, fingers finding fur. "Ulf!"

Ulf licked his muzzle in one fell swoop.

Oh. Oh, yes. Max opened his eyes, feeling gritty and raw.

Ulf was right there, though, the magnificent wolf cleaning him.

"Ulf. Mate."

Ulf barked for him, the sound happy, pleased.

"Oh. Oh, I need something to drink. Water." He needed to get up.

Ulf shifted for him, the handsome wolf turning into a stunning man. "I'll get it for you."

Max pushed up onto his elbows. "Have I slept long?"

"Two days." Ulf padded over to the storage pantry and grabbed him a bottle of water.

"Wow." Max took the bottle, surprised at how his hands shook.

Ulf took the water back and opened the bottle for him before crouching next to him. "I was worried about you, about what they poisoned you with."

"Yeah. Yeah, I dreamed about you. No one else has come?" Had the snows gotten deeper?

"No one has come. I've taken up your patrolling. Our territory is untouched."

"Good." He drank deep, so thirsty.

Ulf's hands stroked his belly. "You're feeling better? More normal?"

"More awake."

Chuckling, Ulf kept touching. "I'm so proud of you, mate."

"Proud of me?" Max leaned into the touch.

"You fought them, you resisted the poison they injected into you." Ulf looked fierce. "You protected your mate and our lands."

"This is my place too." He knew it. His home, his heart.

"It is." Ulf beamed at him, looking so pleased at his words. "Our territory to defend, to live in, to love in."

"Yes." Max leaned in, breathing in the scent of his mate.

Ulf pressed their mouths together, this kiss not

soft or gentle, but telling him all about the need that sang between them. He gasped, opening eagerly, the rush of energy between them amazing.

Pressing him down into the soft blankets, Ulf made him feel so many things. They weren't as scary now, though. Ulf's love excited him; it didn't frighten him.

He could feel the heat and hardness of Ulf's cock lying against his skin. It promised need and pleasure. He reached down, wrapped his fingers around the heavy shaft, and squeezed.

Groaning, Ulf pushed into his hand. "I want your mouth, Max. I want to feed my seed into you."

Max groaned, toes curling at the words and he leaned back, eager. Moving up his body, Ulf straddled his shoulders and rubbed the tip of his magnificent cock against Max's lips. The motions painted him with Ulf's pre-come, the salty, clear liquid exploding with flavor in his mouth. The flavor of Ulf. Of his mate.

When Ulf pushed in, took possession of his mouth, it was coming home and Max put his head back and howled. Ulf answered, the two sounds mixing together, twisting to become one.

Sean Michael, often referred to as "Space Cowboy" and "Gangsta of Love" while still striving for the moniker of "Maurice," spends his days surfing, smutting, organizing his immense gourd collection and fantasizing about one day retiring on a small secluded island peopled entirely by horseshoe crabs. While collecting vast amounts of vintage gay pulp novels and mood rings, Sean whiles away the hours between dropping the f-bomb and pursuing the kama sutra by channeling the long lost spirit of John Wayne and singing along with the soundtrack to "Chicago."

A long-time writer of complicated haiku, currently Sean is attempting to learn the advanced arts of plate spinning and soap carving sex toys.

Barring any of that? He'll stick with writing his stories, thanks, and rubbing pretty bodies together to see if they spark.

For more information on other books by Sean, visit his official website: SeanMichaelWrites.com

Also by Sean Michael

Chosen
Christmas Angel, A Hammer story
Christmas Auction, A Hammer story
Christmas Homecoming, A Hammer story
Control, A Hammer story
Cream
Daddy, Daddy and Me
Deeper, A Hammer novel
Ding Dong Bell, A Jarheads Story
Don't Ask, Don't Tell
Drawn
End of the Line
Eternity
Everyday Stories: Jarhead Shorts
Flying With Dragons
For Love and Money
Forged
Found
Fur and Fang
Golden
Gravity
Hitched, A Hammer story
Homecoming, A Jarheads story
Horsing Around
In Sickness and in Health
Inheritance
Life as a Front Porch
Little Jamie, A Hammer story
Little Square of Cloth
Love and the Farmer, A Velvet Glove story
Love in an Elevator
Love is Blindness
Made to Order

Amber Quill Press

Royal Line
Serving Mr. Right
Silver Edges
Spot the Difference
The Good Life
The Wizard and the Thief
Wallflowers
Welcome Home
Working it Out
Working to Win

Changeling Press

Alec (Shibari Auction House)
Bad Elf, No Candy Cane
Ben (Shibari Auction House)
Brent (Shibari Auction House)
Bringing Her Home
Christmas Elves are Ringing
Every Rose has his Thorne
Howling for Kitty
Jack (Shibari Auction House)
James (Shibari Auction House)
Joel (Shibari Auction House)
Keeping Sir Thorne
Leaf (Shibari Auction House)
Robin (Shibari Auction House)
Sam (Shibari Auction House)
Special Order
Storm in the City
Swinging Along
Tending to Rose

Totally Bound

Almost
Bruised
En Prise (Chess 3)
End Game (Chess 5)
Helpmate (Chess 4)
Malting (Beer & Clay 1)
Middle Game (Chess 2)
Opening Moves (Chess 1)
Size Matters
The Piercer's Game

Resplendence Publishing

Breaking Cover
Drawing Straws: Erik
Drawing Straws: Joe
Guardian Angel
Guns, Leather and Tinsel
In Time of Need
Royal Flush
Service
SWAK: Plugs
SWAK: Pony Play
SWAK: Pushy Bottom
SWAK: Shaving
SWAK: Sounds
The Dog Next Door
Totally Covered

Dreamspinner Press

Cupcakes
The Swag Man Delivers

Ellora's Cave
Brush and Whip
Pack and Mate

OmniLit/All Romance eBooks
The Millionaire's Mistake